BLINDSIDED

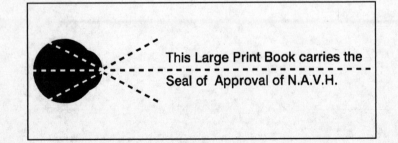

This Large Print Book carries the Seal of Approval of N.A.V.H.

BLINDSIDED

FERN MICHAELS

WHEELER PUBLISHING
A part of Gale, Cengage Learning

GALE
CENGAGE Learning·

Detroit • New York • San Francisco • New Haven, Conn • Waterville, Maine • London

GALE
CENGAGE Learning®

LIBRARY OF CONGRESS CATALOGING-IN-PUBLICATION DATA

Michaels, Fern.
    Blindsided / by Fern Michaels. — Large Print edition.
        pages cm. — (Sisterhood Series) (Wheeler Publishing Large Print Hardcover.)
    ISBN-13: 978-1-4104-6476-7 (hardcover)
    ISBN-10: 1-4104-6476-8 (hardcover)
    1. Female friendship—Fiction. 2. Vigilance committees—Fiction. 3. Judicial corruption—Fiction. 4. Juvenile delinquents—Abuse of—Fiction. 5. Large type books. I. Title.
PS3563.I27B55 2014
813'.54—dc23   2013046047

Published in 2014 by arrangement with Zebra Books, an imprint of Kensington Publishing Corp.

Printed in the United States of America
1 2 3 4 5 6 7 18 17 16 15 14

BLINDSIDED

CHAPTER 1

It was a beautiful autumn day, too nice really to be indoors, but Myra Rutledge had already been out with the dogs. She'd even made a trip to town to run some errands and stopped to have a solitary, boring lunch. At the moment, she couldn't remember what it was she'd eaten. She looked around her beautiful country kitchen and wished, not for the first time, that she had some kind of culinary expertise. She'd wished so many things lately, and none of her wishes had come true; nor were they likely to come true. Sad.

Oh, how she missed what she called the *old days,* when she and the girls were right- ing justice, vigilante-style. The "girls," meaning Nikki, Alexis, Kathryn, Isabelle, and Yoko. But as Charles said, all good things must come to an end. She'd argued the point, as had Annie, but Charles had held firm with his words. After he'd bandied about the word *old* at least a hundred times. Possibly more, until she and Annie had run him off with the broom. He'd retired to his lair in the catacombs, also known as the War Room, beneath the house. Which hadn't changed a thing. At that time. Now, though, it was a different story.

Myra fingered the pearls around her neck, her great-grandmother's heirloom pearls, which she was never without. Her intention had always been to leave the pearls to her daughter Barbara, but that was impossible now. With Barbara's death years ago, her life had changed, and so would the legacy of her pearls. Maybe she'd just donate them to some charity and let it sell them off for whatever they could get.

A heavy gust of wind sent a cascade of brilliant-colored leaves sailing across the backyard. Myra debated a moment as to whether she should go outside and collect a bouquet for the kitchen table. She shrugged and decided that the chrysanthemums in the bright purple bowl on the table still had some life in them.

Myra shivered as she looked across the room at the thermostat. She walked over and turned it up. She flopped down at the kitchen table. The dogs came running, not understanding what was going on with their mistress. She fondled all of them and babbled away about everything and nothing. She missed the girls and the boys, but most of all she missed Annie, whom she had seen every day until Annie went to Las Vegas two days ago. She usually stayed ten days or two weeks, which always left a huge void in Myra's life.

The bottom line was that she was bored out of her mind and had no clue what to do to occupy herself. She could, she supposed, go down to the tunnels and pester Charles, who was writing his memoirs; but he'd make short work of her. She knew that because she'd tried the trick on other days. Writing a memoir such as Charles's had to be tough going since he'd been at it over four years. She had no idea why he was even bothering since he had to be so careful to change names, dates, and places so as not to incriminate anyone. In the end, what was the point? Whatever it was, it kept Charles busy, which was more than she could say for herself. Maybe she needed to write her own memoirs. Like there would be a market for her life story! Then again . . .

The dogs suddenly tensed, the fur on the back of their necks standing on end. Visitors? Intruders? They ran to the door as Myra looked up at the security monitor over the kitchen door. A car was whizzing through the opened gates. Someone with the combination. "Annie!" Myra shouted, as she opened the door and ran outside. "Oh, dear God, you are home!"

Annie hugged Myra. "You missed me that much, eh?"

"I did. I do. I was sitting here going out of my mind missing you and feeling so very sorry for myself. I wasn't expecting you for at least a week."

"I knew you would be missing me, so I decided to come back."

"They kicked you out *again*?"

Annie laughed. "They can't kick me out; I own the joint. Things just go to hell when I'm there for some reason. This time, though, I thought I had it made. I tried sneaking in. Damn if they didn't know I was there before I even arrived. Does that make sense, Myra?"

"Sort of."

"Since Bert Navarro took over as head of security, wind couldn't get through a crack. We have better security than the White House with all those Secret Service agents. If you have secrets, Vegas is the place to be. Which brings me back to what I was saying — they knew I was there before I even got there. It ticks me off. I won seventy-three dollars on my way out of the casino. Do you want to go to lunch? My treat?"

"Anytime one of the richest women in the world wants to buy me lunch, you won't hear me declining the invitation. Where would you like to go?"

"Stop with that rich stuff, Myra. You have as much money as I have, and if the bill is over seventy-three dollars, you're paying the balance."

"Deal. What's wrong, Annie? I can read you like a book."

"Let's get a few drinks under our belts and talk then. Anything going on since I left?"

"Not a thing. Same old same old. The leaves are almost all down. I think there's supposed to be a harvest moon tonight. Before you know it, there will be frost on the pumpkins. I planted some pumpkins just to see if they'd grow. I have six or seven of a good size for the front porch, and Charles will have enough for pies at Thanksgiving."

"That's it! That's your news! Three days is a long time. Seventy-two hours to be precise. I can't believe nothing happened in seventy-two hours."

"Sorry to say it is what it is. I haven't even heard from the girls since you left. How was

Bert? Did you meet with him?"

"He's fine and yes, we met for a drink. He likes the job. He hired a new man a while back who has his own story. I met him and gave my seal of approval to his employment. What that means is Bert has more free time with an extra set of eyes and hands. Having said that, according to Bert, there is never a dull moment. He said Kathryn makes it back to Vegas just about every weekend. Things are okay between the two of them since he's accepted the idea that Kathryn doesn't want to get married, not now, not ever. Once he crossed that hurdle and truly accepted it, he's less stressed, and they just enjoy each other's company for what it is instead of tiptoeing around each other. I didn't see Kathryn. Bert said she was due tomorrow. She thrives on driving that eighteen-wheeler, but then we all knew that.

"He's quite pleased with himself about Harry's agreeing to come to train his troops, as he calls them. Like I said, we have better security than the White House. Does that boggle your mind, Myra?"

"Yes, it does. Kathryn's young, Annie. The young thrive on adventure, and driving overland is an adventure. It's also survival for Kathryn, so we can't fault her. You keep forgetting we're old now. We can't do things like that anymore."

"Says you," Annie snapped indignantly. "Age is a number. Nothing more."

Myra looked at Annie, her eyes sad. "We have to be realistic, my friend. You can't stop the aging process no matter how hard you try, and I know you're trying very hard, Annie. Now, why don't you tell me why you *really* came back home after only three days, and don't try that trick about how they kicked you out, because I'm not buying it."

Annie stared out the kitchen window at the colorful leaves blowing in all directions. Like Myra, autumn was her favorite time of year. She poured a cup of coffee and carried it to the table. "I didn't realize I was that transparent."

Myra's voice turned gentle. "Annie, whatever it is, you can tell me. We've always told each other everything. You know I'm a good listener, and you also know I am not judgmental. Except for that time with the pole dancing," Myra said defensively.

"My eyelashes are falling out."

"What? That's why you came back from Vegas, because your eyelashes are falling out! Everyone's eyelashes fall out, and new ones grow. You can get new ones. I saw it on TV. I don't want to hear that your toenails are yellow, either. That's why they make nail polish. Cut to the chase, Annie."

"Fergus left. He's gone."

Myra's eyes popped wide. "Where did he go?"

"Home. To Scotland. To his family that he has been estranged from for years and years."

"What changed, Annie? Did something happen or change that you didn't tell me about?" She watched the tremor in Annie's hands as she brought her coffee cup to her lips. "You can tell me," she said gently.

"I was blindsided, Myra. I didn't see it coming. And, yes, something did happen, but I promised not to say anything to anyone. When your partner confides in you, you have to keep that private, and a promise is a promise. Fergus won the Irish Sweepstakes. It was a lot of money. I don't know why or how he thought he could keep it a secret, but he did. Somehow, his children got wind of it, and they started making overtures toward him. Blood is thicker than water. We both know that, Myra. It wasn't that he didn't want to share his winnings with his children; he did. The first thing he did was set up trusts for the children and grandchildren. I encouraged him to do that. I'm not sure in my own mind that he would have done it if I hadn't pressured him into it. Regardless, it's water under the bridge now. He's gone."

"Is he coming back?"

"I doubt it."

"How do you feel about that, Annie?"

"Well, Myra, I understand it, but that doesn't mean I have to like it. I would never, ever, stand in the way of a family's reuniting. Nor would you. We both know how important family is since we both lost ours. It is what it is. The sun will come up tomorrow, and that same sun will set later in the day. Life goes on."

"So does that mean you're okay going it alone? Did he ask you to go with him, Annie?"

"No, Myra, he did not ask me to go with him. It's easy for me to say now that I would have declined, but back in that moment of time, I don't honestly know what I would have done or said had he asked me."

"Is there anything I can do, Annie?"

"Not a damn thing, my friend. I have to work this out myself. Right now, I'm up for some *action.*"

"Well, my dear, you've come to the wrong place if you expected action here at the farm. Unless you count taking the dogs out or riding over to Nellie's to watch paint dry. She's having her house painted as we speak.

Pearl Barnes is laid up with a bad case of gout and is meaner than a wet cat, so we can't visit her. Martine, our esteemed ex-president, is in Dubai or some damn place with a lot of sand doing something or other. She left yesterday morning. It's just us, Annie. We can't even count on Charles to entertain us because he's deep into his memoirs and only comes up to cook and most of the times he . . . God, Annie, I'm almost ashamed to say this, but he's been using a Crock-Pot since it does all the work. I'm getting sick of one-pot meals. I might actually have to try my hand with a cook-book."

"Well, that sucks. Everything sucks. Don't mind me, Myra, I'm just cranky. I took the red-eye, and I haven't had any sleep."

"Do you want to skip lunch, go home, and take a nap? Or you could go up to your room here. We could go out for dinner and skip that mess bubbling in that pot on the counter."

"No, I want to do lunch. That seventy-three dollars I won is burning a hole in my pocket. Get your jacket, and let's go. Do you have to tell Charles you're going?"

"You know what, Annie? He won't even know we're gone. He won't be coming up here to check on anything. Like I said, that

16

stupid Crock-Pot does it all."

"Fergus was a good cook, much better than me. I might have to look into a Crock-Pot."

Myra rolled her eyes as she slipped into her jacket. The four dogs lined up, expectant looks in their eyes. "Nope. You're staying home, guys. Here's a chew. See you in a little while. Do not chew anything else while I'm gone."

The dogs, as one, looked at Annie, who burst out laughing. "Sorry, guys, I have no jurisdiction here."

"Hold on, Annie, someone is at the gate. I can't see who it is other than that it's a woman," Myra said, when the dogs rushed to the door. She eyed the monitor and frowned. "I think . . . it almost looks like Maggie." Myra pressed a button on the panel by the back door, and the electronic gate swung open. "It *is* Maggie!"

Myra and Annie followed the mad rush of the dogs to get through the open door. "You wanted some action, Annie! Looks like we just got some. Oh, good Lord, the girl is crying!"

Maggie Spitzer barreled out of the car, stopping to pet each dog before she ran into Myra and Annie's outstretched arms all the while sobbing, as if her heart was breaking.

Back in the kitchen, both Myra and Annie fussed like two mother hens over Maggie, crooning and cooing to their younger charge as they asked questions. Annie moved to make tea, the universal cure-all to everything in life as far as she was concerned. That it never helped was of no consequence. The bottom line was that when someone was in acute distress, you made tea. Tea was the magic elixir to everything. Period. Bottom line.

"Please, Maggie, stop crying. I can't understand a word you're saying. We can't help you if you don't tell us what's wrong, dear," Myra said.

Maggie sniffled, then blew her nose in a wad of paper towels Annie held out. She gulped, took several deep breaths, and blurted out her turmoil in one long, sobbing sentence. Gus Sullivan, her husband, had died ten months ago in Afghanistan when he had been called to help out with a security company.

"Ten months ago!" Annie and Myra cried in unison.

"And you're just telling us *now*! Why?" Myra demanded, as Annie urged the young woman to drink the tea in front of her.

"I didn't . . . I couldn't . . . I was in shock at first. Then I got angry because Gus didn't have to go. He *wanted* to go. Even in the condition he was in, which wasn't all that good health-wise. He was in constant pain, and there was nothing more the doctors could do for him. All he said was, 'I'm a soldier. I have to do this. They need me.' He didn't think twice because some damn company wanted him as a consultant. He didn't even ask me if I was okay with it, he just agreed. We had a horrible fight, and he left. He just packed a duffel. Someone came to pick him up, and he waved good-bye. He *waved*! Do you believe that? He waved good-bye. No kiss good-bye. I didn't see it coming. I felt like I was . . . blindsided, for want of a better term. Six weeks later, the same person who picked Gus up came to the farm and gave me the news, along with his gear. They said there wasn't . . . there wasn't enough of him left to send home for burial. It was a roadside bomb."

"Darling girl, why didn't you call us? We would have rushed to you on winged feet. Did you go through this alone? Was anyone there for you? Oh, Maggie, we are so sorry," Myra said, wrapping the young woman in her arms. She looked up at Annie, whose eyes were wet.

"The girls. Did you tell the girls?" Annie finally managed to ask.

"No. I felt so guilty I couldn't bear to be around anyone. By then I knew I had fallen out of love with Gus. I called Ted in the middle of the night, and he helped a lot. He was there for me. He even came to see me once during . . . the worst of it. The only other thing I did was call Gus's nephew, his only living relative, and told him about Gus's death, and turned over the kennel and the farm to him. He came in a heartbeat, and things finalized the other day. I had nowhere else to go, so here I am. I need a job. Are there any openings at the paper? I'll do anything, even maintenance if that's all that's available. I kept my old house in Georgetown and paid the taxes, but there's a tenant in there I'll have to ask to move."

"Ted knew. He never said a word," Annie said in a disbelieving voice.

"Because I asked him not to. I wasn't in a good place, Annie. I wasn't up to making decisions. It was Ted's idea to turn the farm and the kennel over to Gus's nephew, and the sooner the better. I would like to think that I would have done it somewhere down the road, but having Ted help me was even better. He would check on me six or seven times a day."

"Ted is a good man," Myra said gently.

"Yes, he is," Maggie agreed tearfully.

"Don't get me wrong here. I married Gus because I loved him. Gus married me to belong to someone. He married me for all the wrong reasons. I found that out rather quickly. He wanted a partner. A business partner. Not a wife. I tried to make it work, but you can't make someone love you. If Gus hadn't gotten the offer to go off to Afghanistan when he did, I probably would have called it a day on my own because I fell out of love. It's that simple.

"I told him I would stay until he got back, then I'd file for divorce. I don't know if he even heard me; he was so gung ho on getting back to Afghanistan. That all went down during the big fight. Ted insisted I go to a shrink, which I did. What I got out of all of the sessions was that in his mind, Gus had only one love: the army. He knew he might die over there, and he was okay with it, knowing he was doing what he wanted to do. That was pretty hard to accept. Plus, the shrink said he knew that he had nothing to come home to. That's the guilt I'm carrying with me."

"Oh, no, no, no, darling girl. That's all wrong. Gus made a choice. It wasn't your choice. You can't carry that guilt with you. You said it yourself — Gus was a soldier. It was the only life he knew from the age of eighteen as I recall. It was his choice to return to Afghanistan, and it doesn't matter in what capacity he was going; he made it knowing what he was getting into. Did the two of you communicate while he was there?" Myra asked.

"A few times via e-mail. He was happy, said he felt he was contributing. He asked me not to be angry with him. It was a roadside bomb, and the man who came to see me said he died instantly. There was a huge insurance policy. I wanted to give it to Gus's nephew, but he wouldn't take it. I doubt I'll ever be able to spend the money. I'm trying to come up with a good cause that Gus would approve of to donate it to. Something for wounded vets on their return. I don't know yet. I'm sure something will come to me sooner or later."

"Ted?" Annie said, mentioning her new editor in chief at the paper she owned.

"My rock. I couldn't have made it without him, and no, I don't want his job, Annie. I laughed when he told me he had taken over my old job. He said the chair didn't fit, but he was getting used to it. He misses being out there gathering news, or in his case, *making* news. Espinosa sent me funny e-mails from time to time. He was in on it — the secrecy part. Both he and Ted are better friends than I deserve."

"Rubbish!" Annie exclaimed. "The three of you worked well together. They missed you terribly when you left, but they both stepped up to the plate, and I know every time a crisis reared, they both would ask, 'What would Maggie do?' And then they'd do it. It actually worked. You were on the payroll in absentia in a manner of speaking."

Maggie smiled through her tears. "Thanks for telling me that."

Myra clapped her hands, and said, "Now I think we should all go to lunch. Annie has seventy-three dollars she won in Las Vegas, and it's burning a hole in her pocket. We were on our way to town when you arrived. You're too thin, Maggie. The first thing we need to do is put some meat back on your bones. Or we could drink our lunch if you feel that would be more appropriate."

Maggie blew her nose in a fresh wad of paper towels, dabbed at her eyes, and sat up a little straighter. "I'm your girl," she said with spirit.

"And you're going to stay with me until your house is available. My roommate just relocated, and I'm all alone," Annie said.

"Where's Fergus? Are you saying Fergus

left?" Maggie asked, shock ringing in her voice.

"It's a long story, dear. We can talk about it over lunch," Myra said, shooing Maggie out the door while she tried to hold the dogs at bay for a clean getaway.

Annie drove the way she always did, like a bat out of hell. They arrived at a local bistro that served alcoholic beverages at lunchtime with the brakes smoking and tires squealing.

Myra and Maggie exited the car on wobbly legs. Not so Annie, who smiled with satisfaction, and said, "I got you here in one piece."

"Just shut up, Annie. It's going to take at least an hour for me to calm down after that hair-raising ride."

"I remember this place. We got drunk here, Annie. I can't remember who drove us home, though," Maggie said. "This is like old times. And they were good times, too."

"Well, don't look at me; I'm *old* now and can't remember a damn thing. Just ask Miss-know-it-all Myra," Annie said, glaring at Myra, who glared right back.

They were seated in a ruby-red leather booth in the back of the bistro. Annie suggested they make it simple and order one of everything, which she did. "Three double bourbons and branch water on the rocks. One of everything on the menu."

"Annie!" Myra yelped.

"What? What? There are only four things on the damn menu, Myra. Burgers, hot dogs, fries, and onion rings."

"Oh," was all Myra could say.

"Works for me," Maggie said. "I've been drinking to excess lately. After today, I'm going on the wagon. I smoke now, too," she volunteered.

"Really?" Myra and Annie said in unison.

"They were just crutches to get me . . . you know, through the bad nights."

"Did it help?" Myra asked.

"No. I'll give up the cigarettes after today, too. I hate smelling like a chimney stack, and I hate waking up with a hangover."

"Good for you, dear," Myra said, reaching across the table for Maggie's hand. She patted it to show she understood, as did Annie.

"So, tell me about Fergus," Maggie said, raising her bourbon glass in a toast. The women clinked their glasses before Annie started on her story, embellishing it along the way, which was no surprise to Myra. She knew that Annie was trying to lighten Maggie's dark mood at her own expense.

Twenty minutes later, Maggie said, "So what you're saying is, you're going to miss the sex more than the man himself even though he's a really good cook."

Annie squirmed in her chair and flushed. She shrugged and gulped at the little bit of the bourbon in her glass that remained. She held it aloft for a refill.

"I guess you're thinking there is no one else out there who will rip your clothes off with their teeth. Is that it?" Maggie continued.

"More or less. I might have to settle for a manual slow and easy. We all have to make concessions from time to time," Annie said airily.

Myra wanted to slip off her seat in the booth, her face a fiery crimson.

"But the last time we were in here you said Fergus had a heat-seeking missile that was all yours. What are you going to replace that with?" Maggie giggled.

"A purple vibrator turned on high!" Myra said, deciding she might as well join in the fun at Annie's expense. And just maybe she'd learn something she could pass on to Charles. At some point. Just the thought made her insides all jittery and Jell-O-like.

"You little devil, you! I knew it! The word *vibrator* was never in your vocabulary, Myra, my dear," Annie chortled.

"I've been reading *Cosmo* so I can keep up with you," Myra said defensively.

"Myra, you are so far behind me, it would take you a lifetime to catch up. Now, if you really want the skinny on Fergus's prowess, gather close. I wouldn't want word of this to fall on anyone's ears but yours. Myra, get out your notebook and make notes for Charles."

Maggie's eyes almost bugged out of her head.

"Tell us. Our lips are zipped. Right, Myra?"

Myra nodded. If her life depended on it, she couldn't have made her tongue work.

Maggie Spitzer knew in that moment in time that she was back home, and her life would take on a whole new meaning. Who said you can't go home again? she thought smugly. She was the living proof. So there!

CHAPTER 2

Ted Robinson looked down at the text he was reading, his eyebrows shooting up to his newly receding hairline. He read it three times, committing the text to memory. We need a ride home. We're snookered. Big-time. Come and get us at Mongol's Bistro. Maggie.

"Espinosa!" he roared. "Let's hit it. *Maggie's back in town!*"

Joe Espinosa stood up and looked around. "No shit!"

"You're driving, buddy; c'mon, shake it!"

Espinosa dangled his car keys in front of Ted's glazed eyes. "Articulate, Ted!"

He did as he raced for the elevator, his body shaking, his eyes still glazed. "She needs *me*, Espinosa!"

"Yeah, I got that part, but don't you really mean she needs a ride? Did she specifically say she needed *you*? She did not. She said she needed a ride. So don't go getting your hopes up so high I won't be able to catch

28

you when you fall to Earth," Espinosa grumbled.

"Whatever. The important thing is she's back. Maggie's back in town! Remember that song Bobby Darin used to sing? Damn! I hope she wants this stupid job back. I'll give it up in a heartbeat."

Espinosa slid behind the wheel of his SUV. "Ted, just because Maggie is in town doesn't necessarily mean she's back for good. C'mon, I don't want to see you hit the skids again when she leaves."

"You're wrong. The fact that she's here means she is back. We talked about it. She said when and if she made the decision to return, it would mean she could put the past few years behind her, and that would mean she's ready to move forward. Hey, I'm the one she called. I'm the one that talked to her during those long, dark nights. I'm the one who went to see her and bolstered her. She knew she could count on me. By the same token, I know if I had been in her shoes, she would have come through for me the same way. We have a bond between us. We both went off the rails for a while, but she's taken the next step. I'm not stupid, Espinosa. What will be, will be. In the meantime, I can hope and dream. Stop trying to shoot me down. Can't you drive any faster?"

"I'm going past the speed limit as it is. Calm down, okay? Jeez, you're like some lovesick teenager."

Ted didn't bother to respond, his thoughts on Maggie, their history, and possibly a future with her back in it. Everyone in the whole damn world knew he was still in love with Maggie Spitzer. Even Maggie knew it. Nobody thought she was in love with him. All he could do was hope for the best.

Ten minutes later, Espinosa said, "Okay, big guy, we are here! How do you want to play this? Do we both go in? What?"

Ted shrugged. "I don't know what the protocol is for bailing out three drunk ladies, one of whom is my boss. I guess we'll just wing it, which means come with me."

Espinosa hopped out of his SUV and followed Ted into the bistro. He spotted the happy drunken trio within seconds. They waved and shouted. Annie let loose with a shrill whistle, doing a better job than he ever could have — and he was a guy. He was impressed. His boss's prowess in all things always impressed him for some reason.

"Is the bill paid?" Ted asked, his eyes on Maggie.

"I paid it because Annie only had seventy-three dollars that she won in Vegas and I had to make up the difference because the bill was wayyyyyy higher than seventy-three dollars," Myra singsonged.

"Can you walk, ladies?" Ted asked through clenched teeth.

"Such a silly question, Mr. Robinson. Of course we can walk. We could probably dance if we were asked to. Dance, that is. Isn't that right, girls?" Annie said, her arms flapping every which way.

"Right on," Myra said, twirling around; she would have fallen if Espinosa hadn't grabbed her by the arm. "I have this inner-ear problem," Myra said defensively.

"I-do-not-feel-the-need-to-dance," Maggie said, enunciating each word carefully, her eyes crossing as she tried to focus on the two men standing in front of her.

"And I do not feel like dancing either, so there, young man," Annie said, holding tight to Myra's arm. She leaned over and hissed into her friend's ear, "We have to stop doing this; we're too damned old to get drunk and depend on other people to get us home."

Myra glared at Annie, her expression saying more than any words could have.

It was tough going, but somehow Ted and Espinosa got the three women into the

31

backseat of the SUV. "Where to, ladies?"

"Myra's house. Maggie is staying with me until her tenant moves out, but I just got back from Vegas, and the house is in a shambles. Does that answer your question, young man?" Annie chirped.

All Ted heard was that Maggie was staying and would move back into her house. He mumbled something in response. Life was looking good.

Getting the inebriated ladies out of the SUV proved to be a bit harder than it was getting them in. All Espinosa could see were legs everywhere as the women tumbled over each other. Finally, they were all in the house. Espinosa looked around and decided to make coffee. Ted headed into Myra's family room and built a fire. He ran upstairs for blankets and pillows, which he spread out on the floor. Everyone needed to sleep it off.

"This isn't feeling right to me, Ted. I'm not sure it's a good idea to leave these three alone. Maybe we should stay," Espinosa said.

"I know what you mean, and I feel the same way, but I think when they wake up they'll be happy we aren't here. We'll get them settled and leave. Five bucks says they'll be asleep in minutes. They're pretty damn drunk in case you haven't noticed."

"Oh, I noticed," Espinosa said sharply. "Wonder what got into them?"

"Sometimes you really are stupid, Espinosa. What got into them is Maggie. They had no clue what she's been through. Did you forget that? Whatever their game plan was, it must have worked because Maggie is staying and moving back to her own house."

Espinosa handed out cups of strong black coffee.

"This is just so sweet of you, Joseph," Annie said, calling Espinosa by his given name. "Thank you so much for rescuing us. I'll make sure you both get a very nice bonus in your paychecks."

Maggie swayed from side to side as she tried to focus on the little group in the kitchen. "Ted, I have a line on a story. I meant to tell Myra and Annie but . . . other things got in the way. It's a story the Vigilantes need to know about."

Annie and Myra reared up at the same time. "Someone needs our help? Oh, this is just what we've been waiting for," Myra said, clapping her hands.

"Hoorah!" Annie shouted. Then she lowered her voice, and said, "Marines always say that when something goes their way."

"Tomorrow will be soon enough. We need to be clearheaded when I tell you. I want to go to sleep now, and I can't think clearly," Maggie said, as her legs finally gave out on her and her eyes closed. Ted reached for her, scooped her up, and carried her into one of the nests he'd made near the fire. He made sure the glass doors on the fireplace were closed tightly.

"Ted?"

"Yes."

"Thank you for everything. I'm sorry I hurt you. You know that song, 'I Will Always Love You,' the one Whitney Houston sang? That's how I feel . . ." she said, her words trailing off into nothing. Ted stared down at the only woman he'd ever loved, would ever love, and smiled sadly. He felt something prick his eyelids. He blinked and stalked out to the kitchen, but not before one of Myra's magnificent golden retrievers settled down next to his ladylove. In his mind, there was no greater protection than that of a dog. His love was in good protective paws.

"Maggie's asleep. If you two think you'll be okay, Espinosa and I will be getting back to the paper. Call us if you need anything."

Annie drew herself up to her imposing regal height and fixed her gaze on her two loyal employees. "I trust this . . . this visit is between us, gentlemen."

"What visit?" Ted grinned as he opened the door for Espinosa. "If you need us, call. Smells good in here."

Myra's eyes turned crafty. "Do you think so?"

"Oh, yeah," Espinosa said.

"Well, then, consider it yours," Myra said, pulling out the electrical cord and handing the Crock-Pot over to Ted, who didn't know what to do, so he just accepted it.

Everyone waved good-bye.

"I think you just did a very dangerous thing, my dear. Charles is going to be upset, isn't he, Myra?"

"Ask someone who cares about Crock-Pots. I-do-not-care!"

"Feisty, aren't we?" Annie tittered as she made her way to the family room, where she sank down, closed her eyes, and was asleep instantly.

Myra smiled as she looked at the empty spot on the kitchen counter where the Crock-Pot had been sitting. Gremlins.

Charles Martin stepped into the kitchen and looked around. The first thing he noticed was his missing Crock-Pot, the empty cups on the table, and the absence of his beloved. The second thing he noticed was two strange jackets hanging on the wooden pegs near the back door. Guests!

He called out, and the dogs came running, which was no surprise. But they didn't approach him — the four dogs just stood in the doorway, their tails wagging furiously. "Aha! You want me to follow you, is that it?" He did, his hand flying to his mouth so he wouldn't laugh out loud. "Shhh," he said to the dogs as he backed out of the room. In the kitchen, he opened the door for the dogs. They looked up at him as much as if to say, *Can we trust you to look after the ladies?* "It's okay, I have the picture. Go!" They did and were back within minutes as they lined up waiting for their treats, which they all carried back to the family room.

As smart and as astute as he was, Charles knew *something had gone down* while he was in the catacombs, and it wasn't his disappearing Crock-Pot, although he rightly assumed it had something to do with the ladies' afternoon nap.

Annie was back after only three days. He again rightly assumed she'd been either kicked out of Vegas as she put it or she returned because . . . because . . . Maggie Spitzer was here. He craned his neck to look out the kitchen window to see if Annie's spiffy one-of-a-kind sports car was in the courtyard parking lot. It wasn't. That had to mean someone brought them home from wherever they'd been. It could have been anyone, but if he were a betting man, which he wasn't, he would bet on either Ted Robinson or Joe Espinosa. Or both of those worthy gentlemen.

Something had happened, and he'd missed it. Whatever *it* was. He felt a momentary pang of jealousy that he'd been excluded and all because he was hell-bent on writing his memoirs, an opus that no one would ever read. Even Myra, who said she didn't care to revisit the past in any way, shape, or form.

Dinner. He'd fallen way short on that, too, using the silly Crock-Pot to give himself more time to write his equally silly memoirs. Obviously, he needed to make some changes, and he needed to make them quickly, or he was going to be standing outside the door looking in. Myra could be unforgiving. Annie more so. Maggie . . . Maggie would send him to the dogs and not even blink. Women!

Charles munched on cheese and crackers as he watched the digital clock on the gas range. His thoughts were all over the map as he waited for the time to pass. Somewhere deep inside he knew something was wrong, and the women hadn't seen fit to include him in whatever it was. And that confirmed his thought that he needed to clean up his act. He looked over at the empty space on the kitchen counter. His first clue. Myra meant business.

The minutes, then the hours, ticked by so slowly, Charles wanted to scream. He tried browsing through cookbooks to pass the time, turning the television set on the counter off, then on, then off again because there was nothing even remotely interesting. He debated about baking a cake, then negated the idea even though he'd heard or read that after a drinking bender, the drinker always wanted something sweet.

The bottom line was he was feeling sorry for himself, and he didn't like the feeling. Maybe he needed some fresh air. A walk around the garden might be just what the doctor ordered. He could gaze at the harvest moon and bay at it if he wanted to. He wanted to.

The dogs must have intuitively sensed what he was planning because, even before he could get up, they were at the door, waiting expectantly.

Charles reached for a cigar and some dog chews and let himself and the dogs out the door. The dogs immediately ran off, leaving

Charles to meander through the leaf-strewn garden. He sat down on a bench by a small pond Myra had put in two years earlier and listened to the soft sounds of the pump at the far end. Such a peaceful spot. But he wasn't feeling peaceful at the moment. He was feeling angry. Not at the ladies but at himself.

The wind whipped up suddenly, and within minutes, the pond was covered with leaves. The gas lamp at the far end cast a hazy yellow glow over his surroundings. It looked eerie to his eyes. He looked up at the beautiful harvest moon and wondered if he should make some kind of wish. What would he wish for? Happiness for all his loved ones. What could be better than that? He made his wish and didn't feel silly at all.

"Wake up and smell the roses, Sir Charles," he muttered to himself as he fired up his cigar. His thoughts took him everywhere and yet nowhere as he puffed on the cigar, blowing perfect smoke rings that rose high in the air and skittered across the yard on the wind.

The dogs, not understanding this strange behavior, raced around the yard, yipping at each other as they tried to catch the swirling leaves. From time to time, they would stop and look upward at the night, which was suddenly like daylight to them. Finally, exhausted, they settled down by Charles's feet. He handed them all a chew. He smiled in the moonlight. The dogs were his and Myra's children and treated as such.

Charles didn't know how long he sat there on the bench. Long enough that the wind sent the leaves on the pond somewhere else as the moon inched its way across the sky. His body was telling him it was way past his bedtime. Not that he had a real bedtime; he didn't. He slept when his body told him to sleep. An hour here, two hours there. Rarely, if ever, did he sleep a full night in his bed. A doctor had once told him his brain wasn't programmed to sleep the way other people slept. He'd accepted it because he couldn't come up with a better answer. Now, however, his body was telling him it was time to head into the house and prepare for some rest.

Charles grunted when he got up, his knees and joints creaking. Even the dogs heard the bone-cracking noises. They were on their feet instantly, racing to the kitchen door. He was stunned to see Myra sitting at the kitchen table drinking a cup of tea, the tea bag hanging over the side of the cup. He winced at the sight.

"Did you have a nice walk in the garden, dear?"

"I did. Would you like me to make you some *real* tea?"

"No. This is fine. I gave your Crock-Pot to Ted this afternoon."

"I see" was all Charles could think of to say.

"I hated it, Charles. I'd rather eat a baloney sandwich than that stuff you threw in the pot. I didn't even know we owned a Crock-Pot."

"I ordered it online. Truth be told, I didn't much care for it myself, but it was convenient. Would you like to talk about it, Myra?"

Myra knew he wasn't referring to the Crock-Pot. "Yes, and no. Annie's back, as you can see. She came over to take me to lunch because she'd won seventy-three dollars on her way out of the casino. If lunch was over seventy-three dollars, I had to make up the difference. Just as we were leaving to go, Maggie showed up. Her husband, Gus Sullivan, was killed in Afghanistan by a roadside bomb. Ten months ago! She didn't tell anyone but Ted. Gus went back as some kind of security consultant, against Maggie's wishes. She said their marriage was over even before he left, and she has been carrying around a ton of guilt on her shoulders. Ted helped her through the worst of it. Anyway, she's back to stay and will be working at the *Post*.

"In addition to that, Annie told me Fergus left to return to his family in Scotland. It seems he won the Irish Sweepstakes and didn't tell anyone but Annie. Somehow, the family he was estranged from found out about his winnings and welcomed him back. Annie says she isn't devastated, but she is. That's why we went to the bistro and drank more than was good for us. I swear I will never do that again. Ted and Joseph brought us home. I guess you could technically say they put us to bed in the family room. That's the end of my story. I'm *not* sorry about the Crock-Pot, Charles. You need to know that."

Charles nodded. "Will Maggie be all right?"

"I think so. She might have a few things she has to work through, but she's back with all of us now. One step, one day at a time. Maggie's tough. What she didn't realize was that she is also vulnerable, like the rest of us. She knows that now. Oh, she did say something else when we got back. She said she wants to talk to us in the morning about a possible mission for the Vigilantes."

Charles felt his heart skip a beat. "Really?"

"That's pretty much what I said, too. 'Really?' Oh, Charles, I hope it's something we can sink our teeth into. We have been so inactive, and I can't bear those gold shields getting tarnished and going to waste. We need to *use* them. You know what, darling? I will take some of that real tea now. And maybe something nourishing. Like food. I'll settle for peanut butter and jelly if you make it."

"Consider it done, my dear. Would you like some marshmallow fluff on top of the jelly?"

Myra giggled. "Of course, dear. Sweets to the sweet. Oh, I can't wait for Maggie to wake up to tell us what's on her mind. Have you seen anything on the news lately that would . . . fit into our lifestyle these days, Charles?"

Busy at the counter, Charles stopped to think, then shook his head. "Not that I recall. Everything is political nowadays, or the news is about some movie star's doing something he or she shouldn't be doing. I have no clue."

Myra nibbled on her thumbnail, her gaze on a hanging plant in the window, her thoughts taking her back in time to other missions with the girls. She could feel her heart rate accelerate as she contemplated getting back into action with her peers.

Charles set Myra's plate in front of her, then one for himself. He poured fresh *real* tea and sat down across from his wife. "I have to admit, I'm looking forward to hearing what Maggie has to say." He bit into his sandwich, a wicked gleam in his eyes.

"I knew it! You are just as anxious as Annie and I to get back to work. I swear, Charles, I was beginning to think we were starting to atrophy, and that Crock-Pot just confirmed it. Aren't you glad we're starting with a clean slate now?"

"My dear, you have no idea!"

"Oh, yes, my darling, I do. And so does Annie. And I truly believe Maggie will be up for whatever comes our way. As soon as I finish this lovely sandwich and drink this delicious tea, I am going to text Nellie, Martine, and Pearl to put them on alert. I know they're chomping at the bit just the way Annie and I have been. Unless . . ." Myra let her eyes do the talking. Charles laughed.

"Just so you know, Charles, today at the bistro I was not only drinking, I was listening, and you would be surprised at what I learned. I'm willing to share if you think you can beat me to the second floor."

Before Charles could react, Myra was up and sprinting up the back staircase to the second floor, with Charles hot on her heels.

"Oh, dear, you caught me," Myra said, gasping for breath.

"That I did, old girl, that I did, and I am never going to let you go."

CHAPTER 3

Retired federal judge Cornelia Easter, Nellie to those near and dear, shivered in her easy recliner when a strong gust of wind whipped against the casement windows. The noise was so loud, the cats cuddling on her lap hissed and raced off to more quiet surroundings. She looked over at her husband, retired FBI Director Elias Cummings, and smiled. She wasn't sure if a magnitude seven earthquake could wake Elias when he dozed off after a more-than-satisfying dinner.

The lone cat nestled on her shoulder only stirred when he alerted Nellie that she had an incoming text message. She hated text messages that required a response because the keys were too little, and her gnarled fingers had trouble hitting the right keys. As she read the message, she risked a glance at her husband — still sound asleep. She sucked in her breath, trying to decide if she was excited at what she was reading or dreading the outcome. She did, however, like the part that Maggie was back in town. She fumbled in the pocket of the recliner for a pen and managed to tap off a response that was short and to the point: I will be there. "There" being Myra's for dinner the following day, followed by a meeting in the catacombs for a possible mission. She stared off into space, finally focusing on the fire burning in the fireplace, and came to the conclusion that she was excited at the message she'd received.

She'd been bored for weeks now — maybe it was months, she'd simply lost track of time — ever since the painters had arrived. Either they were exceptionally slow, or she had no patience for perfection, which the painters said was needed when painting such a lovely old historical farmhouse. She couldn't help but wonder how excited her husband would be when she woke him up to go to bed, which was laughable in itself.

She really should get up and put some more logs on the fire. She loved the warmth from the fire. Another sign of old age, along with her arthritis, she thought sourly. The need to feel warm all the time was right up there with wearing three-quarter sleeves even in the high heat of summer, so the ugly brown spots that could no longer pass as freckles couldn't be seen. Old age sucked, as Annie pointed out on a daily basis.

Nellie frowned. Was she losing her mind? Didn't Annie just leave for Vegas a few days ago? She was sure of it. But she was suddenly back home, along with Maggie Spitzer. Aha! For sure, something was in the wind. Her frown deepened. Unless . . . Annie got kicked out of Vegas. Again. More than likely that's what had happened, knowing Annie's track record. Still, the fact that Annie was back so quickly meant something serious was going on. Doubly so since Maggie had also returned.

Nellie struggled to get her new hips, which weren't so new anymore, to work as she got out of her chair to throw more logs on the fire. She watched as the sparks shot up the chimney like a Fourth of July fireworks display.

Outside, the wind continued to whistle and shriek like loons on a lake. She paid it no mind as she tried to imagine what would go down tomorrow at Pinewood after dinner. The frown was knitting its way over her brow again when her thoughts took her to Pearl Barnes, who was suffering through a painful bout of gout. Would Pearl make it to Pinewood? Knowing Pearl, she'd be there if

48

she had to crawl. That left the ex-president, who was in Bahrain or some damn place like that, giving a speech for half a million dollars. How in the world would she get back home in time for a meeting at Pinewood? It would take her days just to figure out a way to shake her Secret Service protection.

Nellie looked over at Elias, who was snoring loudly, another reason the cats had run for cover. She let her hand dip down into the pocket of her lounger and withdrew the soft velvet pouch she always kept near. She withdrew the shiny gold shield. A delicious wave of something she couldn't define raced through her body, then the word *danger* flooded her whole being. Holding the flawless chunk of gold in the palm of her hand had to be the ultimate adrenaline rush. She savored the moment before slipping the shield back into the velvet pouch.

A log dropped with a loud cracking sound. Elias stirred but didn't wake. Nellie closed her eyes and let her memories take her where they wanted to go.

Less than forty miles away, in Alphabet City, the retired justice of the Supreme Court, Pearl Barnes, hobbled around her kitchen in search of food that wouldn't aggravate her condition. She was cranky to be sure because she absolutely refused to take medicine for her condition. She hated pills of all kinds, and it had been over fifty years since she'd even popped an aspirin. She'd researched her condition years ago and knew what she had to do each time a bout flared up. If her calculations were right, she'd be almost as good as new if she could make it through the next day and a half. She'd cut down on her healing time during her last three flare-ups thanks to a bean-and-legume diet, along with gallons of water. In her research and chats online and blogs and tweets and everything in between, there had been one woman much her own age who swore by the bean, legume, and water diet for gout by saying she was good to go in three days after a flare-up. And don't worry, the postscript read, if you have gas for a few days. It's all about ridding yourself of the toxins.

Pearl Barnes hated doctors. Until she needed one. She also hated lawyers even though she was one herself. Until she needed one. The truth was there was nothing much in life that Pearl actually liked other than her part in operating an underground railroad for abused women. She'd more or less retired from that venture when, thanks to ample warning, she got the hell out of Dodge in the nick of time. If she had a love of any kind, seeing the women off to safety was it. She still gave her input, but she was smart enough to know she was under surveillance, so she was extra careful not to do anything that would jeopardize the other faithful volunteers. She missed it, missed the urgency, the danger, the smiles of the grateful women and kids she put her life on the line to help.

Pearl was in the right frame of mind when the text came through from Myra. She responded immediately, saying she would be there with a bell around her neck. And she would be there. When she gave her word on something, there was nothing in the world that could make her go back on a promise. Now for sure she had something to look forward to. And if her calculations were spot on, she might be able to enjoy the gourmet dinner she was sure Charles would be whipping up.

Pearl read the short text again. Annie had just gone to Vegas, and yet she was back. Obviously, she'd been kicked out of her own casino. Again. And Maggie Spitzer was back in town. For sure, that had to mean something. Being as astute as she was, Pearl immediately decided that Maggie's marriage had gone south. A *twofer.* Two words came to Pearl's agile mind. *Danger* and *action.* There were no words in her vocabulary to describe how much she loved both danger and action. She dived into her plate of beans and legumes and ate with a vengeance. She swigged down almost a liter of water and swore to herself that she immediately felt better. Yesiree, by tomorrow she'd be full of piss and vinegar. She would spend the rest of the evening trying to figure out how to shake the man who was constantly tailing her. As she hobbled about the kitchen, her thoughts traveled to Martine Connor as she wondered if she'd be a no-show for tomorrow's meeting. Myra had told her a few days ago that Martine was in the Far East or some damn place surrounded by sand doing God only knew what. Giving speeches for money just to have something to do because she swore on the Bible that she was not going to be one of those presidents who wrote their memoirs and had a library named after them so they could display her book. She liked Marti Connor. Really liked her. The translation of the word *like* meant the ex-prez was her kind of woman. Didn't she get them those fancy gold shields? Now, that took guts, but she'd gone up against the good ol' boys and gotten it done. And it was irreversible.

As Pearl settled herself for the evening in her family room, she admitted she could hardly wait for the hours to pass so she could drive out to Pinewood.

Danger.

Action.

Words to live by as far as she was concerned.

Martine Connor, Marti to friends, looked across at her Secret Service agent and winced. She liked Jessie Palmer, she really did, but she'd had enough of her. This trip to the Far East was it, as far as she was concerned. When she got back to the States next week, she was going to act on her less-than-lame plan to discontinue the service, to which she was entitled for the rest of her life. The bottom line was that Jessie Palmer was cramping her style, and she'd had enough. Enough!

What the hell was she doing in this godforsaken country anyway? In thirty-six hours, she'd given six speeches, eaten shitty food, and pocketed a boatload of cash she neither wanted nor needed. How she had allowed herself to be persuaded to come here was something she still hadn't figured out. But here she was on her way to some putrid luncheon where she would pretend to eat, after which she would give an hour-long speech on a subject she pretended to care about, and which had to be translated for the people who were pretending to listen.

An incoming text made Marti sit upright in the back of the limousine she was riding in. Jessie Palmer looked over at the ex-president of the United States and frowned. She needed to know what the text said, but she knew if she asked, her charge would blow up at her. Blowing up was happening a lot these past few months, and she knew in her gut she was on a short leash. "Good news?" she asked lightly.

Marti burst out laughing as she deleted the message. "You have no idea how good it is. Okay, Jessie, here's the plan. After this speech today, rev up the engines, I'm going home. Cancel everything else. Tell them I have a bellyache, a fungus, a bug — I don't care, but I want wheels up the minute I'm out of that palace. Do not argue, do not ask questions. If you can't do that, I can fly home commercial. Do it! Now, Jessie!"

"But . . . but . . ."

"There are no buts. Just do it."

Jessie wasn't about to give up. "Diplomatic relations . . ."

"Okay, then I'll do it myself and probably

not as diplomatically as you can do it. What's it going to be? You know I never mince words."

Jessie Palmer cringed when she thought about Martine Connor's vocabulary when no one was around, and even sometimes when people *were* around. The lady simply didn't care what she said, when she said it, if she had a point to make she thought no one was getting. With a heavy sigh, she started to tap out text messages. Out of the corner of her eye, she could see the wicked gleam in Connor's eyes as she, too, tapped out a message on her BlackBerry.

Marti felt a giggle in her throat that she did her best to squelch. She typed. Am on the way. Do not start without me.

Marti stared out the bulletproof window. Sand. Sand everywhere. She hated sand. She hated the hot, dry air. She hated the car she was sitting in. It smelled even though it was clean. At least it looked clean. She knew she would smell just like the car until she could shower and change her clothes. Since that wasn't going to happen anytime soon, she knew she would smell until she arrived back in the States. Well, she could live with that since she had no other choice.

She was going home. Thank you, God!

Back to the land of freedom. Back to breaking the law with her sisters to make sure
justice got served. God, just the thought
had her tingling all over.

Charles did his best to hide his grin when
Annie sashayed into the kitchen. "You're
looking well this morning, Annie. I hope
you're up to a good breakfast," he said
tongue-in-cheek.

"Knock it off, Charles. I know how I look,
and yes, I'm up for a good breakfast. What
are you serving? By the way, I heard the
shower going, so I'm thinking Maggie will
be joining us shortly." She looked over at
Myra, who, in Annie's opinion, looked
bright-eyed and bushy-tailed. "How long
have you been up, Myra?"

"Actually, Annie, I didn't go to bed. I took
a middle-of-the-night walk with Charles,
then we sat here drinking tea until the sun
came up," Myra fibbed. "Did you sleep
well?"

"I did. I think I dreamed all night about
what Maggie is going to tell us when she
joins us for breakfast."

"I have to admit that while I didn't dream,
I did discuss the possibilities with Charles,"
Myra said as she fingered her pearls.

The swinging door leading into the dining

room swung open. Maggie, freshly show-
ered, her corkscrew curls still wet, ran to
Charles and hugged him. "Ooooh, this
smells so good. I missed your cooking,
Charles." She turned around and announced cheerily, "It's like old times. Well,
almost."

"Maggie, dear, we agreed yesterday that
yesterday and the days before yesterday are
gone. We're only looking forward from here
on in. You didn't change your mind, did
you?" Myra said.

"No. Absolutely not. I know better than
anyone that you can't go home again. That
doesn't mean that going forward won't be
better. I believe it will be. The memories
will always be there to be looked at when
the time is right or needed. I can do it."

"Of course you can, dear. And you have a
great backup system, that will be here for
you twenty-four/seven. There are times in
all of our lives when we need someone to
help us take the next step. I guess that's
what I'm trying to say, Maggie," Myra said
gently.

"I know that, Myra. Why do you think this
is the first place I ran to?"

Annie clapped her hands. "Okay, enough
of that. Tell us what you hinted at yesterday.
Myra and I can hardly wait to hear what

you have to say."

"I'm sorry, ladies, but whatever Maggie has to say will have to wait. You all know my rule."

"Ah, yes, no business talk at the table. And the reason for that is so we can all appreciate your culinary endeavors. We get it, Charles." Myra smiled.

"Then let's gobble this down quickly," Annie said as she dived into her pancakes, which looked so light and fluffy she thought they might fly upward.

A devil perched itself on Charles's shoulder. "Chew each bite twenty-two times. As you all know, I do not stock antacids in this house. I refuse to accept that my cooking will give anyone indigestion. Chew, ladies. In addition, when one is excited while eating and conversing with excitement, one swallows air, which then leads to gas."

"Stuff it, Charles. We've heard it all before. Look," Annie said, pointing to her plate, "I'm done unless you want me to lick the syrup off the plate."

"I'm finished, too," Myra said, a glint in her eye.

Charles didn't bother to answer when he pointed to Maggie's plate, which was still piled high with his special fluffy pancakes. The mound of crisp bacon was still on the side of her plate and yet to be devoured.

Annie groaned and poured herself a second cup of coffee. She looked at Myra, who sighed in resignation and held out her cup for a refill.

It seemed like forever before Maggie finished her breakfast. Myra and Annie waited a few moments for Charles to whisk away the plates before they started to grill Maggie. "Talk!" they said in unison.

Maggie looked around the table. Suddenly, she felt like she was on display. She took a deep breath. "I don't know if you're going to be interested or not, but I know that when I read about it and saw the media coverage, I thought of you. Do you remember that judge in Pennsylvania a few years ago who was arrested for sending children to boot camps and getting kickbacks from the developers who built the camps? Kids as young as ten who later, it was found out, didn't need to go to such places. One youngster committed suicide. It was all over the news. They were hellholes of misery for those kids. He raked in millions of dollars. Do you remember it?"

"Yes, it was horrible," Myra said. Annie and Charles both nodded that they, too, remembered what she was talking about.

"I saw that poor mother being interviewed. That miserable cretin of a judge showed no sign of remorse at the boy's death, and said the money he was paid was finder fees. The developer said it was a kickback. The judge got sentenced to twenty-eight years in prison."

"If the judge is in prison, what do you think we can do? I don't understand," Charles said.

"I guess I didn't make myself clear. The Pennsylvania judge and what he did was an example, just a starting point. The criminal justice system actually worked that time, and the system took care of him. He'll probably die in prison.

"But something along the same lines is happening in Baywater, Maryland, where I just came from, only there are two judges, and both of them are free as the breeze. They're twins. They preside over family court, juvenile court, and civil court. Eunice and Celeste Ciprani are their names. They come from a very political family that goes back like forever. From what I can gather, they are untouchable."

"No one is untouchable," Annie said vehemently.

"Then you don't know the Ciprani twins," Maggie said. "Listen, I came into this whole thing a little late. Actually, I just started hearing about it the week before I came here. At first I thought it was just local politics, but then I overheard a few things, read a few things, and asked some questions. I got shut down real quick, so my antenna went up, and I came here. I think it's something that needs to be looked into. The local papers are on the side of the twins. There was one weekly paper with a young reporter who took a stab at it, and if I'm right, got shot down; and the weekly printed a retraction."

"What did these twin judges do?" Myra asked, her interest piqued.

"I don't mean to sound vague, but I'm not sure. What I was able to glean from the little I heard and read was something along the lines of that judge in Pennsylvania but on a grander scale. Remember now, I was more or less out of it for ten months and wasn't paying attention to what was going on around me. It was only when I finally came out of the fog I was living in that my reporter instinct kicked in. It's all there. I can feel and smell the corruption. I know I'm right. I'd like to work on it with Ted and Espinosa, then have you ladies step in."

"So what you're saying is the whole court system in Baywater is corrupt, is that right?" Charles asked.

61

"The twins control the courthouse. At least that's what I've been told. In addition, it appears that all the family money was gone. And judges don't make the kind of money to support the lifestyle those two judges enjoy. We would need to delve into that. Abner Tookus can help if he's still in the game. They have a big mansion on Chesapeake Bay. Those don't come cheap. If there's no old family money, where did they get the funds to pay for it? They drive high-dollar cars. And it doesn't hurt that they look like movie stars and dress and act like movie stars."

"Ooooh," Annie said, clapping her hands in excitement. "I'm liking how this is sounding. How old are these twin judges? Do you know?"

"I'm not sure. I've only seen pictures. I'd say early fifties if you discount the Botox. From the pictures I've seen, they both look like they've been nipped and tucked, sliced and diced. Hey, I'm just a reporter. I report what I *see.*"

Annie and Myra laughed out loud.

"Any paramours in the picture?" Charles asked. He looked to the ladies like he wasn't quite getting it. The ladies continued to laugh.

"No clue, Charles. I'm sure you can find

out, though. As I said, I came into this late. I think . . . I really do, that this is something that requires —"

"Our brand of justice," Annie chirped as she finished Maggie's sentence.

"How long will it take you to do a background check, Charles?" Myra asked. "It goes without saying that Annie and I are very interested in knowing more. Nellie, Pearl, and Marti are due back in town this evening around seven. I think we should convene a meeting immediately."

"I can call Abner and ask him to do what he does best. You all probably know what's going on with Abner these days since he married Isabelle. He is still in the game, right?" Maggie asked.

"I believe so. We haven't had an occasion to call him for his services lately. I think you should call him and put a rush on it."

Maggie raised her eyebrows. "Payment?"

"Whatever he asks for. He always comes through for us, and I see no point in haggling and causing stress to anyone," Annie said.

"Okay, but Abner expects me to haggle. I think it's part of his game. As long as he thinks he's sticking it to me, it works for him. Now that he's an old married man, it's possible he changed the rules," Maggie said.

"Do your best, dear," Myra said.

"Then, ladies, if we're finished here, I'll get to work. Dinner will be whatever you can find in the fridge," Charles announced.

"Then I will take Maggie home and get her settled in. I'm sure she has calls to make and things to do until this evening. While she's doing that, I may cook something and bring it over. Is six o'clock okay, or do you want it closer to seven o'clock?" Annie asked.

"Shoot for eight, Annie. As long as you don't plan on bringing hot dogs. Try to be more imaginative, dear. In my texts to the others, I said eight o'clock." Myra smiled to take the sting out of her words.

"All right, ladies. *Dismissed,*" Charles announced, getting up from the table and heading to the huge bank of computers in the room the women called his lair.

Back in the kitchen, Maggie looked around for the backpack that she never traveled without. She said she carried her life on her back because she didn't trust safe-deposit boxes, dresser drawers, or hidey-holes in an attic or cellar to safeguard her life's precious records.

A short conversation ensued as Myra reached for her jacket so she could take the dogs for a run. A smile tugged at the corner of her mouth when she heard Maggie ask Annie if she had her old job as a reporter back.

"Of course, dear. I have to be honest. I don't know what to do about Ted. He's done a magnificent job as the paper's editor in chief. It was hard for him to step into your shoes, but he did it, with a few mishaps along the way. I don't want any hard feelings."

"Annie, look at me. Ted would be happier than a pig in a mudslide if you'd fire him and let him go back to being an investigative reporter. It will be the three of us again. Ted, Espinosa, and I were a team for more years than I care to remember."

"I'll call Ted when we get home. I'll ask him to come by this afternoon, and we can make plans. I just don't know who I can replace Ted with," Annie fretted as she stared out to the parking area at the back of Myra's house.

"Take my car, Annie. Ask Ted and Espinosa to pick up your car and drive it out to the farm when they come to see you." Myra picked up a set of car keys and handed them to Annie.

"John Cassidy, Annie. He'll make a good EIC. Just tell him to stay out of Ted's, Espinosa's, and my hair."

"I can do that, dear. You're sure about John, Maggie."

"I am sure, Annie. He has printer's ink in his veins like his father and grandfather before him."

"All right then, that's good enough for me."

The golden retrievers raced ahead of the women. Myra shivered in the cold. "It feels like the temperature dropped ten degrees in the last hours." She looked overhead at the scudding clouds. A strong gust of wind almost blew her over as she walked Annie and Maggie to her car. "I think it's going to rain later."

"Feels damp," Annie said, climbing behind the wheel. "Call me this afternoon and we'll compare notes."

"Okay." Myra leaned in the open car window. "I'm so glad you're back, Maggie. We all missed you. Call the girls; they'll love hearing from you."

"I will as soon as I get settled. Thanks for being you, Myra. And for whatever it's worth, there are no words to tell you how much I missed you all," Maggie said tearfully.

Myra nodded and stepped back as Annie backed up the car and headed for the gate.

Myra felt tears prick her eyelids.

"Don't cry, Mom. Everything is okay now."

Myra whirled around and clutched at her pearls. "Darling girl, is it really you?"

"It's me, Mummy. Maggie needs you all. Shower her with love the way you used to shower me with love. She needs it, Mom."

"I will. Of course I will," Myra gasped. "I wish I could see you. I wish I could take you in my arms, darling girl."

"I have to go, Mom. I want to watch over Maggie. I love you, Mom. The dogs need you right now."

"And I love you, darling girl." Myra wiped the tears rolling down her cheeks. She barely noticed the dogs sitting at her feet, their heads cocked upward as though they were listening to her spirit daughter. One of the dogs nudged Myra's leg. She looked down and rubbed the dog's sweet spot between her eyes before she turned to walk back to the house. The normally rambunctious dogs trotted along behind her protectively.

"It's all right, girls. That was my daughter. Shhhh. We're good now."

CHAPTER 4

Five miles down the road from Myra's farmhouse, Annie swooped into her own driveway and screeched to a stop. Maggie gasped. "I think that short ride was just like flying in a plane, Annie. You do have a heavy foot. You know that, right?"

Annie sighed. "Everyone is a critic. I have things on my mind. What do you think I should prepare for dinner, dear?"

Her eyes still wild at the crazy trip, Maggie said, "Spaghetti and meatballs."

Annie's heart fluttered in her chest. "Spaghetti and meatballs! I think I can do that. But I'll have to scoot into town to the market for the ingredients. You know where my office is. Go on in and do what you have to do. The key is under the mat."

"Lots of garlic, Annie," Maggie called over her shoulder as she skipped her way up the short flight of steps to the deck leading into Annie's kitchen. She eyed the pumpkins,

68

which were decoratively arranged along with a scarecrow and some bales of hay. She correctly assumed that Annie decorated for Harry Wong's little daughter, Lotus Lily. She winced at the sound of Annie's burning rubber in her haste to get to the market.

Like she was really going to the market. Spaghetti! Meatballs! In a million years, she could never make spaghetti, much less meatballs, that would be edible. Even with a cookbook.

Twelve minutes later, Annie pulled into a parking spot at the Roma Italian Eatery. She bounced into the deserted restaurant and bellowed for Pasquale, who came on the run.

Seeing Annie, he put his hands on his hips, and said, "Company, eh? How much?"

"Enough for seven people. Lots of garlic. And two dozen of your garlic twists."

"How many times do I have to tell you, Miss Annie? Just fry some garlic in olive oil and it will permeate the whole house and make it seem like you cooked for *hours.*"

"Yes, yes, okay. I got it. Just get it ready, Pasquale, and I will be forever in your debt."

Pasquale, a short, chubby, happy little man, shouted a string of Italian. The only thing Annie understood was her name and the word *loco.* At least that's what it sounded like to her.

"You will, of course, return my containers at some point?"

Annie paced the confines of the small foyer. "Don't I always? You better throw in some garlic while you're at it. I don't think I have any at home."

"Of course. Many times I have offered to show you how to cook the sauce. I ask again."

"One of these days, Pasquale. This is just easier. Onions along with the garlic, right?"

"Wouldn't hurt, Countess," Pasquale said, tongue-in-cheek.

Ten minutes later, Annie settled two large shopping bags in the trunk of Myra's car. She cringed at the pungent aromatic garlic wafting from the bags. Oh, crap! Now she was going to stink up Myra's car, and the jig would be up.

Pasquale came up behind her as she was about to close the trunk. He was holding out a large box of baking soda. He shrugged. Annie started to laugh and couldn't stop. She hugged the little Italian and handed over a wad of bills, not knowing if it was too much or too little. If she was short, she'd settle up when she returned Pasquale's containers.

Annie waved as she roared out of the

driveway and headed home. She let out a sigh so loud, she swore the birds overhead started to squawk. She ran into the house and called out Maggie's name. When there was no response, she walked up to the second floor to see what was going on. Maggie waved, her cell phone to her ear as she tapped on her laptop. Annie mouthed the words, "I'll bring up coffee later." Maggie nodded.

Annie galloped back down the stairs and out to the car. She raced back into the kitchen and, within minutes, had everything in the containers transferred to a huge spaghetti pot Fergus had insisted she buy last year. Within seconds, she had garlic and onions smelling up the whole house. She dumped it all into the larger pot and then washed out the fry pan and put it back on the rack.

Her eyes on the clock, Annie bundled everything up into the shopping bags and ran out to the barn with them. Hot dogs would have been so much simpler. She was breathless when she returned to the kitchen to make the coffee she had promised Maggie.

While she waited for the coffee to drip into the pot, Annie took long, deep breaths and exhaled. "I'm too old for these shenanigans," she mumbled to herself. "Next time it's hot dogs, for sure, and Myra will eat them or I'll stuff them down her throat."

"Wow! Annie, you sure do work fast! It smells so good in here. I could smell the garlic all the way upstairs. Oooh, oooh, I can't wait for dinner. I guess you really did pay attention to those cooking lessons Fergus gave you," Maggie said from the doorway.

Annie waved her hands airily. "Half the battle is being organized. I'm organized."

Liar liar, pants on fire. "Coffee, dear?"

"I'd love some coffee. I don't know how you do it, Annie. Ted is on his way with your car. I explained everything, and he's over the moon. He doesn't think it's his place to talk to John Cassidy, so that's something you'll have to do. Do you think you want Ted to stay on to show John the ropes for a few days or just let him plunge in? If you want my opinion, I think John can sit in that chair and not miss a beat. Ted's raring to go. I don't know who's more excited — me or Ted. Oh, Annie, I feel like the weight of the entire world is off my shoulders. Thank you so much for taking me back. And thank you for understanding." Maggie babbled nonstop.

Annie smiled. It was so good to see Maggie smiling and happy. She knew she would have setbacks from time to time, but she knew that in short order, the young woman would move forward and leave the past behind her.

"I called my tenant, and he agreed to move out next week. I agreed to pay his first month's rent on his new place. Nice guy, and he said he understood, so I will be out of your hair by this time next week. Is that okay, Annie?"

"Of course, child. I told you that you could stay as long as you like. I just rattle around here by myself since Fergus left. My housekeeper will be back next week. I gave her the time off because her granddaughter just had a new baby, and I was going to Vegas."

Maggie leaned across the table. "Do you miss him, Annie? Was he the one for you?"

"I do miss him. Was he the one? There were times I thought so and other times I thought, *No, he's not the one.* It doesn't matter now. He's gone, and he won't be back. At the end of the day, dear, family is what's important, and I'm happy that Fergus is back with his children. It doesn't matter what the reasons are. Life is too short for unhappiness and to yearn for something you can't have. That's how I have to look at it, and I'm okay with it. I don't want you worrying about me, Maggie."

Maggie smiled. "I love you, Annie. You always make it right for me. I hope someday I can do something for you to really thank you."

"Dear girl, you don't have to wait for someday. Today, I'm happy if you're happy. Now, how much did you tell Ted about your case?"

Maggie laughed, a joyous sound. "Just enough to get him all riled up and raring to go. I have a good feeling about all of this, Annie."

Annie got up to pour the coffee. "I do, too, child. I do, too."

It was a comfortable silence as the spaghetti sauce bubbled on the stove, the heavenly smell of garlic, onions, and cheese permeating the air, to Maggie's drooling delight.

From time to time, they spoke of everything and nothing as they watched the muted small-screen TV perched on Annie's kitchen counter.

"Maggie, did you call Mr. Tookus?" Annie asked, breaking their comfortable silence.

"I did, Annie, but my call went to voice mail, which I thought was strange. In all the years that I've known Abner, he has always answered his phone. Actually, I think his phone is glued to his ear. I have never had to leave a message. I did leave one, but he hasn't called me back. I'm sure he will at some point."

Annie shrugged. "Mr. Tookus is married now. Perhaps he went on location with Isabelle, who is designing a new shopping mall in upstate New York."

Maggie laughed. "Are you saying his phone won't ring in upstate New York?"

"No, not at all. He might be busy. I think in his other life, he could have been an architect himself. You saw where he lived. We all did. He did that all himself, and it was so good they featured his loft in *Architectural Digest.*"

"I know all that. It doesn't matter what is going on in his life; he answers the phone. It's who he is. Maybe it's me he doesn't want to talk to. Things got rather contentious between us way back when. You should try calling him, Annie, to see if he picks up when *you* call."

Annie pulled her cell phone out of her pocket, scrolled down for Abner's number, and clicked. She listened to Abner's ominous voice telling the caller to leave a name and number, which she did. She rolled her eyes and shrugged as she slid the phone back into the pocket of her slacks. "I guess we just wait to see if he calls one of us back. I'm sure there's a reason why he isn't answering. It could be as simple as being out of the area of a cell tower. It could be anything, dear, so don't take it personally."

Maggie chewed at her nails, a disgusting, hateful habit she owned up to and wasn't able to break. "I can't wait to get started on this. It's been a long time, Annie. I just hope I haven't lost my edge." Her tone was so worried, so fretful sounding, Annie hastened to assure her that the moment she put on her investigative reporter cap, things would fall into place. "It's like riding a bike — you never forget how to do it."

"Two judges, Annie. Twins. You really can't tell them apart, at least in the pictures I've seen. I bet anything that they've stood in for each other on the bench and no one knew the difference. That's a scary thought in my opinion. Not to mention illegal. Think about it, Annie. The plaintiffs, the defendants, the lawyers couldn't tell the difference. If it's true. By the way, I also placed a call to the young reporter on the *Baywater Weekly*, the guy who brought all this to my attention. I called the paper first, and they said he was on a leave of absence, and, oddly enough, they gave me his cell phone number. I left my number and my e-mail address. He hasn't returned my call either. My gut tells me he's hiding out."

"And you think that means what?"

"Why do people take a leave of absence? Why would he hide out? Think about it. Intimidation would be my guess. He's a young guy, so I doubt he's sick. It's obvious to me that he took this leave after his paper printed that watered-down article. I heard something about a retraction, but I don't think that happened. Someone put a clamp on things. He must have talked to the wrong people, asked the wrong questions. I'm just talking out loud. It might be something as simple as taking a late-in-the-year vacation. One way or another, we'll track him down. The *Post* can always use another good reporter, right, Annie? You know, in case we have to dangle a carrot for him when we do find him."

"Absolutely. You do whatever you need to do, Maggie. You think, then, that this young man was or is onto something?"

"I do, Annie. Reporter's instinct. Maybe no one else saw what I saw between the lines. And it is a local weekly paper. People don't devour weeklies like they do the dailies, and the dailies not so much anymore now that people can read their favorite newspapers online."

Annie turned her attention to the back door of her state-of-the-art kitchen. "I hear a car. Must be Ted bringing my car back." She got up and looked out the diamond-shaped panes in the door. "It's Ted and Joseph. Ah, I'm pleased to say that there are no visible signs of dents or bumpers falling off, at least that I can see."

Maggie laughed out loud. "Ted isn't the cowboy driver you think he is. If anything, he drives below the speed limit. Espinosa is worse. He creeps along on the highway, and other drivers blow their horns at him. In my opinion, they are both hazards on the road. You have to keep up with the speed limit. Both of them used to make me crazy because it would take us twice as long to get somewhere as opposed to when I was driving."

Annie smiled. "I guess that's good to know." She opened the door and hugged her two employees. Coffee was offered and accepted. Both men sniffed, and Ted lifted the lid off the spaghetti pot.

"Ah, my favorite food on earth. I could smell it all the way outside." Espinosa seconded Ted's endorsement.

Annie felt out of place as Ted and Espinosa sat down at the table and proceeded to share thoughts and ideas on Maggie's news. Ideas were bounced around at the speed of light as plans and suggestions flew just as fast. The trio were in their element as they relived old times and mapped out an itinerary. At one point, Ted turned to Annie, and said, "I moved all my stuff out of the office, with Espinosa's help. I even watered your plants, Maggie."

"Really! I thought for sure you'd let them die." At Ted's stunned look, she added lamely, "You aren't exactly the watering-plant type, if you know what I mean. Are they lush and healthy?"

Miffed at Maggie's words, Ted nodded and moved on to what he was saying. Like he was really going to tell her he lived in mortal fear of the plants dying and Maggie somehow finding out. He'd nurtured them daily, sometimes hourly, with plant food, new soil, and spraying the leaves so they'd be shiny and healthy-looking.

"You really should call John now, Annie, and tell him about his promotion. I set everything up for him. All he has to do is turn on the computer, plant his rear end in the chair, and he's good to go."

"Since you all don't need me right now, then yes, I'll call John. Stir the sauce once in a while so it doesn't burn, and do not eat it! That's an order."

"Like we would really do something like that," Ted said in mock horror.

Within seconds, three of Annie's favorite people on earth were back to forming and shoring up their plans to take on the Ciprani twins in Baywater, Maryland. *Oh, to be that young again and have the drive and stamina that those three have,* Annie thought.

There was excitement in Maggie's voice that was contagious when she looked at Ted and Espinosa, and said, "We're onto something, aren't we?"

"Oh, yeah. Keep talking, sweet cheeks," Ted drawled, using his favorite nickname for his old love. Maggie laughed out loud. Espinosa's thumb shot upward as he leaned in closer to make sure he didn't miss anything.

"Okay, guys, listen up. This is what I'm thinking . . ."

It was totally dark outside when Myra's guests arrived, the headlights of the various vehicles bouncing off the kitchen windows. It was hard to contain the excitement she was feeling. She looked around to make sure everything was satisfactory. It was. They were eating in the kitchen this evening because it was less formal than the dining room, with the long, polished table where one had to shout to be heard at the end. Kitchens, in her opinion, were for eating and cooking. She wasn't sure, but she rather thought her guests felt the same way.

The large, round, oak table that could seat eight was set with colorful place mats along with decorative colored dishes that seemed to glow in the kitchen light. A bright orange pot of brilliant fall leaves, with a small pumpkin that matched the ceramic pot, graced the center of the table but would be removed and replaced with grated cheese, hot pepper flakes, salt, and pepper, and, of course, the bread tray when Annie served her dinner.

The security monitor above the door came alive as car after car, along with short bursts of their respective horns, announced Pinewood's guests for the evening.

There were laughter, hugs, and comments about how good the food that Annie and Maggie were carrying to the kitchen table smelled. Questions were asked about Nellie's not-so-new titanium hips and Pearl's gout, then followed up with inquiries about Martine's trip to the place, wherever it was, that no one could pronounce.

Things moved with a precision drill as the

food was transferred to bowls that matched the colorful dishes, wine was poured, and more hugs welcomed Maggie home, followed by casual conversation along with a hundred excited questions about what was going on.

It was all casual, friendly, and when Myra said, "Charles is knee-deep in his research down below in his lair, so his rule that we can't talk business while eating is not in effect." Hoots of delight ensued as the guests all helped themselves from the bowl of spaghetti.

Most of the questions were aimed at Maggie, who willingly relayed all she knew, ending with "After our meeting this evening with Charles to hear what he came up with, Ted, Espinosa, and I are going to travel to Baywater and see what we can come up with firsthand and get the lay of the land, so to speak. My gut is telling me we all need to tread very carefully. I think the twin judges are a force to be reckoned with."

"And you think we aren't?" Annie asked testily.

"That's not what I meant, Annie. If I were a betting woman, my money would be on all of you. I'm just saying those two judges are not amateurs, and we all need to keep that in mind. That's another reason why I want to go there and walk the walk and talk to that young reporter from the *Baywater Weekly.*"

The ladies kicked it around some more, their eyes on the clock as they waited for the appointed hour, when they were to meet Charles in the catacombs, better known as the War Room. As women always did when a meal was over, they got up and worked as a team to clear the table, load the dishwasher, and pack away the leftovers into other bowls with lock lids. Myra leaned over to whisper in Annie's ear, "You need to give Pasquale my compliments. It was a delicious dinner."

Annie blinked. Then she smiled, leaned forward, hissing in Myra's ear, "You say one word, and I will snatch those pearls off your neck and shove them up your nose."

"Finally, finally, I one-upped you. Someday you have to tell me how you pulled this off with Maggie at your house. Not to worry, my lips are sealed." Myra laughed.

"What are you two talking about? What's so funny?" Pearl asked.

"Myra was telling me she thought I put a tad too much garlic in the bread. Like Myra knows the first thing about cooking! Although, I do have to say, she does make a decent grilled cheese sandwich." Annie leaned over to straighten Myra's pearls, which draped her neck. "There you go, dear. I just straightened out your pearls. You certainly wouldn't want them to break now, would you?"

"I would be devastated if that happened." Myra smiled.

"I think we're good here," Nellie said as she pressed the WASH button on the dishwasher. "The garlic twists are packed up, and the leftover spaghetti is in the fridge. All Charles has to do is heat it up."

"Then, ladies, I suggest we join Charles. Maggie, dear, check the kitchen door and set the dead bolt."

"I already did it. Front and side doors are bolted."

"Then let's get things under way," Myra said, leading the way to the living room and the secret entrance that would lead the women to the catacombs.

CHAPTER 5

The six women entered the War Room quietly and took their seats at the huge, round table in the center of the room. They looked at each other expectantly, unsure what was to follow. Myra turned to look at Charles, who was at his station next to a long wall of computers, three steps above the floor where they sat. Charles nodded to indicate he knew they were waiting for him. He flicked a switch, and the television screen came to life.

There was a soft, muted humming sound in the air from the high-tech machinery and the overhead paddle fan. The entire area was climate-controlled to protect the expensive machinery under Charles's control.

One wall of the War Room had clocks that revealed the time around the world. Another wall was taken up by the ginormous television screen where Lady Justice presided.

"I find this room absolutely amazing,"

Pearl Barnes said as she looked around. "It's unbelievable how you created all of this here in the catacombs. Must have taken forever from start to finish."

"Not all that long. Isabelle designed it. It took about six months. Since then, it's gotten a lot of use, as you all know. For a short period of time we had an empty chair when our sister Julia passed away. Annie took her place. So many important decisions have been made in this very room that I've lost count. Sisters that we are, we cried here, laughed here, celebrated our victories here. It's good to be back," Myra said, a catch in her voice.

Annie looked around. "Since Charles isn't ready to join us, this might be a good time to have Maggie bring everyone up to speed and to explain why we're all here and what's expected of us. By the way, Marti, how are you going to handle the Secret Service you have protecting you, as far as we're all concerned?"

The ex-president laughed. "I went straight to the top. Meaning Lizzie Fox. As you know, she's my best friend. She's taking care of it just the way she did for you, Nellie, when you wanted your protection gone so you could become Cornelia Easter, private citizen. Lizzie said my protection will be a thing of the past in two days. She said my ace in the hole was the *Post,* where I would give an interview saying I have no need of protection at the taxpayers' expense. I look forward to my unfettered freedom just as you did, Nellie. As far as I'm concerned, it's a done deal — as everything is once Lizzie takes it over."

Everyone nodded to show they were sympathetic to Marti's feelings and that they all understood and accepted Lizzie Fox as Marti's solution.

"Maggie, the floor is yours," Myra said.

Maggie leaned closer to the table, her voice at conversation level. "Okay, here goes. Right now I'm going strictly on my reporter's instinct, which has been dormant way too long. The fact that it kicked in is telling me I am on to something. I want to say right now, at the outset, that I have no proof of anything. Absolutely none. All I have is this gut instinct telling me I'm right, and things need to be investigated. Now, if I'm wrong, which I don't think I am, you can all drum me out of here with a broomstick, but I don't think that's going to happen. There is also the possibility I am reading more into this based on that case in Pennsylvania. I don't think so, but you all need to know there is that possibility. I haven't had any real quality time to do any research. I did a Google search, but the info I managed to get is limited. It's just social networking stuff.

"Baywater, Maryland. That's the location we're going to be working. Two hours from here, perhaps less if you have a heavy foot on the gas pedal. There are two judges who are twins and appear to control the courthouse and the system. There appears, I say *appears* to be no crime whatsoever in Baywater. Because . . . everyone who appears before these two judges is sent to jail, prison, or a work farm. Almost like those camps from the place in Pennsylvania. At least that's what a young reporter was trying to say in an article he wrote in a weekly paper. Being a reporter, I'm trained to read between the lines, and I can tell you that article was a watered-down version of what the reporter wanted to say. I've got calls in to him, but so far there's been no response.

"I might be a little ahead of myself here. The reason that particular article triggered my interest is because I remembered reading, as I'm sure you all read, about the judge in Pennsylvania who was sending kids to boot camps and taking kickbacks." Maggie looked around to see all the women nodding to indicate they remembered the judge in question and the case she was talking about.

"I haven't had the time to do a real background check; Charles is doing that. But what I do know is what I've read recently. The twin judges are Eunice and Celeste Ciprani, famous in the state of Maryland. They call each other Nessie and Cee. No one else would dare call them by their childhood names."

"I'm not getting it, Maggie. What was it that triggered your interest? Twin judges, I grant you, are unusual, but there must be something else to bring us all here at this time," Pearl said.

"Well, for starters, Baywater is virtually crime-free. I drove fifteen miles out of my way to visit Baywater before I came here. It's a *Stepford* town. Remember that movie? The whole town just looked like it had been scrubbed clean. It didn't look real, but it *was* real. Every nerve in my body was twanging as I walked around. The hair on the back of my neck was on end the whole time. I felt like a thousand pairs of eyes were watching me. It was a really creepy feeling, I can tell you that. By the way, the local jail is filled. The three prisons within a hundred-mile radius are filled to capacity. I suppose you could say the town has a kick-ass police department, but I'm not buying that. While I was having lunch, I Googled the town, and that information came up."

"Are you saying that every offender who goes before either one of the twin judges or any judge ends up in prison?" Marti asked.

"I think that pretty much sums it up from my point of view. But I found out something else, and the only reason I found it out was I read between the lines of the article that young reporter had published. He said the twins were land rich. Well, guess what's built on some of that land? Boot camps would be my guess for want of a better term. That's where all offenders who break the law are sent because the prisons are already filled to capacity. Again, I'm not sure of any of this, but I think I'm right, and right now I am stressing here that what I say is just my opinion. I could be wrong. Until we get copies of the actual land deeds, there is no proof. You spit on the sidewalk, you go to one of those camps. That's the way it was in Pennsylvania if you believe the stories. Now, the article in the *Baywater Weekly* did not say that. It's what I read between the lines, and I could be wrong. I'm sure Charles will have more details when he finishes his search and talks to us. With nowhere else to send offenders, they're sent to these camps, with the state picking up the tab. Again, just my opinion. If you think about it, it makes sense. Win-win for the Ciprani twins. Think about this: they lease the land, get rent from the camps and a kickback from the managers or whoever supervises the actual running of the camps. And the state pays for it all. Are you all following me now?"

"Bastards!" Pearl snapped. "Back in the day, which was really just two years ago, I heard something about this from some of the women we were hiding in our underground railroad. I remember one of the mothers was hiding out her son. I can get to some of those women if need be. They might have some firsthand knowledge. As you all know, I'm under surveillance for running the underground railroad, so I have to be careful, but I *can* do it. What you're saying makes sense to me if my opinion counts."

"As long as you're careful, Pearl," Annie said. "We can use all the information we can get. I'm thinking we're going to be going up against some very powerful people, who won't take kindly to our brand of justice."

"Annie, Careful is my middle name. When you take on the responsibility of hiding women and their children so no further harm can come to them, you develop eyes in the back of your head, and your other senses are always on high alert. I know the rules, so don't worry about me," Pearl responded.

Charles took that moment to step down from the dais. He offered a greeting, then clicked on the monster TV. The women stared at Lady Justice with unblinking intensity, a reminder of why they were seated where they were and what they planned to do. Another click, and the full screen came alive with the picture of two beautiful women smiling into the camera.

"Definitely Botox," Marti said. "Too much in my opinion. Especially on the forehead."

"They're not youngsters," Pearl said. "Close in on their necks, Charles." Charles clicked the remote control he was holding several times. "Turkey wattle! That's hard to correct, and it appears to have been done already and needs doing again. That tells me their age is not what is being reported. Add ten more years," she said, authority ringing in her voice.

In the background now, Charles fought with himself not to laugh out loud.

"The hands are a giveaway," Nellie snorted. "Check out the veins and the liver

92

spots. Maybe their surgeon ran out of sutures or that stuff they use to freeze off the liver spots."

"And you know this how?" Annie asked.

"I looked into it. That's how! It's bad enough my fingers are crooked from my arthritis, I didn't want those damn liver spots highlighting them even more. Pearl is right — add ten years, and don't try telling me they have good genes, either. So there, Annie!"

"Did you do it?" Annie asked as she looked down at her arms and hands.

"Hell, yes, I did, but the damn liver spots came back. You can't fight old age. Those two on the screen are sure giving it a try, though. Do we know exactly how old they are?" Nellie asked.

"They admit to fifty-four," Charles said. "Who knows if it's true. If it's imperative to find that out, I can search the birth records. For now, they're admitting to fifty-four."

"Plus ten," Myra snapped. "Any paramours in the background?"

"She means do they have booty calls?" Annie said, tongue-in-cheek.

"I don't understand the term," Charles said, looking perplexed.

"Sex, Charles! Do they have sex? Casual, meaningful, committed." Marti grinned.

"Oh, I see. Well, according to several pictorials as well as various tutorials I was able to access, the ladies seem to go to dinner once or twice a week with men. At this time, I don't know if they're personal dinners or business dinners. I assume you all want me to find out. Is that correct?"

"Yes, dear, that would be extremely helpful. Sex makes the world go round; we all know that." Myra laughed. The others tittered, to Charles's chagrin.

"Moving along here," Charles said. "The twin judges come from a long-illustrious political family in Maryland. At one point in time, around twenty or twenty-five years ago, the family money ran out. I'm speaking of actual money. But the family was and still is land rich. I don't think I'd be too far off the mark to say the family owns half of the Eastern Shore, at least the rich half. I'm referring to raw land. The twins are the only members of the family left and thus make all the decisions about family affairs since it is just the two of them. In one article I read, there was a brief one-line mention of a brother, Peter. I have to assume he passed away, but I will verify that when I get into the family records. The only real family building is a mansion on the Chesapeake Bay. It's been photographed, featured, showcased so many times, I couldn't keep up with it. To say the mansion is magnificent would be an understatement. The twins stay in town at a luxurious condo during the week and drive up to the mansion Friday, when court is over. That's been their pattern for many years."

"The men who dine with them in town . . . are they the same men they dine with when they're at the mansion? Sleepovers?" Annie asked, tongue firmly in cheek.

"Don't know yet. I have queries out to my people. I expect a detailed report by midday tomorrow. Right now there's more we don't know than what we do know."

"Did you come up with anything about the town of Baywater? Maggie said she went out of her way to visit it on her way here. She likened the town to a Stepford town. Is there anything to her opinion?" Marti asked.

Charles clicked the remote in his hand. A picture-pretty image appeared. "What you are seeing is the main square in the town. It's quite pretty, extremely well maintained. They have old-fashioned gas lamps, cobblestone roads around the square. Ivy-covered buildings. What you're seeing is a picture taken in the springtime. Note the colorful flowers everywhere. It all looks like an army of gardeners work twenty-four/seven to keep it looking like it does. There's no sign of litter anywhere. I'd like my own people to do a visual check. Avery Snowden is gathering up his men to do just that. I want to be sure things are clear before any of you go there to do whatever you're planning on doing.

"There was something else that hit me straight out. When I was researching the town of Baywater, one of their claims to fame is their extraordinary police department. They have no crime, or so they would have you believe. The Baywater Police Department has been looked up to by virtually every law-enforcement agency across the country. The chief of police travels around the country giving speeches on how to safeguard citizens. The chief gets paid to do this. Handsomely, I might add. But only when he does it on his own time. He's also one of the men the twin judges have dinner with on a regular basis."

"That's very interesting," Nellie said. "The first word that comes to mind is *collusion.* Do you all agree?"

The ladies nodded as one.

"Charles, how far did you get when you checked the land records?" Maggie asked.

A snort of sound escaped Charles's lips. "I ran into all kinds of problems with the state's Web site. I managed to get to the

Baywater site, then it shut down. I was pulling my hair out in frustration because a virus warning kept popping up and wouldn't let me advance any of my searches. I immediately knew something was wrong. I turned it over to Avery and his experts. So, to answer your question, Maggie, I can't tell you anything."

Maggie's fist shot in the air. "I knew it! I knew it! This is what I think. Like I told you before, I think the twin judges lease out their land to some kind of organization, possibly themselves, that built camps for sentenced offenders and the state picks up the bill. If the jails and prisons are full, what do they do with offenders on an ongoing basis? If you can get arrested and sent away for jaywalking or spitting on the sidewalk, it sure makes sense to me."

Marti sucked in a deep breath. "How many such places do you think there are, Maggie?"

Maggie shrugged. "I have no clue, but I have to think this is not a small operation. I think it's on a much grander scale than the case in Pennsylvania. It's just my gut and my reporter's instinct that tells me that if we're right, the twins went for the max. That's not to say they didn't start out small, got a feel for things, then they went at it full bore. Again, it's just my opinion."

"Maggie, dear, your opinions carry weight with all of us. You're the professional, and we respect your opinions," Myra said.

"Has Abner been in touch, Maggie?" Annie asked.

Charles bristled at the mention of the hacker's name. No one but Myra seemed to notice.

"He just sent a text saying he was out of cell-phone range and is on his way back to the city and would call me in the morning. If Charles is right, Abner will know how to get past that virus thing he ran into. Since land records are available to the public, anyone can go to the hall of records in Baywater and search them out. If we do that, we'll see firsthand if we're being stonewalled. But we would also be tipping our hand."

"Before we do that, we need to create a legend that will bear intense scrutiny. I can get started on that right now. Off the top of my head, I'm thinking of a wealthy European industrialist. I'll leave you ladies to your planning," Charles said. He clicked the remote, and Lady Justice once again reigned supreme over the room.

Myra took the floor. "Okay, ladies, it does look, at least from my perspective, that we are indeed onto something. Let's bat it around and see how you all feel, and if you have any ideas, no matter how bizarre they might seem, we want to hear them. I don't mind telling all of you that I like the challenge I'm seeing here."

"I agree; I'm tingling all over," Annie quipped. "Let's hunker down and get to work."

"Wait a minute. Are you all saying that Ted, Espinosa, and I shouldn't leave for Baywater tomorrow?"

"Not just yet, dear. I think we need to give Charles and his people a few days to get us the real skinny on the twin judges. As well as Mr. Tookus. We certainly don't want to tip our hand ahead of time. Let's take a vote," Myra said.

The near-unanimous vote was six to one to wait.

Maggie, the only dissenting voice, sulked.

CHAPTER 6

Judge Celeste Ciprani looked around her chambers the way she did every day she was in the courthouse presiding over her courtroom. She had furnished and paid for the suite herself because she was addicted to fine things. In her opinion, being a judge made her worthy of fine things. Rich mahogany paneling, the Louis IV desk that had belonged to her great-granddaddy and was worth a fortune. The chairs were Chippendale. She had two, and her twin sister, Judge Eunice Ciprani, had the other two, left to them by their grandfather. A Windsor love seat that was worth more than the two chairs together just went to prove Celeste didn't care if the furnishings matched or not. What she cared about was showing off what she had. Celeste was all about her image. Just like her sister, Eunice, whose offices were just three doors away and furnished almost exactly the way hers were.

Eunice insisted that her plants and ficus trees were more luxurious, something Celeste didn't dispute. Both sisters admitted that they considered their suites as havens away from home.

Celeste and Eunice were the only two judges in the Baywater courthouse who had suites. The other judges, and there were nine, had small, cramped offices with furnishings liberated from some dank, dark place in the bowels of the ancient building. The reason they were small was because the Ciprani sisters demanded the extra room to create suites, and the only way they could be accommodated was to make the other offices smaller. Since the twin judges ruled the courthouse, they had only to ask to have their wishes granted. It was a wise person who kept quiet and sucked up the discomfort because that same person didn't want to feel the wrath of the Ciprani twins.

Celeste hung her pure silk robe on a scented padded hanger. She smoothed the sleeves, fastened the top snap, then ran her hands over the expensive material. Her robes were custom-made, and she had six of them, as did her sister. One for every day of the workweek and one extra, just in case of a spill or something equally disastrous. The robe defined who she was — Judge

Celeste Ciprani. The stand that held the one-of-a-kind robe was an antique and could only hold one item, Celeste told anyone who cared to ask why she had two racks. A judge's robe, she explained, was sacred and deserved its own place. The robe stand was the first thing a person saw upon entering the sacred domain. Well, not exactly the first thing; the solid gold nameplate on the door, appropriately engraved, was the first thing a person saw. The other antique stand had two hooks, one for her coat or jacket, the other for her designer purse and umbrella.

Celeste took a last look around her office. Satisfied that everything was the way she wanted it, she walked over to her desk and pressed a button on the console. "Are you ready, Nessie?" Her twin said she was and would meet her in the hall. They would walk through the courthouse and out to the parking lot to Eunice's car.

Celeste checked the locked drawers on her desk and turned off the light. She checked the door twice — not that she was obsessive-compulsive; it was just something she did every night. Now she was good to go.

The courthouse was quiet, with only the evening workers around. The lawyers and their clients were usually gone by four o'clock, four-thirty at the latest. The other judges were usually out of the building by four-thirty, never later than five, along with the stragglers. The clerks and bailiffs followed on their heels. It was a well-known fact that the Ciprani twins were always the last to leave the building and usually the first to arrive in the morning.

The twins met in the hall, smiled at one another, touched each other on the arm in a sisterly way. "Good day?" Eunice asked.

"Every day's a good day except when it's a bad day, Nessie," Celeste said, calling her twin by her childhood nickname. "I guess I should say, uneventful. How was yours?"

"Same as yours, Cee. I can't wait to get home and have a drink. I called home a little while ago to see what Thelma prepared for dinner. It's warming in the oven. Your favorite, Cee. Rare roast beef, creamed peas and onions, garlic-mashed potatoes, and pickled beets. Oh, yes, yeast rolls and peach cobbler for dessert."

"Thelma is a gem. I'd hate to lose her."

"Why would we lose her? She's been with us forever. We pay her well. She starts at nine and leaves at four-thirty. Did she look at you crossways or something? No one cooks like Thelma, and she minds her own business. If you're thinking of firing her, perhaps you should rethink it. There aren't that many good cooks around these parts."

"Did you forget that I sentenced her nephew to eighteen months at the farm? After that, her attitude toward me changed. I know this may sound bizarre, but I like to think ahead. What if she puts something in our food? The boy is her favorite nephew. She made a point of telling me that. Favorite nephew or not, it's not her concern; it's the concern of the parents who allowed the boy to drink and drive. Think in terms of the boy's sentence as a new Chanel purse, Nessie, and forget about it. Just because Thelma is our housekeeper she has no right to question what we do in court. She needs to remember her place. Regardless of what you say, cooks are a dime a dozen, and there's always takeout."

Nessie shrugged off her sister's comments except for the part about a new Chanel purse. "You're paranoid, Cee."

"Like you aren't!" Cee snapped. "Listen, I need you to cover for me tomorrow morning for two motion hearings. I saw on the roster that the case you were to hear settled at four o'clock this afternoon. I found a wrinkle, and I need to go for some Botox."

Nessie stopped in her tracks and looked up at her twin in the dim light. "Sure. Let me see! Oh, my God! Yes, you do have a new wrinkle. Are you sure Ethan can take you on such short notice? And the next question is, Can you get Botox on top of other Botox? Won't it lump up on you?"

"I'm just going to show up. Trust me, Ethan won't turn me away. He won't even fuss; he'll just have his girls reschedule everyone else. He wouldn't be *the man* to go to for cosmetic fixes if it wasn't for you and me. We put him where he is. I'm not worried about it. I'll be back in time for my ten o'clock hearing. No, it won't lump up on me, at least I don't think it will," Celeste said, but her tone betrayed uncertainty.

Eunice skipped ahead as she pressed a button on her key chain and unlocked the doors to a sleek, black Porsche.

The short ride to their luxurious condo was made in what the twins considered comfortable silence. They were so in tune with each other that words weren't necessary. It had always been that way since early childhood. It amused both women that people couldn't figure out which twin was the alpha. In their minds, they were equal in all things, so there was no reason to speculate even though, if one wanted to get technical, Celeste was born seven minutes earlier than Eunice.

If a private behind-the-scenes-poll were to be taken among the citizens of Baywater, the results would be that the Ciprani twins were rich, vain, manipulative, corrupt, selfish, hateful, man-haters, and *evil*.

"I don't know if this is important or not, Cee, but yesterday I sent my clerk to Eva's for lunch. She told me this morning that there was a stranger having lunch at the café and she was asking questions about the town and about us. And she was Googling Baywater. My clerk could see her laptop. Not that she was trying to hide it or anything. She said she looked familiar but couldn't place her. I had ordered the ravioli, and she had to wait for it, so with nothing else to do, she was doing what she calls people watching. The woman paid in cash when she left and asked for directions to the courthouse. It might not mean anything, and it might mean something."

"Hmm. You're right, Nessie. I don't like strangers coming to town and asking questions, especially when they ask questions about us even though we are famous in certain circles. We'll stay alert, but right now my main concern is this damn wrinkle. *That's* important."

Nessie laughed. She loved how vain Cee was and how she herself had no need of

Botox. She would, however, admit to consulting Ethan for several small injections of Restylane, but she had no need of Botox, and that irritated her sister to no end. It also irritated Cee that she was a diabetic and Nessie wasn't. Cee had her father's genes and Nessie her mama's. It was the only point of contention between the twins.

When they reached their destination, both women exited the racy sports car and walked across the underground garage to the elevator. Both women did what they always did — reached for the cans of Mace they carried in their purses. Even though the residents of the condominium were wealthy, Social Register types, that didn't mean some lowlife couldn't find the way into the parking garage, top-notch security or not.

Once, and only once, after one too many glasses of wine, Cee had confided in her twin that she knew they were not liked or even respected in Baywater. Even though Cee knew she should not drink wine to excess because of her diabetic condition, she did so when she was very stressed. She'd gone on to say they were hated in the courthouse by their peers. Even the janitors hated them. To which Nessie had responded, What difference does it make as long as those same people *fear* us? Cee said she couldn't argue with that and had gone to sleep.

It was Cee's turn to make the weekend drive up to the Chesapeake Bay mansion. While the drive wasn't that long in miles, it seemed to take an eternity for the twin judges to reach their old home. The moment Cee stopped the car on the circular shale driveway, both women heaved a sigh of relief. They were *home*.

"I just love this time of year," Nessie gushed as she climbed out of her sister's Mercedes, her eyes on the cobbled road that led to a dead end. She heard rather than saw the small rusty-looking car with the bad muffler chugging on by. She shrugged. She opened the back door of the car for her designer briefcase, stuffed to overflowing with files, records, and the newspapers she hadn't had the time to read. Her pricey handbag, just as full, was almost as big as the briefcase but cost twice as much.

Cee joined her sister, carrying an identical briefcase and handbag, equally filled. They walked around to the rear door and entered the mansion by way of the kitchen. Nessie ran to the thermostat and turned up the heat. Cee headed for the huge fieldstone fireplace, turned on the gas starter, and added wood. By the time they changed their clothes, the house would be warm, and they could eat the takeout food they'd bought in town.

In this beloved family home, there were no servants, no household help, and for good reason. Neither sister wanted the house tainted in any way by other footsteps, and to that end they had an expensive state-of-the-art security system. They considered this house sacrosanct. Once a month, the twins took one extra day and drove up to the shore house to clean it from top to bottom and lay in staples and frozen food. There was, however, a gardener, but in more than twenty years, the twins had set eyes on him perhaps five times. His routine was Monday through Friday, and the rule was he was to be gone by six o'clock Friday evening. He never worked weekends. He never called his employers; nor did they call him. It was a situation that worked for everyone.

No one ever *dropped* in for visits on weekends. To do so meant they were invading the Ciprani twins' privacy and ignoring the posted privacy and no trespassing signs. That, too, worked for everyone.

The Ciprani twins were not loved and

adored on the Eastern Shore any more than they were loved and adored in Baywater. They were hated and feared by their neighbors and the local citizenry.

Nessie tossed the empty Chinese food container into the fireplace. The grease and little bits of food left in the container sizzled and spit upward. She snuggled deeper into the nest of pillows and pulled out the newspapers she'd brought with her. She looked over at her sister, who was reading a brief. Her concentration was total. She decided not to interrupt her sister's concentration.

A long time later, Nessie asked, "Cee, did you read the article in the *Baywater Weekly* written by someone named Daniel West?"

"Hmm," Cee murmured, so deep was her concentration.

"The thing is, there's nothing damaging or anything to us, it's just who is Daniel West and why did he select us for his article? Normally, the papers give us a heads-up before printing anything. This time they didn't. It makes me wonder why. Are you listening to me, Cee?"

"Hmm."

"Cee, on the drive here, I thought someone was following us. Did you notice anything?"

This time, Cee's head jerked upright.

"What did you say?"

Nessie sighed. "I said I had the feeling someone was following us on the drive here. That's why I asked if you noticed anything. I realize it was dark, but there was that one car that stayed with us right until we pulled into our driveway. I'm not trying to be melodramatic or anything. Once we hit the turnoff, rarely has there even been a car following us. I pay attention to things like that. Only residents take that turnoff. I turned around to see if I could make out what kind of car it was when you pulled into the driveway. It looked like a clunker of some kind with a bad muffler. No one around here drives cars like that. I don't care if that makes me sound paranoid or not."

"I wasn't going to say that at all, Nessie. I commend you on being so alert. I guess my mind was on other things. In the morning, we'll drive around and see if we can see the kind of car you described. It could be something as innocent as a friend visiting some kid. It is Friday night, and kids gather early for weekend activities."

Nessie sighed. "Cee, the only people who live on the lane beyond us are old, and the Matthews house is empty. That leaves the Donaldsons, and they're in their late eighties. Their chauffeur is almost as old, and

111

they have a Bentley. Their nurse or attendant, whatever she is, lives on the premises and drives a Mustang. I've seen her in it, and it's bright red. I wish now I'd had the presence of mind to watch to see if the car turned around and came back."

Cee stared at her sister in the glow of the firelight. She fingered the area where she'd had a Botox injection earlier that morning. She tried to frown, but her muscles wouldn't cooperate. The area *felt* lumpy, and it *looked* lumpy. Unusual, because Ethan always massaged the area after an injection for just that very reason. To her chagrin, her face looked like she'd been stung by a bee.

"Why are you looking at me like that, Cee?"

"I'm trying to decide if we should go on red alert or not. This injection site feels lumpy. It even looks lumpy. It's never been lumpy before. I'll kill Ethan if he screwed me up."

Nessie threw her hands in the air. "For God's sake, Cee! All you have to do is massage the area. That's what you've always said. This could be serious, and you're worried about your vanity."

"There's nothing we can do at the moment, now is there, Nessie? I said in the morning we'll drive around and see if we can spot the car. Someone could have gotten lost. As to the reporter at the *Baywater Weekly,* I will call them in the morning and ask some questions. What that means, Nessie, is there's nothing we can do right now, so it's perfectly all right for me to worry about this lumpy area by my eye. Enough said!"

"Okay, okay, try this on for size, sister dear. I wasn't going to say anything because it was just a weird dream, but it all ties in, in a crazy kind of way. I had a dream about Peter last night. It was so real I couldn't go back to sleep. I spent the night in the kitchen drinking coffee trying to figure out why would I dream about Peter at this point in time."

Cee's voice was so cold, Nessie shivered and clasped her arms across her chest. "I thought we agreed to never discuss Peter. He's dead."

"Only to *us. We* declared him dead. He's *not* dead as in dead, Cee. He's out there somewhere. He can come back anytime he wants and get his pound of flesh. It was just a dream, but dreams have a way of . . ."

"Coming to pass? Is that what you're trying to say? We had him declared dead. We even have a death certificate. Have you been thinking about Peter and what we did,

Nessie?" Cee asked as she massaged the injection site at the corner of her eye.

"No, not really, and certainly not recently. I won't lie. I do think about him from time to time. If he ever comes back, you and I will spend the rest of our lives in prison."

"Peter won't come back. He hates us as much as we hate him. He's out of our lives — get that through your head. This damn lump is simply not moving," Cee whined.

"He has to hate us for what we did to him. There is no court in the land that wouldn't side with him. We hate Peter because Daddy did that old-fashioned, Southern thing and left everything to the firstborn son. And we stole it all away from him. Therein lies the difference."

"Why are we having this conversation, Nessie? Because you had a bad dream? A guilt-ridden bad dream? Or is it the article in the paper or the clunky car you saw? I thought we agreed never to discuss Peter because he is dead to us."

Nessie picked at a rice noodle that had dropped to her lap. She looked over at her sister. "Aren't you the one who always says we need to pay attention to things that happen out of the norm? To pay attention to gut instinct? That's what I'm doing. You should be doing the same thing instead of

114

stewing and fretting over a lump by your eye. It will smooth out. We go through this every time you get a Botox injection." Nessie's tone turned ominous when she said, "Everything happens in threes, you know that. The article in the *Baywater Weekly* no one warned us about was number one, the clunker car following us was number two, and my dream of Peter is number three. Say something, Cee."

"I'm going to put a hot compress on this lump."

"You do that, Cee. I'm going to bed," Nessie snapped. She poked at the fire, then closed the glass doors to make sure no sparks worked their way through the fire screen.

Nessie stomped her way out of the room. Cee watched her go as she worked the skin around her eye. Nessie was so emotional. Then her eyes narrowed as she thought about her brother, Peter, and how much her parents had loved him. At least that's what she and Nessie had been told as they grew up. She stopped just short of adding, And how much our father hated Nessie and me because our mother died giving birth to us.

CHAPTER 7

Maggie turned off the ignition, her weary shoulders slumping. She looked out the windshield and realized it was now totally dark though it was only five-thirty. She had hoped to arrive earlier, but she'd gotten sidetracked. Now she was home. She continued to stare out the window at the total darkness. It was all so normal. The streetlamps casting a yellow spill over the sidewalks, a man walking a small dog, two giggling girls walking arm and arm, drivers looking for parking spaces. Just the way it was every day when she'd lived here a few years ago. The end of the day for tired workers. She wished then that she had taken the time to get to know her neighbors, but when she'd last lived here in Georgetown, she was up and out of the house by six in the morning and rarely got home before eight or nine in the evening. That didn't leave much time for getting to know one's neighbors.

Maggie got out of the car and looked down the street, to where Nikki and Jack Emery lived. Just five houses away. She squinted in the darkness to see if there were any lights on in the house, but she couldn't tell. She turned back to her own house and smiled in the darkness. Her tenant had left the porch light on for her. As far as tenants went, William Yost was ideal. He paid his rent on time and if anything needed fixing, he had it fixed and sent on a bill with his rent check. He had promised to take care of her house as if it were his own. She hoped he had done that.

Maggie popped the trunk and started to unload everything to the narrow sidewalk. Then she ran up and opened the door with her old key. A warm blast of air greeted her. She sniffed appreciatively. She smelled lemon polish, floor wax, and window cleaner. It was not an unpleasant scent, more like it used to smell when she would take a day off to clean house.

It took her seven trips to carry in all her belongings and what Annie called her gear. For now, her plan was to leave everything in the foyer and get Ted or Espinosa to carry her heavy suitcases up to the second floor at some point. Knowing herself, she estimated it might take at least a year to unpack

117

all the boxes and bags. She shrugged.

Maggie walked around, turning on lights, her eyes popping at how neat and clean everything was. There was even a laid fire. She couldn't see a speck of dust anywhere. She walked into the kitchen and sniffed. Food! She saw the bottle of wine, the small vase of fall flowers mixed with colorful autumn leaves. She picked up the note on the kitchen table and read it.

Dear Maggie,

Thanks so much for allowing me to live in your house these past few years. I enjoyed every day I lived here. I did my best to keep up with everything, and hope it meets with your approval. I had everything cleaned, and there are fresh linens (your personal ones I never used) on the bed and clean towels in the bathroom. Dinner is in the oven. I loved cooking in this kitchen. If you ever want to lease again, put me at the top of your list. I'm still working at the Department of Justice. Anytime you want to do lunch, call me, and it will be on me. I forwarded my mail, but some may slip through. Call me, and I'll stop by to pick it up. Oh, I left both keys on the table in the foyer. I also switched the utilities back to your name as well as the phone. It's still connected, but in your name now.

It was signed *Bill.*

Talk about the perfect tenant.

Maggie kicked off her shoes, uncorked the bottle of wine, then looked in the oven. Ah, stuffed pork chops, new potatoes with baby carrots. She could smell the rosemary sprinkled on top of the chops. On the bottom shelf was a berry pie. She knew it was a berry pie because some of the juice had spilled over onto the sheet of tin foil under the pie plate. She could hardly wait to dig in because if it tasted half as good as it looked and smelled, she would be in food heaven. Bill Yost must like to cook. Even before she opened the refrigerator, she knew she would find juice, eggs, bacon, milk, and some fresh fruit. Her fist shot in the air. "You are some kind of guy, Bill Yost!"

An hour later, stuffed to the gills, a little woozy from half the bottle of wine, Maggie tottered into her living room. She struck a match to the laid fire, turned on the TV, and flopped down onto her favorite chair.

If she was smart, she'd go out and walk around the block; but right now, she didn't feel smart, just felt full and content. Why spoil a good thing? She settled herself more comfortably in her recliner, pressed the MUTE button, and closed her eyes, not to sleep but to think.

The past week had moved slowly in her opinion. Charles was still working down in the catacombs, trying to come up with enough background to get her mission under way. It bothered her that it was taking so long. Ted and Espinosa agreed, and they were as anxious as she was to get things moving. Then there was Abner. Abner never took this long to get back to her. A week was actually unheard of where Abner Tookus was concerned. Maybe she needed to cut him some slack. He was married now to Isabelle, so his life probably wasn't the same as it had been. She thought back to his call in the middle of the week, when he asked her if she realized what a hornet's nest she was diving into. She remembered how she'd shivered and passed the question on to Ted and Espinosa, whose eyes had gleamed as hers had. The words *juicy* and *dangerous* came to mind. The stuff all reporters lived to write about.

Maggie cracked an eyelid and saw Nancy Grace on the big screen. As she was debating whether to turn up the volume up or not, her cell phone chirped in her pocket.

She pulled it out to see Abner's code name, *Speed,* on the caller ID.

The voice was hesitant. "Maggie?"

"It's about time, Abby. What's going on?" Maggie said, getting right to it.

"Maggie, it's only been a week. Aren't you the one who told me on more than one occasion to get a life? Well, I finally took your advice, and I got a life. A really good life. I'm an old married man, and with that goes all the things a husband does. I'm liking it, in case you care. But to answer your question, I go back and forth to upstate New York to see Isabelle. My work no longer consumes me night and day. I actually keep regular hours these days. I sleep at night and work during the day. And this will probably surprise you even more, but there are days when I don't work at all. I will admit you are a favorite client, so I always cut you breaks and bust my ass to do what you want."

"Yeah, well, busting your ass had its rewards. You probably own the most ocean-front property in the whole world, all thanks to me."

Abner laughed. "You do have a point."

"So, what do you have for me? Tell me you are going to make me happy."

"Oh, I'm going to make you happy, Maggie. Is your fax working?"

Maggie didn't know if her ancient fax machine was working or not. She decided to take a gamble since she was sure Bill Yost would have let her know if it wasn't working. "Yes. Fax away. Do you care to give me any highlights?"

"I think it's all pretty straightforward. If you have any questions, call me. By the way, all that oceanfront property . . . guess who owns the neighboring lots on some of those properties! I've been approached many times to sell off some of it, but I never responded to the inquiries. Now, having said that, if you want me to, I can make a personal inquiry of my own, you know, to see if the owners are still interested."

"The Ciprani twins?"

"Right on, Maggie. Who knew they'd crop up in my personal life at this particular moment in time?"

"Is it undeveloped land, or are there structures on those plots?"

"Both."

"And your bill?"

"It will be with the fax."

"Ah, Abby, after all that, did you form any opinions?"

"Oh, yeah," Abner drawled.

"You gonna make me pull it out of you? What?"

"Be careful and watch your back. Those two women make their own rules, and they rule by fear. I know you're going to say you're fearless, but let me tell you I don't think you've come across anyone of their ilk before. Just be careful, Maggie. Gotta run now. I always call Isabelle around this time."

"Jeez, Abby, I'm sorry. I meant to . . . I wanted . . ."

"Maggie, Maggie, I understand. Don't sweat it. I'm the one who should be apologizing to you. I'm not good at stuff like that, and knowing you, I thought you wanted to be alone. I knew you'd call if you needed me. So now that we're both clear on the past, let's just move forward."

"Okay," Maggie said, a catch in her voice. "Give Isabelle my love."

"I will, Maggie. She said to give you a hug if we met up. You wanna do lunch one day next week, call me. I'd love to see you."

"Okay, but I'm not sure if I'll be going to Baywater next week or not. Gotta wait to see what the others want to do."

"You be careful, you hear?"

"Always, Abby."

"Okay, see you, Miss Reporter. I'm about to hit the SEND button. Watch for the fax.

123

Any questions, call me tomorrow."

Maggie didn't realize how tense she was until she leaned back and closed her eyes. She tilted her head toward the doorway leading to the stairs to the second floor. She could hear the faint ring tone of her fax machine. So, it was working. She let loose with a loud sigh before she forced herself out of the recliner. She looked toward the TV and saw Nancy Grace still on the screen, which meant it wasn't yet nine o'clock.

Maggie walked out to the foyer, grabbed a small overnight bag and her backpack, and made her way to the second floor. It smelled just as clean as it did on the first floor. She dumped her bags in the bedroom, looked around, and smiled. Home. She peeked into her bathroom, which smelled clean and fresh. She smiled again as she made her way back out to the hall and the spare room she'd converted to a home office. The fax was still slowly inching out sheet after sheet of paper.

Maggie sat down in a deep, comfortable chair and watched the papers creep out of the fax machine. An extensive report. A one-of-a-kind report. The kind of report only Abner Tookus could provide. She could hardly wait to read it.

While she waited for the last sheet of paper, Maggie called Myra, told her the report was coming through and to call a meeting for the following day. Myra agreed, set the meeting for midafternoon of the following day, and said she would notify everyone.

Maggie's second call was to Ted. She explained about the fax coming through and said she would fax it to him the minute she finished reading it. "I'm going out to Pinewood tomorrow, so I'm thinking we can head out to Baywater the day after tomorrow if everyone agrees."

"Read fast. I'll alert Espinosa" was Ted's response.

"C'mon, c'mon," Maggie mumbled as she pulled the sheets out of the fax. She really needed to update this machine to one like she'd had at the *Post,* which would spit out forty-two pages a minute. This pathetic archaic fax machine was enough to drive anyone up a wall. Especially someone like her, who had no patience to begin with. Already it looked like she had close to a hundred pages, and they were still coming. She stopped and placed another call to Charles and repeated verbatim what she'd told Ted. She told him she'd alerted Myra to call a meeting for tomorrow. Charles's response was the same as Ted's — *Read fast.*

Myra greeted her guests the way she always did, with warm hugs and a big smile. She looked at Martine Connor, questions in her eyes.

"I'm just me, Myra. Martine Connor, private citizen. I can come and go as I please, and no one is watching me. I took my security detail out to dinner, gave them all a parting gift, thanked them for watching over me, and we parted ways. There are no words to tell you how good I feel. I'm not the retired leader of the free world any longer. Someone else has that responsibility. I slept the sleep of the dead the first night. I even slept in the next morning. I felt . . ."

"Like you could fly if you wanted to," Nellie said, finishing Marti's sentence for her. "I know the feeling; been there, done that."

"Where's Pearl?" Annie asked.

"I think she just got here," Myra said, craning her neck to see out the kitchen door. "I wish there was something we could do about the people watching her. She's under such pressure, and stress is not good for someone who has episodes of gout."

"It's not the same as a security detail," Marti said. "The people watching Pearl suspect but can't prove that she was operating the underground railroad. Those people never give up, I can tell you that. Can you imagine the fallout if somehow they were able to nail her and prove that a retired Supreme Court justice was doing something like that!"

The silence that followed put everyone's teeth on edge. Pearl took that moment to walk into the kitchen. She looked at the women and winced. "What? Did something happen?" she asked, anxiety ringing in her tone.

"I was just telling everyone that I am now a free citizen, my security detail is a thing of the past, thanks to Lizzie Fox. That led to a discussion about the people watching you. Is it still so obvious, Pearl?" Marti asked.

"Some days it is, and some days it isn't. I think they want me to know I'm being watched. I'm afraid to even use my cell phone these days. I know how that works. I'm sure I was followed here, and if they're watching me, then they've seen you all coming here, too."

"Our weekly or twice-weekly bridge game." Myra motioned for everyone to sit down at the kitchen table. "Charles isn't ready for us, and Maggie isn't here yet. We have fresh sweet tea. Annie, you get the glasses, and I'll pour."

Annie rattled around in the kitchen cabinet, looking for glasses that matched. "You really need something a little nicer than these Mason jar glasses, Myra." She whirled around and smacked at her forehead. "I have an idea!"

"Well, by all means share it with us," Myra sniffed, as she plucked glasses from the cabinet.

"We stalk Pearl's stalkers and take them out," Annie said.

"That's your idea!" Nellie hooted.

"And by taking them out, you mean literally *taking them out*?" Myra asked as she fingered the pearls around her neck.

"Okay, okay, we catch them, then Charles and Avery Snowden can relocate them to the far corners of the world. All of you, stop looking at me like that. It's not like we haven't done it before. Pearl deserves some peace of mind. I think we should vote on it."

Annie whooped in pleasure when she saw all the hands at the table inch upward. "What this tells me, ladies, is that we all want Pearl to have an easier life, so she can continue to do what she does best, helping women and children and getting them to safety. Having said that, and the fact that we're getting ready to start a mission, I have another idea."

Myra clutched her pearls like the lifeline they were. She managed to squeak out the words, "Tell us your idea, Annie."

"Well, I think we will all agree that Pearl deserves one hundred percent of our help. But we can't really do that now because of the twin judges we're going after. Now, listen up, ladies. When Bert Navarro, and you all know Bert, took over the security at Babylon, he came to me and asked me how I felt about his hiring a certain man. He was an ex-con. The FBI Director, Mitch something or other, the one Nellie's husband replaced, framed him with the help of the current director, who was a top agent at the time, and an innocent man did the time. Bert followed the case and did everything he could for the guy, but it was an airtight frame was the way Bert explained it to me. Anyway, this guy is the best of the best, and I gave my okay. He did a stint with the SEALs and he's ex-FBI. We pay him an exorbitant salary, and every casino in Vegas has tried to steal him away, but he's loyal to Bert. I say we bring him here and let him get his pound of flesh for the years he was wrongly incarcerated. We can keep him on the Vegas payroll and pay him for whatever work he does for us, which is getting those people off Pearl's back once and for all."

"Who is this person?" Pearl asked, excitement ringing in her voice.

"His name is Jack Sparrow. I only met him twice, and both times, he kissed my hand. Like I was royalty. He thanked me for having faith in him and believing in him."

"Will Bert give him up even if it's for just a short while?" Marti asked.

"Marti, Marti, Marti! Does the Pope pray? I own the joint. I pay him. Bert works for me, as does Mr. Sparrow. Does that answer your question?"

"What question was that?" Maggie asked as she blew into the kitchen, her corkscrew curls standing on end from the blustery October wind.

"We're going to hire Jack Sparrow to take out the men ruining Pearl's life," Annie said, glee ringing in her voice.

"*The* Jack Sparrow? The one who sued the FBI and won a pot of money? The one we wrote numerous articles about in the *Post* years ago and called him a one-man army? Oh, I am liking this! A lot."

"That's the one," Annie said gleefully. She smacked her hands together, then clapped Myra on the back. "Say something, dear, before I stuff those damn pearls in both your ears."

"I think it's a marvelous idea. I can hardly wait to tell Charles," Myra said, rising to the occasion but only because all eyes were on her.

One look at Pearl, who was kneading her hands with tears in her eyes, was all Annie needed to pick up her cell phone. With Bert Navarro on speed dial, she was talking to her head of security at Babylon within seconds. Quickly and concisely, in a voice none of the others had ever heard before, Annie spelled out what she wanted. Within seconds, she was ending the call over Bert's protests, which she was ignoring by saying, "I'll call and have my Gulfstream V burning fuel within the hour. And, Bert, I won't take no for an answer. I'll arrange to have Mr. Sparrow and whoever he needs to bring with him picked up at the airport and brought out here to Pinewood. Call me with his ETA on my cell."

The women all clapped their hands, Myra the loudest, when Annie ended her call. "Doncha love it when a plan comes together, girls? Pearl, did I do okay?"

"You did. You did, Annie. I feel like I can almost breathe again." Pearl jerked her head toward the kitchen door and the monitor overhead. "They're out there, you know."

"Yes, but not for long." Marti laughed.

131

"Ted and Espinosa can pick up your guests with the *Post*'s van we use for undercover work when you get the ETA," Maggie said.

The house intercom buzzed. "I do believe Charles is ready for us, ladies," Myra said. "Leave the tea, we can clean up later. My dear husband doesn't like to be kept waiting. And I can hardly wait to tell him of this latest development. He may or may not go over the moon when he hears what we're up to."

Thousands of miles away, Bert Navarro looked at his cell phone, offered up a few cusswords that weren't in anyone's dictionary, and sent off a curt text to Jack Sparrow. My office. ASAP.

Five minutes later, there was a loud knock on Bert's door at the same moment the door opened. A tall man who looked like a nerdy college professor, right down to his tweed jacket with leather patches on the elbows and a pipe that was never smoked in his breast pocket, entered the room. He had a silver head of hair that was all his own, capped teeth that gleamed in the artificial light, and a weathered tan that said he spent a lot of time outdoors. He didn't, but he did use a tanning booth. He was tall, well over six feet, thin, and fit. But it was his piercing green eyes that drew one's attention. They said, *I see you and everything about you, so don't give me any crap.* "How's this for ASAP? I was coming down the hall to see you anyway. What can I do for you today, Mr. Navarro?"

He even sounds like a college professor, Bert thought. But then that was Jack Sparrow's stock-in-trade.

"Not me, Jack. Our boss, Countess de Silva."

"Okay, what can I do for the lovely lady that I owe so much to?"

"That very lovely lady wants you on her private Gulfstream along with several of your . . . ah . . . best friends within the hour. Said the Gulfstream will take you to Washington, D.C., where you will be met and taken to Pinewood, Virginia. That same very lovely lady has a *private job* for you. It's one of those jobs where you can name your own price. You can take as long as you need to . . . ah, do what she wants. You will, of course, remain on Babylon's payroll. She did ask me to give you a message, Jack."

An amused expression crossed Sparrow's face. "Which is?"

" 'This is your chance to do some serious damage to the assholes who framed you and

133

sent you to prison for crimes you didn't commit.' "

"Did she now? I love it when a lady like the Countess has my back. When do I leave?"

"Like now. Be selective on who you take with you. Just the best, Jack. Annie and the others won't settle for anything less."

"I hear you, boss. I'm on my way. Should I report in from time to time?"

Bert laughed. "Only if you want to."

"Well, then, guess I'll see you when I see you."

"Yeah, guess so. Listen, you be careful, you hear me, Jack?"

"Uh-huh."

CHAPTER 8

Conversation at the huge, round table in
the War Room was quiet, even a bit subdued
after the earlier exuberance upstairs. The
main reason the women were so quiet and
subdued was that they didn't want to disturb Charles, who was frantically working
on the dais.

Myra turned slightly when she thought
she felt a light touch to her shoulder. A
smile tugged at the corners of her mouth.
Her spirit daughter was letting her know
she was in attendance. Her right hand
reached up to touch the warm spot on her
shoulder. Her head still turned, she looked
up at Charles and wasn't surprised to see
his head rear back. And then, like her, his
hand went to his shoulder. He looked down
and saw Myra smiling at him as she nodded. A slight tilt of his head told her he
acknowledged his spirit daughter's attendance just the way she had.

Myra turned back to the others at the table. A quick glance told her no one had noticed anything out of the ordinary. She wished she could shout out to everyone, to tell them her spirit daughter was here in the room, but she knew she couldn't and wouldn't do that; nor would Charles. She looked up to see Charles descending from the dais, his arms full of files and thick binders and folders. He distributed four sets before he gathered up the remainder.

"Good Lord, Charles, what is all this?" Nellie asked.

"Don't be alarmed, ladies. The bulk of what you have in front of you are the case files on the offenders the Ciprani twins have sentenced in the last five years. To be honest, I ran out of paper. I wanted to go back ten years, and I will, but not until a new supply of paper is delivered. There's no need to go through those files at this sitting. I printed them out so you could read them at your leisure. There's enough there for you to see the pattern of how the judges operate their courtrooms.

"I've separated this mission into sections. I've combined my own research with that of Maggie's source, who works for us from time to time. I also want to say that what you have in front of you is not complete.

136

That means our research is ongoing. Taking that one step further, I strongly oppose any of you going to Baywater until we have everything we need. Also, I have not completed your legends as yet. I know you all want a time frame here, and all I can tell you is we need a few more days, possibly a week, to ensure we have an airtight plan.

"Now, if you'll all open the blue folder and follow along with me, you'll see it is labeled 'Baywater.' What we have here are photographs, aerial and otherwise, of the town itself. It lists population, mileage, a map of the actual streets, the elected officials with their bios, which include the mayor, the city attorneys, the city planners, in short, anyone who holds any kind of office. All town employees right down to the gardeners who work out of the sanitation department are also included. You have in front of you all the information I could gather up to this point on past elections and the outcomes. Some of the bios are extensive, going back to a date of birth, and some of this information was obtained from Facebook and various blogs and tweets. So you are asked to be careful in what you believe and disbelieve. Also, there is a photo of the condominium where the twin judges reside during the week, along with the address. As you can see, a very costly piece of property. It is a very secure building. The other photos are of the ancestral home on the Chesapeake Bay. Before-and-after pictures. As you can see, the renovations were extensive. There are only three houses on the street. One house is empty and the other is inhabited by an elderly couple with a live-in nurse. It's very secluded and has, as does the condo, state-of-the-art security.

"The yellow folder details the lives of the twin judges' family, going back as far as we could. Again, read at your leisure.

"The red folder deals with Judges Celeste Ciprani and Eunice Ciprani. It details their lives with what is in print. There are no personal face-to-face interviews of any kind because there hasn't been time. I'm of two minds in regard to personal interviews. If I send Avery and his people to interview people, we're sending up some red flags. If we wait and let Maggie, Ted, and Joseph do it, we're on the spot to follow through should things go awry. This is something you will decide among yourselves.

"The beige folder will be your legends once they are created. Again, I need a few more days to make sure they're airtight. I want you to talk among yourselves and decide who you will be comfortable being because you will be living that legend, and you have to believe in it so that it's like a second skin. There is also the possibility that we won't even need the legends, and you can go as who you are. In other words, it is yet to be decided.

"The black folder is a financial folder. It contains all the financials we were able to dig up. There are bank and brokerage accounts that Maggie's source came up with that are not out of the ordinary. The accounts are healthy and robust and can be explained away by astute investing and being a bit of a gambler in the stock market. What isn't available is the dollar and cents amounts in the offshore accounts. The main account is in the Cayman Islands. Mr. Tookus believes there are others, and he is still working on that end of it. At one point, going back years and years, there was an account in Switzerland, but that's long gone, along with Switzerland's old banking laws. Mr. Tookus thinks the account was closed, transferred, then transferred back to Switzerland. There are funds in Liechtenstein, there are funds in the Antilles, and, of course, the Caymans. The Bank of Mont Verde to be precise. We do not know the amounts. Our research in this matter is ongoing. What that means is sometimes a bribe will work, but if discovered, it is a career ender for the person we bribe. So the payoff would have to be extremely high. Only time will tell.

"We were able to secure years of travel arrangements for the twins. Eunice appears to like warm weather, the ocean, and sand. She likes to water-ski. She heads to the Cayman Islands at least twice a year, usually during the Easter and Christmas breaks. Celeste likes to ski on snow and heads to Europe. Usually, they meet several days before the end of their vacations. One year, they meet in Europe, and the next in the Caymans. While in Europe, one would assume that Celeste travels by rail to the various banks and countries she wants to check so that there is no paper trail of her travels."

"What about siblings? Wasn't there something about a brother?" Myra asked.

"Ongoing, dear. I'll have more later in the week. Right now, for all intents and purposes, there is no record of his even being born, much less dying. If there was indeed a brother, we'll find him. I, for one, have no idea how something like that could be expunged.

"The last orange folder deals with Daniel West, the reporter for the *Baywater Weekly*. I have to admit that gave me a devil of a time, the reason being the young man's name is Dennis West, not Daniel. He goes by Dennis or Denny to his friends. He's twenty-five and lives with a friend in a garden apartment. He's an intern, so to speak, and he grew up in Chevy Chase. Another reason I couldn't locate him using the utilities as a reference. The only thing I could find in regard to his credit rating is he is saddled with a lot of student loans. He drives a battered old Ford that is obviously paid for and is registered in what I assume is his father's name, and the home address is the parents' address in Chevy Chase. That search is also ongoing."

"Charles, in all your research, what have you come up with in regard to how these judges became so powerful?"

"Fear and intimidation and evoking the family name is the only thing I can come up with. I now have a question for you ladies. Marti, what about your Secret Service detail? Pearl, how are you going to evade the FBI agents who have been tailing you? I need to factor all of that in when I create your legends for your own safety."

Marti laughed, the others joining in. "It's all been taken care of, Charles. I am Martine Connor, private citizen. The detail is gone, thanks to Lizzie Fox."

Annie weighed in on Pearl's problem. She explained about Jack Sparrow and his people, who would be arriving in another — she looked at her watch, and said — "thirty minutes."

Charles nodded his approval as he gathered up his own copies and returned to his workstation.

The women at the round table let loose with a long, audible sigh.

"Well, this is not making me happy," Maggie said sourly. "I was hoping to get on the road in the next day or so, and I know I speak for Ted and Espinosa. Having said that, I understand where Charles is coming from. I guess I'm just anxious to get going on all of this."

"Patience, dear, is hard to come by and something we've all had to learn the hard way. In the meantime, I don't see any reason why you, Ted, and Espinosa can't call or e-mail or somehow get in touch with some of the parents of these children," Myra said, tapping the stack of case histories. "On second thought, don't e-mail. You don't want to leave a paper trail that can be traced back to you. While I myself am not into the social media that are part of the lifestyle for some people, we need to factor that into our game plan once we actually come up with one. I bet that some of these people, perhaps siblings, have posted on Facebook, and you can get a feel for one or more of them. I'm sure that will keep the three of you busy for days on end. Remember, the more knowledge we have, the more power we have."

"Well said, Myra," Nellie enthused, clapping her hands.

"That sounds like a plan," Maggie said.

"Annie, where is Mr. Sparrow being taken when Ted and Espinosa pick him up at the airport? You aren't bringing him here to the farm, are you?" Marti asked.

"Actually, yes; Ted is bringing him here this evening to meet all of you. Then Ted will take him to a hotel that we arranged for. After our initial meeting, there will be no physical or face-to-face contact. All contact will be by phone. When the situation is resolved, Mr. Sparrow will return to Las Vegas, and we'll move forward with our mission. Since this has to happen, it is the perfect time, what with our being in a holding pattern."

Myra looked at her watch. "We need to go upstairs, ladies. We've eaten into the thirty minutes. Ted should be arriving with our guests momentarily. I guess we should convene in the dining room. Does that meet with everyone's approval?"

The women nodded, mumbling and muttering as they gathered up their individual piles of folders. Maggie led the way.

In the formal dining room, Martine Connor looked around, remembering the last time she'd held court here in this very room. At that meeting, she had been the president of the United States and she'd handed out the special gold shields that, to this day, had not been put to use. She felt a small thrill of excitement rush through her as she looked around at the other women. She couldn't be sure, but she thought they were thinking the same thing she was.

"Refreshments?" Annie asked.

"I think later, Annie." Myra looked at her watch. "Our guests should be within a mile of here if the flight was on time. I have to assume it was or we would have heard from Ted by now. Tell me, what do you think now that we've heard from Charles and have our reading material in front of us?"

"I think we're all going to hell in a handbasket," Nellie said. "Unless we send those two judges there first. I hate crooked judges. I find this whole thing extremely intriguing, and I can't wait to get started if my opinion counts."

"Well, I'm raring to go myself. I just want

those agents off my back so I can do what I want. It's going to be tricky is what I'm thinking. I hope, Annie, that you have Mr. Sparrow's pulse down correctly. My people are counting on me to get them to safety. That's my main priority."

"And we'll make it happen, Pearl. Trust me on that," Maggie said.

Annie ruffled through the stack of folders in front of her. "This is a lot of reading to plow through," she grumbled. "Maybe it's a good thing if we all stop to think about it. While reading all of this and getting up to speed, Mr. Sparrow can put Pearl's problem to bed, and when that's all cleared up, we can start fresh. Charles is right. If it comes to that, we have to know our new legends inside out, so we can blend in and make it all work for us. Maggie, dear, do you have any ideas?"

Maggie looked up from a folder she was reading. "A ton of them, Annie. And when I go home tonight, I'm going to lay it all out. I'm taking Ted and Espinosa with me, and we will be burning the midnight oil. We can get a bead on quite a bit behind the scenes. We'll be checking in often during the day to apprise all of you what we are doing and learning."

The dogs, who had been sleeping under

the table, got up as one and raced to the kitchen, letting out the high and shrill barks they reserved for strangers entering the compound.

"I do believe our guests have arrived, ladies," Myra said, getting up to follow the dogs to the kitchen to greet her new guest.

Introductions were made quickly by Ted. Myra didn't know if she was impressed or disappointed at the appearance of their new guest. Until Ted winked at her, which she took to mean everything was A-okay. She led the way into the formal dining room, where introductions were made again. She could tell that the others were having the same reaction she'd had initially.

Pearl's spirits sank at the sight of the man who was to be her savior.

Marti sighed. Nerd. She did her best not to look at Pearl, who looked ready to cry.

Nellie frowned. *I weigh more than he does,* she thought.

Maggie stared the longest. *Perfect. Just perfect,* she thought.

Annie grinned from ear to ear, like she knew exactly what everyone was thinking. They were all going to be so disappointed when Jack Sparrow delivered. She risked a glance at Myra, who was actually beaming. And she was *not* fingering her pearls. *Whoa!*

146

This man, Myra thought, as she studied him, was a man comfortable in his own skin. She knew in her gut Annie had been right, and Pearl would be in good hands.

"Talk to me, ladies. Tell me what I can do for you," Jack Sparrow said quietly.

The women all started to talk at once, but somehow the man standing at the head of the dining room table appeared to make sense out of it all. His eyes remained on Pearl. What he said surprised them all. "I know you. I followed your career." Then he looked at Martine Connor and grinned from ear to ear. "And of course I recognize you, Madam President. If you hadn't pardoned me, I'd still be languishing in prison for crimes I did not commit. You have no idea how badly I wanted to thank you personally, but it wasn't possible, so please, accept my heartfelt thanks. And to all you other lovely ladies, I recognize you also. I'm in awe to be standing here in such distinguished company. Having said that, I'm all yours for as long as you need me."

The women started to babble again. Sparrow tilted his head as he listened. It was almost like the women could see him sifting, collating, and forming a plan right in front of their eyes.

"Okay, I got it. This is what we're going to

do first. Tomorrow, at first light, I'm going to be making a call, a mysterious call, to Justice Barnes. We need to determine if her home and cell phones are being monitored. My guess is they are. I will have one of my people meet Justice Barnes at some out-of-the-way café or park or someplace she knows, then the rest of my people and I will be following whoever it is that follows Justice Barnes.

"My people were dropped off at the hotel we're going to be staying in. There is no need for you all to meet them at this time. Better they're strangers to you. I brought along special phones that we'll be using among ourselves. Ted will bring them to you all tomorrow. With instructions, of course. It's going to take a few days to establish a pattern, a routine, of the agents assigned to Justice Barnes. Are you all following me here?"

The women nodded, their eyes sparkling.

"I want them gone as in gone, never to return. Can you do that, Mr. Sparrow?" Pearl asked, her spirits rising.

"Without a doubt, and at the same time, I just might be able to settle a few scores of my own. I don't want you to get the idea I'm doing this for myself, because I'm not. It's just the icing on the cake, if you follow me, and I think you all understand about vengeance and what it does to the psyche."

"We do! We do!" the women bellowed as one. Ted's and Espinosa's fists shot high in the air.

"Then I think I should be getting back to the hotel and my people. All I need right now are phone numbers and Justice Barnes's address. When I call you in the morning, Justice Barnes, just follow my lead and don't be afraid to talk to me, and respond accordingly."

Jack Sparrow gave a curt nod, then surprised everyone in the room by walking around the table, lifting each woman's hand, and kissing it.

The women preened.

Ted Robinson glowered when he saw Maggie's smile of pure delight. Show-off. Ass-kisser. Brown-noser. He just knew Maggie thought the guy was suave, debonair, and dashing. Jesus, the guy had to be at least in his late fifties, maybe early sixties.

Espinosa paid careful attention to what was going on and seemed stunned at the expressions he was seeing on the women's faces. He really needed to practice Sparrow's move and try it out on Alexis. The guy was *smooooooth.* Something he was not.

The dogs gave the trio a rousing send-off

by barking and wagging their tails as they raced to the van waiting in the courtyard. Sparrow held up his hand for silence and whistled. The dogs, startled, went silent and sat back on their haunches, panting.

"How'd you do that?" Ted asked grudgingly.

Sparrow grinned. "For some reason, dogs like me. I like them, too. Guess they sense it. Best answer I can give you."

Still miffed, Ted climbed behind the wheel and waited till Espinosa and Sparrow were belted in. Then he floored the gas pedal and cleared the gate by a hair.

Back inside, the women were chattering like magpies as they gathered up their files as they prepared to leave.

"I like the guy," Maggie said.

The others agreed, especially Annie, who said, "We're in good hands. Trust me on that."

Myra fixed her gaze on Marti. "This was the first I heard that you'd pardoned Mr. Sparrow. How'd that happen?"

"Bert Navarro happened, by way of Kathryn, who got to Lizzie Fox, who got to me. I took a lot of flak and heat for that, but I'm glad I did it. I hope he gets his pound of flesh. There can't be anything worse in this life than spending time in prison for something you didn't do, especially if you were in the FBI."

"Well, we're here to help him if he needs our help. He seems pretty efficient to me, and his appearance . . . As Bert said, he's one of those people you never look at twice because he's so ordinary, which I think will work in everyone's favor. I don't know about the rest of you, but I'm excited for you, Pearl. I think you're finally going to get those monkeys off your back," Annie said.

"From your lips to God's ears, my friend," Pearl said, as she slipped her arms into her jacket. "Good night, girls, and thanks for all the help."

The women all smiled and hugged one another as Myra walked them out to their cars.

Myra stood in the courtyard watching the line of cars until the last red taillight was just a speck of red in the distance.

"Nice going, Mom. I liked your Mr. Sparrow."

"Oh, darling girl, how sweet of you to visit again. Is there anything I should be worried about? Talk to me, sweetheart."

"Not one little bit, Mom. Pearl is going to be okay. Expect some fireworks."

Myra looked around, half expecting to see her spirit daughter materialize. "Hold my hand, sweetie. I need to feel you next to me." Myra almost fainted when she felt a rush of warmth in her hand, warmth that went all the way up her arm. She wasn't sure, but she thought her spirit daughter had just laid her head on her shoulder. Tears rolled down her cheeks as she savored the moment.

" 'Night, Mom. Get some sleep. I'm going to see Daddy now and tell him not to work so hard."

"Good night, darling girl."

There was a bounce in Myra's step as she herded the dogs into the kitchen. Like she was going to be able to sleep after talking with her spirit daughter. Highly unlikely.

Definitely unlikely. Actually, it was an impossible thought.

CHAPTER 9

Pearl Barnes stood at her kitchen window, her yard lit by the halogen lamps she'd turned on when she came down to the kitchen. It was only four-thirty, and she'd already consumed an entire pot of coffee.

Returning home from Pinewood, she'd been so wired up she knew that sleep was impossible, so she hadn't even tried. Instead, she'd taken a shower and gotten dressed, her thoughts all over the map as she tried to imagine what was going to go down in only a few hours. Her cell phone was in her pocket so that she could catch the call when it came on the first ring.

Pearl craned her neck to see beyond the yellow pool of light on her sheltered terrace. Was it raining? She opened the back door and stepped out to check. Yes, it was raining. Any other time, she would have heard it, as she'd trained herself over the years to be alert to any and all sounds, ordinary and otherwise. She must be slipping. She made a mental note to be more observant.

Pearl walked back into the house. She'd deliberately turned on every light in her house to alert her surveillance that something was about to go down. Let them scramble as they tried to catch her doing something that would warrant an arrest and put a huge feather in the cap of the FBI. *Retired Supreme Court Justice arrested for running underground railroad.* Alphabet City would run wild with that. If that happened, she'd spend the rest of her life in prison with no parole.

Pearl sat down at the table and let her thoughts turn back to the moment in time when her daughter came to her and confided that her husband was abusive and she was afraid he was going to do something to her small daughter. Years of lawyers, court hearings, and wrangling left her daughter an emotional wreck as her little daughter started to regress until Pearl took matters into her own hands. Through friends, and through ex-convicts they knew, she was finally able to make contact with nameless people who ran an underground railroad for people like her daughter. Without a second thought, she'd resigned her seat on the Supreme Court and joined up, so to speak. Her daughter was in a safe place now, and she managed to see her and her only grandchild at least three times a year. While it wasn't an ideal situation, she'd accepted it because in the end all she wanted was her daughter and granddaughter to be safe.

To date, her organization, small as it was, had saved over thirty-nine thousand women and children. She was proud of what she now called her life's work and would do it all over again. It was true, she thought. A mother would go to the ends of the earth for her children and not think twice. In her case, going to prison just wasn't important enough compared to the well-being of her daughter and grandchild and other women and children in the same position.

Pearl looked at the clock. Then she looked outside again. It was still pitch-dark. Dawn wouldn't arrive for another hour. She decided to make fresh coffee even though she didn't want any. It was something to do. She was watching and listening to the coffee drip into the pot when her phone rang. She almost jumped out of her own skin as she fumbled for the phone in her pocket. She struggled mightily to take a deep breath before she answered the phone. She clicked it on in the middle of the second ring. "Hello."

"Ah . . . I know it's early in the morning, and I'm sorry," said a shaky-sounding female voice. "This is . . . this is 39674 . . . and I need your help. Will you help me? I can meet you someplace for . . . for breakfast."

Pearl drew another deep breath. "Of course. Do you have a location in mind?"

"They said you would know where that place is and not to mention it on the phone."

Pearl's mind raced. How would Jack Sparrow know about the place she met her runaway mothers? Was she supposed to give it up on the phone? Unlikely. The voice obviously wanted anyone listening to the conversation to think she knew where the breakfast place was. That had to mean Jack Sparrow would tail her when she left the house, then call the voice on the phone and give her the location. "Of course. I'll meet you there in half an hour. I'll leave right now. Are you okay?"

"At the moment I am. Thank you, thank you, thank you."

Pearl dusted her hands. She turned off the coffeepot in middrip. Feeling like she was back in the groove again, she reached for a hoodie hanging on a rack by the back door. She slipped into it, zipped it up, grabbed an umbrella, and headed out to get her car from the garage. There was no doubt in her mind that there was a tracking device on her car, which would make it easy for her to be followed. Right now, that's what it was all about: making it easy for her surveillance team to follow her.

The pouring rain slashed at Pearl's windshield as the wipers struggled to keep up with the onslaught. It was hard to tell if anyone was following her or not. She could see headlights behind her, but they could belong to anyone. Amazing, she thought, how many motorists were on the road before five in the morning.

Ten minutes later, Pearl saw the huge, high, backlit sign announcing that Betty's Diner was an eighth of a mile down the road. She put on her signal light for Sparrow's benefit so he could alert his operative that, she, Pearl, had arrived at her destination. She took her time turning off the windshield wipers, the heater, and the engine. Then she stalled a little more by pretending to rummage in her bag for something. Finally, she zipped her hoodie back up, settled the head portion more securely on her head, and climbed out of the car. By her estimate, she'd given Sparrow's operative an additional five minutes, seven or eight if she dawdled crossing the parking lot. She took her time.

Betty's Diner was like every other diner around the country. The windows were steamed up, the booths were red plastic with rips in them, the tabletops Formica, the swiveling stools at the counter were red. Domed plates of pastries were spaced out on the counters ten inches apart. Huge Bunn coffeemakers filled the back counter and smelled wonderful. The waitress behind the counter looked tired. Pearl knew from long experience that her shift ended at six.

"How're you doing, hon? Haven't seen you in a while," the waitress, whose name tag said she was Margie, said.

"I've been out of town. Coffee please, and a sticky bun. I'll take the back booth. I'm waiting for someone, a young lady," Pearl said. She hoped the person she was meeting was a young lady. At the moment, she was flying blind, but that would change shortly. The only good thing about meeting on the fly like this was that whoever was tailing her wouldn't have had time to attach any listening devices anywhere near where she was sitting. The doorway was not in her line of sight, but she could hear the bell every time the door opened.

Pearl smiled up at the waitress when she set a plate with a warm sticky bun in front

158

of her. The heavy mug of coffee smelled just the way she remembered it from countless meetings over the years. "I think the person you're waiting for just arrived, hon. I'll send her on back. Enjoy."

"Wait a minute, Margie. I know you're going off duty soon. Here, let me pay now." Pearl pulled a fifty-dollar bill out of her pocket and handed it to the tired waitress. It was to ensure that the waitress didn't talk to anyone who might ask questions about her at some point in time. Margie nodded her thanks.

In the blink of an eye, a young, mousy, wet, bedraggled young woman slid into the booth across from Pearl. Her lips barely moving, she said, "Jack's at the counter, and one of your tails is in the parking lot. In case you don't know it, there's a GPS tracking device on your SUV. Two of our people are checking your house right now for listening devices. Jack said to give you this phone. You only contact him on this phone, not your landline or your cell phone. We have someone in the parking lot watching the agent who's watching you. There's another one, but he or she hasn't surfaced yet."

"How do you know there are two agents?" The mousy-looking woman looked at

Pearl like she'd sprouted a second head. "Because Jack said there were two."

Before she could ask if the young woman wanted coffee, Margie was back with a cup and another sticky bun. The operative wolfed it down. "Jack said not to stay more than twelve minutes," she said, looking at her watch. "I have six more to go. Say something, Your Honor."

"What do I do next?"

"Whatever Jack tells you. Remember, if you want to call him, just hit the number one. You hit TALK if he calls on that phone. Simple. If one of us calls you on your regular phone, just play along with the cues we give you. I probably shouldn't say anything personal to you, but I admire what you do, lady. I have a sister who got tied up with the wrong guy. That's how I got into this. Any questions?"

"I think I'm good. Who do you think they're going to follow, me or you?"

"Both of us. I'll lose him before I head back to the hotel. Not to worry, we got it covered. Nice meeting you. Thanks for the coffee and sticky bun. I haven't had a sticky bun in years."

Pearl blinked, and the contact was gone. She dallied long enough to finish the coffee she didn't want. She balled up several paper

160

napkins just to kill time before she slipped her soaking-wet hoodie back on and zipped it up. She reached for her purse and slid out of the booth. Jack Sparrow was eating scrambled eggs at the counter. She waved to Margie and left the diner. It was starting to get light out, and cars were pulling into the parking lot to go through the drive-through at the side of the diner. She did her best to appear nonchalant and not look around.

Pearl was halfway down the highway when her brand-new phone rang. She clicked it on and listened to Jack Sparrow telling her to go home and wait for him. She clicked it off, and a second later, her regular cell phone rang. She picked it up and said hello.

"Uh . . . ma'am, this is 39674. I want to thank you for meeting with me. I have a message for you. Star 67 said to tell you there will be four at the dinner party. She wants to know what the ETA is."

"Four? I wasn't prepared for four. It's okay, it's okay. I can accommodate four. I'll just have to do some juggling and make a few calls. You need to calm down. But I will have to get back to you on the sit-down time. Is that okay?" Pearl asked, allowing just enough anxiety to alert her tails to creep into her voice.

A choked voice said it was okay. The connection was broken.

The clock on the kitchen range read 6:20 when Pearl entered her kitchen. She saw the note on her kitchen table immediately.

Bug in landline. Bug in light fixture in master bedroom. Bug in vent under microwave oven. Tracking device on your SUV, and a bug in the remote control that opens your garage.

Talk on new phone outside only.

Pearl took the note, shredded it, then tossed it down the garbage disposal. The machine gurgled to life as the water washed away all evidence of the yellow sticky note.

Now what was she supposed to do? For sure she couldn't drink any more coffee. She poured out the pot that she'd been making when the first call came through at four-thirty. With nothing left to do, she washed out the pot and dried it.

Then she waited. But she was good at waiting. Actually, she excelled at the waiting game because the end result was always worth waiting for.

Around the corner, Special Agents Barry and Landry sat huddled in Barry's Dodge, whispering.

Senior of the two, Landry asked why they were whispering.

"Force of habit. I can't believe it, Landry. We've been on this shit detail for eight goddamn months, and today, at four-thirty in the morning, the woman finally makes a move. Eight months! And we sign off in fifty minutes. We've been busting our humps here, and those two are just going to walk into it and get the collar. Tell me, how fair is that?"

"I don't like it any more than you do, but Zander said to wait and brief Mahoney and Palance," Landry said. "Personally, I don't think she's going to be doing anything during the daylight hours but talk on the phone and make plans. I'm thinking if there's any action, it will be after dark. I could be wrong, but I don't think so."

Barry, junior to Landry, was forty-two, buffed and ripped, and, according to him, a real lady killer with no desire to get married. In his opinion, his talents were wasted on this pissy-assed stakeout. Landry, fifty-six, was a bachelor by choice, married to his job, twelve pounds overweight, and ideal for stakeout work. He had two more years to go before he'd be a thirty-year man and retire on a very generous pension.

A Dodge Ram pickup truck pulled to the curb. Two Harley-Davidsons were nestled in the back cargo hold. Two agents bounced out of the truck and slid into the backseat of the Dodge. Mahoney and Palance grinned at the two cranky agents. "What does Zander want us to do?"

Both agents were young and full of piss and vinegar. They were also full of themselves, according to Landry. Early thirties, fit and trim, aviator glasses at seven in the morning even though the day was rainy and dismal. Both were dressed casually in jeans, biker boots, and leather jackets. They were hot shots and didn't care who knew it.

"The same thing you've been doing for the past eight months. Watch the house, watch the woman, listen to her phone calls. This might be nothing, but then again, it could be something. That meeting at Betty's Diner wasn't for shits and giggles. She's up to something. But can we pin that *something* on her and make it stick? Not at this point. No harm in having breakfast with some young girl. The phone calls could be anything. Remember who she is and was before she retired. If anything goes down, this town will cut her miles of slack. Every lawyer and judge will be Johnny-on-the-spot wanting to help her and give the Bureau another black eye. She won't go the local route though, count on it. She'll hire that buzz saw, Lizzie Fox. Then it's all over but the shouting, and we're all fools. Get your lazy asses out of our car so we can grab some shut-eye. See you at seven," Landry said.

The two young agents grinned. Mahoney thought they were cloned from the same mold. One he detested.

When the two younger agents were back in their pickup, Mahoney asked a question. "Who the hell is Lizzie Fox?"

Palance glared at his partner. "You don't know who Lizzie Fox is! Where the hell have you been these past few years? That's one lady you don't ever, as in ever, want to go up against. She has every politician in this town in her pocket. What that means is they all owe her. And she is not above calling in favors. She was and probably still is a personal friend of Martine Connor, the former president of this here United States of America. She was legal counsel to the president. Not to mention she is one hell of a looker. Drop-dead gorgeous. Judges just rule in her favor regardless of what the case is. No lawyer worth his salt will go up against her. You getting the picture here?"

"Yeah, we're screwed from the git-go. Even if we nail Justice Barnes, it won't go anywhere."

"Yep, that's the way it will go. And we'll be the assholes she nails to the wall on the stand. So, I'm thinking here, we should let Landry and Barry do the collar. Ah, I see you still don't know what I'm talking about. Go on your laptop and Google her. Hey, you like Vegas, right? Well, guess who she's married to! Cosmo Cricket. The guy that calls the shots with the Gaming Commission. Now, *that's* the big time! You want to go up against a dynamic duo like those two, be my guest."

Mahoney opened up his laptop and typed in the lawyer's name. He let loose with a whistle. "You weren't kidding, were you? That chick is *smoking hot*!"

Palance slouched in his seat. "How'd you like to be staring at her while she grills you on the stand, Mahoney? You'd be tongue-tied, and you'd wet your pants, that's how you'd do. Then you'll get transferred to Pierre, South Dakota. While you're reading, I'm going to take the bike and go get some coffee. You want anything to go with it?"

"I'm not hungry," Mahoney said, swallowing hard as he envisioned himself on the witness stand answering or trying to answer Lizzie Fox's questions.

"Shit!"

Mahoney could hear Palance laughing uproariously as he gently lowered his bike to the ground.

CHAPTER 10

Pearl Barnes fussed around in her kitchen. First, she emptied the dishwasher. Then she made coffee that she had no intention of drinking. She'd been doing that a lot lately, and she needed to stop. She looked around, her gaze coming to rest on the two cell phones on her kitchen table. She wished they would ring. Anything to get this show on the road. But when nothing happened, she walked over to her kitchen door and looked out at the early-morning sky. The rain had stopped, and the October sun, though weak, was trying to peek from the clouds, but it was a losing battle. The clouds scudding across the sky looked like giant bruises.

She turned back to look at her bright kitchen. She loved her kitchen. It was sunshine yellow, with a wonderful breakfast nook that looked out over a yard that in the summer was a veritable rainbow of color.

When she had time, which she had a lot of these days, she loved digging in the soft, loamy earth. When her daughter was little, they would work together in the garden. Then they would sit for hours in the breakfast nook, her daughter doing her homework, or they would just talk. So many memories. And not even one regret. She wondered how that could be.

Pearl looked at the muted television on the kitchen counter. She had no clue what Matt Lauer was talking about, but he seemed excited for some reason. She wondered when he had started going bald, not that she cared one way or the other. She decided she didn't care what the commentator was excited about either — she had her own problems to deal with. If she turned up the volume, she might not hear the cell phones if they rang. Besides, her hearing wasn't what it once was. In fact, she'd been fiddling with the idea of going to get her hearing checked and possibly getting a hearing aid. Just the thought made her crazy because it was one more indication of her age.

Pearl stared at the phone, willing it to ring. And, lo and behold, it did. Who says a watched pot never boils? *The magic of positive thinking,* Pearl thought as she clicked on the phone, her heart thumping in her chest.

"This is Star 72. We have an update on the party."

"Extra guests? I'm sure it won't be a problem. We have enough time to adjust the menu, don't we?"

"Not really," Star 72 said quietly. "With the extra guest list, we need to move the party somewhere else."

"Any suggestions?" Pearl's mind raced. Did they want her to meet somewhere? She gambled. "I can meet you somewhere if you want to discuss it."

"That's a great idea. Location?" Star 72 asked.

Pearl responded smartly. "Two plus four." Like her words had any meaning at all, she was just making it up as she went along.

"Star 77 will meet you at location three. Confirm."

"I confirm, Star 72. When do you want me to leave?"

"Now. A mode change is in the works. Do you agree?"

"I agree." Pearl broke the connection and pondered the conversation. When she'd been active in the underground, the star numbers were assigned to the volunteers. Their clients just had assigned numbers. It worked for everyone. A mode change meant she was to switch vehicles. Location three if this was all for real would mean the next stop on the relay that only the underground volunteers knew.

Pearl walked into the laundry room and pulled a dark gray hooded sweatshirt from the closet along with a baseball cap that said NY METS on it. She then slipped a bulging backpack over her shoulders; it contained a flashlight, flex cuffs, a gun, and a Taser, all bundled tightly in a fluffy pink towel. She'd used everything at one time or another. As had all the other volunteers. Their mantra was, whatever it took to get their people to safety. The last thing she did was to grab the two cell phones and stuff them into the pocket of her hooded sweatshirt.

Pearl was out the door within seconds. The moment her engine turned over, the cell phone Jack Sparrow gave her pinged. She picked it up, said hello, and waited.

"Don't say anything. Just listen. Go to the Shell gas station on the corner of Dorchester and Shepherd. Drive around to the back. There's a maroon Subaru waiting for you. Park your car, be sure to lock it and take the keys. Get back on Dorchester and stay on it till you come to an empty storefront. The sign overhead says it was once a deli. Pull into the lot and sit there and wait.

Right now I want you to say, 'I understand.' Then hang up."

Pearl did exactly as she was told, her eyes straining to see through the pouring rain that had started all over again the moment she got out to the highway.

Four cars back, the two FBI agents in the pickup truck cursed to each other. "Okay, she's on the move. Stay with her. What the hell! I just heard the cell ring. You heard it, right?" Palance nodded as he concentrated on the road in front of him. "Then how come we can't hear what she's saying? Okay, okay, she just said, 'I understand.' Crap, she's got a burn phone."

"You want a wild guess, Mahoney? I told you she has another cell phone. Get with the program here. This lady is no dummy. You need to call this in to Zander. She's turning into that Shell station. What do you want me to do?"

"Follow her, pretend you're going to get gas. It's self-serve. Oh, oh, she's driving around back." A second later, Palance bounded out of the truck and ran to the side. He was just in time to see Pearl get out of her car and slog her way to where a maroon Subaru was parked. He ran back to the truck, climbed in, and yelled, "She's in a maroon Subaru; she switched up cars."

"Son of a bitch!" Mahoney swore as he peeled away from the gas pump. An elderly lady laid on her horn at the way he cut her off.

"Don't lose her. Stay as close as you can. Crap on this rain. What the hell are we supposed to do now? I could have taken the bike but not in this downpour."

"I told you, call Zander. We're going to need some extra help here. Man, she's cruising for an old lady, especially in this weather."

"You lose her, your ass is grass with the boss. Eight months, and it has to happen today, in this goddamn monsoon." Palance lowered the window and got a blast of rain in his face for his efforts. "You know what, Mahoney? Doesn't it strike you as a little odd that the old man has this running detail on Justice Barnes? Eight months, all those man-hours, the overtime, when he's always screaming about cutbacks and money? If she is running an underground railroad to get women and kids to safety, what the hell is wrong with that? We all know the justice system stinks, especially in this town. We get orders to look the other way on shit that's a lot more serious than this. In my opinion."

"You need to keep those opinions to

yourself, pal."

Palance snorted. "If I can't talk to my partner, who can I talk to?"

"I'm just saying. Damn, she's pulling over. No way I can follow her in. What the hell is this place?"

Palance lowered the window again. "The Busy Bee Café. But it's out of business now. Go to the next turnoff and swing back around. You can pretend to have engine trouble. I'll get out and raise the hood."

Mahoney did as instructed.

Within minutes, a Chevy Yukon pulled into the parking lot; even in the heavy rain, the two agents could tell that the windows had been darkened. Engine idling, the big SUV sat there like a dark monster. Across from it, Justice Barnes sat and waited, her engine also running.

Inside the pickup, Agent Mahoney cursed because he couldn't hear a thing. His gut told him the occupants of both vehicles were conversing on phones that he had no access to. What the hell were they supposed to do? There was no probable cause that he could see and feel comfortable with to intercede. The lady could meet up with whomever she pleased wherever she pleased. Just like she could switch cars on an hourly basis if she felt like it. At this point, he was gut certain Justice Barnes knew she was being followed, and there wasn't a damn thing he could do about it. For now.

Palance climbed back into the truck, drenched to the skin and shivering. "Turn up the damn heat, will you? I'm freezing here. You pick up anything?"

"*Nada.* And no word from Zander either. We need to decide to either move or wait them out. What do you want to do, Palance?"

"Pull out and head down the road, take the first turnoff, and circle back. If we're lucky, they'll just think we had some engine trouble. We need backup." As Palance talked, he was sending out texts on his cell phone. He cursed again when there were no replies.

The rest of the day was, as Mahoney put it, the worst goddamn screwed-up Chinese fire drill he'd ever seen as Justice Barnes led them on a merry chase all over town. She was back at her own house at ten minutes past five. It was already totally dark when she pulled into her driveway, driving a gray, nondescript Nissan Sentra whose license plate was crusted with mud to prevent identification.

Inside, Pearl collapsed on a kitchen chair and stared around at her pretty kitchen with

175

wild eyes. Today was a day she hoped she wouldn't have to repeat, but she knew that was wishful thinking on her part. She'd been sent home to rest for an hour or so. By seven, Sparrow told her, she'd be on the move again.

Pearl made coffee, rummaged in the fridge, and made a baloney and cheese sandwich that she wolfed down. She finished her sketchy dinner with a banana and waited for the coffee to finish dripping into the pot. Her mind raced as she wondered if she could hold up for two or three more days until Sparrow was satisfied that he had all the Fibbies in his net. What would happen afterward was anyone's guess. Even though Jack Sparrow had assured her that when he left to return to Vegas, she would be a free agent and could do as she pleased with no one following her, no one invading her privacy. It all sounded too good to be true. It boggled her mind that in the short time he'd been here, Sparrow had mapped out a course of action, gotten his people lined up, and did what she had believed impossible. She was no fool, though; she knew, thanks to Annie, that this was Sparrow's chance to get his pound of flesh for being railroaded and spending time in a federal prison. That, she thought, had to leave some serious mental as well as physical scars on a person.

Antsy with nothing to do, Pearl wandered over to the door and looked out into her yard. She wondered how many invisible eyes were watching her house. Thank God the rain had stopped, and while the night was crisp and cool, stars were peeking out through the clouds. Another few hours, and the sky would be star-spangled. And it was a new moon. That wasn't so good. Her work called for darkness.

Pearl poured a second cup of coffee, returned to the table, and stared at the two phones. She thought they looked like two malevolent eyes.

Less than three miles away, in Georgetown, Maggie Spitzer was opening cartons of Chinese food and setting the table for herself, Ted, and Espinosa. Ted was setting out silverware in lieu of chopsticks, along with napkins, while Espinosa opened three bottles of Chinese beer.

"This is really like old times, isn't it?" Maggie said, eyeing her two best friends in the whole entire world. Ted and Espinosa beamed and nodded.

"You guys ready to hit the road tomorrow?" Maggie asked.

"I'm chomping at the bit," Ted said. "I have six interviews lined up with the parents of kids sent to those boot camps. I took the youngest ones. How many did you confirm, Maggie?"

"Eight, but two are iffy. The mothers sounded like they really wanted to talk but the husbands not so much. I'll wing those two. When the others see which way we're going with this, they might clam up. Like one lady said, if she talks to me and it gets out, how much worse is it going to go on her son? He's only twelve, and he has nine more months to go at that place he's in. The boy is seriously depressed, and they have him on meds. The lady said he's like a zombie. God, Ted, how are we going to make this right without something going wrong for those kids?"

"The proof will be in Espinosa's pictures, that's how. I don't care how powerful those two judges think they are, the *Post* is more powerful. The ladies are planning a snatch and grab with those two judges. Once we get them out of their comfort zone, it's free fall. At least from where I'm sitting, that's how it looks to me."

Maggie reached for her third egg roll. It crunched when she bit into it. Her eyes rolled in pure delight at the taste. She did love good food. "I sure hope that Charles gets this synchronized down to the last sync because the timing is going to be crucial."

Espinosa opened three more bottles of beer and passed them around. Ted tossed one fortune cookie to him and another to Maggie.

Maggie was biting down on the cellophane to rip it away when her cell phone rang. Startled, she looked across at Ted and Espinosa and shrugged as to who would be calling her during the dinner hour. "Whoa! It's Dennis West, the kid who wrote the story in the *Baywater Weekly*," she whispered.

"Damn it, Maggie, answer it before he chickens out and hangs up," Ted roared.

"Maggie Spitzer!"

"Miss Spitzer, this is Dennis West. I've gotten several messages saying you were trying to reach me. What is it you want to talk to me about?" Maggie pressed a button that would allow both conversations to go to speaker format so Ted and Espinosa could hear what was being said.

Ted mouthed the words, "He sounds nervous." Espinosa nodded, as did Maggie.

"Oh, Mr. West, thanks so much for calling me. Yes, I have been trying to reach you. I'm a reporter for the *Post* here in D.C. I wanted to talk to you about the article you wrote in the *Baywater Weekly*."

"The *Post*! You work for the *Post*!" Dennis West repeated, excitement ringing in his voice. "Do you know Ted Robinson? He's my idol. He's the first thing I read when I go online. Someone said he was the EIC and not reporting anymore. I was crushed. If I had one wish, it would be to be as good a reporter as he is."

Maggie grinned from ear to ear as she held the phone out to Ted, who ran with it.

"Dennis, this is Ted Robinson, Maggie's my partner. Nice to meet you, kid. So, can we arrange a meeting? We're thinking of offering you a job here at the *Post*."

The silence in the room rang in all their ears as they waited for the young reporter to respond.

"Oh, jeez! Holy smoke! I can't believe I'm talking to you. I wasn't lying; you are my idol. Oh my gosh! This isn't a joke, is it? Maybe I'm dreaming. Nope, I just pinched myself, and it hurt. Why me? Holy gee whiz!"

Ted grinned. The kid sounded just like he remembered himself years and years ago when he was in awe of a particular reporter who had gone out of his way to mentor him. Now it was his turn. "So, what do you say?

Can we meet, Dennis? By the way, where are you? We've been trying to track you down for the past few days. Is anything wrong?"

"Right now I'm in Old Town in Alexandria, Virginia. I've . . . ah . . . I've been moving around as much as the clunker I drive will let me. It's a long story, and I suspect that's what you want to talk to me about, right?"

"Did I mention a company car comes with the job? When can we meet up with you?" Ted said smoothly. His eyes shot questions to Maggie, which meant, Can we make this happen? She nodded.

"Oh, gee whiz. Holy cow! I don't believe this. Hey, I'm all yours. I can be anywhere you want in an hour if my car will get me there."

"Tell you what, Dennis. I'll call the *Post* and let the night guard know you're coming. Wait for us in the lobby. There is one thing, though."

"Oh, jeez, I knew it. What? What's the catch? Oh, crap, I knew this was too good to be true." It sounded to all three like the young reporter was going to cry.

"Hey, kid, hold on there. You don't even know what I was going to say. You know the rule, never assume, and you sure as hell never presume. What I was going to ask you is this. Where is your original story on the Ciprani twins? The real story before your paper watered it down?"

"Boy, you must think I'm dumb, Mr. Robinson. I did what you would have done. Ask yourself where my original is?"

Ted reared back and looked at his two partners, then he grinned. "You kept a copy on someone else's computer, right?"

"You got it. When the paper came out, watered-down, those two judges made my boss ask for my laptop. I had no choice but to turn it in. I had like five minutes to send the files to a friend of mine. I paid him for his computer. It's in the trunk of my car. No one knows that but you now. That's why I've been, you know, moving around. The truth is, I've been afraid. So, do you still want to meet with me and give me a job?"

"You know it, kid. We'll see you in an hour. Park right in front of the building. I'll put my tag on your car when I get there."

"Dennis, this is Maggie. Listen, tell me something. Did you get the goods on those two?"

"I thought I did. I guess I did because that's when all my problems started. My boss got fired after that sham article was printed, and there was nothing in it. You

182

don't do anything in Baywater unless those two judges okay it."

"Kid, do you know how to spot a tail?" Ted asked.

Dennis snorted. "I do and I did. But I didn't have my friend's computer then. Someone searched my car. I know this because I wasn't born under a mushroom, you know. I set a trap. There was nothing for whoever searched it to find. That's another reason why I headed up here to Virginia. I have some college buddies here who are letting me bunk with them."

"Okay, we're going to hang up now, Dennis. We'll meet you in an hour. Be careful, okay?"

"Oh, man, you know it. See ya."

The trio looked at one another. "What do you think, Ted?" Maggie asked.

"I think we hit the mother lode, Maggie. I think that kid has just what he says he has, and he's smart. You need to call Annie since I made some pretty rash promises. See if we have her approval. It is her paper, and she's the boss."

Maggie picked up a sugared bun that came with the Chinese dinner and stuffed it in her mouth as she hit the number three on her speed dial. She talked around the bun and waited. Annie's response was what she thought it would be. "Whatever it takes, dear."

"We're good to go, guys," Maggie said, reaching for a second bun.

Ted's clenched fist shot in the air. Then he clapped a grinning Espinosa on the back.

Maggie burst out in joyous laughter. Her adrenaline was at an all-time high. Damn, it felt good to be back!

CHAPTER 11

Maggie, Ted, and Espinosa climbed out of the cab smack in front of the *Post* building. The three of them looked at the junky car, more rust than metal, in front of the cab and grinned at one another. They'd all had cars like what they were looking at when they had started their careers. "For one thing, he doesn't have to worry about anyone stealing that hunk of junk." Ted laughed as he pushed his press card under the windshield wiper on the driver's side of the car.

Maggie was alert as she looked right and left to see if there was anything out of the ordinary. Everything looked normal to her for this hour of the evening. It didn't look like Dennis West had anyone following him. She strained to see into the building lobby and waved for Dennis West to join them. The door opened, and a figure that resembled a soccer ball rushed out to the

185

curb. He was short and squat and dressed in jeans with holes in the knees and a T-shirt that said RAT'S ASS on the front. A battered baseball cap was squashed down on a head of unruly curls the color of cinnamon. Chipmunk-rosy cheeks, denim blue eyes, and pearly white teeth completed the picture of one Dennis West.

Introductions were made.

"You guys weren't joking, were you?" Dennis asked, his tone worried as he removed his cap, smoothed his curls, then mashed the cap back on his head.

"Do we look like we're here for shits and giggles, kid? Move your ass and get that computer out of the car. Do you care if that car gets towed?" Ted asked.

"Not one little bit if you say a car comes with this job."

Ted ripped his press card off the windshield and stuck it in his pocket. He watched as Dennis heaved and heaved until he finally pried the trunk of the clunker open.

"Damn!" the trio said in unison. "How old is that thing?"

"Doesn't matter. It works, and it saved my ass. But to answer your question, it was one of the first on the market. I could probably sell it even now for maybe fifty bucks."

Espinosa tried to slam the trunk shut, but

it wouldn't close. He shrugged.

"You have to tie it down if you want it to close," Dennis said as he struggled with the heavy, ungainly computer. Ted rushed ahead to open the door to the *Post* building, Maggie trailing behind. Espinosa finally gave up after he gave the trunk another hard slam only to have it fly up and hit the back windshield.

In the *Post* newsroom, the trio did their best to try to hide their smiles as Dennis West looked around at the few straggling veteran reporters who hung out far into the night, his expression one of awesome delight. He walked around, touching a chair, peering at a computer, trying out a chair here or there until he finally asked where he would be sitting.

"Right over there between me and Maggie," Ted said, pointing to a bright red swivel chair. "New kid always gets the red chair so we can keep track of him. You gonna set that thing on the desk before you get a hernia?"

"Oh, yeah. Jeez, this is just the way I saw it in my dreams. It feels . . . it feels . . . *awesome.* Like, you know, I belong here all of a sudden. I don't know what to say. How can I thank you? What kind of benefit package goes with the job? Not that I care, but the book says you always need to ask."

"The whole ball of wax, kid. Stop in at Human Resources tomorrow. They'll explain everything. Now, how about plugging that thing in and booting up. In case you haven't noticed, we're kind of anxious to see what you got."

Dennis West fumbled around, muttering to himself as he tried out the red chair and proclaimed it a perfect fit. He swiveled around a few times like a little kid doing a whirly-twirly, and laughed out loud. "I'm really here! I can't believe it! I swear I won't let you down. What kind of car?"

"You let us down, and I'll kick your ass all the way to the Canadian border. It's a black 2011 Taurus. That work for you, kid?" Ted said through clenched teeth.

"Well, gee whiz, yeah. Why wouldn't it?" Dennis asked, as he tapped the keys on the ancient keyboard. "Who pays the insurance? How much . . . what's my salary? I think you're supposed to tell me that."

"Who the hell do you think pays it? The paper pays it. HR will explain everything to you in the morning. Probably ten times what you made at that jerkwater paper you were working at. Come on, what's our problem here?" Ted demanded, losing patience with the young reporter.

"I told you it was slow. I guess that makes sense. What about gas?"

"I'm going to kill you!" Ted roared. "You get a gas card. You just look dumb. That's your stock-in-trade, right?"

Dennis shrugged, turned, and smiled a smile so pure and joyful, the others could only grin. They had all been there, done that, lived through it.

"Here we go. It's all on one big file, just scroll down and read. I labeled every interview, time, date, and if I had to go back a second time for any reason, I logged that, too. I scanned the signed affidavits. Everything is there. I have all the originals in a safe place."

"Okay, Dennis, here's your first job. The kitchen is down the hall, second door on the left. Go there and make us some coffee and bring it back here. We all drink it black. If there are any cookies, bring them, too. *Go!*" Maggie ordered.

Dennis turned tail and made his way to the kitchen. He felt like dancing even though he had two left feet. He wanted to sing, but even his mother and his college roommates told him he sounded like a sick cat in distress. He *needed* to do *something*, so he jumped up and down, clapped his hands like a little kid, whistled off-key, then did a little jig until he got dizzy.

When he came back down to earth, he measured out coffee and poured water into the pot. He looked around. He was really here, and he was making coffee for the guys. At some point, he'd be one of them. One of the guys. Not yet, though, and he understood he would be sitting in the red chair for a while unless he hit a really big story. A Pulitzer. Every reporter's dream. He looked around at the cups on the shelf with the different reporters' names on them. He could hardly wait to see his own cup up there, waiting for him. How in the hell had he gotten so damn lucky?

Dennis's touch was short of reverent when he reached up for the cups that said Maggie, Ted, and Espinosa. They were large mugs, with handles that looked like bent pencils. He wanted one so bad he felt like he could taste it. He also knew he'd need to earn it, and when he did, one of the other reporters would gift him with one. That was the way it worked. Or so he'd been told.

Dennis reached for a colorful plastic tray leaning up against the backsplash next to a sign that said YOU MAKE A MESS, YOU CLEAN THE MESS. He looked around to make sure he wasn't leaving a mess. No mistakes this early in the game. He poured the coffee, then rinsed the pot and dumped the grounds in the trash under the sink. His hands shaking, he carried the tray down to the newsroom, where he stopped dead in his tracks when his hosts stared at him like they were either going to kill him or love him to death. More likely the former as opposed to the latter. The cups rattled on the tray. Espinosa rushed to take the tray from his shaking hands.

"What? Oh, my God, what? You're firing me already? What? I didn't leave a mess in the kitchen. The sign said to not leave a mess. I did not leave a mess. What?"

Ted took the lead and advanced a few steps, his hand outstretched. Maggie did the same, then Espinosa came forward. "Kid, what we read, even though it was a sketchy first read, is some of the best reporting I've seen in a long time. I don't even think I could have done it any better. How'd you get all those people to talk to you?" Ted demanded.

"Oh, God, oh, God! You mean you aren't firing me? You scared the wits out of me. You like what I wrote?" The others watched as the young reporter kept pinching his arms and wincing at the pain he was inflicting on himself.

"We do!" Maggie said, rushing to hug

him. "Listen, Dennis, this is your story. We're just here to help you get it published in its entirety. I don't think I'm off the mark when I say you might, you just might, get a Pulitzer for this. If you do it right. Ted and Espinosa agree."

Dennis West felt his eyes roll back in his head as he slipped to the floor.

It took all three of them to get the roly-poly reporter up onto the red chair.

"This kid is something else," Ted said, sounding like a proud father.

"He's done all our work for us," Maggie said. "He's got it all. Wonder how long it took him."

"Six months," Dennis said breathlessly as he came around to the land of the living.

"Here, drink this," Espinosa said, handing him his cup of coffee. Dennis gulped at it gratefully.

"How did you get all of this, and how'd you get it without tipping your hand to those two judges?" Maggie asked, pointing to the text on the screen.

Dennis West laughed. "Look at me! Some elderly lady told me I looked like her grandson. Old people love to talk, and she couldn't wait to unload on me because I listened. People, as a rule, don't listen to old people. That's a really terrible mistake because old people are very wise. I wasn't a threat to anyone. Someone else said I looked honest. Just so you know, I am honest. I don't cheat. And I would never pad an expense account. I'm ordinary. But the bottom line was all the people I talked to had something to say and wanted to say it. I could read their fear. While all the affidavits are real, the article has bogus names. I had to do that. Reprisals are a terrible thing, you know. What did you think of Miz Charlotte Rushton's affidavit?"

"What's not to like? But the fact that she's in a nursing home and is up there in years may not work to our advantage."

Dennis giggled. "Miz Charlotte put herself in that nursing home. She wanted to get as far away from those evil women as she could get. That's what she called them — evil women. She's sharp as a tack and she gave her doctor permission to talk to me about her and the conditions she does *not* have. She also moved out of state and is here in Virginia. She had enough good sense to do that, so that should tell you she has all her marbles. She worked for the Cipranis for thirty years. She knows all their secrets, and she couldn't wait to finally talk about them. And Jon Eberly, the brother Peter's best friend. I can't be sure about this, but I think

193

he knows where Peter is, and it isn't six feet under either, the way those judges say, even though he vehemently denied it. I don't care if those judges had Peter declared dead or not. I think he is very much alive. No matter what I did, no matter what I promised, I couldn't get any more out of Eberly. He still lives in Baywater and has a business there, so he isn't going to rock any boats. Call it gut instinct, reporter's instinct, but I think he has been in touch with the brother. The guy was nice to me, real nice."

"And all the victims' families? How'd you convince them to talk to you?"

"Told them the truth. I just said I wanted to expose those two judges, but I couldn't do it without help. Like I said, I changed everyone's name. Once I agreed to do that, they were more cooperative. It's all one big, hot, bonfire mess."

"You did real good, Dennis. Real good. We're going to take you now to a condo the *Post* keeps for out-of-town guests. You'll be staying there until . . . well, until we tell you it's safe to move. It could be a while, and you don't have to worry about rent. I'll pick you up in the morning, get you situated here with HR, get your car and everything you're going to need. I don't want you going back to wherever it was you were staying. We'll cut you a check later on to buy anything you need for now. You okay with all this? That means you cut all ties to friends, associates, anyone associated with Baywater. You got that? If it's a problem, tell us now. You make even one phone call that we don't authorize, and you're outta here. You can call your parents and tell them we're sending you on an out-of-town assignment. That's it."

"Well, yeah, Mr. Robinson, I'm okay with it all. I'd pretty much have to be a fool not to be okay with all of this. *This* is the stuff dreams are made of, at least for people like me. I don't know how to thank you."

"I have a question, Dennis," Espinosa said. "Where'd you get the guts to take on those two judges? Weren't you afraid they'd come after you? From what we've been hearing, everyone is afraid of them."

Dennis shrugged. "Yes, and no. I heard about all the people who tried to go up against those two, and I heard the things that happened to them. All explained away, of course. It's all wrong, and no one cares. Or else everyone else is a coward. I might be many things, but a coward I am not. But if you need one thing, then it's this. A buddy of mine has a nephew who got sent to one of those camps. The boy is out now, and he's never going to be the same. The kid goes to therapy five days a week and . . . It's all in there. He's case number sixty-five. It bothers me to talk about it, so just read it, okay?"

"We skimmed through it all, but I'll read it thoroughly when I get back home. Ted is going to take you now to the condo." Maggie moved to the side, and whispered to Ted, "I'm going to stay here, run off copies, and fax them to Myra and Charles. I'll take a cab back to my house. Do you want me to send the file to your iPhone?"

"Yeah, do that," Ted said.

"What about tomorrow?" Espinosa asked.

Maggie chewed on her lower lip for a moment. "I think I'm going to go out to Pinewood first thing in the morning. I'll plan on leaving around six. When I get back, I will either have permission for the three of us to go to Baywater, or I won't. I'm also wondering if we should take 'Jimmy Olsen' with us," Maggie said, referring to the young reporter. "He might be a help. I need to think on that some more. I'll meet you here at the paper sometime tomorrow morning. You'll be busy showing the kid the ropes and getting him settled in."

"Then if you guys don't need me, I'm going to head on home. See ya in the morning. Nice meeting you, kid," Espinosa said, clapping Dennis on the back.

"Hold on, Espinosa. We'll ride down with you in the elevator," Ted said. He hugged Maggie in a not-so-brotherly way. "I'm liking this," he whispered.

"Yeah. Yeah, me, too, Ted," Maggie said softly. She waved airily as she headed toward the fax machine.

Maggie's thoughts were all over the map as she watched the fax eat up the pages she'd printed out from Dennis West's file. In some respects it seemed like she'd stepped back in time, then seconds later she was staring into the future. Life was beyond strange sometimes. Then again, everything happened for a reason. All she had to do was figure out what that reason was.

She turned around and looked at the red chair as she remembered the days and months that she'd sat in it, learning the ropes. They were good days. And a few bad ones, but it went with the territory. She hoped Dennis West would appreciate those same good and bad days. Her gut told her the kid had what it takes. Ted and Espinosa thought so, too; she could tell. Kind of like having a kid brother to look after. She laughed then, a sound of pure mirth.

Life was looking good. Really, really good.

CHAPTER 12

A weak sun was just creeping over the horizon when Maggie walked into her kitchen to start the new day. Should she make coffee or pick up some on the way? She hated making these kinds of earthshaking decisions so early. She was headed out to Pinewood to talk to Myra and Charles. She looked at the empty pot and decided to stop at the first convenience store she came to so she could fuel up on her daily ration of coffee. Decision made, she was out the door and headed for her car moments later. Her neighborhood was stirring even at such an early hour. Two couples were walking their dogs. The good-looking stud two doors down was starting his morning run. She made a mental note to get back into her exercising routine. She always felt better when she exercised. Soon. There were more important things on her agenda right now.

Before unlocking her car, she looked

around, then upward. It felt like rain. Again. And her knee was bothering her. When her knee bothered her, it usually rained within a matter of hours. She was better than any weatherman when it came to predicting the weather. She looked at the huge trees, now bare of their leaves, that lined the sidewalks. Yesterday there had been leaves on some of them, but they were gone. Probably because of the high winds that rattled the house last night. It was, after all, autumn, and wind and rain were daily staples, not to mention goblins and witches. All that remained were skeletons. The trees were one of the main reasons she'd moved to this particular neighborhood in Georgetown. She loved the old trees in the spring and the way they shaded the sidewalks and the front of the houses like giant umbrellas. The trees were one reason, and having Jack, and now Nikki as neighbors, was the other reason she'd snapped up the house she still lived in. She made a mental note to call Jack and Nikki later in the day even though she knew that they knew she was back. One should never slough off good friends like Jack and Nikki.

It was cold, way too cold for late October. She had never liked the cold because she didn't like to bundle up, and she sure as hell hated shivering. If only she'd had the presence of mind to come out and warm up her car. She accepted the fact that she wasn't clicking on all of her cylinders. Soon. All she had to do was shift into her neutral zone and take it from there. Easier said than done.

The ride out to Pinewood was uneventful. Neither Ted nor Espinosa had been in touch this morning. True, they were busy with Dennis West. But Ted always checked in. Always. Well, things were different now, she reminded herself. All she wanted was to get back on her old footing and get on with life.

Maggie heard the dogs as she sailed through the open gate at the old farmhouse. The fact that the gate was open told her Myra was in the kitchen and had seen her car approaching on the security monitor. She hoped the coffee at Pinewood would be better than what she'd picked up at the fast-food dump she'd stopped at. Breakfast would be good, too. But only if Charles was making it. Myra might serve toast with butter and jam, but that was about it. She was way too hungry for just toast and jam.

The kitchen door opened, and the dogs barreled out. Myra held out her arms, and Maggie rushed into them. She savored the feeling of being held close by someone who cared for her.

Myra's arm around Maggie, she led her into the kitchen, where Charles was busy at the stove. "Look who's in time for breakfast!" Myra said happily.

Maggie rushed to hug Charles. She sniffed appreciatively. "I was hoping I wouldn't have to settle for toast and jam." She giggled. "No offense intended, Myra."

"And none taken, dear. Sit! Sit! Tell us how it went last evening with the young man."

"Extremely well. I liked him. Ted and Espinosa fell all over themselves to help him. Hero worship goes a long way with those two, and that young reporter just idolizes the two of them. All Dennis had to say was that Ted was his idol, and it was clear sailing. Right now, as I speak, they should be headed to Human Resources to get him all set up. Then it's to the barber and some department store to outfit him in the manner to which Ted thinks a reporter should become accustomed. They have some banking to do — you know — set it up so his pay can go in as a direct deposit. The guys have it under control."

"He knows his business, then?" Charles queried.

"Do you mean does he have a fire in his belly the way they say good reporters have?

The answer is yes. He certainly isn't stupid. He's gutsy, maybe too much so for his own good, but both Ted and I recognized that in him. Been there, done that, have the T-shirt to prove it. Ted will rein him in if he goes off half-cocked. We put him up at the *Post* condo. I made sure Annie okayed everything. She said do whatever it takes, and we did it."

"He's a definite asset then?" Charles queried again.

"Absolutely. Which brings me to the reason I came out here this early. I want the four of us to head out to Baywater today, as soon as I get back to town, and the guys finish up what they're doing. Dennis has a rapport with some of the families, and we need to use that. Did you come up with legends yet for all of us?"

"I'm almost done. I think it's okay for the four of you to head out to Baywater. I want you to register at the Harbor Inn. Take three rooms. Use your own background when you get there. But only on one condition."

"Name it," Maggie said, eyeing the plate of fluffy scrambled eggs Charles had set in front of her.

"Backup. I'll have Avery Snowden send a few of his people. I'm thinking two women and two men."

Maggie picked up her fork. She knew better than to argue with Charles, who would ultimately go to Annie, who would then side with Charles. "As long as they don't get in our way or stand out. I told you what that town is like. Eight strangers milling about is going to send up red flags."

"You won't know they are there; nor will anyone else. Trust me. Having said that, we need to generate a little curiosity if, as you say, the whole town is buttoned up. Expect to be stopped by the local police the first chance they get. That's so they can get and run your information through all their databases. Make it easy for them. Speed going through town."

Maggie's eyebrows shot upward. "Did I just hear you right, Charles? Are you sure you want us to do that?"

"Oh, I'm sure all right. Avery's people will be everywhere. We need to know how tight the town control is as soon as possible. And remember this, the only words you know if one or all of you get arrested are, 'I want a lawyer.' "

Maggie laughed out loud. "We can do that."

"Where's your special gold shield, dear?" Myra asked.

Maggie stopped eating long enough to dig

203

into the pocket of her wool slacks. She held it up. "I always carry it on my person."

"Don't use it unless you have to," Charles warned.

"Gotcha. Anything else I should know before I head back to town? By the way, what is the latest with Pearl? Are they making any progress?"

"As you say, it's all going on. They're baiting the trap, so to speak. I spoke to Mr. Sparrow around midnight, and he assured me that Pearl should be in the clear in less than forty-eight hours. Unless, of course, something goes awry. No need to go into details here and now. Everything is under way."

"That's good to know. I don't know how she managed to live with all that surveillance for so long. Scumbag bastards!"

Charles nodded and smiled. Maggie did have a way with words. "Stay in touch. Hourly is best, but I'll settle for every two or three hours. Straight up at twelve whenever possible. It doesn't necessarily have to be you; Ted or Joseph can call in."

"Okay." Maggie finished the last of her breakfast, dabbed at her mouth, and asked for some coffee to go.

Myra's eyes sparkled. "I wish I were going with you, dear. Please, be careful."

"Always, Myra. Always."

Ten minutes later, Maggie was back on the road and headed for Alphabet City, also known as the nation's capital. She stopped for gas and sent Ted a text while she waited for her tank to fill. My ETA is one hour from now. Be ready to roll. Sign out the van. I'll leave my car in the motor pool.

The response came at the speed of light. Hot damn. Maggie laughed as she capped her tank, replaced the nozzle, and grabbed her credit-card receipt. " 'Hot damn' is right," she said, swinging onto the highway.

It was thirty minutes past high noon when Ted Robinson rolled the *Post*'s van into the town of Baywater. Maggie rode shotgun, while Espinosa and Dennis West sat in the back. The intrepid reporter had talked nonstop the entire trip. Twice Ted told him to button it up, and he did, but it was impossible for Dennis to contain his excitement or, as he put it, "I can't believe I'm here with all of you and that we're going to make it happen and you actually are going to try to get arrested."

Ted told everyone to be quiet so he could hear the robotic voice on the GPS. "Okay, two lefts and a right should bring us to the Harbor Inn. Did you decide how you want to do this, Maggie?"

"Charles said three rooms. You and I will share one room, Espinosa and Dennis will each have their own. Double beds in our room, Ted, so don't go getting any ideas."

Ted strove for a nonchalant tone when he said, "Works for me." His stomach felt like a beehive of hornets had taken over his intestines.

"How soon do you think we should get ourselves arrested?" Espinosa asked in a jittery voice.

"Not till we get something to eat and map out a plan, which you guys were supposed to do before we got here that you didn't do," Maggie snapped.

"That's not true, Maggie," Dennis West replied. "We said you were going to interview Jon Eberly, Peter Ciprani's friend, because I think he knows more than he told me. You can actually walk to his office from the Harbor Inn. The three of us are going to go to the outskirts of town, where some of the people I interviewed live. Properties here are really spread out. We need wheels. Maybe we should rent another vehicle."

"I think the kid is right. I saw an Easy Rental office right on Main Street, next to some insurance office," Espinosa said.

"Yeah, yeah, that's Jon Eberly's office, the

guy Maggie is going to see. Then it will make sense for her to rent the car," Ted said. "Okay, guys, we're here. Bail out. Let's get situated and meet in twenty minutes in our room. A word to the wise. Do not leave anything in your room you don't want anyone else to see. That goes for the van, too, so take everything with you."

Espinosa shot Ted a baleful look and pointed one by one to everyone's backpack. "Duh."

"Okay, okay!" Ted shot back.

Registration wasn't anything out of the ordinary, the foursome decided, when they met in Maggie and Ted's room twenty minutes later.

Maggie was perched at the end of the bed and looked at her colleagues. "I hope we didn't make a mistake using the *Post*'s credit card."

"The way I see it is it has an upside and a downside. Take your pick," Ted said, looking around the spacious room, which was clean and neat as a pin. The spreads and drapes were bright chintz and looked to have been freshly laundered. The furniture was hard rock maple and polished to a high sheen. There was an Internet hookup, a twenty-six-inch TV, and a DVR plus an honor bar. The floor was heart of pine with braided rugs. Two comfortable easy chairs were positioned at each end of the bay window that overlooked a small garden with colorful, painted Adirondack chairs. The bathroom was simply a bathroom, with over a dozen towels stacked on a portable shelf. It was all he could do not to stare at the two beds and what they might possibly come to mean where he and Maggie were concerned.

"Okay, let's hit the road. Ted, you call into Charles every two hours. I'll take the hour in between since we're splitting up. You guys check in with me. Just send a text. Dennis, which way is Mr. Eberly's office?"

"Go out the front door, walk down the driveway, and make a left, then a right, and that will put you on Main Street. What time are we going to meet?"

"Six sounds good to me. I'll go first, you guys wait ten minutes, then leave. Try not to get arrested until later."

Ted hooted as the door closed behind Maggie. He eyed the red numerals on the digital clock on the table between the two beds. *Shit! Two beds. Double shit!*

It was a blustery day with dark clouds scudding across the sky, but so far it hadn't rained. The way her knee ached, Maggie knew it would rain by midafternoon. Traffic in the center of town was light. She didn't see a single pedestrian and thought it strange. She did, however, feel unseen eyes on her as she walked along, looking up at the names on the plate-glass windows.

There were benches under the streetlamps along the promenade that were already lit on that dark, gloomy day. Huge urns of colorful fall flowers stood outside all the stores and offices. She thought the town must have a very active garden club. All in all, it was a neat, tidy town. Too neat. Too tidy. For her liking.

She stopped, read the lettering on the window, and again on the double-hung door. She opened it and walked into a small foyer, where a middle-aged woman sat behind a plate-glass cubicle. "Can I help you?"

"I hope so. I'd like to speak with Mr. Eberly on a personal matter."

"And your name is . . ."

"Maggie Spitzer. I'm from the *Post*. In Washington, D.C. I'm a reporter." Before the woman could say anything, Maggie handed over her *Post* credentials for perusal.

"Yes. I see. Please have a seat, and I'll see if Mr. Eberly can see you. He's been tied up all day so far."

"I have nothing else to do, so I can wait. All afternoon if necessary." *Tied up, my foot,* she thought. She settled herself in one of the uncomfortable chairs and whipped out a tattered paperback novel she carried with her for just such occasions. She'd been reading chapter seven for the past ten years, and if asked what the novel was about, she would have said she didn't have a clue.

The receptionist cleared her throat to get Maggie's attention. "Mr. Eberly said he can spare fifteen minutes. If you need more time, he suggests we arrange an appointment."

"Fifteen minutes is fine," Maggie said, jamming the paperback back into her backpack.

Maggie's first thought was that she had been right. Eberly, Peter Ciprani's best friend, wasn't busy and had probably been playing on the Internet. There wasn't a file, a folder, or any kind of paper on the man's desk. She couldn't see what was on the computer because it was angled away from her line of sight.

Jon Eberly was an ordinary-looking man with a receding hairline. He was pale and had liver spots on his cheeks and chin. He had soft brown eyes, a pleasant smile, and was dressed casually, his button-down shirt rolled up to his elbows, his tie loose at his neck. He walked around the desk and held out his hand. A tall man, wearing pressed khakis and boat shoes. Definitely casual.

"Jon Eberly."

Maggie was surprised at the firmness of his handshake. She exerted pressure of her own and saw the man wince. Strike one for her side. *I am not a helpless little woman.* "Maggie Spitzer. I'm from the *Post* in Washington."

"Well, that's not exactly around the corner now, is it? Did one of my clients get into some kind of trouble in the District, and you need verification of their insurance? Glad to help if that's the case. Please, sit down. Coffee, soft drink?"

"No thanks, I'm fine. None of the above, Mr. Eberly. I'm here, as are several of my colleagues, but they're off doing other things right now. We're planning an in-depth story on Peter Ciprani. Supposedly deceased. Turns out he isn't deceased at all. He's very much alive," she lied, hoping to see some kind of reaction. "He's the brother of two judges here in Baywater. But then I suspect you know that since you and Mr. Ciprani were best friends growing up and through college. It's wonderful to have such a long-lasting friendship."

Maggie had always prided herself on not only her reporter's instinct but also on being able to read people, especially when you blasted in like some avenging bird and hit your quarry with a broad assault. To his credit, the only thing that changed on Jon Eberly's face was a slight tightening of his lips.

"Wherever did you come by such a statement? It's cruel. Peter has been . . . dead for many, many years. Why would the *Post* be looking into something like this? I'm sorry, but this is in such bad taste. I don't think I want to discuss this any further."

"Well, that's entirely up to you, Mr. Eberly. It's not just Peter Ciprani we're writing about. We're actually planning an . . . exposé of his twin sisters. I'm told he plans to cooperate. It doesn't matter to me right now one way or the other if you talk to me today or not. People saw me come here. I and my crew are registered at the Harbor Inn. Tomorrow and the day after tomorrow, there will be more of us descending on this quaint little town. We at the *Post* think the good citizens here in Baywater have lived under the Ciprani-style rule of law way too long. I always like to lay my cards out on the table, so all parties know exactly what's going on. Do you still want me to leave?"

Jon Eberly ran his hands through his thinning hair. Suddenly, he looked like a deer caught in the headlights. He sucked in his breath and let it out with a loud swoosh.

"You up for a little walk in this crazy weather we're having right now, Miz Spitzer?"

The last thing Maggie wanted was to take a walk, but if a walk was what it took to get Jon Eberly to say something, she'd gallop down the street. "I'd love to go for a walk, Mr. Eberly."

CHAPTER 13

Myra Rutledge paced the kitchen, the dogs doing their best to keep up with her frantic movements. What she really wanted to do was go down to the War Room and shake Charles until his teeth rattled. What *was* taking so long? In the past, when a mission came up, he had a fairly good plan within hours, and usually a Plan B also, and everything laid out, meaning *everything* was covered six ways to Sunday. What *was* he doing down there in his lair? They'd done other missions far more complicated than this one. A small, hateful thought crept into her mind. Charles was losing it. Charles was getting older. Charles didn't really care anymore. *What?* In her heart of hearts, she knew none of that was true.

Myra thought about all the phone calls she'd gotten during the course of the day. Annie chomping at the bit. Nellie expressing the same doubts she'd just thought of.

Marti wanting to know when they were going to *move.* And the last phone call, just minutes ago, from Pearl, who sounded as mean and nasty as a scalded cat. Like this was all her fault. Maybe she did need to go down to the War Room and rattle Charles's cage, figuratively speaking.

The antique grandfather clock chimed in the living room. Six o'clock. Annie said she would be over at six. The clock on the range read 6:02. Myra wondered which one was right. Annie was always prompt if not early. The dogs ran to the door, which meant Annie had arrived, which then meant the grandfather clock had the real time. The kitchen clock was two minutes fast. She needed to remember that and adjust it at some point. Charles was a stickler for the correct time. Hence the clocks in the War Room that gave the time all over the world.

Anyone, anywhere, could set their clock by Annie. She said it had to do with Las Vegas because there were no clocks in the casinos. *Whatever . . .* she thought as she opened the door to admit her lifelong friend. They hugged because they always hugged.

"You look as frustrated and antsy as I feel, Myra. I think it's time to take Charles by the ear and lead him somewhere or make him do something. Oh, my, how stupid did that just sound? I'm just not good at sitting around twiddling my thumbs.

"By the way, Pearl called me a while ago. She said she had tried to call you but the call went to voice mail. You were probably out with the dogs. Then she tried to call Nellie, but Nellie had to drive Elias to the eye doctor because they were going to dilate his eyes. Pearl told me something very interesting. Listen to this, Myra. She, Pearl, was at home waiting for . . . whatever Mr. Sparrow's next move was going to be, and she was reading the paper. She said on page three there was an article about Judge Henry Rhodes retiring after serving fifty years on the bench."

"I never heard of him," Myra said.

"Me either. But, Myra, here's the kicker. Judge Rhodes sits on the bench in the town of *Baywater.* Pearl and Nellie both know him. Pearl said he came to both her and Nellie's retirement parties. They have a history of sorts going back to law school although Pearl was quick to point out that Judge Rhodes was a lot older than both of them. She said he also did not come from a life of privilege. She went on to say he was the youngest judge ever to sit in Baywater. An accomplishment in itself. Think about

216

it, Myra. Fifty years sitting on a bench and rendering decisions day after day after day."

Myra frowned as her fingers worked at the pearls around her neck. "And this means what, Annie?"

Annie sighed. "I think it means what Pearl didn't want to say on the phone knowing we'd figure it out. Mr. Sparrow called yesterday to say Pearl's house, car, and phone are bugged. Think Baywater. I'm thinking now because she said I should tell the girls and maybe we could help her and Nellie plan a surprise retirement party of our own for Judge Rhodes. Damn, now I can't remember if she said it or I said we should plan a party. It doesn't matter who said it, it's a good idea. Don't you think, Myra?"

"I do. I do. Do you know any more about what's going on with Pearl?"

"No, other than she's tired. She tried to say things, but they were so vague, I couldn't make heads or tails of the conversation."

"Coffee, Annie? How about a ham sandwich?"

"Yes to both. Do you think we should tell Charles? He might be able to incorporate this new development into whatever he's working up."

"I think so," Myra said as she bustled

about the kitchen. "We can go down to the War Room after we eat. Anything else?"

Annie shook her head.

"Charles did come up to the kitchen for a late lunch," Myra said, "and reported in on Maggie and the boys. The boys are just confirming the interviews Dennis West did and setting eyes on the kinds of people affected by the twin judges. It appears that Maggie may have hit pay dirt — those were Charles's words, not mine — in regard to Mr. Eberly, who was Peter Ciprani's best friend. Charles said Maggie went at him full bore. That was the last I heard. What's Marti up to?"

"Not much. Loving her private-citizen role and chomping at the bit to do something. I'm supposed to call her this evening. I am so ready to get into the swing of things, Myra. If we don't get moving we're going to start to atrophy."

Myra handed Annie the plate with the ham sandwich. She poured coffee, then sat down across from Annie at the table.

"I feel the same way, but we both know there is no point to hassling Charles. Do you think Pearl meant to plan a party for all the judges except for the twins? Or do you think she meant to plan and include them so we can get their measure?"

"I think she meant to *exclude* them. Can you imagine having the ex-president of the United States, a retired justice of the Supreme Court, and Nellie, who was a federal judge, all attending your retirement party, and the guest list is so exclusive that the twins are not invited. Of course," Annie said, chomping down on her sandwich, "that would just tick them off royally, I'm thinking. The daily paper would be sure to play that up, and Maggie could do a bang-up job at the *Post.* The AP would pick it up, and those two would be out in the cold. I have to say, I really like the idea. You know, we could Google Judge Henry Rhodes. I meant to do that at home but got sidetracked. Good sandwich, Myra."

Myra preened. She rarely, if ever, got compliments where food was concerned. She did, however, get many comments — complaints — when her culinary expertise came into question. Not that she cared. Well, sometimes she cared, she corrected the thought. "Thank you. I do like coleslaw on a sandwich. Nellie is the one who said if you fix a sandwich that way, you'll never go back to mustard. She's right."

"We're done eating, Myra. We don't smoke, so there is no reason to sit here and . . . and do nothing when we can bedevil Charles. I say we go down to the War Room *NOW.* We can clean up later."

"That works for me," Myra said. "You do know he's going to be like a wet hen, don't you? He hates to be interrupted."

"Ask me if I care, Myra. I do not. We can be just as cantankerous as he can. And do not overlook the fact that there are *two* of us to *one* of him. I rest my case."

"I do like the way you think sometimes, Annie."

Myra looked down at the dogs, knowing they thought they were going out for a run. "Later, guys. Here's a chew for each of you. When we get back, we'll go for a long run in the yard. You know how you like making Annie run after the ball! Especially in the moonlight!"

Annie burst out laughing. "Myra, do you remember the night of your birthday years ago, when you and I got really tanked after the official party and everyone went home? We ran naked through the sprinklers, and Charles caught us!"

"Lord, how could I ever forget *that*! That was the first time Charles saw the tattoos on our butts that you said we needed because we were going to invest in ink. He didn't speak to me for two whole weeks! As I recall, it was two very peaceful weeks. He thinks you're a bad influence on me, my dear."

Annie leaned against the wall until she stopped laughing.

"Okay, okay, we have to get serious now so we can ream him out. Stone-faced. We don't give him an inch, and we demand, yes, demand, a progress report. You got that, Annie?"

"I do, Myra. I got it. The big question is do *you* get it? You always weasel out when it comes to Charles, and I end up having to play the heavy."

"Not this time. I choose my battles wisely. You taught me that, Annie."

"Showtime!" Annie hissed in Myra's ear as she led the way down to the War Room. Tiny bells could be heard with the movements they made as the air circulated. Bells that Myra and Annie had strung when their daughters played down here as children. She felt a lump rise in her throat, and she knew Myra was feeling the same emotions she was. Amazing how all these years later, the bells sounded crystal clear.

"Ladies! To what do I owe the pleasure of your company at this hour?" Charles chirped happily from his position behind the row of high-tech computers that looked like they belonged at NASA.

Myra blinked. Annie's jaw dropped.

"Would you believe we got lonesome, dear?"

"Not for a minute, Myra, my love. I'm thinking you came down here to prod me, to chastise me for not working faster. Well, I have good news. Shall we go upstairs? I'm rather hungry right now."

"Only if you rescind that silly rule of not discussing business while eating," Myra snapped. "We want to know *now!*"

"Of course you do. Come along, ladies," Charles said, tongue-in-cheek. Annie just rolled her eyes. Myra shrugged her shoulders, satisfied that they'd won this round.

In the kitchen, Myra literally shoved Charles onto one of the kitchen chairs. Annie clamped her hands on his shoulders while Myra slapped together a sandwich any which way, then plopped it in front of her husband. "Talk and eat, and neither Annie nor I care if it's bad manners."

"Testy, aren't we, ladies? Ah . . . this is . . ."

"*Delicious* is the word you're looking for, darling, but we already know that. Talk." Myra looked over at Annie, who still had Charles's shoulders in a vise grip, and winked.

"Yes, yes, I'm ready. Listen carefully, *girls.*"

"You cannot sweet-talk us. Get to the point, Charles. We've waited long enough," Annie all but snarled.

"The Ciprani homestead on the bay where the twins go every weekend is where I concentrated my efforts. The homestead, which was refurbished and has been written up several times in *Architectural Digest,* is quite beautiful. There are only three houses on the lane. I just outright bought the Matthews house because it's been standing empty for almost four years and is sadly in need of repairs. Unfortunately, I grossly overpaid for it, but time was of the essence. The heirs were quite impressed that the ex-president of the United States wanted their house. They snapped up my offer. How we will ever unload it later on is still a mystery that is plaguing me. The paperwork is in process, but the heirs agreed that we could take possession immediately.

"The Donaldson house at the end of the lane proved a little more difficult to negotiate. The couple are elderly and have a nurse/ companion to see to their needs. I had my people offer a three-month cruise around the world if they would temporarily let us use their property to film what we led them to believe was the next *Gone With the Wind.* I was told by my people that the nurse/

companion talked them into it. I think I should be congratulated on getting all this done in just a few days. The Donaldsons were on their way as of three this afternoon. The lane now only has one resident: the Ciprani twins.

"As far as the world knows, Marti still has her Secret Service detail. No reason to alert anyone otherwise. Avery's people can fill that hole quite nicely. What that means is that, by the weekend, there will be so many people on that little lane that the twins will be pulling out their hair. We may be moving a contingent of partying college boys, rowdy college boys, into the house sometime on Friday, where they will party nonstop. It's one possible plan, but we might not have to resort to it. Things might move faster, take a different turn, and we'll scrap it. I was also able to find out that the authorities in that little town of Waterton are not enamored of the Ciprani twins any more than the people in Baywater appear to be. I say 'appear.' "

"What good will the Donaldsons' house do us since college is in session?" Myra asked.

"Myra, Myra, Myra! College students party on the weekends. They'll descend in droves come Friday. Secluded beachfront mansion, waterfront, two sailboats, well-stocked pantry, and no one will be driving anywhere. It's not carved in stone. We can resort to it if need be. Avery's people or the new bogus Secret Service detail will see to that. We set down the rules for the fraternity, and they all signed off on them. Now, if it doesn't go off, those college youngsters have three months to use the house. Tell me you are impressed," Charles said, stuffing the last bite of his sandwich into his mouth.

"Let me make sure we have this right, Charles. Setting this all up gives us the time, the opportunity, and the wherewithal to take over the Ciprani household. What about their security? I'm sure it's state-of-the-art. How do we circumvent that?" Annie demanded. To Charles's relief, she relaxed her hold on his shoulders.

Charles clucked his tongue. "One of Avery's men knows the company that installed the system. He said he can dismantle it so it will just appear to be a glitch that the company will get to . . . eventually. Which in our case is never. Are you still impressed?" He twinkled.

"I am, dear. I think Annie is, too." Annie's head bobbed up and down. "Would you like another sandwich?" Charles nodded agreeably. He loved it when his wife smiled at him.

"Were you able to come up with anything in regard to the brother, Peter?" Myra asked as she sliced ham for a second sandwich.

"Sorry to say, no. I think he was or is a missionary. If not a missionary then some kind of dedicated serious volunteer. I checked with every Christian group that he was affiliated with. No one could give me any kind of concrete information. By the same token, each person I contacted said that they think they would have heard some way, somehow, had Peter died. Sometimes the conversations didn't ring true, but it could have been the phone connection. If Peter wanted to remain out of sight for whatever reasons, I'm sure his people would cover for him. Maggie is convinced he's alive and that Jonathan Eberly knows where he is. Our young reporter thinks the same thing. We just have to find him. It just might not be as quick as you'd like. The search is ongoing. I should be hearing from Avery's boys shortly. The last time I heard from Maggie was around five o'clock, and she said she put the fear of God into Jon Eberly. She also asked me to have Avery's people put a tail on him. She thinks he's going to do something. She also said they haven't had any luck getting themselves arrested yet."

Charles looked at the two halves of the neat sandwich. Nothing dripped out, and there was no mess on the plate. He sighed. Why were women so transparent?

"When can we go to Waterton?" Myra asked.

"Anytime you want. Marti is on her way out here now from the city. She was quite amused that she now owns the Matthews's old homestead. She wanted to know when she could hang curtains. She said no house is worth moving into until you hang curtains."

"And she's right," Annie and Myra said at the same time, before going off into peals of laughter.

"Where's Nellie on this?" Annie asked.

Charles looked up at the monitor. He pointed a finger at it. "Ask her yourself. She just drove through the gate. Marti should be here in another thirty minutes."

"But what about Pearl?"

"She'll catch up. She has to take care of her own personal business first. A day, a day and a half at the most should do it. I think I'll leave you ladies now. Thank you, dear, for the lovely sandwiches. Next time a little less coleslaw." Myra threw the dish towel at him. He chuckled all the way back to his lair.

Myra and Annie welcomed Nellie with open arms, literally dragging her into the kitchen. "Charles figured it out. We can go to Baywater tomorrow if we want. Will you be able to leave Elias for a few days?"

"I don't see why not. As long as the television doesn't go out, and no one steals the ton of food in the freezer, he should be good for . . . oh, I'd say, ten months or so. That means no problems. Where's Marti?"

"On the way. Pearl, of course, is taking care of business. Coffee, Nellie?"

"Black please. So tell me what we have to look forward to."

"Let's wait for Marti, so we don't have to go through it twice. I think it's pretty foolproof. That means we can make it work for us. First, though, I think we're all going to be going to a party for your old friend Judge Rhodes as soon as we plan it."

"Isn't it amazing how sometimes things all come together at just the right time to make it work for us?" Nellie beamed.

"Amen to that," Annie cackled.

Chapter 14

It was well past the witching hour when Pearl Barnes sat down and curled her legs under her, on her favorite window seat and stared out at the dark night. Another ninety minutes, and she would be getting into still another strange car and heading to the old, abandoned train depot at the outskirts of town. The gravel road leading to it was now overgrown with young trees and scrub, and one needed four-wheel drive even to get close to the ramshackle building. Jack Sparrow liked having a "meeting" of the secret underground railroad at the old train depot.

She had no complaints about Sparrow and his small but mighty crew. She had been stunned when he told her that the FBI was using so many agents on her case because it was convinced she was laundering money via the underground railroad. "Or at least that's what they want people to believe. In reality, they're trying to set you up the way they set me up. I did a stretch in a federal prison for something I didn't do. Zander saw to that, and he's moved up in the ranks. He wants to be the next director of the FBI. If Bert hadn't gotten President Connor at the time to pardon me, I'd still be in prison. The bastard is trying to do the same thing to you. Nailing a retired justice of the Supreme Court for such nefarious deeds would get him a three-inch black headline. Above the fold. You would not do well in prison, Justice Barnes. If he succeeds, he's one step closer to achieving his goal of making that happen. Bert told me before I came here that the current director has some serious health issues and is contemplating stepping down. Zander is the logical choice. He's made a name for himself, and he's on a first-name basis with the current president. On rare occasions, they even hit the links together. No one is quite sure how that all came about, but Zander trades on it. The agents under him hate his guts, but like all good agents, they do what they're told."

Pearl admitted to being nervous. Sparrow told her it was understandable. However, his words did not relieve the anxiety coursing through her. All she could think about were the women and children in a holding pattern as they waited for word it was time to be moved to safety.

Pearl stared into the dark night. She was glad the rain had finally stopped, but even so, there was cloud cover. There would be no moon or stars tonight, and she was grateful. She'd been fighting the dark side, and, ironically, only felt safe on nights like this. She went over again in her mind what she was to do. At exactly 2:20, she was to use her personal cell phone and call a number that Sparrow had given her earlier in the day. He had written out an entire script for her, which she had memorized.

Waiting at the depot would be thirty-three women and nine children waiting to be taken to safety. The children weren't children at all but fully dressed manikins that could be picked up with ease. In the dark, her tails wouldn't be able to tell the difference. Everyone, including herself, would climb aboard a bus at a given signal, at which point the agents would close in and arrest everyone. Sparrow said that was why he wanted the agents to know the exact time it was going down so they could set up a perimeter. What the agents didn't know was there was another perimeter set up by Sparrow and some of Avery Snowden's operatives. "That's when we get the drop on them." The rest, Pearl knew, would mean she could return home, knowing that she was safe and that her privacy would never again be invaded by a rogue agent of the FBI.

What no one knew, not even Sparrow, was that Charles had recalled Ted Robinson, Espinosa, and the new cub reporter from Baywater for the festivities. They, too, were waiting in the dark, and once more Ted would get his headline and his byline. Above the fold. Espinosa would be nominated for his photography, and Dennis West would be ecstatic to be included with the pros.

It was all a go.

Pearl shifted her position on the window seat and looked down at her watch. Almost time to get ready. She thought about eating something but didn't know if all the butterflies in her stomach would appreciate food. Perhaps a power bar on the way to the old depot. Her eyes still on the numerals on her watch, Pearl waited.

At the right moment, she hopped off the window seat and walked around the house per Sparrow's instructions. First, she turned the downstairs bathroom light on, then off; next, she turned the kitchen light on for three minutes, then turned it off; next, she turned the upstairs bedroom light on and off, went downstairs, called a certain number on her regular cell phone, and said, "I'm on my way." Finally, she went outside and got into a dark green Toyota SUV and left, not turning on any lights till she got out to the main road.

Pearl's heart kicked up an extra beat as she turned on the lights. She'd made the same kind of run a thousand times, and she always felt the same way — fearful yet exhilarated. Today was no different. The only difference was Sparrow's dire warning that she wouldn't do well in a federal prison. Like she didn't know that already. Breaking the law, even for the betterment of innocent women and children, was still breaking the law. Long ago, she decided she didn't care and would suffer the consequences if she was caught. Saving those women and children from lives of misery was all that mattered.

She was on her way now. There was barely any traffic, and what was there was going the other way. If anyone was following her, they didn't have their headlights on.

Not that it would have mattered one way or another. There was no backing down now.

Less than twelve miles away, Jack Sparrow used various birdcalls to communicate with his people. He always laughed to himself at how as a child he had perfected that little feat. With a name like Sparrow, how could it be otherwise. This place, he thought, as he looked around from his position in the tall grass, was just about as perfect as it could be. Birds nested everywhere. Yesterday, he'd seen some wild ducks that had clacked their own symphony.

Sparrow looked to his right. He heard noises, but they weren't being made by his people. His people were trained. Zander's people were not into wildlife. He looked to his left. What he saw made him rear back: Bert Navarro, his boss! Harry Wong, the second-highest-ranking martial-arts expert in the world! Jack Emery, Zander's nemesis, with a score of his own to settle with the section chief. Son of a bitch! The goddamn cavalry was now at his beck and call. He wished he could laugh out loud. He did manage a wicked grin and a one-finger salute the others acknowledged.

"We are locked and loaded. Hoo rah!" Sparrow, an ex-Marine, muttered to himself. Suddenly, he felt infallible. With backup like he was seeing, Zander was dead in the water. Not that he had any doubts before, this was just the confirmation he needed.

Sparrow was low to the ground, so he heard the vibrations of vehicles on the rough road long before he saw them. Overhead, birds started to squawk. To Sparrow, it was the sweet sound of victory.

The big yellow bus rumbled in first. The engine died in a slow, struggling cough.

The big yellow bus was followed by a variety of old trucks, clunky cars that made way too much noise at ten-minute intervals. Women, carrying make-believe children, scrambled from the assorted vehicles and clamored aboard the bus. Pearl Barnes was in the last vehicle to arrive, a dark green Toyota SUV. She hit the ground running.

Sparrow looked over at Bert, Harry, Jack, Ted, Espinosa, and the young kid.

Sparrow mouthed the word, *Showtime.* Still, he didn't move. He held his breath as he waited for the gaggle of agents to tighten their perimeter and identify themselves. He mouthed the words, *"FBI, freeze!"* Ah, right on target.

In a nanosecond, floodlights lit up the old depot like the Fourth of July. Still, he waited until all the agents were in place. He counted seven in total. Piece of cake. Still, he waited until all the women were herded into a circle, with Pearl cautioning everyone to say nothing.

That's when Sparrow and his people moved, quickly and stealthily from their own perimeter, until there was an operative behind each FBI agent. "I-don't-think-so, boys! Your turn. Hands up, and the first one who doesn't follow orders gets his kneecap blown out. Which one of you bastards wants to go first?" Sparrow singsonged.

The curses and the expletives rang in the bright light. He had no volunteers.

"You bastard!" Agents Barry and Landry said at the same time. "You fucking set us up!"

"Ah, you recognize a setup. Is that what you're saying?" Sparrow spit out. "How does it feel, you piece of shit? Tell me. I want to know. How does it feel?"

"Eat shit, you crud! I'm not telling you anything," Palance roared, the veins in his neck bulging with his rage.

"Wanna bet?" Sparrow spit out the words a second time. The Taser in his hand sizzled. Palance dropped to the ground. The Taser sizzled a second time, and Barry fell forward.

Ten minutes later, gasping for breath, Barry finally managed to clear his throat, his face a mask of pain, fear, and apprehension. "C'mon, Sparrow, this isn't going to get you anywhere. They'll lock you up and throw away the key. You did one stretch and lucked out. That won't happen a second time."

"Is that what Luther Zander told you when you lied at my trial? I want you to call him right now. Tell him you ran into some trouble, and he needs to get here right away."

Barry did his best to sneer at Sparrow. He didn't pull it off. He did manage to spit out, "Like I'm really going to do what you say."

Harry Wong stepped forward into the blinding white light. He looked questioningly at Sparrow, as much as to say, "How long do you want him out?"

Sparrow grinned. "Ten minutes. Make sure when he wakes up he's in a world of pain. I hate that son of a bitch."

Harry stepped forward and reached out. He squeezed the soft spot under Barry's nose, then stepped back as the agent toppled to the ground. "That'll be ten grand, Sparrow. Deposit it in my offshore account," Harry said, an evil look on his face.

Sparrow made a mental note never to get on Harry Wong's bad side.

Bert Navarro burst out laughing. "Harry, you're such a card sometimes. Card. Get it? Card, Vegas. You know, gambling cards. Aw, forget it. You need to develop a sense of humor, Harry." Harry just looked disgusted as he stepped back to where Jack Emery was standing.

Jack Emery looked over at Sparrow, and said, "Got all the cell phones, all the sleeve and collar mikes, all the guns. Tidy little pile, I'd say."

"Flex cuffs intact. Both wrists and ankles," Bert said.

Espinosa could have doubled as a monkey as he hopped about taking the pictures that would bring him fame and fortune.

Ted Robinson kept waving his recorder to make sure he was getting every last sound of dialogue. Dennis West was so wide-eyed he looked like he was going to black out. "Who are these guys?" he managed to gasp as he jerked his head in the direction of Bert, Harry, and Jack.

"The good guys. No one you need to know. Now or ever. Now zip it up, kid, and stay out of the way," Ted growled.

"Yeah. Yeah. I got it. I'm way over here. I'm outta your way. See, I'm way out of your way. Way out. Oh, Jeezus!"

The agents started muttering among themselves. Sparrow and the others listened to the comments. Their grins were just as evil as Harry's.

"Who is that guy?"

"Who set him up? Barry, Palance, Mahoney, and Landry?"

"If that's true, I can't say I blame the poor bastard."

"Yeah, well, I always wondered how Zander got moved up so fast in the ranks. It never computed to me."

"This is the end of our careers with tomorrow's headlines. You know who that guy Robinson is, right? And that dude snapping all the pictures! Christ on a raft!"

"Is this where we grovel?"

"FBI agents do not grovel."

"Bullshit! This agent will grovel if he has to. The only thing I did was follow that asshole's orders. I'm not taking heat for something I didn't do."

"Shut the hell up. We go down, you go down. There is no in-between."

"You should listen to that guy," Jack Sparrow said cheerily. "He's so on the money, you can take it to the bank."

Sparrow's foot nudged Agent Barry none too gently; Barry only twitched. He kicked again with a little more force, and Barry twitched again. "Hey, Harry, I said ten minutes. How come this slug isn't waking up?"

"Sometimes I don't know my own powers. Blow up his nose, he'll be on his feet in a second."

"I'm not blowing in that guy's nose. Oh, who gives a shit. Palance, get your ass over here and you make the call. Chop-chop."

Palance looked around, saw Harry take a step forward. He hustled and reached for the phone Sparrow had in his hand. "I'm going to tell you exactly what to say. You try anything smart, and Mr. Wong here will see that you go to sleep for a *very long* time. You'll be brain-dead when you wake up." Sparrow laughed at the silliness of his own statement. "That *is* your phone, isn't it?"

"Yeah, it's mine. It's 3:40 in the morning. What if Zander doesn't answer?"

"You better hope he does or it's nighty-night for you, pal. In other words, you keep calling until the bastard answers. Now, this is what you say. 'Things got out of hand. You need to come here right now. And you need to come alone. We got blindsided. They want you.' Then you hang up, and if the phone rings again, you let it ring. Okay, repeat what I said." Palance repeated Sparrow's words verbatim. "I got it, Sparrow."

"Tone of voice is crucial. I'll be right next to you. You slide off-key, a bad nuance, and my pal Harry here will make you wish you'd listened. Tell me you understand."

"I understand, you bastard. What you need to understand is I don't have Zander's home telephone number. None of us have it."

"Surprise! Surprise! Here it is." Sparrow rattled off the numbers to Palance's dismay. He tapped in the numbers, aware that Sparrow had pressed the button that activated the speakerphone.

The moment the phone was picked up after eight rings, Palance went into his spiel. "Boss, things got out of hand. You need to come here right now. And you need to come alone. We got blindsided. They want you." Palance broke the connection, sweat dripping down his face. "Satisfied?" he snarled.

"Only if the son of a bitch shows up. One more thing. Where's the money?"

"What money?" Palance tried to bluff. Harry took a step forward. "Okay, okay, it's in the back of the justice's SUV."

"How much? Where did it come from?"

"Ten million. As to where it came from, you'll have to ask Zander. All I know is that it's clean, unmarked money. You can't trace it anywhere. At least that's what he told us."

"Justice Barnes, can your little organization use five million dollars?"

"Yes, sir, we can, and my people will be forever in your debt," Pearl said smartly.

"It's yours," Sparrow said. "Okay, guys, squat and form a circle. On your knees.

241

Someone knock those damn lights out. Leave one set burning. Everyone else, get into position. Zander should be arriving momentarily, depending on how fast he drives."

Fourteen minutes later, a low-slung sports car roared up the rough road, rocks and debris spitting in all directions. Gun in hand, Luther Zander approached his men, his face a mask of fury as he cursed in several different languages. "Answer me, goddamn it. What the hell happened here?" When none of his agents responded, Zander turned around and set off a deafening volley of shots high in the air.

"Well, that certainly got my attention, Zander," Jack Sparrow said, coming up behind him. Bert swooped in from the left and kicked the gun out of the assistant director's hand. Sparrow grabbed his arms and jerked them backward. The assistant director howled in pain and outrage. Sparrow drove him to the ground, then hauled him to the middle of the circle, his legs straight out in front of him. "Now, I'm going to tell you once, and once only. Tell these fine agents how you railroaded me for your own purposes. Those that don't know, that is. Three by my count. All the rest lied the way you did. And tell these same fine agents how you planned on doing the same thing to Justice Barnes so you could step into the director's chair."

"You're insane. A court of law found you guilty. I demand that you release me and my men immediately. Do you hear me, Sparrow?"

Sparrow's gun spit; he hit Zander's left kneecap straight on. Zander screamed. "One more chance." When there was no response, Sparrow's gun spit a second time and blew out the assistant director's right kneecap. The agents in the circle stared, mesmerized at the pain they knew their boss was going through, wondering if their own kneecaps would be blown out. "The next shot is going to go through your foot — they'll have to amputate it, and you'll have a stump to walk around on. Talk, you son of a bitch! And make sure it's loud and clear so we can all hear what you're saying. Robinson, front and center. Make sure you get his permission to tape what he says."

Ted obliged.

The agents listened, their eyes as wide as saucers. Barry and Palance couldn't believe that their boss was throwing them to the wolves. Then the cursing started all over again.

Sparrow reached into his hip pocket and

yanked out a piece of paper that he'd typed up earlier with Zander's, Barry's, and Palance's confessions. He handed out five more and told the agents to fill in their own names on the blank affidavits. "Sign it, boys!"

"Like hell!" Barry blustered.

"Don't be like that, Agent Barry." Sparrow brought his gun up, and said, "Center mass, and you're dead. No one will grieve for you. Sign the damn paper." Whatever the agent saw reflected in Sparrow's eyes made him rethink his words. He nodded that he would sign the paper. Jack Emery removed the flex cuffs, and all three men signed their names. The remaining five followed suit.

"Now what?" Bert asked.

"Now we load all these guys in that big old yellow bus. I do believe that a man named Avery Snowden is waiting down the road to . . . ah . . . take his passengers somewhere that I am not privy to. Think of it as a relocation service."

"My people are on the way," Pearl said, hugging the man she thought of as her savior. "What will you do now?"

"My boss," Sparrow said, jerking his head in Bert's direction, "said I can take a week's vacation. I'm thinking Monte Carlo sounds good. Give me some insight I can take back to Bert. You're good, Justice Barnes. Call me if you even think you have any problems, and I'll be there. You know, like the song says, call my name, and I'll be here."

"Harry, Jack, nice seeing you again. Bert . . ." He shrugged, not sure what to say.

"By the time you get to the airport," Bert said, "there will be a private jet waiting to take you wherever you and your friends want to go. By the way, Barry lied to you; there was twelve million dollars in the SUV. I liberated some for you. After the justice takes her five, I thought we'd use the rest to provide for these schmucks' families. Anonymously, of course." Bert tossed Sparrow a canvas bag and turned to leave.

Bert, Harry, Sparrow, and Jack Emery moved off to the side.

"You okay with all this, Sparrow?" Bert asked. Sparrow nodded. "Good. I'm going to call Lizzie Fox and have her handle the FBI. She's an expert when it comes to those guys. And get this, she and her husband, Cosmo Cricket, are in D.C. for some symposium in regard to a foundation for children they set up. She'll hop right on this, and, Sparrow, you are home free. I for one am proud to shake your hand. Be honest with me, okay? It goes without saying the

Fibbies will give you your job back now if you want it. Do you?"

"Hell, no! I can't believe you asked me such a thing. All I wanted was to be cleared, and the *Post* will do that for me. Thanks for helping out. I owe you, Bert. Harry, what can I say? Thanks. Jack, there's no one better I could ever want to watch my back. So, thanks to you, too."

It was clear to everyone that the party was over. Ted, Espinosa, and Dennis West stood alone outside the circle of light.

Espinosa was holding up Dennis West and grinning from ear to ear. He'd downloaded every last picture and knew he'd struck the mother lode. Ted was preening like a peacock. "Biggest sting since our last one, Espinosa. This will make four special editions to our credit. That's if you're counting, and I, for one, am counting. What's wrong with you, Dennis?"

"Who are those people? Where are they taking those agents?"

"Dennis, Dennis, Dennis. If I tell you, then I'll have to kill you. Do you still want to know?"

"Of course not. But just so you know, Mr. Robinson, I have a very active imagination."

"I do, too, kid. I'm seeing you with two blown-out kneecaps, bald, and hooks for hands. That means in my vision you can't text and you can't e-mail. So, what say we grab some breakfast and head back to Baywater. We should get there just as the sun comes up. Maggie is going to be so livid."

"Oh, Jesus, oh, Jesus. How can you even think about eating?"

"Because I'm hungry, that's how," Ted and Espinosa said, as they each grabbed the young reporter by the arm and dragged him down the makeshift road to where they'd hidden the *Post* van. They shoved him inside, then climbed in.

"Doncha just love it when the good guys win?" Ted cackled as he settled himself behind the wheel.

"I don't know how you can tell the good guys from the bad guys. They shoot guns, they threaten and . . . and . . ." Dennis babbled.

"Eat young cub reporters for breakfast. That means shut up, Dennis, and go to sleep. We'll wake you when we get to Baywater and you, my friend, are springing for breakfast." Ted continued to cackle. Espinosa rolled his eyes as he grinned from ear to ear.

That, Dennis decided, as his eyes started to droop, had to mean only one thing. He had passed his initiation and was now one

of the guys. Jesus. How lucky could one guy
get?

CHAPTER 15

Annie de Silva sprinted across Myra Rutledge's parking lot like a young girl, the strong blustery October wind pushing her forward. She had a stack of newspapers under one arm and was waving another in the air. Myra opened the door and slammed it shut.

"*Special edition,* ladies!" Annie shouted to be heard over the barking dogs. The ladies each grabbed a copy and immediately started ooohing and aaahing over what they were reading.

"Where's Pearl? I thought she would be the first one here. She must be one happy camper today. Damn, I wish I had been there for that takedown," Nellie said.

"She's on her way. She needed to get some sleep," Myra said, as her eyes devoured the newsprint in front of her. "I wish I had been there, too," she mumbled.

Marti weighed in. "I knew I did the right

thing when I allowed Bert to convince me to pardon Mr. Sparrow. I'm so glad he's exonerated now. Sometimes the end does justify the means. Looks like another shake-up at the Bureau. Wonder who's going to handle things until a new director can be appointed."

Nellie started to laugh. "I have the scoop on that. Just as I was leaving the house the president himself called Elias and begged — I'm saying *begged* — him to sit in until that can all be arranged. The current director can't take the stress and was admitted to the hospital a few hours ago. As you know, Elias was director a few years back."

"Is he going to do it?" the women all asked at once.

"At first he said no, but the president wore him down. He finally agreed to six weeks, and the president accepted that. He was on his way to town when I left to come over here."

"Nellie, what about . . ."

"His early Alzheimer's? Elias didn't see fit to mention that. What he did say was he couldn't screw up things any worse than they are right now, even with his handicap." Nellie giggled like a schoolgirl, and the others giggled right along with her.

"Where do you think those men are going

to end up?" Marti asked.

"This is where we do not ask questions. It's all being taken care of. That's one of our rules — when a mission, either run by us or others who are helping, when it's over, we simply move on. Nothing will ever come back to bite anyone. Over the next few days, there will be a dozen different spins put on what happened. The only thing we make sure of is that the families are taken care of, and they will be. They'll all be given new lives somewhere with no financial worries, so the children and wives won't be targets of the media. Shame for something that is no fault of their own is a terrible thing for children to have to endure," Myra said.

The dogs reared up and raced to the door. Myra looked up at the monitor. "Pearl's here." She opened the door, and a swirl of leaves blew in. The dogs tried to catch them as they tumbled over one another.

Pearl slammed the door shut and burst out laughing. "We did it, girls! Oh, I wish you could have been there. It was kind of crazy for a while. Mr. Sparrow had his people synchronized down to the last sync. In a way, it was almost effortless, but in reality, it was just a well-executed plan. There are no words to tell you all how grateful I am that we can continue to help all those women and children. As we speak, forty-two women and children are being moved to safety. I'll get back into the swing of things when we return from Baywater. Anything new on that?"

"Plenty, Pearl, but right now we need to get on the road. We're expected in Baywater by two o'clock. You're going to ride with Nellie. Annie and I are driving together, and Marti is driving alone because she's going to be driving to Florida when she leaves Baywater. She wants to experience the freedom and the open road. We'll be our own little caravan, so make sure we stay together. No hotdogging on the highway. We roll into town together. Nellie will fill you in."

"Okay, girls, saddle up!" Annie said. "I always wanted to say that, but somehow the appropriate time just never came up. Everyone go to the bathroom *NOW* so we don't have to make pit stops. Myra made each of us a thermos of coffee, so don't walk out without it. Take a mental check. Do you have everything you're going to need?"

"You sound like our old first-grade teacher, Annie. It's yes to everything. Now, can we get started?" Myra said tartly.

Annie huffed and puffed. "You, Myra, are the worst offender. You always forget something, and you're always the first one who wants to make a pit stop. I like to think ahead."

"Everyone out, so I can settle the dogs." The minute the door closed behind the women, Myra sweet-talked and petted her beloved dogs. She thought they looked sad, and they were, so she doubled up on the treats. Then she blew kisses. Tails wagged and thumped. "I'll be back before you know it, I hope," she muttered under her breath.

The caravan left Pinewood. The time was 12:15.

Judge Eunice Ciprani slipped into her coat. She eyed the clock on her office wall. If Lyzette wasn't too busy and could fit her in, she would be able to get a minifacial, eyebrow waxing, and still have time to pick up Cee's dry cleaning and her own and be back in time to hear her first afternoon case.

Normally, she would walk to Henry's Salon from the courthouse, but because she needed to go to the dry cleaner's, she opted to take her car. The fact that she didn't have an appointment at the salon didn't bother her at all. Appointments were for people who had time to make schedules or did not lead busy lives. She, on the other hand, had to do things when opportunity knocked.

Eunice parked her car in the rear of the lot and entered the salon through the back door. She knew she was a snob but didn't care. The facial room and the eyebrow-waxing corner were in the back, separated from the main part of the salon by a beautiful beaded curtain. She liked it because she didn't have to gossip or make small talk with the citizens of Baywater. She had absolutely nothing in common with any of them, so it was better that she stay aloof. She wisely refused even to think about the fact that those same citizens hated her and her sister. The back room just worked better for everyone concerned.

Lyzette, the tall, redheaded stylist, was reaching up to the cabinet for something when Eunice walked in the door. Her first thought was, *Oh, crap, this is one customer I do not need today.* Her second thought was she would happily forgo the judge's meager ten percent tip if she'd just turn around and leave. She forced a smile on her face and asked what she could do for the judge.

"I know this is last-minute, Lyzette, but I have fifty minutes to spare. Can you do a minifacial and wax my eyebrows? I don't know if it's the cleanser I'm using or what, but my skin is breaking out. You know how I hate zits."

Maybe if she weren't in such a cranky mood, thanks to the speeding ticket she'd gotten on her way to work, Lyzette would have chosen her words more carefully. Right now, though, she didn't care. Plus, she had two other customers waiting in the meditation room. "I'm sorry, Judge. I'm booked solid today. You should have made an appointment."

"I never make an appointment, Lyzette, you know that. I never know what my schedule is. Can't you fit me in?" she wheedled. "Surely, your other two customers won't mind waiting."

"Yes, they will mind, Judge. And I have to pay attention to the time because they need color. Look, I can get one of the other girls to do you, or I can just wax your eyebrows, but I simply do not have time for the facial."

Eunice's face tightened. Her eyes narrowed as she contemplated her next move. Should she give in gracefully? Should she intimidate the stylist? Or should she stomp her foot, say she'd never be back, and leave?

The decision was momentarily shelved when the interior salon erupted in sound as everyone started talking at once. Both women strained to hear what all the excitement was through the beaded curtain.

"I saw them. Four black Chevy Suburbans. Full of Secret Service agents."

"President Connor is in town."

"She rented every room at the Harbor Inn. Or her people did; that's what I heard."

"She's hosting the retirement party for Judge Rhodes. Do you believe that? The president, even though she's left office, is here in our town and hosting Judge Rhodes's retirement party? How cool is that?" another voice chirped.

"My sister works at the Harbor Inn, and she said the invitations were delivered to the Inn, along with the guest list, at eleven o'clock this morning. There was a TOP PRIORITY stamp on the package. And under it she said it was stamped PROPERTY OF THE UNITED STATES GOVERNMENT. The party is by invitation only, and wait till you hear who is *not* on the list. My sister said you have to show your invitation at the door, so the Secret Service sees it."

A chorus of "Who's not on the list?" filtered back to Eunice and Lyzette, followed by hoots and giggles of laughter.

"The two Ciprani judges, that's who," came the shrill response, followed by what sounded like roars of applause.

"My sister said everyone, right down to all the janitors, are invited. Read the paper when it comes out."

"There are four *Post* reporters staying at the Inn. That's the *Post* in Washington. Something big is going down or is going to go down," said another voice.

"I heard that woman who retired from the Supreme Court is going to be there and a retired federal judge named Cornelia Easter. She's married to the former director of the FBI. This whole town is buzzing like a beehive."

The bell over the front door tinkled, and a new customer walked in. The decibel level rose as the woman shouted happily, "Guess what I have in my hands, ladies! Champagne! Last night, in just a few hours, I sold the Matthews house in Waterton. And guess who I sold it to? The president of the United States. Ex-president, actually. And she didn't quibble about the price. Beaucoup dollars, ladies!" Janet Myers literally screamed, her shrill voice echoing off the walls. "Bubbly for everyone!"

Lyzette watched as Eunice slipped on her coat. "I think I'll let you get back to your other customers and come back some other day, when you have more time."

"Be sure to make an appointment, Judge. Otherwise, the same thing might happen, and your eyebrows are a mess." She loved how the judge's face lost color. The minute the door closed behind Eunice, Lyzette locked it and raced into the salon. "This is all just too juicy. Guess who heard every word you ladies said. Judge Eunice Ciprani!"

The laughter was contagious.

Every woman in the world knew that beauty salons were hotbeds of juicy gossip. The kind of gossip that strained lives and made others run for cover. And the women in Henry's Salon were no exception.

Eunice Ciprani was shaking with rage when she climbed into her car. She tried to fish her cell phone out of her purse, but her hands wouldn't obey her mind. Cee was going to chew nails and spit rust when she heard what was going on. She commanded her hands to work as she searched the console for a cigarette. Her secret vice. Even Cee didn't know she smoked. Weed, too, sometimes. Maybe it would calm her down. It did to the point she was able to start the car and drive out of Henry's lot. Instead of going back to the courthouse, though, she drove to the Harbor Inn. She choked on a mouthful of smoke when she saw the four dark Chevy Suburbans parked in the circular driveway and all the activity that was going on.

She drove on and turned the corner. Still

shaking with rage, Eunice pulled to a stop for a red light. She puffed furiously on the cigarette that was now down to the filter. She tossed it out the window. She looked around to see if anyone saw her ditching the cigarette. That's when she saw a man standing on the corner staring at her. He waved. A horn sounded behind her as the light changed. Eunice blinked, and in that split second, the man was gone.

"Peter!" she screamed as she floored the gas pedal.

"Peter!" she screamed a second time.

By the time Eunice reached the court-house's underground parking lot, she was choking on her own saliva. The moment she turned off the engine she called her sister and started to scream. "You need to come down here to the parking garage right now, Cee. *Right this goddamn minute! Do you hear me, Cee?*" she screamed into the phone.

Eunice got out of the car and fired up a cigarette. She didn't give a hoot if her sister saw her smoking or not. Her hand was shaking so badly she could hardly get the cigarette to her mouth. When she did, she started to choke on the smoke, tears running down her cheeks. She whirled around when she heard her sister's heels clicking on the concrete.

"Is that a cigarette I see in your hand? What's wrong with you, Nessie? Are you having a meltdown?"

"Get in the damn car, Cee, and shut up. Yes, this is a cigarette, and yes, I have been smoking for years, and yes, I'm a nicotine addict or whatever you call people who smoke. I also smoke weed. Yes, I am having a meltdown and so will you when I tell you what just happened." Somehow Eunice managed to blurt out everything she'd heard at the salon. She got a perverse sort of pleasure watching her sister's face turn white. "Just to make sure, I drove by the Harbor Inn, and the place was swarming with Secret Service agents. They all look alike, they talk into their collars and cuffs and wear aviator glasses. The black Chevy Suburbans were all lined up. They rented the whole damn Inn."

"And we're not invited?"

"That's what you got out of everything I just told you? That's what you're concerned about, that we weren't invited? You are more stupid than I thought, Cee. Who cares about the damn party? Not me. Listen to me, they're onto us. What the hell do you think the chances are for this to happen at this particular time along with the president's buying the Matthews house? Are you listening to me, Cee?"

"I think you're overreacting and angry that Lyzette didn't accommodate you. Next time, don't tip her," Celeste said in a strange-sounding voice that Eunice barely recognized.

"Jesus, Mother of God! Okay, okay, I'm going to allow for the fact that you're having a stupid day. Here's the kicker, Cee. I saw Peter. I saw our brother standing on the corner, and he waved to me. He goddamn well waved to me. Now say something."

Cee's mind raced. Was her sister really having a meltdown? As much as she wished it was true, she knew her sister was working on all her cylinders. She needed to keep a level head and calm Nessie down. First things first. She whipped out her cell phone and called her clerk to cancel court for the rest of the day. She cited an emergency and instructed her clerk to notify her sister's clerk.

"Get out of the car, Nessie. You are in no condition to drive. We'll go home and talk this through. First, though, I'm going to drive by the Harbor Inn. It's not that I don't believe what you said, but sometimes a second set of eyes can get a better perspective."

Eunice got out of the car, walked around to the passenger side and got in. She fired up yet another cigarette, her eyes defying her sister to admonish her. She didn't, but she did roll down the window the moment the engine kicked over.

Celeste Ciprani drove slowly, her eyes taking in the excitement she was seeing on Main Street. Nessie was right. Something was going on. Was it just that old fool's retirement party? Why would the president of the United States, retired or not, host a party for the old geezer who had never done a worthwhile thing in his life but sit on the damn bench for fifty years? It didn't make sense. Nor did it make sense that a retired justice of the Supreme Court would attend said party along with another federal judge from Washington, D.C. Clearly, something was up.

Celeste flicked her turn signal and rounded the corner, only to have a Secret Service agent wave her off. Nessie made a strange sound in her throat. Celeste nodded and drove on. "Satisfied? You thought I was lying, didn't you?" Nessie snarled.

Celeste sucked in a deep breath. "No, Nessie, I did not think that. I simply wanted to see for myself. You know how I am. I have to *see* something before I act."

"So what you're saying is you believe this part of it, possibly you believe Connor bought the old Matthews house, and will be our neighbor, but you *don't* believe the part about me seeing our brother, Peter. Is that what you're saying, Cee?" Nessie screamed.

Celeste spoke through clenched teeth. "Pretty much, Nessie."

"Well, guess what, Cee. We both know Peter's not dead even though we had him *declared dead.* We never had a body. You need a body to be dead. Are you listening to me? He's back, and I saw him. All of this happening is too much of a coincidence, don't you think?"

"I don't know what to think, Nessie. Okay, we're home. I'm going to send Thelma home so we can talk and decide what we're going to do." In response, Nessie fired up another cigarette, not caring that her car stunk to high heaven.

"This could all be one giant coincidence," Celeste said tightly.

"There is no such thing as coincidence, and you damn well know it, Cee. Look at me. The shit is going to hit the fan and, excuse my language, but that's what's going to happen. We need to pack up and *go!*"

"We are not going to do any such thing. Flight is an indication of guilt." Celeste coughed from all the cigarette smoke she was breathing in. "Put that damn thing out right now!"

"Make me, Cee! I'll pound you to a pulp if you lay a hand on me."

Celeste knew that her sister meant it. She'd never seen Nessie the way she was now. She supposed that seeing Peter, if it was true, would have had the same effect on her.

Celeste climbed out of the car, coughed again, and inhaled a great gulp of fresh air.

"Come along, Nessie. We'll talk inside."

"I'm done talking, Cee. I told you this day would come, but you wouldn't listen. You just got us deeper and deeper into this thing. I told you months ago that we were . . . Never mind, you never listen, and I'm not in the mood to waste my breath."

"You need to relax, dear. You're mainly upset because you didn't get your eyebrows waxed. You know it, and I know it. What's her name, Lyzette, embarrassed you, and you're cranky. When we get inside, I'll call Martin at the Department of Health and tell him to shut Henry's down because of rat infestation. Three weeks or so of no income will bring those people to their senses. Now, cheer up. I want to see that old Nessie smile of yours."

"I'd tell you to kiss my ass, Cee, but you'd need a compass to find it," Nessie snarled as she stomped her way to the elevator.

"Then be like that," Cee said, resignation ringing in her voice. She felt so light-headed she wondered if she would black out before they could get inside the condo.

CHAPTER 16

"Annie, what in the world are you doing?
We need to talk. Seriously."

Annie's fingers were moving at the speed
of light as she sent out text after text.
"Hmm," she said.

"I just had a thought. We can't roll into
town with Marti driving her own car. We're
going to have to pull over as soon as I find
a good spot so she can get out and drive
with Nellie and Pearl. You can drive Marti's
car. She can't be seen alone with no Secret
Service guarding her. Why didn't we think
of that earlier?" Myra fretted.

"Hmm," Annie said, clicking away.

"What *are* you doing? You need to listen
to me, Annie."

"I am taking care of business, Myra. I do
that sometimes. You know like when I go to
Vegas and rear up and cause trouble. I'm
texting my financial advisor to keep him on
his toes. Do you have Apple? I heard every-

thing you said. Contrary to what you might think, I can do two things at once. It's called multitasking."

"If you wanted me to bring apples, why didn't you say so? You claim you're in charge and think of everything, so if you wanted apples, you should have said something. I just bought some winesaps the other day at the market, and they are so juicy. Charles said he would make some pies."

"Apple, Myra. A-P-P-L-E! It's a stock. It closed yesterday at six hundred and twenty dollars. I have two hundred thousand shares. Do the math, baby!"

Myra blinked. "Oh, my!"

"I have the same number of Google shares. You do know what that is, don't you?"

"I do know that," Myra said smartly.

"I bet you own it and don't even know it. You should call your financial advisor and ask. I can tell you what to say and how to act so he won't think you're stupid. What about Facebook? I hope not, because so far it's a disaster. How about Intuitive Surgical?"

"Are those best sellers? I'll have to order them."

Annie sighed. "It's not a book, Myra, it's a . . . never mind. I'll educate you later.

Now, you were saying . . ."

"I said we need to pull over. Call Nellie and tell her and have her call Marti. We're about seven miles outside of Baywater. Then call the kids and make arrangements to meet up as soon as possible."

"By 'kids' I assume you mean Maggie and the boys."

"Yes, Annie, that's who I mean."

"I'm starting to get excited, Myra," Annie said as her hands flew over the keys. Myra heard the pings from Annie's special phone indicating she was getting responses to her texts. She wished she was as high-tech-capable as Annie, but she wasn't. She still used an old-fashioned flip phone. She hated it. Actually, she hated all things digital. And to everyone's dismay, she used ten-dollar Kodak throwaway cameras to take pictures of the dogs. "I'm going to pull over up ahead."

"The shoulder looks capable of handling three cars, and there's hardly any traffic."

"You are a Neanderthal, Myra," Annie snapped.

"And that means what? As long as you can screw things up, Annie, why shouldn't I do the same thing? What is Facebook?"

Annie ignored the question and sighed as the car came to a stop. She unbuckled her seat belt and got out and walked over to the car Nellie was driving. She waved to Marti, who climbed into the backseat. She waved back as she climbed behind the wheel of Marti's car. She slipped it into gear and waited for a break in traffic before she pulled out onto the road.

Fifteen minutes later, Myra, following the robotic voice on her GPS, turned and drove up the long driveway to the Harbor Inn, where Avery Snowden's bogus Secret Service agents directed her to the back of the property. The transfer from all three cars went smoothly, and, within minutes, the three women were whisked to their suite on the top floor with no one seeing a thing.

"That was pretty slick," Annie said.

"Now what?" Marti asked.

"Now we take care of business," Annie said.

A knock on the door startled the women. They looked at one another. It was Pearl who went to the door and opened it to admit Avery Snowden.

"Thought you might like to know that both judges, at different times, drove by the Inn. The first time Eunice drove by on her own. I ran her license plate. The second time both sisters were in the same car, but Celeste was driving. And both judges canceled whatever court sessions they had for this afternoon. I sent one of my operatives over to the building where they live, and the car is in the underground parking garage. It would appear that both of them are upset. Why else cancel court and run for home?"

"Do you know where Ted and Maggie are?"

"They should be back by four. Maggie said they were driving out to one of the boot camps to check it out. I'm not quite sure what their plan is. I want you all to stay here until I say you can go out in public. We need to check things a little more. If you want food, call me, and I'll have one of my people bring it up. Do not put through any calls using the switchboard. Use your cell phones. Believe it or not, cell-phone reception is quite good here."

When the door closed behind Avery, Myra clapped her hands. "Okay, ladies, let's get to it. We have a kick-ass party for Judge Rhodes to plan, one that will make those two monsters turn green with envy that they were not invited, and we do not have all that much time."

"I do love a party," Annie chortled. "Girls, let me tell you about a few I planned and carried out in Vegas."

Marti laughed. She loved Annie's stories.

■ ■ ■ ■

Fifty miles away as the crow flies, Maggie Spitzer was chewing her nails. "Are you sure it's a good idea to go in cold turkey like this, Ted?"

"It's the element of surprise, Maggie. You of all people should know that."

Maggie continued to chew on her nails. "I do know that, Ted. What has me concerned is that whoever is in charge is going to be making some phone calls as soon as they see us. Dennis told us that there are NO TRESPASSING signs everywhere. We are going to be trespassing. God, this place is really out in the boonies, isn't it? And this road looks like it was cut out with a machete."

"Twenty acres," Dennis said. "You ain't seen nothin' yet. Wait till you see the twelve-foot-high fence with razor wire on top of it. We're talking kids here, the oldest being seventeen. The commandant — that's what he calls himself — is meaner-looking than a junkyard dog. He dresses in camo and desert boots and carries a rifle. I had pictures, but the paper didn't print them. I repeat, they're just kids. I'm ashamed and embarrassed to admit he ran me off the property. It was the rifle that did it."

"Don't apologize, Dennis. When you're staring at the wrong end of a gun, you do what's best for you."

"He's a mean one. Piggy little eyes, shaven bald head. I guess he thinks it makes him more menacing. He's built like a brick outhouse. He doesn't walk, he stomps. He leads by intimidation. I figured that out real quick. I Googled him. He's skirted the law but was never convicted of any crime. He appeared before both the Ciprani judges several times and got off each time. There are six counselors. All big, strapping guys who look like bodybuilders. It's all about intimidation."

"I think we're getting it," Ted said. "Okay, I can see the fence in the distance. About another mile, maybe a mile and a half, and we'll be coming up to the guardhouse. That's what it is, right, Dennis?"

"Yeah, there's a guy who sits in there reading *Playboy,* and he has a rifle, too. Big buff guy. At least that's who was sitting in the booth when I came out here. There's a homemade crude barrier that he has to open manually. He had a walkie-talkie of some kind hooked to his belt. There's a good chance he won't let us through. When I was here, I came by myself. Yeah, yeah, I know it was stupid, but at the time, I had no idea what was going on. Now that I do, I'm not sure even four of us will get through. They might think we pose a threat."

"What I'm worried about is will the commandant call the judges for instructions?" Maggie said.

"That would be like his admitting he can't handle things. I think he'll play it by ear, then make the call," Espinosa said.

"I agree with Espinosa. But, and here's the but, Dennis wasn't big-time, he was just the *Baywater Weekly,* which most people don't even bother to read and the judges can manipulate. The *Post* is big-time, and there are *four* of us. Everyone, and I do mean everyone, is going to wonder why we're sniffing around. D.C. is not exactly around the corner from this place," Ted said.

"Start clicking, Espinosa. Get a good shot of the guard. He is big. You were right, Dennis," Maggie said as she watched the guard strut his stuff as Ted approached the guardhouse. "Everyone, get your credentials out. Be polite but firm."

"Gotcha," Ted said. He felt an adrenaline rush as he brought the *Post* van to a complete stop.

"This is private property, sir. You need to turn around and leave. Unless you have an appointment with the commandant. Do you?"

"No, actually I do not have an appointment. We're reporters from the *Post*. That's in Washington, D.C. We're here to investigate a charge of brutality and to talk to whoever cares enough to be heard. We at the *Post* pride ourselves on covering both sides of an issue."

"Listen, smart guy, there are no charges pending or otherwise on brutality here. And I do know where Washington, D.C., is and I also know and even read the *Post*. Online. We don't get a paper out this far on a daily basis. No appointment, you don't come in. So be good little boys and girl and turn around and head back where you came from."

Ted's response was slow and easy, the cadence never changing. "I think maybe you should rethink what you just said and use that gizmo hanging off your belt to call someone in authority to come out here and talk to us. Yeah, yeah, I think that's what you should do. Otherwise, I'm going to have to call Judge Ciprani myself. Think about it, big guy. How's that going to look? Then, see, here's the other thing. Your not letting us in might make us think something really is going on here that you don't want getting

274

out. I'm looking at all that razor wire, and it's starting to make me wonder why a kids' camp needs all that plus someone like you. You following me here, Ace? Because if you're not following me, then we're all in a world of trouble."

The guard chewed on his lower lip. He squinted, then reached for everyone's ID. "Wait here and don't make any moves." He turned his back and entered the guard shack.

"He's actually calling someone," Dennis hissed. "Man, you were *smooth,* Ted. You actually scared him enough to make the call."

"The commandant said you can go through. He can give you fifteen minutes. That's all he can give you without an appointment. He's a busy man." The guard handed back the ID cards and opened the gate for Ted to drive through.

To Maggie's amusement, Ted offered up a sloppy kind of salute. *Smooth.*

They saw the commandant coming down the steps of a log-cabin-type building, and he was dressed just as Dennis had described.

"That's him," Dennis hissed from the backseat. "I told you he was scary."

Ted opened the door, and they all piled

out and introduced themselves to the commandant, who said his name was Bob Szmansky.

"I can give you fifteen minutes and that's it. We stick to a very strict schedule around here. That's what makes it all work. My guard said you're here to investigate a charge of brutality. What charge? This is the first I'm hearing about it."

Ted fell back into his smooth role and took the lead. "I believe the charge is being filed as we speak by one of the parents of a child sequestered here. At this time, that's all I can tell you. Retaliation in a place like this can be a terrible thing for a child no matter what age he is." To make his point he turned to look at the high fence and the razor wire.

Szmansky's shoulders stiffened. "Since I don't know what you're talking about, what is it you want? Be specific."

"Round up all the kids and let us ask them as a group. If they say nothing has happened, we're outta here. Oh, and we want a tour. I want to see the *Hut.*"

Something flickered in Szmansky's eyes but was gone almost immediately. "We don't have a hut. Maybe you're thinking of one of the other camps."

"Yo, Dennis! Tell the commandant about

276

the hut," Ted said.

"It's over there, past the copse of pine trees and brush. It's where you send the kids who break the rules. No lights, no sanitation, and no food. I took a picture of it, so don't go saying you don't have a hut."

"Oh, that building! That's where we store the bird feed. It would be inhumane to put a kid in there, and I resent the implication."

"So then, I can quote you on that?" Ted said, still in his smooth mode. "Are you going to call the kids out here or not? You might want to rethink that fifteen-minute deadline. The last thing I want is to report to the reading public, which last I heard includes the governor and the attorney general of this fine commonwealth, that Commandant Szmansky refused to allow reporters to meet with the inmates at a work camp for children sentenced by the Judges Ciprani that he runs."

The last thing Bob Szmansky wanted to do was cave in to this bunch of creeps, but he had his orders, which were always to cooperate and make sure there was no collateral damage. If they knew about the damn hut, then they knew other things as well. Better to bite the bullet now. His stomach rumbled, then tightened into a knot. He didn't like what he was seeing, and he sure as hell didn't like what he was hearing. These people were not the second team. He knew who they were because he'd been reading stories with their bylines for years. Definitely the kind of reporters you didn't want to piss off.

"Of course. Just let me call my point man to order a roll call."

The four reporters waited patiently as a three-note bell rang from somewhere in the back of the compound. They could hear running feet and loud voices.

"Front and center, guys!" Szmansky roared. A whirlwind of movement followed until all the boys — it looked to be well over a hundred or so — stood in precise lines. "At ease, boys. We have visitors today."

Espinosa started clicking his camera. He walked up to the precise lines and took shots from all angles as he tried to gauge the ages of the boys. He wanted to make sure he got every face. When he got to the back row he hissed to the tallest boy. "Listen, kid, we're going to be getting you all out of here and back to your families. It might take a week or so, but don't give up. Spread the word among your buddies and keep it quiet. Tilt your head to the right to let me know you understand what I said when I get up front. Then I want you to tilt it to the left if kids get put in that damn hut."

"Mr. Szmansky, a shot here in the back to show you towering over your . . . ah, troops." Szmansky walked around just as the tallest kid in the back tilted his head first right, then left. "Okay, let's all smile, wave your arms. Before you break ranks, my boss has a question."

"My name is Ted Robinson. I'm a reporter for the *Post* in Washington, D.C. We got a complaint and it is being filed as we speak by a parent charging that one or perhaps several of you have been brutalized. Raise your hand if this is true." Ted was not the least surprised when no hands shot in the air. "The other thing is this. Have any of you been sent to the Hut? If so, raise your hands." No hands rose in the air. *Surprise! Surprise!* Ted thought as he looked around, wishing he could wipe the smug look off Szmansky's face.

"Okay, boys, break formation. Ah, that's good. Great! Super! Thanks, guys," Szmansky said, sweat beading on his forehead.

The reporters watched as the kids raced off. Maggie stepped forward. "I'd like to talk finances with you, Mr. Szmansky. We also want to see the buildings, the sleeping quarters, the Hut, of course, and the schoolrooms, the kitchen along with the menus, and, of course, the bathrooms."

Szmansky drew back, his beady little eyes squinting into the last afternoon rays of weak sunshine. "Don't you need a warrant for something like that?"

"Only if you have something to hide. I can get one," Maggie lied. "It might take a few hours to have it delivered while we wait. The point is, I *can* get one."

Szmansky's first thought was *The shit's going to hit the fan sooner rather than later.* His gut told him it was the beginning of the end as he knew it. He thought about the Porsche he'd just bought, the sailboat he had up on the Bay, and the summer place he was planning to buy that winter with his six-figure year-end bonus, when the real-estate market really slumped.

"Like I said, Mr. Robinson, there's nothing hidden here. Go ahead, take the tour. Look at whatever you want. I'm not even going to escort you because I don't want you saying later on I only showed you what I wanted you to see. You've screwed up my day anyway, so go for it."

The minute the reporters were out of sight, Szmansky was on the phone, his back to the log cabin. The phone rang six times before a strangled-sounding voice answered.

"It's Szmansky, Judge. There are four reporters here from the *Post*. They said they were here on a report of brutality. I've cooperated, and they already knew about the Hut." He listened to a rant that ran for two full minutes before he said, "With all due respect, Your Honor, it's my ass that's on the line here. If you want me to say that, then I will, and I will also say *you* told me to say it. I just follow orders. *Your* orders. Look, you can't have your cake and eat it, too. They can't prove anything unless those kids talk, and, trust me, not a one of them is going to. Yeah, I'll call you when they leave."

Inside the log cabin, the reporters walked around. "That was a little too easy, doncha think?" Dennis said.

"Yep. Way too easy. But we're here, so let's give it a thorough going-over. Dennis, check the Hut since you know where it is. See if there's any bird seed in there. Or if ever there was any bird seed in there. There's bound to be some on the floor. Espinosa, follow him and take pictures. Maggie and I will do the tour."

Espinosa held up his hand and told them in hushed tones what he'd told the tallest boy. "He's a good-looking Hispanic boy. Looks to be about sixteen or so. Make sure he's behaving normally. I sure as hell don't want him getting into any trouble."

Maggie waited until Dennis and Espinosa were out of earshot before she looked up at Ted, and said, "I'm getting bad vibes here. Something's wrong. Do you feel it, Ted?"

"Oh, yeah," Ted drawled.

CHAPTER 17

Pearl Barnes was like a schoolgirl as she settled herself at the round table in the Harbor Inn's lone suite of rooms. "This is like a hen party, girls!" The others agreed as they pulled their chairs closer to the table. Then they all looked at one another and burst out laughing.

"Well, girls, here we are," Myra said, fingering her pearls. "The first thing on our agenda is to plan the party for Judge Rhodes. Annie, give us a status update."

"Well," Annie said, sitting up a little straighter, "you all know how I like to delegate, and that's what I did. I called a caterer in Washington that I know, and he will be delivering the food Friday afternoon. We opted for heavy canapés, hot and cold. No one will go home hungry. We have everything from crab-filled shrimp, sweet-potato-crusted lobster, filet-mignon medallions, sesame chicken in a white-wine-caper sauce, and all manner of cold canapés, cheeses platters, veggie platters. You name it, and it will be there. I also ordered an ice sculpture with a big fifty carved into it, along with the scales of justice. The space here in the Inn simply won't accommodate sit-down dinners. I did this all online, by the way. We'll be serving only champagne and beer. The caterers will send an advance team to pretty up the hall with balloons, streamers, ribbons, and whatever else they decide to use. Of course, there will be a huge retirement banner. I found a DJ who promised to play nothing but Golden Oldies. The party will last three hours."

The women all clapped their hands in approval.

"Gifts?" Marti asked.

"You're pretty much the gift, Marti. Having the president, retired or not, at your party, is about all a person could want in the way of a gift. But everyone deserves a package with a big red bow, so the gift will be a month-long trip for two to Hawaii. The judge can take a companion. I think that covers it except for a photographer, who will be Espinosa. Everyone there will want their picture taken with you. I hope you don't mind. All we have to do is address the invitations and have one of Avery's men take them over to the courthouse to distribute. We have a list of every person in the courthouse, so no one will get left out. I don't know if they will all attend or not. I'm thinking they will. Except for the Ciprani twins, that is," Annie said.

"It will be my pleasure to pose with all the guests," Marti said. "I really mean that."

"Of course you mean it; otherwise, you wouldn't have said it, Marti. I'd like a picture with you myself. Now, if we divide up the invitations, we can have it done in no time," Nellie said.

"Then what?"

"Then we have to decide whether we drive up to Waterton now or wait till tomorrow to see the house Marti just bought. I'm thinking we should wait till morning. If we leave now, it will be dark by the time we get there, and we'd just have to turn around and come back. Besides, I think we want to be on hand to see and hear what Maggie and the boys have to say when they return. We can certainly all have dinner here, possibly Chinese or Italian. Avery said his people would arrange it. Which makes sense since we don't want to be seen in public. Yet," Myra said.

"We need to have a foolproof plan on how we're going to free all those children at the same time. The camps are twenty-five miles apart and cover a radius of a hundred miles," Annie said, nibbling on the end of a pen she was holding.

"What's our time frame here?" Marti interjected. "What about a jamboree sponsored by some do-gooder group that will be delighted to have its name attached to something so worthy that an ex-president is sponsoring it? We pick one camp and have the children brought there. I'm thinking the time frame is going to be crucial, which leaves the question of how soon we move in on the twins. I think it all ought to go down simultaneously. Am I wrong, or am I right, girls?" Marti asked.

"No, dear, you're right. We really haven't had much time to discuss an actual plan. Time this go-round is not of the essence. Well, it is when you think of all those children in those camps, but we need to do this right. I for one would like to check out the living quarters of the twins. They have state-of-the-art security in both places, but Avery is on that. Still, we're going to need a few things," Myra said vaguely.

"I don't think Myra and I should attend the festivities on Friday night," Annie said. "Our pictures have been plastered all over the country, the world, too, as active members of the Vigilantes. It will be better if we stay in the background. Charles is working on legends for us, but even so, we can't attend."

"Annie's right," Myra said. "No sense blowing any cover we might be able to use."

"I think I want to know more about the brother, Peter, the one who supposedly died. Or, at least, the twins had him declared dead. I don't know why, but I think he has a part in all this. A big part. In a good kind of way," Pearl said.

"Maggie's on that. She's spoken with Peter's best friend. She's convinced the brother is alive and that the friend, whose name is Jon Eberly, knows more than he's letting on. He has an insurance office right on Main Street. A storefront office. If there's anything to find out, Maggie will find it," Myra said.

"I have one little worry, girls," Marti said. "Do you think there is anyone in this town who is smart enough to figure out that ex-presidents do not travel with a contingent of Secret Service agents the way I am? Not to mention I requested the removal of all protection last week, and the request was granted."

"Not to worry. The Secret Service will not let on you have no protection. Trust me on that. As for the contingent, no, I don't see a problem. Everyone expects it, our taxpayer dollars at work. Worst-case scenario, they're moaning and groaning about those dollars." Annie chuckled.

"By the way, did Maggie's friend Abner manage to locate any more of the offshore accounts he was certain the twins had?" Nellie asked.

"I think it's ongoing, Nellie. It's only been a few days if you stop to think about it. I'm sure he'll come through the way he always does," Myra said, confidence ringing in her voice.

A knock sounded on the door, two sharp raps with a gap, then two more sharp raps. "It's Avery or one of his people with lunch," Annie said, rushing to the door. She returned with two huge shopping bags filled with food. "Looks like sandwiches, salads, soft drinks, and lots of coffee. Guess we should eat first, then write out the invitations. What do you think, girls?"

"I'm so glad we aren't back at the farm. Charles disapproves of us talking business over a meal. I find it more satisfying to talk business while I chew, bad manners or not." Myra laughed. "Let's talk about those two crazy judges and what we're going to do to them when we get them alone," Myra said as she fished around in the bag for a sandwich to her liking.

"I love it when you talk like that, Myra," Annie said, chomping down on a six-inch-long sub. "And I have a sterling idea for their punishment. We'll just have to place an order with Charles for a few things and have him overnight it here to the Inn. Listen up, ladies, and tell me what you think. . . ."

As Annie described in exquisite detail the punishment the five of them would administer to the evil Ciprani twins, the others stared at her, their jaws dropping, their eyes almost popping out of their heads. When they high-fived one another, Annie preened like a peacock.

While Myra and the girls devoured their lunch and plotted the downfall of the two judges, Celeste and Eunice Ciprani were pacing the confines of their spacious condominium like wild animals. They snapped and snarled at each other between gulping at the wine in their glasses. They were on their near-empty second bottle of wine, with a third, the cork already removed, waiting its turn on their outrageously priced granite countertop.

Celeste very carefully set her exquisite wineglass down on the kitchen table, making sure the wine didn't spill. She'd poured too much with her trembling hands. Once again, a stressful situation had overpowered her common sense about drinking excessively due to her diabetic condition. She had to take a deep breath and calm down, but it was hard, with Nessie screeching in her ears. The sickly-sweet smell of the funny cigarette Nessie was smoking wasn't helping either. She turned around and turned on the exhaust fan over the range.

"Everything is going to hell in a handbasket. Daddy used to say that. I never knew what it meant, and I still don't know how everything can go to hell in a basket. A handbasket is small. You carry it on your arm. Explain that to me, Cee."

"Shut up, Nessie. You're drunk."

"Like you aren't?" Nessie screamed. "Look at you! Your hair is standing on end, your face is splotchy, you're drooling, and you're wearing only one shoe!"

Nessie was right, Celeste thought as she stared at her reflection in the shiny surface of the Sub-Zero refrigerator. She licked at her lips and made an attempt to smooth her hair back from her flushed face. She kicked off her one shoe, sat down at the table, and primly folded her hands. "Nessie, sit down. Please. And will you please put out that cigarette. We need clear heads here, and we need to talk without screaming at each other. Please, Nessie."

Nessie blinked, walked over to the sink, and turned on the water. She held the cigarette under the spray, then tossed it into the trash. She lurched her way to the table and sat down. A moment later, she burst into tears. "I saw him, Cee. Clear as a bell. It really was Peter. Don't tell me I didn't see him because I did. God, why don't you ever believe anything I tell you?" she screeched at the top of her lungs.

Celeste nodded. "Enough already, Nessie. I'm sorry I said I didn't believe you. I believe you saw Peter, and yes, I do believe he came back. What we did was legal. After seven years, you can have a person declared dead. Why he came back at this point in time is something I can't tell you. Yes, he is going to want his share of things. Fortunately, if that's what this is all about, and I'm talking about what has been happening, we can pay him off. We certainly have enough money to do that. Peter was never adversarial, so I don't think he's going to muck things up now. Unless he has some kind of secret agenda that he's been harboring all these years. Money was never important to Peter, you know that."

"Get real, Cee. The first thing Peter would do would be to get in touch with his old friend Jon Eberly, and Jon will tell him everything as he knows it and put his own spin, as well as the town's, on everything we've done. Peter won't accept that. Peter has integrity. Something you and I misplaced along the way, and don't try to deny it, Cee."

"Don't go there, Nessie. Let's just not argue, all right? We need to discuss what is going on. Actually going on, not what we *think* is going on. Can you at least agree with me on that? And I do not want to hear any more about us packing it in and hightailing it."

Nessie clenched and unclenched her closed fists. Her jaw set stubbornly. "Fine, Cee. Where do you want to start?"

"Well, it seems to me it started with Henry Rhodes's retiring at the end of the week. There was supposed to be a general party in the cafeteria after court on Friday night. We were both going to go, as I recall. You said you would buy our gift. Then word filtered out that the party was canceled, and suddenly, out of the blue, there is another party being planned by none other than the former president of the United States, along with a retired justice of the United States

Supreme Court and another federal judge, whose name escapes me at the moment, but who happens to be married to a former director of the FBI. Do you recall her name, Nessie?"

"Cornelia Easter," Nessie snapped.

"Yes, that's it. Moving right along here. The next thing is you hear that the two of us are not invited to this swanky once-in-a-lifetime party for Judge Rhodes. And you hear this in, of all places, the beauty parlor, where everyone in the front room hooted and hollered when they heard you and I were not invited. Which means we are not loved and adored in this town. But then we already knew that. That is a pure fact because you were there and heard the thunderous applause at the news. How am I doing so far, Nessie?"

"Everything you said is correct so far, Cee," Nessie grudgingly admitted.

"The retirement party is being held at the Harbor Inn, where the president and her Secret Service are staying. She or someone reserved the entire Inn. No one comes or goes unless the Secret Service okays it. We both saw with our own eyes that the entire Inn and surrounding area have been cordoned off. That is another solid fact.

"Fact number three. You yourself heard

that President Connor bought our neighbors' house from their estate in Waterton.
Since it is a fact, we can't argue it. All we
can do is ask why the president picked Baywater to plan a party. Why did she pick Waterton to buy a house? What connection
does she have to Waterton, or Judge Rhodes,
and Baywater for that matter?"

"Because Justice Barnes knows Judge
Rhodes, and in her opinion, anyone who sat
on the bench for fifty years deserves something special. Barnes and Easter are friends.
Obviously, somehow, some way, they know
Judge Rhodes. Just like we know tons of
judges from all over the country. Since
President Connor appears to be a good
friend of those two judges, possibly of
Rhodes, too — although I don't know how
that could be — they are all here to throw a
retirement party. On the face of it, nothing
about the party, other than our exclusion,
should raise any eyebrows. Standing in our
shoes, however, things look very different,
and it is understandable that our eyebrows
are up to our hairlines," Nessie said as she
downed the last of the wine in her glass.
She poured more, emptying the second
bottle.

"Facts and suppositions. But we can live
with that. We can also live with being

snubbed. Which then brings me back to the fact that the president bought the Matthews house from the estate. Our old neighbors' house. I told you we should have bought it a long time ago, but you said no, it needed too much work. So now we will never, as in never, have any privacy when we go there weekends. That's another fact. Now we need to know the why of it. Why Waterton? Why Baywater? They go together like salt and pepper, shoes and shoelaces, sugar and spice. And everything nice," Celeste couldn't help adding.

Nessie shrugged as she stared at the cherrywood kitchen cabinets in her line of vision. "She paid full price for the Matthews property and didn't quibble. What kind of fool would do something like that? Years ago, we got an estimate of seven hundred and fifty thousand dollars just to get it up to almost livable. In today's economy, and the wear and tear and weathering, the cost has probably doubled. That's just for renovations."

"She must have a lot of money," Celeste murmured. "Either that, or she's going to write a book the way all presidents do, and make a fortune. On the face of it, it means nothing other than a real-estate deal being consummated and a party going down that we were not invited to. I'm not actually see-ing red flags here, Nessie."

Nessie raised her glass. "I notice you left the best for last, and the last is also a fact, Cee. Are you going to tell me those report-ers from Washington going out to the camp to see and talk to Szmansky is a fluke, a co-incidence? Citing charges of brutality. By the way, I think they're still at the Inn. Explain to me as a fact, how that can be, Cee, unless this is all one big . . . conspiracy? The president and her people took over the whole Inn, yet those reporters are still there. I could hear Szmansky because you put him on speakerphone. He was nervous. When guys like that knucklehead get nervous, you know there's trouble coming down the road."

"He got rid of them."

"They'll go back. And I also notice you haven't mentioned that twit reporter who was with the three stars from the *Post,* the one who wrote that story for the *Baywater Weekly.* Szmansky said he saw his creden-tials, and he now works for the *Post,* too. I'm sure that's how that all came about. He went up to Washington, told his story to those reporters, and they think there's a story here. And guess what? Here they are. Oh, and one other thing — no reporters

from our daily paper are permitted anywhere near the Inn, on the president's
orders. The *Post* has it buttoned down tight.
They get the story. They're Pulitzer Prize-
winning reporters, Cee. We have to pay attention to that."

"And you know this . . . how?"

"You are out of it, Cee. I made as many
phone calls as you did when we got home.
People tell me things. While you were so
damn busy calling the Health Department
to shut down the salon, I was ferreting out
all the information I could gather. People in
this town dearly love to spread gossip, and
today there is plenty to spread around."

Celeste raised her brimming glass of wine
to her lips. When she set the glass back
down, without spilling a drop, she'd consumed half the wine. "We have to pay attention to everything, Nessie. I'm glad you
did what you did. I was angry with those
people for making you wait. They'll be
closed for close to a month. No revenue for
a month will hurt their bank accounts.
They'll think twice about making you wait
the next time you go there. We have to dis-
sect everything you found out, separate fact
from gossip and wishful thinking, and go on
from there. We should eat something."

Nessie opened the refrigerator and pulled

out a bowl of grapes and a block of cheese and set them on the table. She rummaged in the cabinets and finally found a box of crackers. "I'm not hungry."

"Neither am I. I just said we should eat something," Celeste said, popping a grape into her mouth. "What do you think we should do, Nessie?"

"My first thought when I panicked was to cut and run. You're right, though. If we do that, it will look like we're guilty of something. I don't know, and I'm being honest here, if I have the stomach to try and brazen this out if it grows legs. And then there's Peter. What are your thoughts, Cee?"

"My thoughts are all over the place. Why now? Why is this all happening now? Did something happen we don't know about? If it really is Peter, and he's back for real, is it possible he set all this in motion? We can't even factor in Judge Rhodes's retirement. That's been in the works for the past six months. Rhodes isn't even a catalyst, he's a prop. The question is, a prop for what?"

"We let ourselves get too complacent, Cee. Don't even try to deny it. And this is where we are right now. What's our next move?"

"You are so right, Nessie. Now what we're going to do is sober up, make some coffee, eat something, and settle down to figure things out. It will be okay, Nessie. You'll see."

Nessie forced a smile. She didn't believe one word her twin said. Not one word.

CHAPTER 18

The lobby of the Harbor Inn was quiet.
There were no new guests registering, no
activity in the dining room, no housekeep-
ing maids bustling about. It was like a tomb
even though the television in the corner was
turned low. Ellie Stephens, the daytime desk
clerk of the Harbor Inn for the past eight
years, personally watered the lush plants
just to have something to do. She'd finished
the novel she was reading, skimmed through
the old magazines on the rack, and completed three crossword puzzles. All she
could do was sit behind the counter and
watch the Secret Service agents outside the
plate-glass window.

She thought they were very unfriendly,
never smiling, never making small talk. All
in all, a mean-looking, tight-lipped group of
people who made her nervous. The tall,
barrel-chested agent stationed at the front
door had warned her even before the presi-

dent arrived that they would be monitoring the switchboard, and she was not to give out one iota of information concerning the president or any members of her party. When she'd gotten up the nerve to ask why the reporters from Washington were being permitted to stay in the hotel, the agent had glared at her and said it was a matter of national security and none of her business, and if she liked her job, she was not to mention the matter again. Ellie took that to mean the president okayed the reporters' stay. Big-time reporters. Not like Sara Kingston or Abe Martin, who worked at the *Sentinel,* Baywater's daily paper, and who called every fifteen minutes to ask if they could at least come by to talk to the Secret Service. She made short work of the calls and dutifully reported each and every one to the agent standing at the door.

Ellie knew that when this was all over, and the president and her people left, she herself would be friendless. All the calls she'd ended, made short work of, were local people expecting her to part with juicy tidbits. Yes, she would be a pariah, and probably lose her job in the bargain.

Ellie sensed the activity before she saw the small cluster of people by the front door. The big-time reporters were back from

wherever they had gone and were now hud-
dling with the Secret Service. She wondered
if they were friends. She scribbled a note on
a registration card along with the date and
the time that the big-time reporters arrived.
Maybe when this was all over, and she lost
her job, she could sell her notes to one of
the tabloids and make enough money to
tide her over until she got a new job. She
looked up at the wall clock, a jagged gilt
sunburst affair that was part of the decor.
Her shift would end in half an hour. Manny
Salas would relieve her and work through
the night. Next week, it would be her turn
on the night shift. If she still had a job, that
is. She kept scribbling, her head bent over
her task.

Maggie Spitzer took that moment to look
through the plate-glass window. She knew
in her gut that the desk clerk was making
notes. She just knew it. She tapped one of
the bogus Secret Service agents, then jerked
her head in the direction of the desk clerk.
To his credit, he understood exactly what
she was saying. She looked over at Ted,
jerked her head again, then whispered, "The
girl is making notes, I guarantee it. Let's
pretend we're having an argument, and one
of you go around the back and come in
from the side and catch her red-handed."

It worked like clockwork because Maggie and Ted were so in tune with one another. The bogus agent held up a card, while a tearful, jittery desk clerk wrung her hands as Maggie and her little band swept through the lobby. They stopped at the desk and stared at the quaking woman. "You want to give us your side?" Ted asked.

"No, she doesn't want to do that. Do you, Miss Stephens?" the bogus agent said.

"Stephens? That's your name?" Ted said, scribbling in the notebook he was never without. "First name?"

"Ellie. Ellen. People call me Ellen, I mean Ellie," she blubbered. "Oh, God, are you going to publish my name? I'm sorry. Please don't do that. I need this job. I'm getting married in December. This isn't . . . my family . . . Oh, God, I'm sorry."

"Treason is a terrible thing," Dennis West said solemnly. "Who were you going to sell your information to? Spit it out! Now!"

Maggie and Ted gaped at Dennis, their jaws dropping.

"Treason!" The single word was like a gunshot. "No one! I don't know. Whoever would pay for it. That's not treason." Ellie took a sobbing breath and started to babble. "This isn't treason. I'm not a terrorist. All I did was write down what time you all left

303

and got here and how many phone calls came in through the switchboard. What's treasonous about that? *I WANT A LAWYER!*" she cried suddenly, her voice rising to the point that her face turned red.

Avery Snowden's bogus agent stepped forward. "I bet you do. Think about this, Miss Stephens. If you didn't do anything wrong, why do you need a lawyer? Lawyers cost a lot of money. You said you needed money. How can you afford a lawyer?"

"I could make time payments. Because . . . because . . . that guy," she said, pointing to Dennis West, "said I was committing treason. All I did was make some notes."

"This is what we're going to do, Miss Stephens. You said you gave me all your notes. Is that a true and accurate statement?"

"God, yes. I did. Search the desk if you don't believe me."

"If I let this slide . . . and I said *if,* do you promise never to mention this to anyone, and that means your family and your boyfriend?"

"Yes. Yes, of course. I will never ever mention this to anyone. I swear on the Bible. I could go to one of the rooms and get one if you want me to. We have Gideon Bibles in all the rooms here at the Inn. I'm sorry, really sorry. I like the president. I even voted for her. Honest," Ellie continued to babble hysterically.

The bogus agent looked at the reporters, and asked, "You guys okay with letting this slide? Ask yourself what does it do for your reporting when it comes right down to it. A line in the paper, and her life is ruined."

"A hell of a lot, that's what!" Dennis said. "She looks guilty to me. Who's to say she won't do it again? Huh? Who's to say? Just tell me that."

"Me. I say we quit while we're ahead and give Miss Stephens time to calm down and see the error of her ways. She knows the power of the press, especially the power of the *Post.* Don't you, Miss Stephens?" Ted said.

"I do. I absolutely do. Oh, God, thank you. Thank you so much."

"All right then; no harm, no foul," the agent said as he stuffed the two registration cards with the desk clerk's scribbled notes into his pocket. "Go about your business now, folks."

Ellie Stephens collapsed onto her stool and dropped her head between her knees.

The reporters scattered to the elevator. The moment the door closed, Ted grabbed Dennis West by the scruff of his neck, and said, "Do you have any idea what would have happened if she'd insisted on a lawyer? Well, do you, Dennis?"

"I got carried away," Dennis bleated. "It won't happen again. I promise."

"See that it never happens again. You need a muzzle," Maggie said. "From now on, you don't talk unless we tell you to talk. You got that, Mr. Newbie Reporter? Treason! Good God!" Espinosa burst out laughing. Ted openly guffawed.

"Yes, I got it, and my lip is zipped. What's so damn funny?"

"You, you idiot!" Maggie said.

"What's our game plan?" Ted asked.

"I'm going to shower and change. You guys call Myra and see what they want to do. Call me on my cell and tell me wherever we're to meet."

Ninety minutes later, Martine Connor's suite was full of people all talking at once. It took another forty minutes to bring everyone up to speed on the day's activities and what had just transpired in the lobby with the desk clerk.

"Do we have any kind of dollar figure where the twin judges are concerned?" Pearl asked. "I'm referring to the camps and the revenue they bring in."

"This is what we know for a fact," Ted said, referring to his little tattered notebook. "The boot camp properties are like twenty to twenty-five acres each and are owned by the Ciprani judges. The properties came to them upon the death of their brother, Peter. At one time, the Ciprani family owned a goodly part of the state of Maryland. Those four parcels of land plus several up on the Bay, along with the family home, were all that was left after they fell on hard financial times. The twins lease the boot camp properties to the state for an astronomical sum of money. Call it rent. The twin judges paid for the actual structures themselves. The state has five-year leases that have been renewed three times. I don't have the exact amounts as yet but I do know it's in the millions. High millions. Plus the state pays for every person incarcerated at the camps. We're all working on getting precise amounts. I think by tomorrow we should have something concrete."

"The camps are solid, at least the one we saw. Log-cabin style. The bedrooms are dormitory style. Each bunk has a foot locker for personal items. There are six dormitories and four communal bathrooms. The place is very clean and neat. The kitchen was clean; I saw plenty of food, and I also looked at the menu tacked on the wall. Good solid, nutritional food. Vitamins are given to the kids. At least that's what one of the signs on the bulletin board says. There's a pool, a tennis court, a gym. Appearance-wise, it looks like a perfect place to send kids. Almost like a summer camp. Except for the fence and the razor wire," Maggie said.

"And the commandant with the rifle," Espinosa said. "Of the one hundred and sixty kids at that camp, Dennis West spoke to a hundred and twenty of the families. When you read the files, you can readily see that not one of those hundred and twenty kids should have been sent to that camp or any other. I'm sure that if Dennis had had the time to interview the other forty families, he would have come up with the same results. Those kids simply did nothing serious enough to be ripped from their parents and sent to a boot camp. This is all about greed and money."

The ever-practical Nellie asked what the expenditures were per month.

"We're working on that, too, Your Honor. We'll have it down to the penny, trust me on that," Ted said. "I know you're working on it, too, so whoever gets it first speak up, so we don't duplicate the effort."

"And this has been going on for how

long?" Annie asked.

"Almost twenty years as far as we can tell. You need to factor in the age of the twins as well as the brother. Some of the info is on the fuzzy side. The five-year leases have been renewed three times, so whenever the current lease is up, that will be twenty years. One of them is up in February. We haven't been able to find out the incorporation date as yet. Another thing we haven't been able to get the details on is when Peter Ciprani disappeared. He traveled a lot and was back and forth, then he just never returned. We do know the year the twins had Peter declared dead. That's the year they probably incorporated. We just aren't sure."

"These camps . . . Are just children from Maryland sent there or do they take children from other states?" Myra asked.

Dennis West raised his hand, his lips clenched tight.

Ted tried to hide his smile. The kid did listen. "Go ahead, Dennis."

"There are some kids there from Virginia and Delaware. As soon as there is an opening, someone makes sure the spot is filled. They actively recruit agencies in Virginia and Delaware, but the vast majority of the enrollment is from Maryland."

"Why hasn't someone done something

before now?" Annie asked. "How did they get away with this for so long?"

"Fear," Dennis said.

"I understand the fear factor, but once a kid leaves, serves his sentence, why didn't the parents do something then?"

"Same answer — fear," Dennis responded. "The judges are powerful and have a lock on things, and no one wanted to go up against them."

"What about the brother, Peter?" Myra asked.

"We have a picture of him, and we're working with an age-progression program to see what he would look like today."

"I think Peter is alive, and what's more, I think he's right here in Baywater," Maggie said, as she related her conversations with Jon Eberly, Peter's best friend from years past. "He knows more than he's saying, which is basically nothing. I admire loyalty, I really do, but I could not convince him to give up anything. He's lying; I'm sure of it."

"Just out of curiosity, who runs this place?"

"There is a hotel manager named Franklin Pervis, but he's on a medical leave due to a hernia operation. He's due back in ten days. It's off-season, and the employees have all been here for years and years, so they're taking care of things. It's not like there's an influx of guests in October. Actually, we're the only guests, and there are no reservations on the books until Thanksgiving. Avery told me that.

"And the Inn is owned by an elderly lady named Martha Eisendorf, who resides in Chula Vista, California, and just uses the Inn for a tax write-off. Avery told me that, too. We're good to go here if you're thinking there's a problem or that one might crop up. The reservation clerk jumped at the chance to rent out the entire Inn even for a short period of time. That the reservation is in the name of the president is even better."

Annie nodded. "When we are on a mission, I like to know all the facts, and I do mean all, even if they are mundane and picayune." The others nodded in agreement.

With that said, laptops and iPhones came out, and the group got down to work.

Myra moved away from the group and called Charles, who picked up on the first ring. She spoke quietly, not for secrecy but not to disturb the others' concentration. "Which one of Avery's people can get us into the judges' condo? Annie and I are going to want to go through it to see what if anything we can come up with. We're going to need the same person when we head up

311

to Waterton to the old family home. There have to be records, and we need to see them. Another thing, Charles. Are you going to be able to get us everything we asked for?"

Myra listened to her husband, a smile tugging at the corners of her mouth as he complained about the dogs and what he had to do and promise to do to get them to go out in the rain. She listened a while longer and finally hung up when Charles promised a package would be delivered to Avery for early-morning delivery.

Myra joined the group in the sitting room and opened up her laptop. She looked over at Annie and nodded.

It was close to eleven when Marti looked up and rubbed her neck. "I think I'm going to call it a night if you all don't mind."

"I'm with you," Pearl said. "I'm thinking we all need our beauty sleep for tomorrow. Let's decide right now what our schedule is."

"Myra and I are going to do a little B&E tomorrow at the judges' condo here in Baywater. After we do that, depending on what we find or don't find, we're going to drive to Waterton to do the same thing."

"Nellie and I are going to the courthouse

and introduce ourselves, make contact with Judge Rhodes and possibly visit the twins' courtrooms. Just to throw them off their game a little. And we're going to walk the main street, possibly have lunch. Get the lay of the land, so to speak," Pearl said.

"I'm staying here and holding down the fort," Marti said.

"I'm going to dog Jon Eberly early. At least until midmorning. Depending on how that goes. I plan to go with the guys to the other boot camps. We're going to be calling the judges for comments as soon as we can come up with a plan we think will work for all of us. My thought is the other commandants will be calling the judges after our visits. They'll be ripe for some kind of comment at that point. Now, I'm going to go for a walk before turning in. Avery said this was a safe town to walk around in.

"Myra, tell Charles we haven't had any luck getting ourselves arrested. Who knows, maybe it will happen tonight." Maggie giggled at what she'd just said. The ladies smiled.

The women blew kisses as the reporters left the suite.

Tomorrow was another day.

Out in the hall, Ted asked if Maggie wanted company on her walk.

"Sure. I want to clear my head. There's way too much we have to keep track of, and by now, we should have had some kind of contact with those judges. This is not our style, Ted. We're in-your-face reporters. Why is it different this time?"

"We just haven't formed an ironclad plan. It's like you said. There's a lot we have to lock down first. Then we'll zero in and get in their faces. What's up with this walk anyway? Since when do you have to take a walk to clear your head? In the old days, you would eat nonstop until you figured out whatever it was that wasn't computing."

"You do know me, don't you? It's the brother, Peter, that is bothering me. You know what I think, Ted, and I have to warn you, it's bizarre."

Ted laughed. "I think you're thinking that the old friend Jon whatever his last name is, is hiding Peter Ciprani in his offices. That the guy only comes out at night or there's a back entrance, and Peter uses it. If he is back, he can't very well stay out in the open even if he looks different these days. I doubt the friend would take him home and harbor him there. That just leaves the offices."

Maggie stopped short in the circular drive. "Damn, Ted! That's exactly what I think."

"You warm enough, Maggie? The temperature must have dropped fifteen degrees from when we got home."

"I'm fine." Maggie linked her arm with Ted's. It felt right. It felt like old times. What could be better than revisiting her comfort zone with old times?

CHAPTER 19

As Maggie and Ted strolled along in the brisk autumn air, Maggie was shivering. Ted instinctively wrapped an arm around her, drawing her close. His heart kicked up a beat when he felt Maggie lean in toward him.

The town appeared deserted, at least the section of the main street where they were walking. No cars passed. The silence was total, except for the gusts of wind that swirled about them.

"It's like a ghost town," Maggie said. "They must roll up the sidewalks as soon as it gets dark."

"It's almost midnight. Do you think that might have something to do with it?" Ted chuckled.

"Well, yeah," Maggie drawled, a hint of laughter in her voice.

"Maybe they have a curfew, and this is how we're going to get ourselves arrested. I can't say I'm keen on that idea. What do you think Charles had in mind when he suggested that?"

"Everything and nothing probably. I don't think he was all that serious. Like you, I have no desire to go behind bars. I think he wanted to see if the police, in this case, the sheriff's office, is in the twins' pocket. Let's keep our noses clean and obey the letter of the law," Maggie said, peering into the different shop windows.

"I think the only law in this town is Ciprani law. How much farther, Maggie?"

"Mr. Eberly's office is right there," Maggie said, pointing to a store front next to a shop advertising homemade candy. "I can't be sure, but I think the buildings go back farther. To me that means he has one or two rooms behind the main office. As I told you, he appears to run a one-man agency. He has a secretary or a receptionist who sits in a glassed-in area as soon as you walk in the door. I just think he's hiding Peter Ciprani in the back. He'd have a bathroom, and maybe even a minikitchen. He could pull that off. I can't figure out if the receptionist is in on it or not. She'd almost have to be. At some point, she'd want coffee or have to use the bathroom."

Maggie pressed her face up against the

plate-glass window, hoping to see a crack of light, something to indicate activity in the back of the office. All she could see was total darkness. She could make out vague shapes of furniture from the faint glow from the streetlamp three doors down.

Ted, who claimed to have better eyesight thanks to LASIK surgery, cupped his hands over the sides of his face and stared into the darkness. "Well, this is a bust. C'mon, let's head back to the Inn."

"Not so fast. There must be a back entrance, a parking lot, or an alley. Where do the shop owners park their cars? Obviously not on the street. Let's look for an alley."

"Maggie, it's past midnight."

"Ted, don't be a *wuss*. All we're doing is walking around. We aren't carrying weapons, and we don't have drugs on us. We're just a couple staying at the Inn and out for a late-night stroll. My gut is working overtime here. Look, there it is. It even has a name. The alley, that is. What's it say, eagle eye?"

"Main Alley. You sure you want to do this, Maggie?"

"I am sure. It's well lit. Hey, we're new in town, and we just want to get a feel for things. That's what reporters do, and that's our story if anyone asks. As soon as we check it out, we'll head back to the Inn. This is our best chance, Ted. We would really cause suspicion if we did it in broad daylight."

Main Alley was short, only running the length of the row of buildings. The buildings were all two stories, with additional offices on the second floors. "Did you count the buildings, Ted?"

"Seven," he whispered.

"Why are you whispering?"

"Because we're doing something stupid, and I do *not* want to get arrested. Even if Charles thinks it's a good idea. Let's check this out quick and get the hell out of here."

"Here it is. At least the trash can says 'Eberly' on it. Shoot! There are no windows in the back. I was hoping there would be." Maggie stooped down to see if any light, even a crack, could be seen under the door. Everything was as dark as the front.

Before Ted could stop her, Maggie banged on the door, three hard knocks whose sound ricocheted around the alley. Ted almost jumped out of his skin. "Jesus, Maggie, what the hell are you doing?"

"What's it look like I'm doing? I knocked on the door. Calm down. There's no one around here that heard me knocking." She pressed her ear against the stout metal fire door to see if she could hear any sounds within. She couldn't. She knocked again and waited. Still nothing.

"Are you satisfied now? Even if Peter Ciprani is in there, do you think he's going to open the door when he's gone to such lengths to hide out, if he's even here in town? I-don't-think-so!"

"Guess you're right. I'd leave a note if there was space under the door, but there isn't."

"Are you nuts? Why would you do something like that?" Ted asked as he hopped from one foot to the other in an attempt to keep warm.

"To show him and his buddy Eberly that we aren't going away, and the smart move might be to talk to us. I'm coming back here first thing in the morning and putting the squeeze on Eberly. When I left him earlier in the day, he was a nervous wreck. We need to play on that."

"Let's just get out of here, okay?"

"Okay," Maggie said agreeably as she took one last look around. "Hold on! We need to check out his garbage. Bet they didn't think anyone would do that. If the guy is staying here, we might find something. Just be quiet when you tip the can. I'll go through it."

Ted tilted the huge trash can, keeping a

tight hold on the rear end, which had wheels on it. Maggie immediately started to paw through the contents. "Lots of food containers in here. Takeout from the looks of things. Eberly must have one heck of an appetite if he's the one who ate all of this. It's hard to see, but I'm convinced now. Someone is staying here, and Eberly must be bringing in food for him. It has to be Peter Ciprani. And newspapers. A couple of editions of the *Post*. Shows they have some class at least. Okay, we can go now. I've never seen you so twitchy, Ted. What's wrong with you?"

"Nothing. Everything. This whole town just gives me the creeps. Think what you want, Maggie, but I want out of here."

"Okay. I'm done. Let's go."

The town was just as silent and dead as it was when they first hit Main Street for their evening stroll. It also seemed colder, and the wind was whipping up. The few stars they'd seen earlier had disappeared, as had the moon. *It feels like rain,* Maggie thought, as her knee started to ache.

Ted pulled Maggie close as their pace picked up to almost a trot. They made it back to the Inn in record time. One of the bogus agents held the door for them just as Maggie's cell pinged. She yanked it out of her pocket and walked over to a secluded corner to read the text coming through. She held up the phone so Ted could read it at the same time.

"Call me ASAP."

Maggie and Ted both blinked at the same time as the sender's name rolled off their lips. *Speed. Aka Abner Tookus.*

"I'll call from my room," Maggie whispered, as the two reporters beelined for the elevator. Earlier they had decided, or Maggie had, over Ted's objections, that he was to bunk with Espinosa. Maggie won the shouting match.

Maggie ran to the thermostat and turned it up as she danced around trying to get rid of the chill in her bones. Finally, she whipped out her phone and pressed the digits for Abner's number. She wasn't surprised when he responded on the first ring. Neither of them apologized for the late text and return call.

"Talk to me, Abby."

"It pains me, Maggie, really pains me, that for the first time since I began my . . . ah . . . illustrious career, I came up dry. That means I have not been able to find out where the judges have their money. I have everything leading up to it in the Caymans and in Switzerland, but that's as far as I can

322

go. And . . . before you start screaming at me, let me say I think I know how we can get the account numbers, but it is going to require some travel and beaucoup bucks. You wanna wait till morning or get it in gear now?"

Maggie sucked in her breath. She rolled her eyes for her own benefit. "What kind of travel and who will be doing it and how much money does beaucoup mean?"

"I will be traveling to the Caymans and Switzerland. I owe you that much since I was unable to fulfill my end of the bargain. Beaucoup means enough for two people to make clean getaways and live out their lives far, far away in safe havens. Because getting fired as well as prosecuted is a given if they're around after they divulge the information we're seeking."

"I have to get back to you on that, Abby. This is not a decision I can make on my own. You going to bed anytime soon?"

"No. I'll be awake. Isabelle is in upstate New York. I had a nap earlier, so I'm on my own. I'll wait for your call."

"Half hour tops, and I'll get back to you," Maggie said.

Maggie's fingers moved at the speed of light as she sent Annie a text. The message was curt and short. Meet me in the hall ASAP.

By the time Maggie got out the door and ran down the hall, Annie was rounding the corner. They literally ran into one another. "What?" Annie hissed.

Maggie told her about Abner's text and her return call. "I can't okay something like that; only you can do that, Annie. I told Abby I'd get back to him in half an hour. He's one of those night owls, and he's working as we speak. What should I tell him?"

"You tell him to do whatever it takes. I will call Conrad in the morning, get the routing numbers for wire transfers, and have the money in place for Mr. Tookus to pay out whatever amount is necessary. Not to worry, dear; once we get the judges' money, we'll get ours back. We simply cannot allow those two women to benefit off the backs of those children and their poor families."

"Annie, there are two people, one in the Caymans and one in Switzerland. The dollar amount could be quite high," Maggie said, her brow furrowed in worry.

"I expect so, but when you're asking someone to do something illegal and give up the lives they are leading, they deserve to be compensated. I'm fine with it, dear, and so will the others when I tell them. The object is to put a stop to what those twins are doing, and this is a necessary means.

Now, run along, it's late. Call Mr. Tookus, then get some sleep. Tomorrow is going to be a busy day for all of us."

"Annie, wait. I'm convinced that Peter Ciprani is staying at the insurance office. Ted and I went there this evening, and my gut is telling me he's hiding out in the back part of the office. I went through the trash can, and there was a ton of take-out food containers, way more than Eberly could eat. Someone is there. Ted agrees with me. By the way, this is a ghost town at night. No pedestrians, no traffic. It's almost like there is a curfew or something. I have no idea what that means or if it even means anything. The stores do not even keep nightlights on inside."

"We'll figure it out tomorrow, dear. Run along now. Try and get a good night's sleep." Annie hugged the reporter and kissed her cheek. "We're going to make this all come out right for the families. Trust me."

Maggie grinned. "I know, Annie. It's like old times all over again."

"Yes, it is, and I am enjoying every minute of it. Night, sweetie."

Annie watched as Maggie scampered back to her room. She was deep in thought as she traced her way back to her room, where

Myra was waiting for her. She related the conversation.

"Wise decision, Annie. Once Mr. Tookus gets the account numbers, we can move the money to a safe place, repay you, and distribute the rest to the families. There is no way on this earth I or any of the others are going to let those skanky judges profit from the misery of those children and their families."

"I'm so glad you think like I do, Myra. Whatever would I do without you?"

"That's my line, old friend."

"As Charles says, we're two peas in a pod. I like that. Is everyone asleep?"

"Or pretending. We should try — I said *try* — to get some sleep ourselves."

"Okay," Annie said agreeably as she followed Myra into the room they were sharing. She slid under the covers and was asleep before her head hit the pillow. Myra just smiled as she pulled up her own covers. She knew she wouldn't sleep — her mind was going a hundred miles an hour as she tried to see down the road to what might go wrong. Eventually, exhaustion led to sleep.

Myra and Annie looked at one another and burst out laughing. The others openly giggled as Myra put the finishing touches to

326

what she called her Shirley Temple wig. Annie's fashionable hairstyle was now covered with a very bad Cher wig. A little latex here, a little there, and they no longer even remotely resembled the matronly women they were.

"And your game plan is . . . ?" Nellie asked.

"To go downstairs, out the back exit, and get into one of the Chevy Suburbans, where Avery's men will take us to the Ciprani condo. He has a card reader that will get us into the garage, and he knows how to pick locks. He also knows how to disarm the security system inside the condo. It seems there is some kind of electronic gadget that can do that in sixty seconds. It's amazing," Myra said, twirling around again so the others could admire her totally tacky outfit.

"Either get rid of those damn pearls or cover them up," Annie snapped. Myra instantly obeyed the order, a sheepish look on her face. She squared her shoulders and marched to the door, Annie hot on her heels.

Forty minutes later, Myra and Annie were standing in Eunice and Celeste Ciprani's kitchen. Avery Snowden's operative looked around. "I'll be out in the stairwell. If you need me, call. I programmed my number into your phones. Remember to set the code before you walk out the door. If the phone rings, do not answer it. I know I don't have to tell you that, but some people just can't stand to hear a phone ring. Remember, I'm just outside in the stairwell."

"Nice kitchen if you're into cooking. Some megabucks went into this." Annie sniffed. She opened the refrigerator. "They eat well, that's for sure. Want a snack, Myra?"

"I do not," Myra said, looking around. "They must have a housekeeper. Everything is shiny clean. Spotless actually."

A voice out of nowhere said, "Those two are hell on wheels and can spot a spot, no pun intended, a mile away. Thelma Thurman, the housekeeper," a tall lanky woman with bright, shiny eyes said as she extended her hand.

Myra and Annie gasped, their faces turning white. Annie reached for her phone.

"Don't bother with the phone. I heard the dude giving you instructions. I'm not going to turn you in. I do have a question, though. Aren't you two a little . . . ah . . . old to be burglars? You can take those silly wigs off right now."

"How did you get the drop on us?" Annie demanded.

"You turned the alarm off, that's how. My

employers have court this morning and demanded I be here at six o'clock. That's how your person missed me. I got here before he did. So" — hands on her hips — the stringy woman said, "Do you want me to show you where the good stuff is, or are you maybe more interested in records and the safe?"

"All of the above," Myra said smartly.

"Believe it or not, I've been dreaming about this day for years. For some reason, though, I thought it would be two burly men who would tie me up and make me tell them everything. I never expected two . . . ah . . . mature ladies like yourselves. Just for the record, I hate my employers. But I need this job, and jobs are not plentiful here in Baywater. Plus I get to take home a lot of food for myself and my sister."

"Why do you hate your employers?"

"Why not? They're evil. Everyone knows that but are afraid to go up against them. I tried when Celeste sentenced my nephew to over a year out at one of those farms. He's sixteen, and some of his friends managed to get a six-pack of beer from somewhere; it was in the car, but it wasn't opened. And none of the youngsters were drinking when they were arrested. All four of the boys were arraigned and sentenced to a year. Then my nephew got a little too mouthy, and she upped it to eighteen months. I asked the judge if she could cut us a break, and she said no. Just no. That was the end of the conversation. My sister almost had a nervous breakdown. Danny is a good kid, straight A's on his report cards. Great at sports. Do you want the records or the safe first?"

Annie shook her head as if to clear it. Myra looked dazed. "I don't suppose you know the combination," Annie snapped.

"Sorry. They have a safe up in Waterton, too. I think they keep stuff in both places. Everything's locked up tight. I had to go to Waterton a few times when they were having a party and needed help. I looked around. I always keep my eyes open. One of these days, I'm going to write a book about those two."

"Show us the safe. I know how to crack safes," Annie said.

"Wow! I am impressed, ladies. Way to go. I bet you two lead real interesting lives."

"We do! We do!" Myra said in a strangled voice.

"Too bad you didn't . . . ah . . . come by yesterday. They both canceled court and flew in here like two scalded cats. Eunice was high on pot, and Celeste started drinking the minute the door closed. They sent me home and told me to be here at six this morning. Something happened. I heard in town yesterday afternoon that the two of them were not invited to some judge's party. And President Connor is going to be there, and she's the one throwing the party. The whole town is buzzing about that. Some other judges are going to be there. They even invited the janitors. You want to ask me any questions? Sometimes they talk around me like I'm not there."

"Show us where the safe is."

Thelma led them to a study of sorts and pointed to what looked like a heating grate. "Behind there. The grate is a decoy."

"Do you know anything about their brother, Peter?"

"Only that Eunice dreams about him, and that makes her sister livid. They were talking about it just the other day when I was preparing breakfast. He's dead."

While Annie sat on the floor and fiddled with the knob on the safe, Myra walked around, then asked, "I don't suppose you know where the key is to these filing cabinets, or do you?"

"I do, actually. It's on Celeste's key ring. So is the key for the file cabinets up in Waterton. If your friend over there can crack a safe, don't you think she can figure out how to open those file cabinets?"

Myra sucked in her breath. "Now why didn't I think of that?" she said sarcastically.

"Because you obviously need to get into another line of work." Thelma laughed. "I'm thinking you're going to need some boxes. Am I right?"

Myra was saved from a reply when Annie cackled. "I got it!" Myra and Thelma rushed over to where Annie was looking up at them, proud as a peacock.

"What's in there?" Myra asked.

"Bundles and bundles of papers. Are we taking them?"

"As soon as our little helper here finds us a box. Any cash?"

"Oh, yeah," Annie drawled, "lots and lots of cash. Getaway money would be my guess."

Neither woman had noticed that Thelma was gone until she returned with a huge black box. "Eunice got a new Chanel purse a few days ago. It came in this box. I saw the receipt. She paid fifty-six hundred dollars for a pocketbook. Only a crazy person would do that. I just didn't have time to take it out to the Dumpster. You can jam a lot in here."

"You are so helpful, Thelma. I don't know how to thank you," Annie said, getting up and heading over to the file cabinets.

Myra looked at the bundles of hundred-dollar bills. Then she looked up at Thelma. "Go get a trash bag, Thelma."

The trash bag was black, and that was good, Myra thought as she dumped the money into it and tied it with a knot. "This is a bonus for you. When we leave here, we'll put it in the trunk of your car. Use it for you and your sister and your nephew."

"How . . . how much is in there?"

"About three hundred grand. That's a wild guess, I'm thinking more. Probably upward of half a million," Annie chirped from across the room.

"Oh, my God!" Thelma said, sitting down on the floor and hugging her bony knees. "Oh, my God! My sister is going to go over the moon. She can quit that shitty job of hers that only pays pennies. Oh, my God! You two are angels! You are!"

"Okay, I got it open! Oh, Myra, there's no way we can take all of this with us. There is a ton of files here."

"I'll help you. You must have a lookout somewhere. Call them and have them come in. What's wrong with you two? We're women! Didn't anyone ever tell you women can do anything?" Thelma grinned.

"I love this woman!" Annie said as she started pulling the files out of the cabinet while Myra hit her speed dial.

Twenty-eight minutes later everything was secured in the Chevy Suburban, and the money from the safe was stashed in Thelma's trunk, under her spare tire.

"We have to tie you up, Thelma, but as soon as we get to Waterton, do what we have to do and are on our way back, we'll call the cops to come get you. It has to be that way so we can clear out the family home before they can go up there. You okay with that?"

"Sure. Just turn on the TV so I can watch my soaps."

Annie tied Thelma to the desk chair with some panty hose she found in one of the dresser drawers. "Just make up whatever story you want when the cops get here. We'll watch the news tonight to see how you perform. One last thing, Thelma. Don't go crazy with that money. And don't put it in the bank. Think about relocating soon."

"Got it. Nice working with you ladies."

"Nicest, cleanest job we ever pulled." Annie giggled. Myra burst out laughing.

"You still need to get into another line of work," Thelma cackled.

"We'll take it under advisement, Thelma. By the way, how often do they go into the safe or the file cabinet — do you know?"

"Not often. I dust and can usually tell. Maybe once a month. 'Course when I'm not here, they could open everything every single night."

"Oh, well, when the cops get here, it won't matter. We just have to be in and out of Waterton before that happens," Myra said.

"Have a safe trip. Nice meeting you two," Thelma cackled again as she settled down to watch her soaps.

CHAPTER 20

Annie and Myra arrived back at the Harbor Inn in Baywater a few minutes before six. Following them were two of Avery Snowden's men, carrying boxes and files that they'd confiscated from the Ciprani ancestral home in Waterton.

"It looks like you were successful," Pearl said. "Did you have any trouble?"

"Piece of cake, Pearl. Avery's man had us in the house within seconds. We were out of there in an hour and on our way back. There wasn't a soul around. The three houses on the lane are all empty," Annie said as she headed for the bar sink to wash her hands while Myra headed for the bathroom to do the same thing.

"Hurry, the local six o'clock news is about to come on. They've been showing teasers as to what the news will be at the top of the hour. They're calling it breaking news. Which in our case means *local* breaking news," Marti said. "By the way, did you find a stash of money?"

"We did," Myra said, taking her place at the table. "We didn't count it, but there were the same number of bundles. Why do you ask?"

"I think we should compensate all the Harbor Inn employees who were sent home so we could have the Inn to ourselves. It's only fair. And maybe a bonus. I don't want people dissing me after we leave here. I want to leave a pleasant taste in their mouths when they talk about me. I can't afford any bad publicity," Marti said.

"I agree, and that's exactly what we'll do. We can have Avery's people parcel it out after we leave. And, of course, Maggie and Ted will mention your generosity when they write up the story," Annie said, sitting down next to Myra.

Nellie turned up the volume on the television as the others started ladling out the food. "Five minutes of commercials, and they'll get to it. Are you sure the housekeeper is someone who will come through for us?"

"Absolutely," Annie and Myra said in unison.

"Shhh," Maggie said as a picture of Thelma Thurman appeared on the screen.

She'd tidied up and was wearing a simple shift dress. Her hair was tied back in a tight bun. Glasses were perched on her nose. She appeared nervous, but she looked directly into the camera.

"Tell us, Miss Thurman, what happened to you today."

Thelma swallowed hard. "Well, I went to work early today at my employers' request, and I was busy in the bedroom changing the sheets when I heard the alarm being disabled. It gives two short chirps of sound when it's turned off, so I assumed it was one of my employers coming back for some reason. I work for Judges Celeste and Eunice Ciprani and thought one of them was coming back because she had forgotten something. I just kept on doing what I was doing, and then something made me look up. And there they were!"

"Who are 'they'?" the news anchor asked in a hushed voice.

"The two burglars who robbed my employers and tied me up," Thelma said in a voice that was just as hushed as the anchor's.

"So that means you got a good look at the people who broke in. How did they get the code to the alarm system? I understand it was a state-of-the-art system."

"That's what my employers told me, state-of-the-art. Yes, of course, I got a good look at the two women."

"Women! Did you say women?"

"Yes. And they were mean-looking. Big ladies. Each of them weighed close to . . . I think around a hundred and seventy pounds each. They were light on their feet, I have to say that, and they moved very fast. It was like they knew exactly what they wanted and where to find it. One of them had a . . . I don't know what it's called, but it helped them open the safe and the file cabinets and it also helped them turn off the alarm. One of them had a small map they referred to. You know, the layout of the condo."

"What did they take?"

"I don't know. You'll have to ask the judges. They left with boxes, but they didn't pack things up till they tied me up. They were nice to me, and even turned on the TV for me to the soaps I like to watch. They told me to go to the bathroom first, though, because it might be a while before someone came to untie me. They were very courteous and even kind when it comes right down to it even though they were mean-looking."

"Did you ever see either one of these women before?"

"No, never. For all I know they could have been men dressed up like women. The more I think about it, the more I'm convinced they were in disguise. I told that to the sheriff. The sheriff's office had me work with a sketch artist. I did the best I could. The sketch artist said my description sounded like aliens."

"Did the perps talk among themselves?"

"They did, but in another language. It could have been Spanish or Italian maybe, and they didn't call each other by name, if that's your next question. They didn't talk much; they were too busy. I don't have an ear for languages. When they spoke to me, it was in English."

Annie and Myra hooted with laughter.

"And you asked if we could trust her. Does this answer your question?" Myra said. The others smiled, enjoying the interview.

"So, Miss Thurman, how long was it before someone came to the condo?"

"Several hours. Maybe four. I'm going by how many episodes of the soaps I watched. Then the judges came home. They were . . ."

"They were what, Miss Thurman?"

"They were livid, like somehow it was all my fault. They cursed at me, threatened me, and said they were going to fire me. That might have been their intention, but I quit on the spot, and they did not pay me for the day either. Tell me how that's fair. Even the sheriff said my life was in danger, and for that, they were going to fire me! That's just not right. I might just be a cleaning lady who cleans up their messes, but I have feelings, and I didn't appreciate their attitude. Plus I was tied up for four hours. The robbers treated me better than my employers. At least they were kind and considerate. And for all your watchers out there, who might have missed the beginning of the program, my employers are Judges Eunice and Celeste Ciprani. I repeat that just in case one of you is inclined to apply for my old job."

"Way to go, Thelma!" Annie said, her closed fist shooting up in the air.

"Wow!" Ted said as he bit into a crispy shrimp roll. "She came through for you with flying colors."

"We told you she would," Myra said. "Now, we need to figure out how we're going to alert the judges to the robbery at the ancestral home in Waterton," Annie said.

"Can I do the honors?" Dennis West asked. "At least they know my name. This time I can tell them that I'm with the *Post.*"

"Where will you say you got their phone

number? Their landline is unlisted at the condo."

"Call Thelma. I bet she has their cell-phone numbers in case of an emergency. She's probably listed in the telephone book. She didn't strike me as a high-tech kind of person. You can say you spoke with her after the cops were done interviewing her," Annie said.

Dennis came up with the number. Myra blocked the call on her cell and punched in the numbers that would connect her with Thelma Thurman. She identified herself as one of the strange-speaking, mean-looking robbers who tied her up and asked for the number. Thelma laughed and rattled off both judges' numbers.

Dennis dialed one of the numbers as the others stopped eating to listen to his end of the conversation.

"Judge, this is Dennis West of the *Post*. I'm calling to ask you if there is any truth to the rumor that your home in Waterton was burglarized the way your condo was? We received a call-in tip that two people were seen carrying boxes out of your home." Dennis held the phone away from his ear so the others could hear the judge screaming into the phone.

"Can I quote you on that, Judge, even

though it's not fit for a family newspaper? Of course I can bleep out all those bad words. She hung up on me!" Dennis grumbled.

Annie was laughing so hard she could barely catch her breath. "She hung up on you because she and her sister are now on their way to Waterton. Anyone want to bet?"

"That's a sucker's bet." Marti giggled. "I'm thinking we just stirred up a giant hornet's nest."

"What else happened while we were away today?" Myra asked.

"Nellie and I sat in on both courtrooms. Both judges just marked time and ruled from the bench, always in the prosecution's favor. At some point, they got a message from someone, and court was adjourned. We had lunch in town, then came home. People stared at us, but no one came up to us or asked questions. That was our day until Avery's men dumped all these files and boxes with us. We've been going through them one by one," Pearl said.

"The boys and I hit the other three camps and found pretty much the same thing we found in the first one. All four are filled to capacity. It was obvious that the three commandants had been warned we might be coming by. They were definitely hostile, and the kids were jittery. Espinosa managed to do what he did at the first one — alert one of the oldest kids to pass the word that they'd be let loose real soon but to keep the info to themselves. We got back here around five and have been helping with the files. That was our day," Ted said.

"I guess I'm last," Maggie said. "I put the squeeze on Jon Eberly. I think I scared the pants off him. I threatened him with a charge of obstructing justice, and he turned pale. I also told him his face was going to be above the fold of the *Post* with the obstruction charge under his name if he didn't produce Peter Ciprani by nine o'clock tomorrow morning. I also said I would see to it that a charge was filed against Peter for defrauding the insurance company to collect a death benefit.

"He didn't buckle, but I think my reporter's gut instinct is on the money, and by morning, both men will be waiting for me when I stop by. The other update I have is that Abner has been in and out of the Caymans and is on his way to Switzerland. He said everything is a *go* in the Caymans but did warn me that we will only have at best a three-minute window when the judges' account can be accessed and the funds transferred to an account of our choosing. He volunteered to do that for us but needs to know where he should wire the monies. I told him I had to talk to all of you first. He's going to call me around eleven this evening our time. And, he said, it took two million dollars to bribe the bank official, who, by the way, wants the money in his account ASAP. Abner told him half now and the other half when the three minutes are up. He expects Switzerland to go the same way except possibly for more than two million. He said the bankers over there are used to a higher standard of living. He's thinking double the guy in the Caymans. The bottom line is we're in good hands, and Abner knows what to do so things don't get botched up. When he calls at eleven, I need an account number and the routing numbers to give him."

"I'll call my financial man right now," Annie said, getting up to leave the room.

"I guess that takes care of business," Nellie said. "Other than cleaning up this dinner mess, that is. Oh, Elias called a while ago. Nothing new is going on at the FBI, and he said if something pops, he promised to screw it up. He wanted to know what I was doing, so I said I was baking cookies. Not to worry. He knows it was a lie because I can't bake anything to save my soul. Well, I can bake, but what comes out of the oven is not edible."

"Charles has not called. That concerns me. Although I did hear that a storm was due to hit there around now. Possibly the power went out, but even if that happened, the generators would have kicked in," Myra said.

"I'm sure he's busy with Avery's men and solving any and all problems resulting from what we're doing. Or maybe he's taking a nap," Pearl said cheerfully.

"That leaves us with this mess," Marti said, motioning to all the scattered Ciprani files they'd put on the floor so they could use the table to eat their dinner. So let's get to it!"

"Did you see that? Did you hear what she said? I can't believe that woman turned on us like that. How could she open her mouth and say such things?" Eunice screamed as she rummaged in the drawers for a cigarette. "I just bet she's involved with those people who broke in here. Mark my words, Cee," Eunice continued to scream. "All the money is gone! Are you listening to me? I told you we should have left. We need to go up to Waterton right now. At least we can get that money. Why aren't you saying anything, Cee?"

"What do you want me to say, Nessie? Let me guess! You think our beloved brother, Peter, is behind this. You think he came back to ruin us, steal our money, and make sure we both go to jail for what we've done. There, I said it. Are you happy now?"

"Only if you believe it. Which you don't. You think that stupid cleaning lady did it or was behind it. She doesn't have the brains to do something like this. For God's sake, she cleans houses for a living. You don't need a brain to do that. Now, are you coming with me or not?"

"Let me get my purse. I'll drive. You're acting too crazy right now to get behind the wheel."

"You're the crazy one. All that money for those security systems and for what? By the time we get to Waterton, we're going to find the same thing, minus Thelma. And if I'm right, that leaves us with no readily accessible cash other than what's in our checking accounts. I don't want to go to prison, Cee. I'd never make it."

"Stop it, Nessie, right now. We have a small stash of money in our safe-deposit box. We are not penniless. If worse comes to worst, you can always sell all your Chanel handbags on eBay. We need clear heads. If it is Peter, we can talk to him, we can appeal to him. He is our brother after all."

"You're such a fool, Cee. After what we did to him, do you really think he'd show either one of us one ounce of mercy? You need to get real here. We're done. Finished. We either need to go to the Caymans or Switzerland right now, or better yet, split up — you take Switzerland, and I'll take the Caymans — and we can meet in Argentina the way we planned. Or did you change your mind on that, too, and didn't bother to tell me?"

"I'm trying to think, Nessie," Celeste said as she roared out of the garage. "I'd appreciate it if you'd just sit there and smoke your funny cigarette until you fry your brain. I said I need to think."

"Oh, wouldn't that be just the right answer. Then you can take all my money and you'll be the last man — in this case, woman — standing," Nessie snarled as she puffed on her funny cigarette.

"Shut up, Nessie. If I hear one more word out of you, I will stop this car and dump you out on the side of the road. I told you, I need to *think.*"

"You said we'd never get caught. You said Peter would never come back. You swore to me, Cee. And now look at what's happening. How could you have been so wrong?"

"I don't know, Nessie. It all started with that boy reporter with that weekly paper no one reads. In his case, it seems everyone read it. Then things snowballed. We are going to leave. I'm just not sure when that time will be. We don't want it to seem like we're taking flight. We can't unring any bells. We'll split up like you said, possibly as early as this weekend. That will give us a two-day head start on the workweek. I'm not sure yet. We'll live just the way we've been living here, only better, in Argentina. Now, aren't you glad that I talked you into buying that gorgeous estate in Buenos Aires? The only difference will be we will not be working judges. We'll have every day to ourselves. We'll be welcomed into society and have whole new lives. We'll finally be able to make friends, to socialize. We won't be pariahs. We have enough money to last us several lifetimes. Now, does that make you feel better?"

"Yes, and no. You make it sound too easy. When something is easy, that's when it all goes to hell. We both know that."

Celeste did know that. "Nessie, we have new identities. Tomorrow, when we get back, one of us will go to the safe-deposit box and get them. Remember how you pooh-poohed me when I told you we needed to do that? They are beyond a doubt the best forgeries I have ever seen, and I've seen as many as you have over the years. They might have cost a fortune at the time, but they were worth every penny. And it's nice to know the forger is in a federal prison and can't interfere with us. No one would ever tie us to him. Are you relaxing now, Nessie?"

Instead of answering her sister, Nessie asked what time it was.

"After six. Why?"

"I just like to know the time. Are we staying the night or driving back? I hate going and coming from Waterton in the dark. I don't know why that is; it just is," Nessie whined.

"We're driving back tonight. We have court tomorrow. We have to act normal so as not to give off any vibes. We got away with today because we were robbed. We canceled court yesterday after that episode with your eyebrows. That certainly sent up a red flag. Relax, we're ten minutes from the house. We'll be back on the road in thirty minutes."

True to her words, Celeste pulled into the shale driveway ten minutes later, just as her cell phone rang. Frowning, she clicked it on. She listened as Nessie walked up to the door and opened it. Even from where she was standing in the yellow glow of the sensor light, Celeste could see the panic on her sister's face. And that could only mean one thing. She identified herself and listened to the voice on the other end of the phone. She felt her shoulders slump and her knees sag. She almost blacked out, but she held on by sheer willpower.

CHAPTER 21

It was close to ten o'clock when Maggie rapped on the door of what she called the presidential suite. Annie opened the door, a sheaf of papers in her hand. "What's up? Avery's people just delivered a huge urn of coffee. Do you and the boys want some? We also have some pastries and fresh fruit."

"If it has my name on it, I'm ready."

"Did someone mention coffee?" Ted asked, elbowing his way into the suite, followed by Espinosa and Dennis West.

Everyone started talking at once. Myra wanted updates on Abner Tookus, to which Maggie said she had not heard anything, and Abner had not called at eleven o'clock last night as he had promised he would. "His flight could have been delayed; he might not have made contact with the banker he was to see. It could be anything, really. He'll call; I just don't know when.

"Oh, this is good. The jelly pastry, I mean.

The coffee's good, too. It's almost like an early-morning picnic. What are you all going to be doing while we go to Eberly's office?"

"You're looking at it," Pearl said, pointing to the boxes and files. "This is going to take all of us the entire day. And we might not get through it all. You four plan on coming back here to help, right?" Her voice sounded hopeful.

"Absolutely, we'll be back. Having said that, we should be on our way. Anyone want to give us some advice?"

"Kick ass and take names later," Nellie said.

"We can certainly do that, Your Honor." Dennis West chuckled. "It's what we reporters do. Right, guys? Ah, and girl."

Maggie gave Dennis a shove that sent him flying toward the door. "Move!" she shouted to Ted and Espinosa. "Bye, ladies."

"I so hope that young lady is not disappointed when she gets to Mr. Eberly's office and Mr. Ciprani isn't there," Marti said.

The women laughed.

"You don't know Maggie very well then. If she says her gut is telling her Mr. Ciprani will be there, he *will* be there. The big question is what will she do once she lays eyes on him? Maggie never takes prisoners. Nor does Ted. Joseph is their backup, and the young reporter is a wild card," Annie said, her tone gleeful.

Myra sighed. "I don't think we have to worry about the youngsters. We need to get a handle on all of this." She waved her arms around at the sea of white paper. "No more talk. It's time to get to work."

The women fell to it, grimacing and grumbling as they bent their heads to the task at hand.

Less than a mile away, at the Baywater Courthouse, Eunice Ciprani opened the safe in her office and deposited the accordion-pleated folder containing bogus passports, fake international driver's licenses, and bogus credit cards, along with a bundle of cash inside. Cee was wrong when she'd said she thought there was $10,000 in the safe-deposit box. There was actually $47,000. Enough to pay cash for plane tickets and get them settled somewhere. For the first time in her life, Eunice actually felt like a criminal. "That's because I am one," she muttered under her breath as she twirled the knob on the safe back to the zero setting.

Within minutes, Eunice was on her feet and slipping into her robe. She was like a runaway stallion as she hustled to her courtroom, where she apologized profusely to the lawyers and their clients. "Root canal." She massaged her cheek to drive home her excuse.

"Court is now in session. The Honorable Eunice Ciprani presiding."

Four doors down the hall, Judge Celeste Ciprani, sporting dark circles under her eyes, wearing no makeup, and with the collar of her blouse askew at the neck of her robe, rapped her gavel as she finished upholding a defense objection.

Good God, how many more hours can I sit here and do this? Every nerve in her body was screaming at her. She looked down at her cell to see the text her sister had just sent. While cell phones were prohibited in the courtroom, Celeste and her sister ignored the rule. Rules were for other people. The single word she saw on the text didn't make her feel one bit better. Done.

Celeste only half listened as the lawyers for both sides prattled on and on about a case that should never have made it to her courtroom, her mind on what she'd experienced when she'd entered the courthouse earlier. No one looked at her. No one said a word, not even the security guards. Didn't they care that her home had been invaded,

355

didn't they care that she'd been robbed? How could people be so callous? On her way to the courthouse, she'd rehearsed a little speech she'd give to everyone who inquired. Such a waste of time. Who cared what those dimwits thought anyway? Certainly not her.

"Sustained. Can we get on with it, Counselor; you're starting to sound like a broken record." The attorney who was the object of the judge's rebuke glared at her. Celeste glared back, a look that said, *Do not try my patience today.*

Celeste's mind wandered. Tomorrow was Halloween. Now, where did that thought come from? Halloween meant absolutely nothing to her other than in a week or two she'd see dozens of teenagers standing in front of her for some kind of vandalism. On the other hand, she didn't expect to be here, so why was she even thinking about rulings and handing out punishments? Maybe it was a good thing. She let her mind travel four courtrooms away to Eunice and wondered how she was faring. Sometimes Nessie could be such a wimpy, whiny child. Other times she was a devil on wheels.

"Your Honor, I object. Mr. Hatfield is deliberately impugning my client's integrity."

"Get over it, Counselor. Objection over-ruled."

Celeste looked at the bottom of her computer to check the time. She almost groaned out loud. Two more hours till the lunch break. Maybe she could throw a quick twenty-minute recess into the mix. She sent a text to Nessie. Twenty-minute recess. NOW.

"Gentlemen and ladies of the court. I'm going to take a twenty-minute recess so the two of you can get your stories straight. Get your ducks in a row, or I will do it for you, and dismiss this case, which never should have been brought to trial in the first place. There will be no more squabbling and verbal slurs below the belt in this court-room. Tell me you both understand what I just said." Both attorneys nodded sheep-ishly.

"All rise!"

Celeste almost flew out of the courtroom. She didn't bother to remove her robe. She ran down the hall to her sister's office. One of the clerks giggled to another clerk that Judge Celeste looked like Batman from the rear the way her robe billowed out behind her like a cloak.

Eunice looked like she was going to cry when she trudged into her office. She flopped down on her ergonomic chair and closed her eyes. "Everything is in the safe, Cee. You were wrong, though, about the money. It was a little more. I counted quickly but I think there's close to forty-seven thousand dollars, possibly a little more or a little less. Certainly enough for us to charter a plane one way. Listen, Cee, I don't know if I can get through the rest of the day."

"You have to get through it, Nessie, just the way I do. Do you think it's any easier on me? Well, it isn't. I thought I would start screaming if I didn't call a recess. We can call an early lunch. Instead of the usual ninety minutes, let's go for two hours, saying we need to look up some case law. Instead of shutting down at four, we can shut down at three. If we do that, we can both hold on. Do you know tomorrow is Halloween?"

"I thought it was today. Is it important, Cee?"

"No."

"Then why did you bring it up?"

"I don't know, Nessie. If it's tomorrow, then it's Judge Rhodes's party. Strange to have a party like that on Halloween. Don't pay attention to me, I'm just babbling. Of late, things just pop into my head. Out of nowhere. Tell me you're going to be okay."

"I'm going to be okay, Cee. You look terrible."

"So do you," Celeste snapped. "On that lovely note, I'm going to head back to my courtroom. Are you clear on lunch and early out today?"

"I am clear, Cee. Since we're taking a long lunch, do you want to go home, where we can talk freely?"

"What makes you think it's safe to talk in our home?"

"Oh, God, I never thought of that. Well, if that's the case, we can just ride around and pick up some food and eat in the car. We didn't eat yesterday or this morning."

"I don't think I could eat anything, Nessie, I really don't."

"Okay, we'll just ride around and talk." Eunice looked around, but her sister was already gone. She got up on shaky legs, straightened her robe, and made her way back to the courtroom. She fought the urge to cry all over again. Cee looked so . . . beaten. Just the way she felt. She forced her mind to think of other things as she settled in to what she called her judge's chair. How was she going to get all twenty-three of her Chanel handbags to Buenos Aires? Cee had said they wouldn't be taking anything with them, just carry-on bags. Maybe she could ship them somehow. Well, at least now she had something else to worry about.

While the twin judges were holding court, Maggie and her fellow reporters walked into Jon Eberly's office. She smiled when she saw a strange man get up from what was probably the receptionist's chair. He held out his hand. "Peter Ciprani. I must say you are tenacious. Look, this is not what you think it is. At least I don't think it is."

Maggie introduced the others, then they all headed to what Eberly referred to as his kitchen, which had a table and chairs as well as a fold-out camping cot. Everything was tidy and neat as a pin. He offered coffee but had no takers.

Peter Ciprani was a tall man. He looked to Maggie like he'd been ill but was on the mend. It was easy to see that he'd once been rugged and deeply tanned. His hair was white, curling slightly around his ears, and he had the brightest blue eyes she'd ever seen. She waited for the twinkle she knew was coming, and it did. And then he smiled, and the whole room lit up. His voice was kind and gentle.

"I guess you want me to go first. Is that it?" He smiled.

"It would be nice," Maggie said.

"I'm sort of a missionary. I don't have any paperwork that says that. I'm affiliated with several missions and have been for twenty-five years. I'm more a volunteer and go where I am needed at my own expense. I was in Peru until a few months ago, when I picked up a very wicked parasite that no one there knew how to treat. I was sent back here to Georgetown University Medical Center, where I was until two weeks ago. Under quarantine, I might add. I'm cured now, so don't worry about catching anything contagious from me.

"As you might guess, spending all that time in a hospital with nothing much to do except watch television, I turned to the Internet and checked on things. That's when I found out my sisters had had me declared dead. I called on Jon, and he filled me in on life here in Baywater and brought me up to date on all my sisters' activities.

"I had no idea I was supposed to be dead. Of course I checked that out and found out my sisters had me declared dead years and years ago. I have to admit I found it very disconcerting. More so when I read my own obituary. I also found out my sisters helped themselves to my holdings. I wish you could have seen Jon's face when I showed up on his doorstep, and he realized I wasn't dead and buried.

"To a certain extent, I can understand my sisters' hatred of me. And it is hatred, make no mistake about that. Our mother died giving birth to Eunice and Celeste. My father . . . I guess the term today is *shut down.* He didn't want anything to do with two babies, girls at that. He doted on me until I was about twelve, then he realized I wasn't going to be a jock, a star athlete, or anything close. I was into the arts and the church. Something he couldn't understand. Refused to understand is probably more like it.

"We had nannies. Dad did look after me. We played chess, he liked opera, and so did I, so we did have a few things in common. I was a good student; he was proud of that. The twins were hellions. That he did not like. They were left to run wild, which they did. I tried to do the brotherly thing, but they hated me, so I quit trying. Flash forward. I went to an all-boys academy when I turned fourteen and from there to college. My father was land rich. He sent me a letter the last year of high school and said he was selling off some land and putting money in a trust for me. I said thanks. At that point I couldn't have cared less. I was into other things, and finance was not one of them. And then he fell on hard times.

I have to say he was a smart man or else he knew the real-estate market. I went back into the records and saw how he made some astronomical deals money-wise. He set aside money for the twins to go to college, and after college, they were on their own. He died of natural causes shortly after he made all those land deals.

"After he died, I never went back to Waterton. Nor did I ever touch the monies in the trust. I had other personal funds I lived on during those years. I just recently found out how much was in the trust before I was declared dead. And my father left the ancestral home in Waterton to me, too. Was that fair? No, it wasn't. I was off doing my thing with the missions. It just wasn't important to me. Working with the missions is my love and will always be my love. I was always sure to leave information with the offices of whatever mission I was working for in case anyone needed to contact me. No one ever did. Ever. I also sent certified letters to the twins telling them that's how they could contact me if they needed to. I still have the return receipts provided by the post office, with each of their signatures saying they did indeed receive the letters. I'll be happy to provide them to you if you need them. I never heard from either one of them. The missions, knowing we work in volatile areas sometimes, are more than careful to keep records if loved ones inquire about us. We are always notified as quickly as possible. To my knowledge, no one ever inquired about me or asked after my well-being.

"After my stint here in the hospital and all the searching I've done, I am at a loss as to what I should do. Eunice and Celeste are, after all, my sisters. Blood is blood. I just assumed that if either one of them needed anything like money, the house, whatever, she would have found a way to contact me. But instead, they stole it and had me declared dead. It hurts me deep in my soul to hear and see how they have misused their profession out of greed."

"How much money was in your trust, Mr. Ciprani?" Dennis asked bluntly.

"Thirty years ago it was well over twenty-eight million dollars. It's worth a great deal more today. My father hired excellent financial managers. The old home in Waterton is prime real estate and is valued, Jon told me, at nine million. Of course, the twins updated the actual structure, but it's the land that's valuable, and it is secluded. As I said, prime real estate, even in these hard times."

"What's your game plan now?" Ted asked.

"Actually, I don't have one. I was thinking of going to see the twins, but thinking about it was as far as I got. I went for a walk the other day and saw Eunice in her car. I waved to her, but she drove off. I have no idea if she recognized me or not. I guess I'm going to have to get a lawyer. I don't do well with confrontations."

"Well, I know just the lawyer, and she's licensed to practice in practically every state in the union. Her name is Lizzie Fox. She lives in Las Vegas these days, but your case is right up her alley. She and her husband were in Washington this past weekend, but I don't know whether they left. I can give you her number and call her myself to tell her to expect your call," Maggie said.

"I would truly appreciate that, Miss Spitzer. So, now where does that leave us?"

"Do you know the full extent of what your sisters have been doing all these years?"

"From the sound of your voice, I'm thinking the answer is no. Jon told me a few things, I pieced together other things, and here I am. Would you care to enlighten me?"

"I don't think it is my place, but how would you like to come back to the Harbor Inn with my colleagues and myself? There are people there who can explain things better."

"Of course. But first let me change my clothes. I just bought some new ones yesterday. Jon has been good about lending me his up till now."

Ten minutes passed before Peter Ciprani made his entrance decked out in pressed khakis, a white, button-down shirt, and a navy blue blazer. Maggie thought he looked good enough to model for *Town & Country* or *GQ*. She blurted out the thought, and Peter threw his head back and laughed. The sound was contagious.

The consensus of the four reporters without giving voice to the words was that Peter Ciprani was a stand-up guy who could be trusted.

"I guess my blood has thinned out. I can't seem to get warm in these parts," Peter said as he walked briskly along with the others. "I can't wait to go back."

"When will that be?" Maggie asked.

"The first of the year. The doctors said they wanted to keep a watch on me, run more blood tests in the months to come. I'm okay with that. I'll rent an apartment now that everyone seems to know I'm back, so I don't have to impose on Jon anymore. He's a good and loyal friend. By the way, was that you in the alley last night going through the trash can?"

Maggie laughed. "It was."

"Oh, my, what is all this security for? Did something happen at the Inn? My first prom party was held here at the Inn. I wore my first tux. A lifetime ago."

"The president is here," Ted said.

Peter's eyes popped wide. "Of the United States? Here in Baywater? Good heavens!"

"Ex-president. Her name is Martine Connor, and yes, of the United States. First female president. You're going to be meeting her in a few minutes. I think you'll like her."

"Then for sure I'm glad I changed my clothes. I've never been anywhere near a president in my whole life. Is there anything special I should do or not say?"

"Try the universal smile. Works every time." Maggie laughed as she ducked under the yellow tape and nodded to the bogus security guards.

"I can do that," Peter said.

CHAPTER 22

When Maggie and her entourage entered the suite, the women stopped what they were doing, thankful for the reprieve. Eyes popped at the handsome man waiting to be introduced. Maggie did the honors.

Later, Annie summed it up for the others. She said it was as though time stood still for a moment as Martine Connor shook hands with Peter Ciprani. The air, she said, was suddenly electrified. The hush that came over them all was thunderous. Nellie, never a romantic, clucked her tongue and blamed it on the antique heating system clicking on.

Whatever it was, Myra said, Martine Connor and Peter Ciprani somehow merged into one entity.

When Marti finally withdrew her hand from Peter's, she knew she wouldn't be traveling to Florida to meet her new maritime friend in the hopes of finding a soul mate. She'd made way too many wrong choices in her life where men were concerned, Hank Jellicoe being the last one. Time to concentrate on what was standing right in front of her.

Annie's cell phone rang at the same time that Myra's cell chirped. Both women moved off, out of earshot, to take their calls. Annie mouthed the words, "It's the governor." Myra mouthed the words, "It's Charles."

The group all started talking at once, no one paying the least attention to Annie and Myra.

"Well, Lawrence, I only hear from you when you want something," Annie said to the governor, who was a friend of long standing. She listened for a moment, then said, "And you knew to contact me about this because Charles Martin said it would be a good idea? Of course, of course, but Lawrence, I'm not a miracle worker. How can I possibly pull that off in a day and a half?" She listened again. "Ah, yes, flattery will get you everywhere. And, no, I don't care that you lost money in my casino. Governors are not supposed to gamble." She laughed. "Absolutely it will make a wonderful photo op. And you already called the twin judges. And they agreed to the photo op? Oh, you had to get someone else to do it. I see. And might I ask what you said to be so persuasive? Relocating the boot camps to a more structured and less expensive locale, and it was time to renegotiate the leases with the Cipranis. I see. Yes, that would do it for me if I were the twin judges."

She listened again, and said, "You want me to do what?" Annie listened again. "Provide the food and beverages for the jamboree along with prizes. I can have my people do that. Your people are transporting the youngsters to Camp One tomorrow. A sleepover and the jamboree gets under way at dawn on Saturday. I've got it, Lawrence. Do I ever! Yes, it was nice talking to you, too. Give my regards to Helen and the kids, who aren't really kids anymore, are they? How many grandchildren? Nine! You must have wonderful holidays," Annie said, wistfulness ringing in her voice.

Annie ended the call at the same time Myra finished talking to Charles. "I think we're on the same wavelength here. Right, Annie?"

"Yep. That was the governor. We know one thing for sure now; the twins will not be taking off in the next few days. I think the governor was quite firm about their attending the jamboree."

"I don't know, Annie. Saying they will be attending is one thing. Showing up is another thing. If they suspect — and I don't see how they could not — that the jig is up with the two break-ins, they could be on their way to God knows where even as we stand here talking to each other."

"You have a point. Surely Avery and his people are on top of that. Maybe I should make a phone call, or you could call Charles to put them both under surveillance. We want to get to them first. We need to make them pay for what they've done to all those children just to fatten their bank accounts. Lawrence didn't say, but I wonder how much he knows. Do you think Charles clued him in, Myra?"

"Absolutely I do. The governor is doing damage control. He needs to come out of this smelling springtime fresh. Think about it, Annie. How will it look for the governor of this fine state to have to admit he was duped by two crooked judges whom he endorsed? Like I said, damage control. Think election year."

Annie nudged Myra and looked over at Marti and Peter, who were having an animated conversation. She quirked an eyebrow. Myra just smiled as they sat back down at the table. Conversation stopped so they could bring the others up to speed on their respective phone calls.

"How are we going to handle all of this?" Ted asked. "Everything is going to happen at once. We aren't exactly an army. We can't be spread so thin."

"I think it's time for us to call the local television station and have Marti give a short interview. Maggie, can you arrange that? Mr. Ciprani, are you with us here or not?"

"I am. Just tell me what you need me to do, and I'll do it." He was responding to Myra, but he seemed unable to take his eyes off Marti.

Maggie was already on the phone, but she nodded.

"I was thinking along the lines of you being Marti's date for Judge Rhodes's retirement party tomorrow evening. Peter Ciprani back from the dead, that kind of thing. However Maggie thinks we should play that. It's an idea, but I think we need to take a vote before we actually spread the word," Myra said.

"Oooh, Myra, I do love the way you cut right to the chase. I think that's about as perfect as it can get. Marti? Peter?"

Marti laughed, a sound of pure joy. Peter grinned from ear to ear.

"Okay, ladies and gentlemen, Channel Three said they are sending their star reporter here at eleven-thirty and it will go live at twelve noon. I told him it had to be in the lobby and no more than a five-minute take. Five minutes is a long time on TV. Ted, you need to head to the courthouse with Espinosa and Dennis and spread the word that a bombshell interview is going off at noon. And that you need to do an interview with the twin judges to get their reaction. Get going right now!"

Dennis West started to babble that he knew the courthouse inside and out. He was so excited, his face kept turning colors until Espinosa clamped a hand over his mouth to shut him up.

"Someday, that kid is going to be famous," Annie said, tongue-in-cheek.

"Only if the guys don't strangle him first," Nellie said, cackling.

"Back to work." Pearl groaned to make her point.

"If you all don't need me," Maggie said, "I'm going to go down to the lobby to check on things. Marti, you and Peter come down at exactly eleven-fifty. I need to talk to your Secret Service guys to make sure nothing goes awry. This is our show, and we don't want the locals screwing it up." She looked at Marti and raised her hands, palms upward, meaning, *Are you listening and do you agree?*

"Not a problem, Maggie. We'll be right on time," Marti said, her eyes sparkling, a huge smile on her face. Peter, Maggie thought, looked to be in some kind of daze. She felt a giggle coming on, so she turned away in time to see Annie wink at her.

Love was blossoming right under everyone's noses, Maggie thought as she made her way down to the lobby to grill the bogus Secret Service agents in her inimical style.

It was eleven-fifteen when Eunice Ciprani called a twenty-minute recess in her courtroom. Having sent a text to her sister, Celeste, she knew her twin would be waiting for her in her office. Even though she was absorbed in her and Celeste's problems, she was aware that something was going on in the courthouse. People did not chatter or laugh or carry on in these hallowed halls, but that's what they were doing. She was tempted to stop and ask someone but thought better of the idea.

Eunice eyeballed her sister, her eyes full of questions, to which Celeste shrugged.

"You have three new liver spots on your face, Cee. You need to get them singed off."

374

"Like I need you to tell me that right now. What is going on out there?"

"And you think I know. Is that it? Well, I don't know. Ask someone. Where's your clerk?"

"She wasn't here when I called the recess." Whatever else she was about to say was cut off when a knock sounded on Celeste's door. Eunice opened the door to see Judge Calvin Jones, all ninety-two years of him, standing in the doorway, scowling, as he peered over his glasses at her. Calvin Jones nominally ran the courthouse or at least he thought he did. Actually, his staff ran the courthouse and allowed him to pretend to be doing it. While his mind was as sharp as ever, his body had given up the ghost years ago. He walked with great difficulty, with two canes, but he walked. And he was fond of saying he would never retire, that the powers to be would cart him off when it was time for him to *go.* Unless, of course, he *went* in his sleep, something he said he had no control over.

"Judge Jones! What . . . what a surprise!" Eunice squeaked as she turned to stare at her sister, who was coming around the side of her desk.

"What brings you out of your ivory tower down here to the first floor?" Celeste inquired. Just what she needed right now, this ancient, doddering old fool who nipped his lunch out of a silver flask.

"I wouldn't be here if it wasn't important. I was asked to deliver a message to you, so I thought I would do it in person. Your presence is expected at the entrance to the courthouse promptly at twelve o'clock for a news conference. Don't even think about trying to get out of it." The old judge's voice was sharp, without a trace of shakiness.

"Just like that you want me to cancel court?" Celeste said briskly, her mind racing.

"Both of you are to cancel court. You've both been doing it on a regular basis of late. What? You thought I didn't know? You should know by now I know everything that goes on in this building."

"What other judges are attending this . . . this command performance?" Celeste barked.

"Just the two of you, and do not ever use that tone with me. Hang up your robes. You have ten minutes to get down to the lobby. Don't even think about trying for the back door. The bailiffs are on duty at each entrance and exit. Why are the two of you looking at me like that? And why are you still standing here? I thought you women loved seeing yourselves on television. Hustle now, ladies."

Judge Calvin Jones stepped aside so the two women could go through the door. He was right behind them but walking slower. Even so, he could hear Eunice hissing to her sister, "You should have listened to me, but did you? Oh, no, you know everything. We could be . . . *there* by now if you had listened to me. And guess what, Cee. Those three liver spots are going to show up like beacons. Serves you right," Eunice growled.

Calvin Jones smirked. It had been years since he'd seen a good catfight, not that he was going to see one now, but one never knew what to expect from the Ciprani twins, and that old saying — you never know — came to mind.

The lobby of the courthouse was full to overflowing with defendants, plaintiffs, and lawyers milling about as the local news affiliate set up its equipment for the hastily called news conference.

The normally unflappable Celeste was indeed flapping now, at least in her sister Eunice's eyes. She watched as Celeste shouldered her way through the throng of people and out the door. She zeroed in on one of the technicians and demanded to know what was going on and why Channel

Three was interrupting her court schedule.

"Nice to see you, too, Your Honor," the technician said airily. "Twice in two days you get to go on the tube. Some people would kill for the exposure. It's just a three-minute segment. Relax."

"Does this mean the authorities found the people who broke into our home yesterday?" Eunice asked.

The technician stopped what he was doing and stared at Eunice. "I have no idea, Your Honor. I'm just getting the light right. Allan Scanlon will be doing the interview, so you can ask him."

"Where is he?"

"In the van getting his makeup on and fixing his comb-over. It's windy out here today," the technician, whose name tag read BOBBY, said.

"Well, it's twelve o'clock. What's the delay?" Celeste demanded.

The door behind the judges opened. The twins heard, "Hey, check this out! Listen to what they're saying." The twins swiveled around to stare at the television set hanging in the lobby in time to hear an excited voice saying, "And not only is Peter Ciprani, brother to Judges Celeste and Eunice Ciprani who had him declared dead, now back from the dead, but he's arm in arm with

378

our illustrious past president, Martine Connor. And we were told just seconds ago that he will be her escort at the retirement party for Judge Henry Rhodes tomorrow night. And now we're going live to the courthouse to hear the reaction to this wonderful news."

To say the twins were like two deer caught in the headlights was to put it mildly.

The reporter with the rosy cheeks and bad comb-over smiled, showing enormous, blinding, white-capped teeth. "Your comment, Your Honors."

"I never thought I'd live to see a miracle like this," Celeste said in a strangled-sounding voice as she tried valiantly to paste a smile on her face.

"I agree with my sister; this is indeed a miracle," Eunice said in a voice so shrill, she saw the reporter flinch. She struggled for a smile that looked as sickly as the one Celeste was flaunting.

Somehow, the twins managed to find their way back to Eunice's office. She closed and locked the door, then slipped to the floor as tears rolled down her cheeks. "God, Cee, why didn't you listen to me? We could have been in Argentina by now or at least in the air. I told you I saw Peter. Why didn't you believe me?"

"I don't know why, Nessie. I guess because

I never thought Peter would come back. Good God, it's way over twenty years. Okay, okay, I screwed up. I'm sorry."

"Sorry won't cut it, Cee."

"I have an idea, Nessie. How about if we leave now, drive up to Waterton, take the work truck the gardener keeps in the garage, and drive to New York? We can be there in seven hours. We can get lost in New York. With our new passports and a disguise, we can leave from Kennedy or LaGuardia. How does that sound?"

"Stupid. It sounds stupid, Cee. The press is going to be hounding us, following us. Didn't you hear those *Post* reporters screaming at us outside? They never give up. They'll wait outside for us until the moon comes out. I really hate those spots on your face."

"Ask me if I care. Do you have a better idea?" Celeste said, swiping at her eyes. "It can't end like this, Nessie, it just can't."

"Did you get the text from Bob Szmansky this morning? Nessie asked. "I think he copied you."

"No. What did it say?"

"Are you lying, Cee? It said he copied you."

"Well, I didn't get it. Can't you ever just respond in the proper manner?"

"It said the governor has arranged for a jamboree at Camp One. The youngsters are going to be bused in tomorrow night, the kickoff will be at dawn on Saturday, and our presence is requested. It seems some countess in Virginia is springing for the tab. The reporters from the *Post* will be there, along with President Connor. It wouldn't surprise me one bit if Peter shows up. The governor said it's time to renegotiate the fees the government is paying. That has to mean they want a reduction, and if we don't comply, they'll send the kids somewhere else."

Celeste rubbed at her temples. Hot tears burned her eyes.

Eunice started to sob as she clutched at her sister. "There's no way out, is there, Cee?"

"I just don't know, Nessie. I just don't know."

Chapter 23

Myra rubbed at her throbbing temples. "I can't do this anymore," she said, waving her hands at the disarray in the suite. Stacks and stacks of loose papers, files, and legal pads glared at her from every corner of the suite like malevolent eyes.

"I'm with you," Marti said, brushing the hair back from her forehead. "I think what we have is more than sufficient. Let someone else sift through this stuff and make the final decisions. We have enough now to take matters into our own hands. Pearl, you said earlier you can put all this on a spreadsheet and print it out, right?"

Pearl waved a yellow legal pad in the air. She looked as tired as the others. And she was hungry. Her left foot was starting to tingle, a warning that her gout was going to flare up shortly. She did her best to ignore the tingly sensation.

"Tell us what you have, Pearl," Annie said.

Pearl perched her reading glasses on the end of her nose and started to read from her notes.

"The Maryland government leases the four boot camps from four different corporations. We tried tracking them at first, but there are so many holding companies and dummy corporations along with the trust that I had to give up because I couldn't keep them straight. A forensic accountant is called for here. What we do know is the four properties where the camps are at one time belonged to Peter Ciprani and were legally transferred to the twin judges when they had him declared dead. Each camp is a separate entity. Following the paperwork is just too mind-bending. Suffice it to say, *we* know that the twins are in control of the entire shebang because we are looking at files we confiscated from their homes. No one else would have all of these files. Having said that, the government pays forty thousand dollars a month to lease each camp. That's one hundred and sixty thousand dollars a month. So, the rental per year comes to $1.92 million. As far as these records go, it looks like the twins have been in business for over nineteen years, so that brings our total to roughly $36.5 million, give or take.

"From every indication in these files, the camps are always at full enrollment, which is one hundred and sixty youngsters to each camp, or six hundred and forty kids. The government pays two thousand dollars a month for each child's care or $1.28 million a month. I have no idea on what basis anyone came up with the number two thousand. To my way of thinking, two grand per child per month is excessive, but when it comes to government, they probably think they're getting off cheap. For twelve months it equals out to $15.36 million. Over nineteen years that would bring it in around $291.84 million, give or take a little on either side. That is an awful lot of money no matter how you look at it.

"The outlay for utilities, food, upkeep, salaries, uniforms, laundry, vehicles, insurance, maintenance, et cetera, barely eats into it. From what I can tell, the commandant who oversees each facility is only paid sixty-five thousand dollars a year with a large yearly bonus. The counselors are paid at twelve dollars an hour. They also get robust yearly bonuses. Of course, room and board are included, as well as driving privileges on company cars, which are leased through separate corporations. It's a dizzying trail to follow.

"It gets especially interesting when you come to the food part. Restaurants and farmers in the outlying areas donate tons of food seasonally. The key word here is *donate*. And yet the food bills remain pretty much the same. I guess you could call it kickbacks or something of that nature. Two sets of books. One for public viewing and one for what we have right here in front of us. We're talking a boatload of money, ladies."

"I had no idea," Annie gasped.

Myra fingered her pearls, her eyes glassy. "And they got away with it all these years. Amazing."

"Who paid for the construction of the buildings? That had to be expensive," Nellie asked.

"The twins. A lot of it could be written off. And it was all done with Peter Ciprani's money on Peter Ciprani's land once they had him declared dead," Pearl said. "So, their return on investment is infinite since not a red cent of their own money ever had to be put at risk."

"And they got away with it all these years," Annie said, repeating Myra's words. Her eyes flashed dangerously. "And if it weren't for Dennis West, they'd still be getting away with it. No, I am not discounting Maggie's gut feelings, but it's doubtful we would have come this far without that young man. Oh, I am seeing a very bright future for young Dennis."

Myra's cell chose that moment to chirp to life. She answered it, a smile tugging at the corners of her mouth when she heard Maggie's voice. "We were just talking about you, dear. Do you have news?" Myra listened. First she frowned, then she grimaced, then she smiled. The others relaxed when their fearless leader let go of her pearls.

The moment Myra ended the call, she said, "The good news is Abner was finally successful with his Swiss banker. He said the man took it right down to the wire and didn't give Abner his answer until two minutes before the bank closed. The bad news is his fee is triple what the man in the Caymans asked for," Myra said, her eyes on Annie, who simply waved off her words as of no importance.

"Then we are good to go here, right?" Marti asked. She got up, unkinked her neck, and did a few stretching exercises. "Let's pack up this stuff and get it out of here. I am so sick of looking at it, I can't stand it."

The women fell to the task. An hour later, all the boxes and files were stacked neatly in the foyer with just a narrow pathway to get to the door. Avery Snowden's men would pick them all up at some point and make sure it all got to the right people. Again, at some point.

"I'm tired. If no one is going to use the shower, I'm going to go first. And then I'm going to bed. Tomorrow and the day after promise to be . . . challenging," Myra said.

The others agreed. As they waited to take their turns, they passed the time talking about Judge Rhodes's retirement party, the proposed mass exodus of the youngsters at the boot camps, the punishment and removal of the twin judges, and last, but not least, Peter Ciprani.

They all slept dreamlessly. Except for Marti, and the less said about her dreams, the better.

CHAPTER 24

Maggie Spitzer fought her way out of a deep sleep as she automatically pawed the nightstand to find her cell phone, which was ringing so loudly she thought for a moment she was in church hearing the bells toll. She cracked an eyelid and saw bright end-of-October sun shining through the slats on the window blinds. She was going to kill Ted. The last thing she'd said to him before they parted company at her door last night was not to call her early in the morning and he'd agreed. "What did I tell you?" she snarled into the phone.

"I don't know. What did you tell me?" Abner Tookus asked.

Maggie's eyelids flew up as she struggled to sit up. "Sorry, Abby, I thought you were Ted. What's up?"

"I need you fully awake, Maggie, so you can understand what I'm going to tell you. Are you fully awake?"

"I am now," Maggie said, as her stomach muscles crunched themselves into a tight knot. "Fire away."

"The money here in Switzerland is gone. It was wired out last night, your time. My banker friend called to tell me. That's the bad news. The good news is he wired the advance money I paid him back into Annie's account. I have a call in to the guy in the Caymans, but he was in a meeting, and there is the time difference between here and there, so he hasn't gotten back to me yet. If this account is gone, I'm pretty sure the one in the Caymans will be gone, too. Those women are not stupid. The only way to track it now is if they themselves give you the routing numbers. I'm sorry, Maggie."

Maggie struggled to find words, but none came. She finally managed something that sounded like, "It's not your fault, Abby."

"I know, I know. I'm sorry, Maggie. I've spent the last few hours trying to see if I could figure out where the money was wired, but I've come up dry. Talk to your people and tell me what you want me to do. If there's nothing more for me to do here, I'd like to head on home. You okay, Maggie?"

"I'm okay. Abby, don't take this personally. Sometimes things just can't be helped, and like you said, the banker paid back the money. I didn't think those two women were that smart. Guess I was wrong. Thanks for calling. I'm giving you permission to leave. I know the others will agree. As soon as you know about the Caymans, let me know."

"This is just my opinion, Maggie, but I think your principals are about to take it on the lam. They're clearing the decks for a getaway. Keep that in mind."

Maggie squeezed her eyes shut as her mind raced. The breaking and entering Myra and Annie had done must have terrified the judges. She knew in her gut that Abner was right, the twins were getting ready to head to unknown parts. The question was how soon?

Maggie took the quickest shower of her life, ran a toothbrush across her pearly whites, dressed, ran down the hall to the presidential suite, and rapped on the door. It was opened almost immediately by Pearl. The others were up but still in their night-clothes. They were drinking coffee. Annie quickly poured a cup for Maggie.

Between sips of coffee, Maggie relayed Abner's news. "I agree with him, they're ready to hit the road. What's our next move?"

"I'll call Charles," Myra said.

"I'm calling Avery to tell him to put surveillance on them immediately," Annie said.

"I'm calling Peter!" Marti said. Everyone turned to her, their eyes full of surprise and questions. "Think about it for a minute. Who but Peter can ensure they stay here? By now, the word is out all over town that he's returned from the dead, thanks to all those interviews. The twins can't afford to ignore him. There hasn't even been a face-to-face meeting yet. We need him to do that as soon as possible to see what he can get from the conversation."

"Do it then," Pearl said. The others nodded.

The phone calls completed, Annie poured more coffee for everyone. A plate of pastries sat in the middle of the table, thanks to Avery Snowden. Maggie helped herself. "I really hate to eat and run, but I want to get the guys together so we can all descend on the courthouse demanding interviews with the judges. One of us will alert the local TV station to have someone there for the big reconciliation with Peter. If we put the twins on the spot, they can't make a move without our knowing about it. See ya!"

"I'd pay to see that," Marti said wistfully.

"I'm getting cabin fever."

"I think you just want to see Peter again," Nellie teased.

Marti blushed. "That, too."

"Then do it, Marti. Take as many of your bogus Secret Service people with you as you want. No one is going to challenge you. If anything, it will be more in your face for those two . . . awful women. I say, do it!"

Myra's fist shot in the air. "Absolutely you should do it. Hurry, Marti. Get dressed, and wear something fetching. Dress presidential."

"You could lend her your pearls, Myra," Annie said slyly.

Knowing the saga of Myra's pearls, Marti was quick to respond. "That won't be necessary. I have my own pearls. I bought them at JCPenney a hundred years ago with my first-ever paycheck. I think I was sixteen at the time."

"Every woman should have a string of pearls," Myra said huffily.

More phone calls were outgoing and just as many were incoming before the women scattered to shower and dress. The only one singing in the shower, however, was Martine Connor.

During the morning recess, both court

clerks informed their bosses that Channel Three had reporters in the lobby along with the *Post* reporters, who were in attendance to cover the Peter Ciprani reunion with his twin sisters. "Judge Jones insists you be on time," one of the clerks said.

"Calvin has no right to issue an order like that," Eunice said. "I am not giving any personal interviews. Celeste and I never give personal interviews, and we are not going to start now, Peter or no Peter. That's private and personal."

"My sister is right, but we will gladly comply with Judge Jones's *suggestion* that we attend, but that's all we're willing to do. At which point I hope the doddering old fool keels over," Celeste said coolly. "I guess that's too much to ask for, now isn't it?"

The two court clerks remained stone-faced and silent. They knew better than to argue with their bosses.

"Judge Jones also told us to remind you that court is going dark at two o'clock this afternoon so everyone can get ready for Judge Rhodes's retirement party. He realizes you won't be attending, but everyone else will be, and he has to accommodate the majority," Celeste's clerk said timidly.

"Fine! Fine! Does the old tyrant have any other orders?" Celeste snarled.

"No, that's it, Your Honor. You have two minutes to get back to court."

Celeste saw the look of panic on her sister's face. She smiled, but there was a warning in her eyes that clearly said, *Keep it together.* Eunice gave a slight nod as she turned to head to her courtroom.

Celeste looked at the two clerks, and said, "I don't understand why this meeting couldn't take place in chambers. It is, after all, a private family matter."

The two clerks shrugged, their expressions blank before they walked off.

Celeste moved quickly, her black robe billowing out behind her own breeze as she swooped into her courtroom.

"All rise! Court is in session, the Honorable Judge Celeste Ciprani presiding."

The first person Celeste noticed when she sat down and peered out into the courtroom was her brother, Peter, and standing next to him was the former president of the United States, flanked by a dozen Secret Service agents.

She could handle this. She really could. She peered into the shiny surface of her computer to see if the liver spot on her nose was noticeable. She was startled to see that the makeup she'd applied to cover the spot had worn off.

Celeste banged her gavel. "Call your next witness, Counselor."

The next two hours crawled by, then it was time to take the noon lunch break. "Court will reconvene at one o'clock. We will go dark at two o'clock according to Judge Jones so everyone can get ready for Judge Rhodes's retirement party, so, Counselors, make that one hour work for you or we'll be revisiting this case on Monday morning."

"All rise!"

Celeste ran to her chambers, shed her robe, then reapplied her makeup. She fluffed up her hair, grabbed her purse, and raced to her sister's chambers. Eunice was waiting for her. "Peter and the president were in my courtroom. He looks the same, just older. He glared at me the whole time. I stared him down. Listen, Nessie, stay calm, okay. We can handle this. We really can. Smile a lot. Remember, we are beyond delighted to be welcoming our brother back from the grave. I don't care if it kills you, Nessie. You smile, and you don't stop smiling until I tell you to stop," Celeste said in one breathless gasp. She took a deep breath, and continued. "If you screw this up, I *will* personally kill you myself. Do you understand, Nessie?"

"I'm really getting sick and tired of you telling me what to do, Cee. I really am."

"I'm sorry, Nessie. I saw the panic on your face when the clerks were telling us what to do. I know you can carry it off. If it's any consolation, I feel like there is an army of ants crawling around my stomach. Come on, time to beard the lion."

Eunice gave her sister a sour look. "You better hope that lion doesn't decide to roar for the media."

"Just follow my lead and try to look happy," Celeste snapped.

Celeste saw it all in one glance: the television camera, the reporters from the *Post,* a gaggle of court staff, all nine judges, and, of course, her brother, the president of the United States, and the phalanx of Secret Service agents. In that one quick searching glance, she looked for something that might indicate forgiveness in her brother's expression. She didn't see it and knew that this was not the Peter of yesteryear.

She was in midstride in her rush, Nessie at her side, so she couldn't have stopped her momentum even if she tried. Arms outstretched, what she hoped was a joyous expression on her face, she squealed her brother's name, Nessie echoing her. They both started to babble about the miracle they were experiencing along with the rest of the world.

The twins wrapped their arms around their brother to his chagrin as they played to the media. And it was all captured on film. The tearful, starry eyes of the twins, the grim face of the dead brother come to life, and the president looking on, smiling benignly.

Maggie and Ted approached and demanded a few words from each of them. She had to shout to be heard, what with the bogus Secret Service agents shouting orders to which no one paid attention.

Ted was in time to hear Eunice saying, "Ohh, Petey, we have so much legal work to do to give you back all that is yours. When can we do it? Can we do dinner this evening? We need to make this all right as soon as possible."

"Can I quote you on that?" Ted demanded.

Eunice blinked. She started to stutter. She was left with no recourse but to say, "Of course you can quote me."

"Peter," Celeste gushed, "I'll even cook. Who knew cooking would be one of my talents? All of your favorites, whatever they are these days. Oh, darling brother, I can't believe you're here standing right in front of me after all these years. God has been so generous in sending you back to us." She gave another bone-crushing squeeze to her brother. Nessie did the same thing before they stepped back to look up at their brother.

He's not buying into this dog and pony show, Celeste thought, a sinking feeling in the pit of her stomach. Maybe she should have cried like Nessie, but if she had cried, her makeup would run and the damn liver spots would show up.

Oh, God, I've never seen such cold eyes. He hates us. He doesn't believe one word either of us uttered, Nessie thought, wondering how Cee was going to make everything come out right.

Ted tried to elbow his way past the TV reporter, only to be shoved back. Espinosa captured the twins' dismay when they stepped backward. He had the perfect caption racing around in his mind. He angled forward and to the right so he could snap photos of Peter Ciprani. He captured disgust and disbelief. Neither boded well for the twin judges in his opinion.

Dennis West had somehow managed to inch his way until he was behind the judges. He tapped Celeste on her shoulder and asked if she was going to deed the four boot camp properties back to her brother, and transfer the hundreds of millions the properties had taken in over the past years.

Dumbfounded, the twins froze in place. Peter grabbed Dennis by the arm, and said, "This isn't the time or the place to discuss this, but I will talk to you when this is over. Say, one hour at the Dog and Duck."

"Yes, sir, I'll be there. You can count on me. You absolutely can count on me, and I will give you as much time and space in the paper as you want. One hour. I'm going there now, so I won't be late. Thank you. You are a prince, Mr. Ciprani." Then he hissed just loud enough for Ted and Maggie to hear, "Your sisters are not princesses." He continued to hiss in the man's ear, "What I can tell you will curl your hair, but I can see that your hair is already curly. So, I'll just blow off your socks. I'm going. I'll see you there. Are you bringing the president? Never mind, that's not my business."

His face red as a beet, Dennis backed up until Ted grabbed him by the scruff of the neck and dragged him outside. Petrified, Dennis winced, expecting a dressing-down by his idol. "Nice going, kid."

Inside, Maggie was patiently waiting for Peter Ciprani to respond to his sisters. His voice was soft, gentle. "I'd love to have dinner with you both. Don't fuss. I'm used to eating whatever is put in front of me. I'd like to bring my lawyer if that's all right? The president has other plans, I'm sorry to say."

"Lawyer? At dinner? Can't we arrange that for next week? Monday would be perfect. Nessie and I were hoping for a family reunion, just the three of us. Time to catch up and get to know one another all over again. Lawyers will interfere with our private time."

Peter didn't give his sister an inch. "I have time now. We could go to your chambers and discuss the legalities, but I have to call my attorney first. We should be able to discuss everything and draw up papers in three hours or so until it's time for me to escort the president to Judge Rhodes's retirement party. I'll contain my appetite for a late-night dinner with my two favorite sisters. What do you say, ladies?"

Like you are really going to tell me what to do. "Well, that can't happen today, Peter. Nessie and I both have commitments we can't cancel. As I said, Monday will work just fine and give us time to gather everything together so you can present it all to your lawyer. Look, we have to go now. Let's just leave it if you can manage to come to dinner, you'll come. If not, we'll meet on Monday."

Nessie rushed in and hugged her brother a second time. "Do your best to come tonight so we can catch up. It is soooo good to see you again, Peter."

"Judge! Judge!" Maggie shrieked. "Give us a comment for tomorrow's paper."

"Sorry," Nessie called over her shoulder. "Another time perhaps?" Out of the corner of her eye, she saw Cee crushing her brother to her chest.

Back in Celeste's chambers, both women collapsed against the wall as they struggled to get their breathing under control.

"That did not go well," Nessie gasped. "Oh, God, did you see his eyes?"

"I did. He's out for blood, Nessie."

CHAPTER 25

Dennis West bounded down the street and around the corner to where the Dog and Duck bistro was located. He'd eaten there before with friends but had never been impressed. Bar food was just that: bar food. He liked to wrap his lips around good solid food by way of a hamburger and fries and a milk shake. He wasn't into spring rolls, stuffed mushrooms, curly sweet potatoes, or deep fried vegetables. What he liked about the Dog and Duck was the outside patio and portable bar. In cooler weather, like now, the manager turned on the gas heaters on poles spaced around the tables. It was like eating at the beach. He opted for outdoors when he saw the gas heaters were in operation. He flopped down on a chair and wondered if he should order a beer to appear worldly or go with a soft drink. Coffee would be good, too, but the Dog and Duck's coffee was awful. He finally decided on a ginger ale.

Dennis spent the next fifty minutes watching the few pedestrians meander up and down the street, wondering what kind of lives they led in private. There were few customers to observe since it was past the lunch hour. He drummed his fingers on the tabletop, scratched at his neck, took deep breaths, then yawned. He almost blacked out when he saw Peter Ciprani approach the table. Dennis was quick to note that the man looked weary. Frail, actually. He stood up, shook hands, and motioned for the older man to sit.

"Dennis. It's Dennis, right?" Dennis nodded. "I wonder if I might ask a favor of you. I'm not sure if you know this or not, but I just got released from the hospital a few weeks ago. I'm on the mend, but I tire easily, and right now, I am very tired. I am supposed to avoid stress, and I've had a stressful day. You see I had a deadly parasite that they were not able to treat in Peru, and that's why I came back to the States, to Georgetown, where I received excellent treatment. Having said all that, I was wondering if we could postpone our talk until I'm feeling a little stronger. I promise to give you . . . I believe the term is an *exclusive.* I'll be honest and tell you anything you want to know because if nothing else in this life, I am honest. Sometimes to my own detriment."

Dennis took only a moment to make a decision. He liked this man, he really did, and he did look tired and worn. "Sure, Mr. Ciprani. I understand. Do you need help getting back to where you're staying?"

"I was staying with a friend, but the president said she would get me a room at the Harbor Inn. My friend that I was staying with promised to take my things there earlier today. I think I'll just move in there until the doctors cut me loose, but to answer your question, I could use a ride if you have some wheels. I don't think I can make it on my own. Plus, I forgot to take my noontime pills."

Dennis pressed the number two on his phone. Ted answered and Dennis explained what he needed. "Be right there, kid."

Fifteen minutes later, Ted, Dennis, and Espinosa had Peter Ciprani settled in a suite of rooms directly below where the ladies of Pinewood were staying. While Ted made sure the man took his meds, Dennis raced out to the closest deli and brought back a ham sandwich, some chips, and a container of potato salad, along with some pickles.

"That should hold you until the party

tonight, Mr. Ciprani."

Peter's eyes were starting to droop, but Ted kept him awake by saying, "This medicine says you need to eat when you take it, so please, sir, eat this sandwich. We aren't leaving you until you do." Peter obliged.

The boys helped him into the bedroom. The last thing Peter said before dropping off to sleep was, "Are my sisters as bad as everyone says they are?" He was asleep before any of them could respond.

"Nice old guy," Ted said.

"I don't think he's that old, Ted. I think his illness has drained him. I think he's just a few years older than his miserable sisters," Espinosa said.

"He promised me an exclusive," Dennis said jubilantly. His mood turned sour in an instant. "He is going to be okay, isn't he?"

"Yeah, kid, he's going to be okay. Today was a game changer for the man. Plus, I think he's falling in love with the prez."

"Wow!" Dennis said, making sure the door locked behind him as he left the room.

Annie summed it up when the party was over. "For such short notice, we did a hell of a job with this party. Judge Rhodes was in his glory, especially when Marti asked him for the first dance. What a memory for that kind old man. I'm so glad we did it, Myra, aren't you?"

"And the best part was we both were able to attend in our disguises so no one would associate us with the Vigilantes. None of our plans seem to be working out. Have you noticed that, Annie? We don't need the legends Charles spent so much time creating. Marti's being who she is has helped us immeasurably. The rest just seems to be falling into place for us."

"Except for Mr. Tookus's striking out. I really didn't see that coming; did you, Myra? Once I heard Switzerland bombed out on us, I knew without Abner needing to confirm it that the Caymans would go the same way. We'll just have to sweat those twins to get the account numbers. With what we have in mind, I feel confident they'll part with the information once we set the wheels in motion. Did you see that coming?"

"Can't say that I did, Annie. He's never failed us before. But you know what they say, there is a first time for everything. This is our first. It pains me to say this, but we almost didn't need Charles for this mission. Aside from Avery and his people, of course. I agree a hundred percent that we can make the twins talk and give us what we need.

But we are not capable of the cleanup like Avery's people are."

"Where did Nellie and Pearl go?"

"They were in the party bar with Judge Rhodes, playing catch-up. I think it's a judge thing. Judge Rhodes was in no hurry to leave. I suspect he's lonely since his wife passed away. I heard him say he's going to take his housekeeper with him to Hawaii. If there's anything to get out of him in regard to the twin judges, Pearl and Nellie will ferret it out." Annie wiggled her eyebrows as much as to say, just because there is snow on the roof doesn't mean there's no fire in the chimney. Myra burst out laughing. "I hope they have a wonderful time. I'm ready for bed, Myra."

"Me, too. The others don't need us to tuck them in when they get here. Annie, when do you think the twins are going to take off?"

"I'm thinking Sunday. They have to go out to the boot camps tomorrow for the governor's command performance. This is just my opinion, but I think they're going to brazen it out and wait for just the right moment to take it on the lam. I'm sure they have a plan. I'm also sure that they had to know this day might come. Meaning, of course, they had an exit route planned.

"Well, that day is here now. Avery's people have them under surveillance, so we'll know the moment they make a move of any kind that's out of the ordinary."

"Do you think Peter is going to go to dinner with them? I think I might be afraid to eat anything they cooked."

"I don't know any more than you do, Myra. If I had to guess, I'd say no, he didn't go. He was cozying up to Marti when you and I came upstairs. Right now, I think she's his top priority. I so hope that works out for both of them. It doesn't appear to me that he's in any hurry to sit down and talk to his sisters. He's also wise in wanting a lawyer with him. I almost bit my tongue off when he said that. I don't think the twins were expecting that."

The old friends said good night to one another, with Annie mumbling that she couldn't remember the last time she'd gone to bed at nine o'clock, and Myra's responding that morning would arrive before they knew it.

Eunice Ciprani paced around the exquisitely set dining-room table. She gazed at the priceless table settings, the splendid crystal, and the heirloom silverware. The peach-colored candles only had an inch and a half to go before they burned out, the melted wax was pooling on the silver candleholders. The ice in the wine bucket had melted earlier and had been replaced.

"He's not coming, Cee. We should clear the table."

"Do you want to eat, Nessie? We went to a lot of trouble to cook this dinner. It's a shame to throw it down the disposal."

"I couldn't eat, Cee, if my life depended on it. We were such fools to think Peter would actually show up. He sounded so sincere."

"As sincere as we sounded to him. No, I'm not surprised. In a way, I'm relieved. Let's go into the office and finish up the paperwork. I'll call a messenger service to pick it up tomorrow from our letter box for delivery to Peter on Monday morning. If things work out, we'll be . . . never mind," Celeste said, mindful of the possibility of bugs in the condo. Nessie bobbed her head to show she understood.

"Quit claim deeds on the properties our father left to Peter that we took over after we declared him dead." Mindful of the possibility of the bugs, she rushed on. "The properties should be returned to Peter as per our father's wishes. We did the paperwork for revoking the death certificate.

Everything is in order. From there on in, it's Peter's problem. We're doing the right thing. So, let's get to it so I can package it up and put it in our letter box. I'll send a text to the messenger service to alert them to the pickup. Then we can go to bed, get up, and go out to that damn jamboree. I'm thinking, Nessie, that we should drive up to Waterton after the jamboree instead of coming back here. What do you say? Or if you don't want to go to Waterton, we could go to Washington, D.C. We haven't been there in a while. Let's leave our options open, okay?"

"Good idea, Cee. Okay, let's get the paperwork out of the way." Playing to the unseen ears, she continued. "I am so disappointed Peter didn't come over. I think he would have liked the dinner we prepared. He looked frail. Don't you think? But he still looked like the old Peter, and he has all his hair. He always was handsome. I wish he'd acted more like a big brother to us when we were growing up."

Celeste crunched her face into a look of disgust. "I wish that, too," she said sweetly.

Twenty minutes later, Eunice deposited the package for messenger pickup in their letter box. She leaned against the wall and fired up one of what Cee called her funny cigarettes. She wished that she could turn back the hands of time. She'd lost count of how many times in the past weeks she'd wished for the past. Eventually, she ceased to care about anything as the pot dulled her thoughts. She stubbed the roach out on the wall and stuck the butt in her pocket. On wobbly legs, she made her way to the elevator that would take her back to where her sister waited for her.

It was pure, unadulterated chaos at the boot camp, with wall-to-wall kids. There were a dozen big yellow buses spread out along the road to the camp. The kids were yelling and screaming and running all over the place despite the counselors and teachers blowing their shrill whistles for order. And the weather was not cooperating. It was cold, gray, and foggy. A light drizzle was starting to fall. Wet leaves swirled and twirled in wild gusts of wind. The scent from the forest of evergreens vied with the cooking smoke from all the campfires. "It smells like Christmas," Ted said through quivering lips. "Damn, I hope it warms up soon. We're all going to get pneumonia."

"That's not going to happen," Maggie said as she stomped her booted feet, trying to keep her circulation working. "Would you look at those two judges in their designer suits and high heels! Look lively, boys. Here comes the governor and his people. Espinosa, do your thing. Dennis, mingle with the kids and spread the word. Discreetly, Dennis. Do you hear me? Don't tip our hand. If you screw this up, I will personally rip your skin off."

"She means it, kid," Ted said.

Dennis shivered. "Gotcha," he said, moving off in his quest to find the older boys Espinosa had alerted the last time they were at the camps. He looked over his shoulder to see if anyone was paying attention to him. No one was. Ted, Maggie, and Espinosa were clustered around the governor and the twin judges. Even though he knew the judges were freezing, they still managed to look chipper. *Chipper?* The governor looked grim, but at least he was dressed warmly. His aides were busy talking to the four commandants and some of the supervisors. He couldn't help but wonder if any of them had a clue as to what was about to happen. There was stupid, and then there was *stoopid.*

Celeste wondered what the temperature was there in the forest. She couldn't remember ever being so cold. She decided to take the initiative. "Governor, would you mind if we went indoors? I'm sure we could all use some hot coffee."

"Nonsense! You're here to see that these kids have a good time today. After all, you put these youngsters here. I'm just sorry I can't stay myself. I was a Boy Scout back in the day, you know. There's a governor's conference today that the president is hosting at the White House, and we certainly can't be late. I promised these reporters a photo op, and that's what they're going to get. I expect both of you to stay until the jamboree is over at four. Now, let's all smile pretty for the cameras. I'd like to get some shots with some of the kids. And, of course, hear what they have to say about their respective camps. Smile, Your Honor!"

Celeste knew in that moment that she was capable of killing. She plastered a sickly smile onto her face, as did Eunice, when a gaggle of boys was brought forward. Maggie jumped right in and started asking questions as Espinosa clicked his camera. Dennis was in the gaggle and appeared to be whispering to some of the boys. Ted shouted questions at the judges, who ignored him.

Suddenly, it all went quiet when Maggie asked a tall, thin boy how he liked boot camp and how much longer he had to go. The boy, who said his name was Jeff, said

413

he was thirteen and he hated the boot camp. He said he had six more months to go before he could go home. "What did you do to be sent here?" Maggie asked.

"I beat up a boy who was bullying me on the playground at school. My dad said I could only hit him if he hit me first. He hit me, and I hit him back. Everyone started to fight, and they said I was the ringleader and I got expelled and had to go to court. That lady said I had to come here." He pointed to Eunice, who glared at him with hate-filled eyes.

"What happened to the rest of the kids? Are they here?"

"Some of them. Those same boys beat me up here, too, and I had to go to the Hut. We aren't allowed to talk about the Hut."

At the mention of the Hut, pandemonium broke loose, a ruckus that the counselors couldn't contain. The youngsters, most of them with tears running down their cheeks, surged forward. The twin judges ran for their lives as Espinosa moved like lightning, snapping pictures that would cover the front page of the *Post*'s next edition.

"Governor, a comment, please?" Ted demanded.

The governor threw his hands in the air. "I'm sorry I can't stay to sort this out, but

414

the state will not be renewing the contracts on this facility or the other three camps. I was going to serve notice on the judges, but as you can see, they skedaddled. Call my office if you need further comment. I'm late now and, as much as I hate to leave, I must. The president is expecting me, and one does not ever keep the president waiting."

The reporters gaped at the governor as he and his entourage climbed into their caravan of SUVs. They continued gaping until the SUVs were out of sight. There was no sign of Celeste or Eunice Ciprani.

The reporters looked at one another, then at the kids, who were shrieking and hollering at the top of their lungs. Ted lunged toward one of the counselors and ripped the whistle that was around his neck. He blew it until his face turned red, but finally, the kids quieted down just as Avery Snowden's men showed up. Horns blasted as men barreled out of the long, dark vans. Avery himself marched forward and held up his hand until even the sobs and murmurings turned silent. A contingent of his men rounded up the commandants, counselors, and teachers and told them to stand down.

"Okay, kids, you're going home today! You'll all be transported back to Baywater, where your parents will be waiting for you. Some very good, kind people have been on the phones all night long calling your parents. The camps are going to be shut down. So, for those of you who have been staying at this camp, get your things together. I'm sorry that the rest of you won't be able to take your personal belongings, but we'll make up to you for what you leave behind. You all know which buses you came on, so get aboard now, and as soon as everyone is checked off on our roster, you'll be on your way home."

Shouts of pure happiness rang in the air as the kids made a mad scramble to do as ordered.

"Who the hell are you people? What gives you the right to do this?" shouted one of the commandants.

"Do you really want to know, big mouth? No! I thought so. Consider yourself lucky that you aren't going to jail. I'm giving you ten minutes to get your gear and clear out. This camp is being shut down as of now. If any of you are expecting a paycheck or bonus, get that thought out of your mind right now. Ten minutes! Go! And leave the firearms behind," Avery shouted.

Espinosa's last shot was of the commandants and counselors running like rabbits to gather their belongings.

"You guys can leave," Avery said to the reporters. "We have orders to shut this place down, turn off everything, and lock it up tight for the new owner, who I have been told was someone named Peter Ciprani."

"Were you able to reach all the parents?" Maggie asked.

"Believe it or not, we were. Baywater will never be the same again once they all descend on the town. We did a good thing here. A real good thing."

Dennis West was beside himself as he helped usher the kids onto their respective buses. Maggie felt her eyes tear up when she saw some of the younger boys hug him and cling to him. He took his time with each one, grinning from ear to ear.

Maggie tapped Ted on the shoulder. "You do know this is his story, right? Without Dennis, these kids wouldn't be going home."

"I know, Maggie. He's got what it takes. We'll nurse him along for a little while until he's ready to spread his wings. I don't have one bit of trouble giving him the byline."

"Me either," Espinosa said.

"Then it's unanimous," Maggie said. "I think our job here is done." She dusted her hands dramatically to prove her point.

"I want to stay until the last bus rolls out of here. I need to get it all on film," Espinosa said. "I want the readers to *see* it all. Then I want to get back to Baywater before the buses so I can capture the arrival with all the parents."

And that's what they did; they stood huddled together as one bus after another rolled down the road, horns blaring, kids shouting and waving.

Dennis swiped at his eyes when the last bus started toward Baywater.

"You did good, kid. We took a vote, and the story is *yours.* You get the byline."

Dennis West fainted, a smile on his face.

Four hours later, the streets of Baywater were lined with anxious parents as they waited for the buses bringing their children home. The excitement stopped just short of being a carnival atmosphere. The four reporters from the *Post* moved through the crowd, explaining that before the month was over, the families would all be compensated financially. There were no smiles, no delirious exclamations of approval, or, as one mother put it, "Like money is going to make this right. It is not going to give my son and my family the time that was stolen from us."

A sound so loud, so thunderous, shook

the air as the long line of buses rumbled down the main street, blocking traffic. A group of Avery Snowden's men climbed out of the first bus with clipboards in hand. They called out name after name as the kids ran to their parents. Espinosa captured it all: the tears, the smothering hugs, the grateful look of the parents as they looked around, wanting to thank someone before they hurried off to their homes, where they could all be a family again.

Two hours later, the buses were gone, as were the families, and only the four reporters were left standing in the rain. It was hard to tell if the beads of moisture on their faces were tears or raindrops.

Soaking wet, chilled to the bone, they walked off, arms linked, to go back to the Harbor Inn, knowing they'd successfully completed a very small miracle for the families of Baywater and the surrounding area.

CHAPTER 26

Myra woke, unsure what it was that awakened her. She lay quietly, listening to a strange sound she couldn't quite identify. She looked over at her small travel clock with the bright red numbers. It was two o'clock. She blinked. Whatever the sound was, it was coming from the sitting room off the little compact kitchen in the suite of rooms. She swung her legs over the side of the bed, tiptoed to the door, and peered out into the sitting room. She was stunned to see Marti curled up on the sofa crying into a wad of tissues. She rushed to her and took the ex-president in her arms. "What is it, dear? What's wrong? Tell me so I can help."

Marti swiped at her eyes and squeezed Myra's arm. "It's Peter. We were downstairs in the bar. He collapsed, and Avery called 911. He's at the local hospital. Actually, it's more like a fully staffed clinic, is what Avery told me. They only have ten rooms, and it's

420

more for emergencies than anything else. They wouldn't let me go with them. For my own good, they said. How can that be for my own good, Myra? The minute I met Peter, something happened to me. He said he felt the same way. It's like we were . . . meant to meet, to begin new lives with each other. I . . . as you know, I haven't exactly made wise choices when it came to the men in my life but this . . . this was so different, I instinctively knew it was right."

"Give me a few minutes to get dressed, and I will drive you to the hospital. Who cares what they said about its being for your own good or not."

"Myra, it's the middle of the night!"

"What difference does that make? You're the president! The waters will part if you show up at the hospital. I personally guarantee no one will turn you away."

"Ex-president, Myra."

Myra waved off her words with a wave of her hand. "Five minutes!"

Back in her room, Annie was sitting on the side of the bed grumbling about the time and asked what was going on. Myra briefed her as she pulled on her clothes.

"And you were going without me? I-don't-think-so." She hustled out of bed and was dressed before Myra.

"Well, hurry up then," Myra said as she bent over to tie the laces of her sneakers.

When both women appeared in the sitting room, Marti broke out in fresh tears. Arm in arm, the three women walked out of the suite and took the stairs to the ground level, where they climbed into Myra's car. They made the short trip to the local hospital within minutes.

Other than coping with the stunned surprise of the guard at the door, the women had no problem taking the elevator to the second floor, where Peter was in a private room. The night nurse blinked, did a double take, and did everything but curtsy when the president walked up to the desk to ask about Peter and whether it was possible to see him.

"He's resting, and we hydrated him when he was first brought in. He bounced back within an hour, but the doctor on call wanted him to stay overnight. He was in touch with Mr. Ciprani's doctors at Georgetown. The bottom line is he overdid it yesterday and admitted it. You can go in, Madam President. You other ladies will have to wait in the lounge. Will that work for you?"

"Can I stay?" Marti asked.

"Yes. I see no reason why you can't.

Anything that will help the patient is what we're about."

Marti whirled around. "Do you mind?"

"Of course not, dear. Call us when you're ready to come back to the Inn. Someone will come to pick you and Peter up if they discharge him in the morning."

If Marti heard, she gave no indication, as she was already running down the hall to Peter's room.

Annie looked at Myra. Myra looked at Annie.

"This is just a wild thought, Annie, but I think we just lost one of our members."

Annie smiled. "I think you're right, Myra. We'll manage."

"I hope it all works out for the two of them. From what I observed, I think Marti and Peter are meant for each other."

"I'm hungry. There's an all-night diner down at the end of Main Street. What say we go get some greasy bacon and eggs, cold toast, and bad coffee?"

"Why not? We certainly aren't going to go back to bed."

Both women were incredulous when their early-morning breakfast arrived. The bacon was crisp, just the way Charles made it. The eggs were fluffy and tasty, the toast was piping hot, and the coffee was fresh roast and delicious. They wolfed it down and grinned at one another. Annie shrugged. "Who knew?" she quipped.

"Be sure to tip well, Annie."

"You're kidding, right? I didn't bring my handbag. I don't have any money on me."

"Oh, good Lord. I didn't bring mine either. I didn't even bring my cell phone. Did you bring yours?"

"Nope. What are we going to do, Myra?" Annie asked anxiously.

"Guess we have to ask to use the phone and call Maggie to come and pay our bill. Unless you have a better idea."

Annie sighed with relief. "That works. Do it, Myra. Ask for a refill on the coffee while you're at it."

"Why do I always get the ratty detail, Annie?"

"Because you're the one that woke me up."

"Oh."

As Maggie Spitzer's credit card was being processed at the diner, Eunice and Celeste Ciprani were standing in their state-of-the-art kitchen, having decided not to drive to the nation's capital after the debacle at the work camp.

"I don't know if I'm going to miss this

place or not," Eunice said. "Probably not. I wonder what will happen to it since we paid it off two years ago. Will Peter claim it, do you think?"

"That really is a stupid question, Nessie. Of course he'll claim it. We bought it with his money, so he'll feel justified in claiming it. Now, one last time, do a walk-through to make sure you have everything you want or need."

"I did that three times already, Cee."

"Well, do it one more time. Then we are out of here. Two hours to Waterton, we pick up the truck, and we'll be in New York by noon if the truck doesn't break down. Move, Nessie!"

Huffing and puffing, Nessie marched to her bathroom, checked out the medicine cabinet for the fourth time, and looked under the vanity. There was nothing she wanted or needed. In her bedroom, she looked inside her walk-in closet. Her eyes immediately went to the two shelves that held her pricey Chanel handbags. She wanted to cry since she was leaving them behind. Twenty-three in total at over three to five grand a pop, so she was leaving behind a small fortune. She loved those bags, she really did. Her gaze dropped to her shoe racks. Another small fortune left behind. Damn, she'd just bought those Louboutin shoes, too. Her Jimmy Choo shoes glared at her, all thirteen pairs of them in every color of the rainbow. She squeezed her eyes shut so she wouldn't cry.

"Are you having a wake in there or what?" Celeste shouted. "It's time to go, Nessie! It's going to be light out soon. I told you I want to drive in the dark. Are you listening to me, Nessie?"

"The whole complex can hear you, for God's sake. I'm ready, and no, I did not forget anything. Don't set the alarm."

"I didn't plan on setting it. I'm ready if you are. All the lights are off. There's nothing in the fridge but wine, bottled water, and a few bottles of diet soda, but I left all the appliances turned on. In case anyone decides to come here to check on things."

The air in the garage was cold, and Nessie shivered. "I feel sad, Cee. Say something nice so I don't feel so bad," she said, dumping her two bags into the trunk of her sister's car.

"We're taking the first step into our new lives, Nessie. By this time tomorrow, the sun will be shining, and we'll be in some Tiki bar having colored drinks with little umbrellas and toasting each other. Is that good enough for you? If it is, get your ass in the car so we can get out of here."

"Sometimes, I actually hate you, Cee. This is one of those times."

Celeste ignored her twin as she turned on the engine and backed her car out of the parking space.

The moment she started the engine, Avery Snowden was on the phone to Myra.

"They're on the move and headed to Waterton. We know thanks to the bugs we planted in both the condo and the cars. My men are on the way to Waterton and will arrive before they do. Get your posse together and burn rubber. We'll hold the fort till you get there."

"All right," Myra said.

"What? What?" Annie barked.

"Showtime, ladies!" Myra bellowed as she started to gather up her belongings.

"Hold on! Give me five minutes to get the guys ready. Don't leave without us!" Maggie demanded, blasting out of the room.

"Does that mean we aren't coming back here?" Pearl asked as she massaged her right foot. She'd so hoped she wouldn't have another flare-up until after this caper was over. Mind over matter, she decided as she zoned in on what she had to do.

Nellie waved her cane about like a magic wand. "I've been packed since we got here."

She cackled. "Where's our *stuff?*"

"Our *stuff,* as you put it, is in the trunk of my car. No. Pearl, we are not coming back here. Marti is going to see to settling things. We can talk about all this on the ride up to Waterton. For now, just make sure none of you leave anything behind," Myra said.

Down the hall, the boys were dressed in the blink of an eye as they fought each other at the vanity to brush their teeth. "You're not going, Dennis, so let us use the sink. You need to stay behind because . . . well, just because," Ted said as he tried to brush his teeth and smooth down his unruly hair at the same time.

"What do you mean I'm not going? You said this was my story. That means I get to be there at the finish! I know what's going on even if you think I don't because I haven't said anything. I know those two old gals are members of the Vigilantes. I've known that from the beginning. You know how I know that, Ted? Because those women were my mother and sister's idols. They had their pictures plastered all over our refrigerators, and we had two refrigerators. I know the other two, the two judges, the *good* judges, aren't just along for the ride. Five will get you ten Pearl has her own agenda; she's got something going on besides her gout. Otherwise, why was that guy Sparrow brought into things? As for Nellie, I don't know what she's all about yet, other than her husband used to head up the FBI, but there's something there. Which brings me to *my* bottom line. Either I'm in or I'm out. If I'm out, I'm taking my story to the *New York Times.* I do know how to keep secrets. Well?"

"You talk too damn much, Dennis. Okay, okay, you can come along."

"No! I can't just *come along.* Either I belong or I don't. Tell me now!" Dennis said, his face red with indignation.

"Dennis, you do belong. Ted is just cranky. He gets that way when you wake him up in the middle of the night. You are definitely one of us, and I'll strangle anyone who says differently," Maggie said, patting the young reporter on the shoulder.

"I'm sorry, kid," Ted said.

"You should be," Dennis said. "Just don't do it again, okay?"

"You got it," Espinosa said. Under his breath he muttered, "Who knew we had a prima donna in the group?"

"This is where the ladies take matters into their own hands, dole out their brand of justice, and the bad old girls are never seen or heard from again, right? Damn, I can't wait to see what they have in store for those two," Dennis said, nearly salivating over the prospect of witnessing Vigilante justice.

"That makes four of us left wondering. Understand this, Dennis. We never, as in *never,* question the ladies." Maggie giggled. "Come on, you guys, we need to hit the road. Get all your stuff, since Myra said we are not coming back."

By the time the reporters hit the parking lot in the back of the Harbor Inn, the women, their engines running, were backing their cars out of their respective parking spaces. Only Marti's car would remain in the lot.

The time on the dashboard clock read 4:59. "We made good time — no traffic at this hour of the morning," Celeste said, as she slowed the powerful car to make the turn into the road that would take them to their ancestral home. In the time it took her to make the right-hand turn, the entire area was lit up like a night game at a football field. She stomped on the brakes when a well-dressed man stepped in front of the car. She stomped harder on the brakes just in time to avoid hitting the man. She pressed a button, and the window rolled down. She could feel her sister's anxiety.

Celeste dredged up every ounce of indignation that was in her. "Who are you? What's the meaning of this? My sister and I live here! Why are you stopping us? Oh, good Lord, don't tell me the president is here *again*!" Her heart beating like a trumpet, Celeste drew a deep breath and waited. She could actually feel Nessie's shaking body even though she appeared to be sitting perfectly still.

"Secret Service, ma'am. Sorry for the inconvenience. We're here to secure the premises. Contractors will be arriving at first light. We need to secure the grounds. I'll need to see some ID from both you ladies. Step out of the car, please."

"I will not step out of this car. I live here, and you damn well know it. Here are my credentials. As you can see, I am who it says I am. And this is my twin sister, Eunice. Here are her credentials. We're tired. Can we just get to our house? Please."

"Not until you step out of the car, ma'am, and we check out this car. That means the trunk and of course the undercarriage as well. And the glove compartment."

"This is outrageous! I'm going to call my congressman and senator and the goddamn current president if I have to," Celeste stormed as she crawled out of the car.

Nessie did the same. She was shaking so badly she could barely stand.

The bogus Secret Service agents took their own sweet time going through the trunk, looking under the car, and going through the twins' purses and briefcases. Celeste had to fight not to faint when the agent gave them the okay to get back in the car and drive on. Neither woman said a word until they were safely inside their old home. "Thank God, we were smart enough to wear our money belts. I was so sure they were going to strip-search us," Celeste said in a shaky voice.

"Now what are we going to do? We can't leave for a while. It will look suspicious if we turn around and leave now after the fuss we created. This is not working out right, Cee," Nessie said as she rummaged in a kitchen drawer for one of her marijuana sticks. Her hand was shaking so hard, Celeste had to hold the lighter for her sister.

"If ever there was a time for you to take a hit of this, it's now," Nessie said, holding out the cigarette for her sister, who stunned her when she took a deep drag from the sweet-smelling cigarette. She almost laughed as Cee started to cough and sputter, but she didn't. She'd probably never laugh again. "I'm going to make some coffee.

Since you claim to be the brains of this outfit, start figuring how we're going to get out of here in that damn truck without those people seeing and stopping us. Another thing, Cee. Isn't the gardener going to want his truck back? How did you get him to leave it here anyway?"

"I sent him a check for a new truck. I paid him for the week and told him to take a vacation. He said he left the registration and tags in the glove compartment. I didn't have to twist his arm. I'll take another puff of that cigarette, Nessie."

Nessie handed over the cigarette, then poured coffee neither wanted but drank anyway. "How long should we wait, Cee?"

"At least an hour. We'll say the gardener had an accident and we're going to the nursery for peat moss and fertilizer or something. They already stopped us, and we're leaving, not arriving. Did that make sense, Nessie?" Cee asked dreamily.

"I guess so. Drink the coffee, Cee. No more hits. We need to focus. We also need to change our clothes so it looks like we're in gardening mode."

"Good point, Nessie! Let's do that right now."

Twenty minutes later, the twins were dressed in jeans, flannel shirts, and Timber-

433

land boots, and were standing in the kitchen eyeballing one another. The cannabis smell hung in the air. Nessie turned on the exhaust fan over the range. Then she sprayed Lysol around the kitchen. At Cee's questioning look, Nessie said, "Just in case those agents come up here for something."

"Oh, another good point, Nessie. You are soooo on the ball toooodayyy," Celeste twittered as she danced across the kitchen floor. She finally sat down across from her sister. They stared at one another for a long time, neither speaking.

Almost calm now, Nessie looked at the clock on the kitchen range, then gathered up her handbag and briefcase and motioned for her sister to get a move on. The money belt itched, but there were worse things in life, she decided. Cee hadn't said what they were going to do with the belts once they got to the airport and had to go through security. She hoped she had a plan. "I'll drive," she said, looking at her dancing sister. "You aren't very good with a stick shift."

"Okayyyy."

"God, you need some fresh air. Come on, Cee, shake it. Time's up!"

A knock sounded on the kitchen door just as Nessie slung her briefcase over her shoulder. Both women froze in their tracks. "Don't answer it, Cee. We'll go out through the garage, where the truck is. The kitchen still reeks of pot."

"If it's that agent, he knows we're here. We have to open it!"

"Cee, no, we do not have to open the door. This is our home, our castle. He has no jurisdiction in our home. Do not open it. Come on, we're going out through the garage. Let them knock all day. Shape up, Cee."

The knocking turned louder, more insistent. Nessie, high on weed, opened the garage door. Let's go, Cee!" she hissed.

"Your Honor! Open the door. You have guests. We escorted them up here. We cleared them."

Nessie turned around and mouthed the word, *Guests*? "Oh, God, he's looking in the window! If you had moved your ass, Cee, we'd be on our way. Now you have to open the door. Or better yet, talk to him through the door."

Celeste straightened her shoulders and walked over to the door. "Agent, we're much too busy for guests. Furthermore, we are not expecting any guests. How dare you bring someone to our home, strangers at that, after what you put *us* through with a thorough search? Now, get off my property, or I'm calling the police. In fact, I'm calling them anyway because my sister and I do not like your attitude. We pay your taxes, Agent."

Celeste, her heart beating so fast she could barely breathe, yelled to Nessie. "Call 911 and have them send someone out here. Right now, Nessie!"

Nessie had the phone in her hand and was starting to peck out the numbers when the kitchen door splintered and crashed open. She dropped the phone when a gaggle of women and men barreled into the kitchen. Stupefied, the twin judges could only stare, their jaws hanging open.

"Good morning," Myra said cheerfully.

"Did the call go through?" Pearl asked as she snatched up Nessie's phone from the floor. She shook her head for the benefit of the others.

"That's a relief," Annie said, dropping the bags she was carrying. "Okay, boys, we have it under control. We'll call you if we need you. Stand by."

Celeste finally found her voice. "Who are you people? Why are you here? What do you want? It's a home invasion, Nessie. Well, guess what, you're too late, we were robbed just days ago, and the thieves took every-

436

thing, so there's nothing left. Who are you?" she demanded again, but this time more shrilly. The sound was like fingernails scratching a blackboard.

"Does 'We're your worst nightmare' work for you?" Nellie asked, waving her cane around.

"What . . . what do you want?" Nessie squeaked.

"We want the money you wired out of your accounts in Switzerland and the Caymans," Myra said quietly. "Give us the account numbers, and we'll leave." *Like that's really going to happen. Oh, Myra, you are such a liar.*

Celeste drew in her breath, as did Nessie. Myra thought the kitchen suddenly felt like all the air had been sucked out of it.

"I don't know what you're talking about. What accounts? Are you people crazy? I'm not going to tell you again; get out of our house!"

Nessie turned white. She reached out to grasp hold of the back of one of the kitchen chairs. *They know. Oh, God, they know about the money.* She wanted to look at her sister but couldn't manage it. Was Cee feeling what she was feeling? Her future flashed in front of her. She wondered who would be wearing her designer shoes and carrying her

437

Chanel bags. She wanted to cry.

"Maggie! Tell these nice ladies what you know about their offshore monies."

Maggie smiled and rattled off everything Abner Tookus had told her. "So you see, ladies, there's no point in lying to us. Just give us the routing numbers, and we'll leave you to whatever you were doing before we got here."

"Scum!" Celeste spit. "I'm not telling you anything because there is nothing to tell. You obviously have us mixed up with someone else."

Pearl moved her laptop onto the kitchen table. She looked over at Maggie, who rattled off a string of numbers for the old accounts. Pearl tapped them into the computer and turned the screen around so the twins could both see it. Celeste's right eyelid twitched noticeably. She brought up her hand to still the movement. Eunice stared off into space.

"Guess we don't have you mixed up with anyone else. These accounts are yours, as you can see. Now, we're going to ask you one more time for the routing numbers. We won't ask again," Annie said, starting to lose her patience.

"You can ask until hell freezes over and neither my sister nor I are going to tell you anything. This is a setup of some kind, and we are not going to play your games. So, do whatever you're going to do or get out of here and leave us alone."

"I guess in the interest of time, we should get on with our plans since these two fine judges don't see fit to cooperate with us," Myra said.

"Annie, tie the ladies to their chairs. Pearl, you help! Nellie, keep that cane handy. Maggie, guard the door."

Celeste bounded off her chair at the same time Nessie did. Arms flailed. Feet shot out, screeches and curses filled the air. But in the end, with Nellie swinging her cane, the twins were subdued and tied to the kitchen chairs. "Lookie here, they're both wearing money belts," Maggie said, as she ripped at the Velcro strips. "Looks to me to be a bundle of getaway money."

"Looks that way to me, too," Annie said as she dragged a large black trash bag over to the sink. She rummaged in the cabinets until she found a measuring cup. All eyes were on her as she ripped at the bag inside of the trash bag. She scooped out a cup full of gray powder.

"I think you need something bigger, dear," Myra said as she pulled a syringe out of another bag. All eyes were on her as she

439

waved the syringe under the noses of the judges.

"What . . . what's that?" Nessie whispered.

"It's a syringe, honey."

"Make sure you add enough water so it can go through the syringe, Annie," Pearl called out.

"When we tested it, it was four to one, wasn't it?" Nellie asked.

"What is *that*?" Celeste demanded. Her voice sounded strong, but there was fear in her eyes. Nessie looked to be in a daze.

Annie finished at the sink. She washed and dried her hands. Then she walked over to the twins and cupped their faces, one at a time, in her hands. "Who has the marker? I don't want to make a mistake. After all, I am not a plastic surgeon."

"What in the damn hell are you talking about?" Celeste said, rearing back in her chair. "Don't you dare touch my face."

"You certainly have had a lot of *work* done, haven't you, dearie?" Annie observed, peering closer at Celeste's face. "Those liver spots are quite ugly. You can have them singed off. Did you know that, Your Honor? Oh, dear, what's that lump by your eye? Ah, a little too much Botox, me thinks. Oh, well, don't you worry. We're going to make sure we *even* you up. No one will even notice that little bump when we're done with you."

"What . . . what are you talking about? Don't you dare touch my person! Don't you dare!"

"Put a cork in it, *lady*. I'm tired of listening to you. And I am through addressing you as 'Your Honor,' since whatever honor you ever had disappeared years ago. Correct me if I'm wrong, bitch, but aren't you tied to a chair? And aren't you at my mercy right now? To me that means I'm in charge, and I'm calling the shots," Annie said as she moved over to Nessie.

"Yes, what are you talking about?" Nessie asked as she tried to jerk her head out of Annie's grasp. Annie held on, knowing full well she would be leaving bruises on the judge's face. When she finally released her hold, Nessie gasped, "What are you going to do to us?"

"We're going to give you a face-lift, dear. Oh, don't worry. We aren't going to be doing any slicing or dicing. We all detest the sight of blood. We're going to be giving you injections. Think of it as a body overhaul."

Nellie started to laugh and couldn't stop. Maggie looked over at the kitchen sink and started to giggle.

"Myra, be aware of the time. That stuff hardens really quickly. You don't want to lose the consistency, or it won't go through the syringe," Pearl said.

"We have five minutes. Girls, strip the ladies down to the buff. We'll start with their rear ends the way that doctor did to that woman who wanted a more curved tush."

"Oh, sweet Jesus," Nessie started to blubber. "Celeste, that's cee-ment they're mixing in the sink."

Celeste thought her eyes would pop right out of her head. She started to curse and bellow, but Pearl gave her a backhand slap while ripping at Celeste's clothes.

Myra filled the syringe and stood between the two women. "I'm going to use up one minute of my time, so follow me here. Give us the routing numbers. Then I want you to tell us all why you think you're here under our control. The clock is ticking, ladies."

"You're insane, all of you. I don't know what you're talking about. As to why we're here, it's because of our crazy brother. Don't you dare touch me!" Celeste screamed.

"Oh, for God's sake, Cee. Give it up already. They know. You want to drag your ass around loaded with cement, go ahead. I don't want to end up in a freak show, because that's where we're going to end up. Don't inject me. I'll tell you anything you

442

want to know."

"Nessie, shut up."

Annie loosened the ties that bound Celeste to the chair and jerked her to her feet. A second later, she watched as Myra jammed the syringe into the judge's left buttock. Celeste howled in rage. Myra withdrew the syringe, refilled it and jammed it into the other buttock. "Those two lumps will be as big as oranges. Pretty hard to sit down." She eyed Myra, who was busy filling the syringe for the third time. "Two more should do it for her rear end. Where's the smaller syringe?"

"In the yellow bag. Maggie, dear, will you fill it? We'll do her forehead and chin next, then get the medium-size one and fill it. Quickly, sweetie. We've almost used up the five minutes. Face and then breasts. When we're done with her, she'll look like she has four boobs. This designer judge will be one lumpy mess when we're through. By the way, lady, the lumps on your face will be nickel-sized, just so you know. You might get an infection. Did that woman get an infection, do any of you know?"

"I'll mix up a new batch for the sister," Nellie said as she tapped her way over to the sink. "Hurry, Myra, it's starting to harden. No, she didn't get an infection. She

443

just couldn't walk; her butt was too heavy to drag around. They said she had close to forty pounds of cement in her rear end. It was really pitiful. They were pushing her around in a wagon."

Celeste sagged against the chair. She glared at her sister, whose eyes were rolling back in her head. "You open your mouth one more time, Nessie, and I *will* kill you. Do you understand that?"

Maggie looked at the bag within the trash bag and did her best not to laugh. It wasn't cement. It was gelatin, which would dissolve within eight hours. Not that anyone would inform either one of the judges.

Myra walked over to Celeste and held up the smaller syringe. "Last chance, bitch!"

"Screw you!"

"Anatomically impossible, lady. Hold her tight, Annie. This is going to sting, and we don't want it going in her eyes and blinding her."

The needle went in again and again until Celeste weakened and fell into the chair. She was sobbing when Pearl handed her a mirror. Celeste fainted. Nessie started to scream and couldn't stop. "I'll tell you. Leave her alone."

"Are you sure?" Myra asked. "If you give

us the wrong numbers, it won't go well for you."

"I'm sure, I'm sure. Oh, God, what kind of people are you?"

"Isn't the question more like what kind of people are you and your sister to do what you did to your very own brother and all those kids out of pure greed? And you would have kept right on doing it if that young reporter, Dennis West, hadn't gotten wise to you. It's thanks to him that we're here right now."

Celeste came to with Annie slapping her face a few times. She started to cry when she heard her sister rattling off the bank codes.

Maggie quickly dialed Abner Tookus and was relieved when he picked up on the first ring. "Pearl is going to be sending you an e-mail any moment. You know what to do. Call me when it's all confirmed."

Nessie started to cry. "I'm sorry, Cee. I don't care about the money. I just don't want to look like you. I don't ever want to look like you. You can do whatever you want to do, but I'm going to throw myself on Peter and hope he takes pity on me."

"Shut up, Nessie. You make me sick. Get real; they aren't going to let us go. How stupid can you be?"

Nessie looked at Annie and Myra, her eyes pleading with them to dispute what her twin had just said. Annie and Myra smiled and shrugged their shoulders.

"Get them dressed," Nellie bellowed. "I'll call Avery for the pickup. Maggie, take their purses and briefcases and put them in one of our cars. Call Espinosa in here to take Celeste's picture as soon as we get them dressed."

Maggie nodded, then called for silence when her phone rang. "Done. The money is safe. We can start setting up a system to compensate people for the evil those two despicable pieces of something unmentionable did. And contribute to solving the unemployment problem. Doing justice is expensive."

A hoot of laughter filled the room as Myra and Annie started to clear up the mess they'd made at the kitchen sink. They dragged the heavy bags to the kitchen door.

The kitchen door opened, and suddenly the room was filled with people. The judges started to scream and lash out. One of Avery's people whipped out two hypodermic needles and jabbed both sisters in the arm. They went limp within seconds, but not before Espinosa clicked his camera.

Dennis West looked down at the woman

446

with the strange bumps all over her face. His eyebrows shot up to his hairline when he saw her backside before one of Avery's men picked her up. He swallowed hard. He himself had dragged out the heavy black bag with the cement bag inside. He swallowed again as he felt Ted and Maggie's eyes on him. He waved *them* off as he looked around to see if there was anything left behind.

"We're good to go, guys," he said in his normal voice. He wondered if he'd ever be the same again.

Outside, in the brisk November morning, Myra looked around, then down the road to the house that now belonged to Martine Connor. "Which house do you think Peter and Marti are going to live in?"

"It has to be Marti's house. I cannot imagine that Peter is going to want any reminders of his sisters. Speaking of which, what kind of story do you think will satisfy him?" Annie asked.

"The one the *Post* prints, which will be that his sisters managed to take it on the lam before the authorities could snare them. No one will ask questions. Trust me on that. As to where they're going to end up, I don't want to know. Do you, Annie?"

"No, I don't want to know. Did you call

Charles?"

"I did, and he's happy for us. He said he's making a delicious dinner for all of us."

"Oooh, I can hardly wait," Maggie, the bottomless pit, said.

"Should I lock the door, Myra?" Pearl asked.

"No. Let's make it easy for Peter when he decides to come here. Did anyone call Marti to see how Peter is doing?"

"I did earlier," Annie said. "Marti said the doctors told him he can go home tomorrow. Marti is going to take care of him. Isn't that wonderful? All's well that ends well."

"Do you think we should start planning a Pinewood wedding?" Nellie asked.

"I think so, I really do," Myra said.

The ladies of Pinewood offered up high fives before they climbed in their cars to head to Pinewood and one of Charles's fabulous dinners.

In the car, Annie started to grumble. "Now what are we going to do, Myra?"

"Wait for someone who needs our help to reach us."

"I guess we don't have any choice. I'm not good at waiting around."

"I have an idea, Annie. Let's you and I go to Vegas and cause some trouble."

Annie perked up immediately. "Do you

mean it, Myra?"

"I do."

"Okayyyyyy."

ABOUT THE AUTHOR

Fern Michaels is the *USA Today* and *New York Times* bestselling author of *Classified, Gotcha! Breaking News, Tuesday' Child, Late Edition, Betrayal,* and dozens of other novels and novellas. There are over seventy-five million copies of her books in print.

Fern Michaels has built and funded several large daycare centers in her hometown, and is a passionate animal lover who has outfitted police dogs across the country with special bulletproof vests. She shares her home in South Carolina with her five dogs and a resident ghost named Mary Margaret. Visit her website at www.fernmichaels.com.

The employees of Thorndike Press hope you have enjoyed this Large Print book. All our Thorndike, Wheeler, and Kennebec Large Print titles are designed for easy reading, and all our books are made to last. Other Thorndike Press Large Print books are available at your library, through selected bookstores, or directly from us.

For information about titles, please call:
(800) 223-1244

or visit our Web site at:
http://gale.cengage.com/thorndike

To share your comments, please write:
Publisher
Thorndike Press
10 Water St., Suite 310
Waterville, ME 04901